ELYSIUM

A NOVEL BY

PIERCE KELLEY

ISBN 978-1-955156-27-1 (paperback)
ISBN 978-1-955156-28-8 (hardcover)
ISBN 978-1-955156-29-5 (digital)

Rushmore Press LLC
1 800 460 9188
www.rushmorepress.com

Printed in the United States of America

Other Works by Pierce Kelley

The Jesus Trail (Westbow Press, 2019);

Pilgrimage (iUniverse, 2018);

Hiding in America (AuthorHouse, 2017);

Hunted (Xulon Press, 2017);

Massacre at Sirte (iUniverse, 2016);

To Valhalla (iUniverse, 2015);

A Deadly Legacy (iUniverse, 2013);

Roxy Blues (iUniverse, 2012);

Father, I Must Go (iUniverse, 2011);

Thousand Yard Stare (iUniverse, 2010);

Kennedy Homes: An American Tragedy (iUniverse, 2009);

A Foreseeable Risk (iUniverse, 2009);

Asleep at the Wheel (iUniverse, 2009);

A Tinker's Damn! (iUniverse, 2008);

Bocas del Toro (iUniverse, 2007);

A Plenary Indulgence (iUniverse, 2007);

Pieces to the Puzzle (iUniverse, 2007);

Introducing Children to the Game of Tennis (iUniverse, 2007);

A Very Fine Line (iUniverse, 2006);

Fistfight at the L and M Saloon (iUniverse, 2006);

Civil Litigation: A Case Study (Pearson Publications, 2001);

The Parent's Guide to Coaching Tennis (F & W Publications, 1995);

A Parent's Guide to Coaching Tennis (Betterway Publications, 1991).

ACKNOWLEDGMENTS

In this book, I explore the human condition of aging through the eyes of a young man studying to become a clinical psychologist. I have chosen Ireland as the setting for the story, and I walked over a hundred miles across and around what is called the Ring of County Kerry to gather insight and details to help me better describe the "Emerald Isle," though the story could be set in any country in the world. It is a universal topic.

I thank the many people from Ireland who I met along my walk for their kindness and welcoming nature. I heard it said that they consider themselves to be the 51st state. Ireland has sent tens of millions of its sons and daughters to the US over the last few centuries, most never to return.

Specifically, I acknowledge and thank the following people in no particular order: Leo, the taxi driver from Cahirseveen; Jim, Mary, and Monica from the Green House in Sneem; Michael from the Ferryman's guesthouse in Portmagee; Pat and Mike, the two men from Portmagee who ferried me to Skellig Michael on two occasions; Maurice and Dean from Ireland walk/hike/bike; Cathy from the Stone Lodge in Cahirdaniel, and Flourinella from Kenmare. I also thank Kathleen Lamanna, an Irish woman from Coeur d'Alene, Idaho, who added much to the final product. Most of all, though, I thank my two traveling companions, Patrick and Marlene Doherty, who made the arduous journey a much more enjoyable one.

I read a number of books to prepare myself for the task of writing this book, including the following: *The World of the Druids*, Miranda J. Greene, Thames & Hudson, Ltd., 1997; *The Celts*, Frank Delaney, Little, Brown and Company, 1986; *Loss of Self*, Carl Eisdorfer and

Donna Cohen, W.W. Norton, 2002; *The Thirty-Six Hour Day*, Nancy L. Mace, M.D., and Peter A. Rabin, M.D., The Johns Hopkins University Press, 1985; *The Immortal Irishman*, Timothy Egan, Houghton Mifflin Harcourt (2016); *Irishisms*, Ronan Moore, Gill books, 2017, and *Anam Cara: A Book of Celtic Wisdom*, John O'Dohohue, Harper Perennial, 1998.

INSCRIPTION

"To everything, there is a season, and a time to every purpose under the heaven."

—Ecclesiastes 3:1 (King James Version)

DEDICATION

This book is dedicated to my parents, Robert Pierce Kelley and Marjorie Sullivan Kelley. His family hailed from County Clare and hers from County Kerry. Most members of both families came to America during the "famine" years of 1845 to 1853.

Chapter One

Birth to Early Adulthood

Brendan Sullivan here, and I'm about to tell you a story of an extraordinary man I met when I was beginning my career as a clinical psychologist and how he changed my life. I expect that everyone has someone in their life who has played an important role in determining who and what they became. For most, it's a parent or relative. For me, more than any other non-family member, it was him.

First, allow me to tell you a little bit about myself. I was born on September 4, 1998, in the village of Sneem, County Kerry, in the Republic of Ireland. It is so named because the Sneem River noisily and turbulently flows right through the heart of what is a small village in the southwest corner of the island into Kenmarc Bay, and then out into the Atlantic Ocean. Places where fresh waters of a river unite with the saltwater of an ocean or a sea are called estuaries, and that is one of the many unique qualities of my hometown.

It's a village of barely five hundred people at the moment, and it isn't likely to grow much bigger any time soon. In fact, it might even shrink some. The so-called Celtic Tiger of the 1990s never arrived in Sneem and the prospects for growth aren't good. Most of the young people move away from Sneem, and all of Ireland for that matter, as soon as they can, never to return except for the occasional visit every now and again. Though they leave the country, the country never leaves them—that's a forever kind of thing.

So far, I've only made it to Cork, barely a hundred kilometers away, but who knows what the future holds for me? I might stay forever right where I am. Why not? I love where I live, but that's a story that is still unfolding and yet to be told.

Because it has changed so little over the years, it provides a glimpse into the Ireland of centuries ago. Problems such as pedophile priests and abusive nuns are found only in the newspapers and on the news . . . not in the homes of the inhabitants or their places of business, nor in their daily conversations, and definitely not in their hearts. It's a magnificent place, full of beauty and wonder, nestled between picturesque hills and valleys which surround it on three sides with Kenmare Bay and the mighty Atlantic on the fourth.

We have no shortage of fairies, leprechauns, and spirits from the past in Sneem. Ancient beliefs and traditions remain firmly embedded in the hearts and minds of all who live there, as do past grievances against the Vikings, the Anglo-Saxons, and of course, King Henry VIII, Oliver Cromwell, Margaret Thatcher, and all of the rest. We hold firmly to a hope that the six counties in the north will, one day, join the Republic so that it will be, as the song goes, one nation once again. In that regard, it is a typical Irish town.

Tourism is now Sneem's primary stock in trade as it is one of the major stops on the Ring of Kerry. Dozens of tour buses descend upon it every day from the first of April until the end of September every year to take in all of the charms that the village has to offer. Not much happens between October 1 and the end of March, however.

The winters are cold and windy though temperatures rarely dip below freezing. That anomaly is due to the fact that warm waters of the Atlantic and the Gulf Stream surround the island, which isn't all that far from the arctic circle. Turf fires in the homes, restaurants, and bars, of which there are plenty, provide the primary source of warmth for all who live there.

As it is throughout all of Ireland, many shades of green dot the landscape due to frequent rainfall, but the buildings in the village provide a kaleidoscope of colors, too. Houses and places of business are painted with different colors. Bright yellows, reds, blues, and various shades of green, among others, adorn the buildings.

It's a mystical place, rich in history and deeply steeped in the traditions and beliefs of the Catholic Church. The "troubles" of the past thousand years with their neighbors to the east are barely below the surface. They haven't gone away and aren't likely to go away anytime soon, but a fragile truce remains in place in Northern Ireland at the moment, which remains separate and apart from the Republic.

Nowadays, the issue of Brexit and Boris Johnson, and how it will affect the border between the two countries, is the talk of the town. The past continues to exert a powerful influence upon the present, however. That may never change.

There is little dissent in Sneem, though, or anywhere else in the Republic, for that matter. For the most part, all are fervent Catholics. Even in the northern six, Catholics are growing in numbers. We're still outnumbered, but it's by an increasingly smaller number—less than a percentage point or two. Maybe things will change when there are more of us than them.

My father, Patrick, was a teacher at St. Michael's National School Sneem where he taught Mathematics and our native Irish language, Gaelic, to the fourth, fifth, and sixth graders for years. It has had about a hundred students in it rather consistently for decades, but that number is decreasing lately. He was a graduate of St. Michael's as were his parents and all of his brothers, sisters, uncles, aunts, cousins, and all the rest of his side of the family. Now, he is the headmaster there.

All students wore uniforms and were required to say prayers and attend Mass daily back then and they continue to do so to this day. Even though the country is in the process of separating the church from the state, those things haven't changed yet. It remains a Catholic school where the students continue to observe religious practices on a daily basis despite the fact that it is a state-sponsored school. Implementation of the laws requiring the separation is still a work in progress.

My mother, whose name is Margaret, was a "stay-at-home" mom, and I was the youngest of seven children. My oldest brother, Rory, is eighteen years my elder. He's old enough to be my father and has children who are about my age. Siobhan is sixteen years older than I am; Patrick is fourteen years older; Diedre twelve; Kevin ten, and Maura eight. I was an accident, as Rory and Kevin like to tell me from time to time.

She was different. Neither she nor any of her family was from Sneem as most people who live there are. We don't get much "new blood," and not all that many move away. Everyone knows everyone else and no one minds only their own business.

She met my father in Cork while he was attending University College there. She had completed her second level of education as required at age sixteen but had not gone on to the next level. She was a few years younger than he.

They were married before my father received his teacher's degree and, as I later figured out, Rory was born many months before the wedding. That may have had something to do with why she didn't go to the next level in school, but I never asked and she never said anything about it. Her family was from Cork.

But she was different in other ways, too, as I found out at a very young age. She wasn't a Catholic! In a country where nearly ninety-eight percent of the people were Catholic at the time, it was rare to find anyone who wasn't. That has changed now, as more and more things are coming out about so many of the priests being pedophiles and how the nuns abused young girls for decades at the Magdalene Laundries, also called asylums. Many have turned away from the church as a result. Despite that, the church is surviving the crisis and the Republic of Ireland remains overwhelmingly Catholic.

Irish Catholics have clung to their religion as a badge of honor for centuries. It's a wonder, actually, how they, or we, I should say, did it, enduring so much. King Henry VIII broke from Rome in 1534 when, by his decree, the Act of Supremacy went into effect. It declared that he, the King of England, not the Pope in Rome, was the "supreme" leader of England in all matters, including religion. The Church of England was created soon thereafter, and that is when the "troubles" began.

Over a hundred years later in 1649, when Oliver Cromwell invaded Ireland and "dispossessed" most Irish Catholics of their land, the problems intensified to an unspeakable degree. He invaded with an overpowering army and killed every man, woman, and child in two large cities that opposed him. He completely subdued the country shortly thereafter as no one dared to oppose him. Some historians have said that he killed nearly half of the people in Ireland in the process of solving what was called the "Catholic" problem.

Penal laws were put into effect whereby Catholics were prohibited from owning land in Ireland. We were, in effect, trespassers, unwelcome wherever we went. In doing so, millions of people were left homeless. They were left to wander the land, living in barrel-shaped wagons pulled by horses and came to be known as "tinkers." Some continue to do so to this very day though they're now living in RVs and their numbers have shrunk considerably.

There were small pockets of Ireland where the laws weren't enforced, such as the poorest land in the country, located west of Shannon, in the province of Connaught. The expression "to hell or Connaught," came into being, said to be uttered, quite proudly, by Cromwell himself. He didn't bother to pursue Catholics in what was called the "West." It was, and still is, "boggy" land, not good for much of anything, at least not as far as he was concerned.

The "Penal Laws," as they were called, designed to punish those who refused to renounce Catholicism, prohibited Irish Catholics from practicing their religion, voting, holding public office, speaking their native language, or attending school, among many other things. Priests were hung if caught saying mass. Those laws remained in place for nearly two hundred years until Daniel O'Connell, the "Great Liberator," began the movement which ended them.

To me, the most amazing and unbelievable part of that period of time in our history was that Irish Catholics could have avoided those hardships if they had agreed to convert to the Church of England and deny their Catholic beliefs. The main difference between the two religions was the issue of the infallibility of the Pope in Rome. Some Catholics did so in order to survive. It was called "taking the soup." That meant that they received food, usually in the form of hot soup, if they renounced their faith.

Irish Catholics endured centuries of hardships to keep their faith. It would take more than some pedophile priests and cruel nuns to shake that faith. Many preferred to die rather than deny their beliefs.

None of that applied to my mother, however, to my knowledge, although some of her ancestors must have been Catholics too, but

I'm not sure about that. Her mother wasn't nor were any others of her family that I met. I never knew her father who died before I was born. She certainly had no love for the English, though. Druids, what few there were back then, were treated just as badly because they, too, refused to accept the teachings of the Church of England and went into hiding, or ceased to exist, for hundreds of years.

She attended Mass with my father and raised all of the children, including me, as Catholics, though. No one ever knew that she wasn't a believer until later. None of my brothers and sisters ever knew until I unwittingly told them. I was a young child at the time.

I was the first in the family to find out, I believe, although I'm sure our father knew. He must have. How could he not have known? It was only after her secret came out, because of me, that most people found out about any of that.

In 1995, the country of Ireland voted to allow divorces. Five years later, in the year 2000, she filed suit to end her marriage with my father. She was one of the first to apply for one in Sneem and all of County Kerry from what I later learned. Before that, people in Ireland were married for life or until "death do us part" because that was not only church doctrine, it was also the law of the land.

It was quite a scandal for her to do what she did. Not being a Catholic and then filing for a divorce, she might as well have put a scarlet letter on all of her clothes or had it stamped on her forehead. For centuries, Druids were quite secretive about their beliefs. Now, they can practice their religion openly without fear of recourse.

As a result, my family was split up. Actually, it was only the two of us who were separated from the rest. All of the other children stayed with my father in Sneem. I went with my mother back to Cork to live with her mother.

She continued to take me to church, and I attended a Catholic school, but that was, as I later found out, because the final divorce decree required her to do that. I don't know if she would have done that otherwise. Even now, we don't talk about those things. She allowed me to make that decision for myself once I was old enough, and I chose to be a Catholic.

However, when I was still a youngster too young to choose for myself, I went with her on many, if not most, weekends to her places of worship, which weren't in churches or buildings within a city, town, or village. Their ceremonies were all out in the woods surrounded by rocks and trees, for the most part, with few exceptions. She would dress me up in a white gown and drag me along with her wherever she went to meet with her Druidic brethren.

At the time, I was too young to protest, but I didn't really mind it at all. At least, I have no recollections of anything bad that happened at their ceremonies—there were no animals being sacrificed, as had been the practice years before. As my mother explained it to me, the Druids worshiped all things of nature—the moon, the sun, the stars, the animals of the forest, rocks, plants, and trees—especially the oak trees. I have mostly favorable recollections of those days even though I was too young to understand what it was all about.

Things changed when I was six or seven after I made the mistake of telling some of my friends in school where I had been one weekend. They all started to make fun of me and called me names. The priests at my school were really upset with my mother once they found out about it.

After that, I began to spend most of my weekends with my father in Sneem. I don't remember going with her anymore to Druidic events once that happened, though. I still lived with her, but I attended the Saint Luke's National School in Cork from the first to the sixth grades, and not with him, at his school, as he wanted. There, I received a "Catholic" education and that satisfied him, apparently.

My parents argued about where I should go to secondary school. My mother wanted me to go to a public school that wasn't run by the Catholic Church. He, of course, wanted me to go to one that was. She wanted me to go to a school with both girls and boys. He preferred an all-boys school.

I wasn't opposed to attending a school run by the priests, but I wanted one where there were both boys and girls, not just boys. Ultimately, I was sent to the Christian Brothers Secondary School, which was for boys only. I think they might have gone back to the divorce court to resolve that issue, but I never knew that for sure.

Secondary School was a bit of a blur. I was still spending most of my weekends in Sneem with my father, so that prevented me from doing things with my friends in Cork. Most of all, though, it prevented me from playing Gaelic football or hurling. Those were the two things I loved to do the most. The games were always on Saturdays and I was almost always away.

My father was a big fan of the Kerry Kings, the best team in all of Ireland, winning more All-Ireland Championships than any other county in the country, including the north at the time. When I became a fan of the Cork City team, he was sorely disappointed in me. More than anything else I ever did with my father, going to the games between those two teams with him was the best, even though we argued vigorously over which team was better. Kerry was my second favorite team.

Hurling was another matter entirely. If he could have, he would have prevented me from ever picking up a caman. If he found one of my sliotars lying around, he'd throw it away. My older brother, Rory, had been hit in the head by one during a game and sent to the hospital when he was in school. My father didn't think he was ever the same after, but I loved playing it as a boy despite that.

The Gaelic Athletic Association or GAA sponsored both football and hurling, among other sports, but it steadfastly refused to support any sports that weren't considered to be Irish, like soccer, rugby, or tennis. They still do. What's most interesting about that is that the six counties in the north are a part of the GAA, but only Catholics are allowed to participate, even now.

So, I played football and, when my father wasn't around, hurling. He was quite insistent about that. He absolutely forbade it.

For years, playing soccer was strictly forbidden, too, and I never played it as a child. Things have changed, and all of his grandkids now play soccer, but I never had much interest in it anyway, though it's now quite big in Ireland, what with the World Cup and all. People play rugby, tennis, and other sports nowadays, but they're not sanctioned by the GAA.

One of my biggest thrills, ever, was going to Fitzgerald Park in Killarney with my father to watch Kerry play Cork in an All-Munster final, even though it wasn't much of a game. That was in 2007 when I was eight-years-old. Cork was trounced. I was hoping that they'd be able to keep it close, but they couldn't. The stadium was packed with nearly forty thousand screaming Irishmen. It was mad. To this day, I've never seen anything like it.

My mother had no interest in sports whatsoever, though she loved to watch me run and play. I don't think she cared if I won or lost; she just loved being with me and seeing me happy. She had no interest in the Cork City team and thought that hurling was simply disorganized crime.

As much as I enjoyed playing the games, it was unfortunate that I wasn't better at them. I wasn't bad, but I wasn't too good, either. I was good enough to make the teams at my school, and that is when I got to play. When my school days ended, that pretty much ended my athletic career, such as it was. I was still a fan, though, and I still am.

After graduation from the Christian Brothers Secondary School, I chose to continue my education at University College Cork. Since I wasn't born into a wealthy family, I chose it because I could stay at home and not have to pay for housing. Tuition was free for me, as it is for everyone else who is an Irish citizen. I chose psychology as my intended major.

My father wasn't happy with my career choice, and he made his displeasure clearly known. He wanted me to be a teacher like he was, and come back to work with him and live in Sneem. Two of my sisters had done so, and I was his last chance for that as far as any of his sons were concerned.

I guess I had an independent spirit, and I was determined to prove to him that I could do better, though there is nothing wrong with being a teacher. In fact, as I look back on things, I think I turned to psychology, not teaching, because of my father and mother divorcing and all of that. It confused me and put my life in turmoil for years . . . it still bothers me. I think it made me want to try to understand it all better and help people get through those kinds of things, especially the kids—kids like me.

Becoming a psychologist wasn't easy, though, as I soon found out. To get accepted into a graduate program, I had to do very well in school. Again, I was pretty good, but not great. I was, by no means, at the top of the class.

In May of 2019, at the age of twenty, soon to be twenty-one, I received a degree called a Higher Diploma in Psychology, which

I obtained with honors. That made me eligible for acceptance into a post-graduate program and for admission to the "Registered Membership with the Psychological Society of Ireland." One had to be a member of it before being allowed to become a psychologist in Ireland.

Shortly after graduation, I decided to accept a job at the St. Stephen's Psychiatric Hospital, located in Cork. It wasn't my first choice, but it was the best of what few choices I had. My pay was to be 25,000 euros per year, which seemed like a small fortune to me.

I was to be under the supervision of licensed clinical psychologists and I was on a career track to become one myself after three years at the hospital, which included some further classwork as well. I would be doing a wide variety of things, including some work with children, though not as much as I wanted. I was delighted. That is where my life as an independent, self-supporting man would begin, and that is where my story begins.

CHAPTER TWO

St. Stephen's Psychiatric Hospital

St. Stephen's is one of the few teaching hospitals in all of Ireland. As such, it has some of the best professors, many of whom are at the forefront of research on various issues in the country. It is a vibrant place full of bright people of all ages. It is also the largest place, by far, which provides care and treatment for those with mental health problems in the southwest part of Ireland. It was a good place for me to begin. I was fortunate to get a job there.

The first month or so went by quickly. Between finding myself a place to live, starting the new job, and learning all of the names of the people I would be working with, I was absolutely for the birds—pure cracked. For the most part, I was just being asked to tag along and observe how things were supposed to be done. Colin O'Riordan was my immediate supervisor and, most of the time, I followed him around.

He was in his third year at St. Stephen's, well on his way to finishing up. He could hardly wait for it to end and he didn't seem to mind letting people know how he felt. Once he completed his three years of clinical education, he was ready to move on to the next stage of his career and begin making much more money in the private sector.

According to him, that meant making at least twice as much, if not more, than he was making at St. Stephen's. He never said exactly how much that would be, but it sounded pretty grand to me. I couldn't imagine it. I was happy to be making what I was.

He quickly became more than just my mentor. He also became a friend. There were no airs about him. He didn't take himself too seriously. He was still a student, learning, as we all were, and he understood that. He didn't act as if he knew it all and we knew nothing, though he did say as much on more than a few occasions. He was a large man, about my height, but much more girth. He had a great belly laugh and most everyone seemed to like him. He made people laugh.

At first, he used to call me a "spanner" because I was always doing something stupid, like forgetting to lock a door after leaving a restricted area or putting down my phone and not knowing where I left it, things like that. He didn't mean it in an unkind way; he was just having fun with me.

Up until that point in my life, I'd never had much of social life, being passed around like I was as a youngster, and then working as hard as I did to receive my degree, with honors, no less. Living at home with my mother and grandmother didn't help much with that, either. So, when I joined him for a pint at a local pub, he was quickly able to see that I was a real rube. He called me "full shilling."

Now that term, actually, is a very complimentary one. It means that the person is top-shelf, brilliant, capable, competent, and an all-around fine person. That isn't the way he meant it with me, though, and everyone knew it.

It was true . . . and it always made people laugh when he called me that. Some of his friends called me a "muppet" for a while because I rarely had anything to say in response to defend myself. Mostly, I just sat there, smiling, listening to what everyone else had to say, enduring the abuse.

I didn't defend myself or fight back. Maybe I should have, but I didn't. I was just glad to be there, part of the gang, so to speak.

Besides, most of his friends were like him, older than me and with much more experience than I had. I listened intently when they talked, even though they were, at times, insulting me. It was all in good fun or at least that's how I took it. I was a "newbie," and I knew it. I accepted that as a fact.

The other thing he did, besides guide me on how to become a good clinical psychologist, was introduce me to girls. I was beyond shy. I was backward.

My living arrangements, and going back and forth from my mother's place to my father's place as I did, made it difficult for me in that regard, too. I never had any real girlfriends. Going to an all-boys school, as I did, didn't help. I was retarded in that regard.

Going out after work to a pub and drinking pints of Guinness with the people I was now working with was, by far, my favorite activity. There was no close second. I looked forward to those occasions, but they didn't happen every day.

Technically, I was still a student working toward another degree. I still had classes to attend, at night, and much studying to do. I had to do well in those classes, too. Three nights a week I was in a classroom. Colin had a few more classes to finish, but he was actually teaching some classes to lower-level students like me when the professors weren't available.

Besides, he had a girlfriend and had an active social life. I was only able to join him and his friends a couple of times a week whenever he invited me. I never went there by myself. I was too shy for that. Between work and the pub, I was interacting with girls more than I ever had in my life, and I was enjoying that. It was, as I said, a totally new experience for me.

There were about fifty other people who were in the same situation I was in, although not all were studying to become "clinical" psychologists. We were all graduates who were just beginning to work at St. Stephen's in one department or another. I knew only a few of them because most had come from different schools across Ireland, not just Cork City.

Most were men, but maybe a third were women, which was a novelty for me. I hadn't gone to school with girls since primary school. It was different in a good but distracting way.

There was this one tall, red-haired girl named Saoirse, who had started the same time I did, who caught my attention. She came from Trinity College, Dublin, and was very pretty. I was immediately attracted to her and I had to try hard not to stare whenever I saw her. She, too, was studying to be a clinical psychologist.

After a few weeks of awkwardly eyeing her, I finally found an opportunity to talk to her one day in the lunchroom where most of the employees ate. We talked about how the job was going and how difficult it was to work full-time and still go to school. We both had a statistics class, but not together, and she was having difficulties with it, as I was.

Other than talking to Colin, and a few others at work and the bar, I pretty much kept to myself. I didn't have time for much of anything else. I was pleased when I broke the ice with her and could exchange greetings when we passed each other in the hallways.

I had found a nice, little, one-bedroom apartment not far from the hospital. It was more like a cottage, actually, which sat above a garage where a family by the name of Geagan parked their cars. Their house was about twenty meters away and I had a bit of privacy. It wasn't too expensive and I could walk to work in ten minutes. It was perfect.

Gradually, I began to fit in. It took me a long time to learn everyone's names and what their job responsibilities were, let alone figure out exactly what was expected of me. It was a good six weeks before I was allowed to do interviews and prepare reports on my own that the medical doctors, psychologists, and psychiatrists would see. My work would be closely scrutinized by Colin and others, but it was "my" work and I felt much better about things when I reached that stage.

For the most part, I was required to fill out forms. The questions were there for me to ask, so that wasn't the hard part. Talking to a person who was in some sort of crisis and usually not completely coherent wasn't easy. I had to be objective and sort through what was fact and what was fiction. I had to think like a psychologist, not the twenty-one-year-old student that I was.

We were all required to take a course called Research and Writing to help us fill out the forms properly. The hospital was in the process of going to a fully operational computer system where manually filling out the forms would no longer be permitted. It wasn't quite there yet, so writing legibly was critical, but what one had to say was obviously most important. Being concise and putting down only the most relevant things was demanded.

When I initially applied for the job, I was told that I would need a car as there would be times when I would be required to do some traveling. I didn't have one when I was hired, but I was allowed a thirty-day period to obtain one after I started. So, after I received my first paycheck, I bought a used Skoda Octavia. The Geagans allowed me to park it next to their garage, not inside it.

The Skoda is made in Czechoslovakia and is quite common in Ireland. They're much less expensive than most other vehicles, even the American or Japanese-made models. It has a fuel tank that holds about fifty liters and can run for about a thousand kilometers before a fill-up. It wasn't long before I put it to use.

I didn't mind the traveling part at all. It gave me an opportunity to get out of the hospital and be on my own for a while. Part of our responsibilities included going to outlying areas to service the rural hospitals and mental health facilities, which was why a car was necessary.

Full-fledged, certified clinical psychologists were too few and too busy to send out to all the little towns and villages scattered around Munster, so they would send people like me to be their investigators, so to speak. We were mostly factfinders and we would report back to our supervisors what we saw and heard. We weren't allowed to do any counseling, though, since we weren't properly certified yet.

In 2000, Ireland's government passed a Mental Health Act which provides rules and procedures to deal with people with mental health problems. Two years later, it established a Mental Health Commission. One of its responsibilities is to ensure that all citizens can receive quality mental health services, no matter where they live or how much money they have. It's easier to do that in the big cities like Dublin, Cork, Killarney, Galway, and some of the others, but not so easy in places like Sneem.

Actually, clinical psychologists work closely with psychologists who did not do the "clinical" work, and that was, I learned, a separate department at St. Stephen's. I never had to interact with them or at least I hadn't just yet. Our job, as clinical psychologists, was to identify any emotional, mental, or behavioral problems from what we observed and from the tests we performed. The psychologists were the ones who made the formal diagnosis as to what the mental illness, disease, or disorder was. It was a team approach and people like me were a part of that team.

Once a diagnosis was made, a treatment plan would be developed. When the hospital took on a person as a patient or client, the team would work with that person to help them develop some goals, identify what had to be done to accomplish those goals, and then work toward achieving them. Sometimes, the problems were pretty obvious, and most of the problems I saw were alcohol-related.

Alcoholism is now considered to be a disease, although it's really nothing like what most people think of when they hear the word "disease." It's not like diabetes, pulmonary heart disease, Alzheimer's, cancer, tuberculosis, Lyme disease, or any of the other things people know of that are called diseases. Most people think a person who drinks too much made a "choice" to do so. Now, the medical profession treats it more like the person was no longer making the decision to drink—he or she was compelled to do so.

I think of it more like an overwhelming desire that pressures a person to drink alcohol. It's no wonder that an Irish man would feel that way when scattered all across the country are about a million signs saying "Guinness is Good for You!" That's more like a national motto or a collective goal! It was something that was expected of you.

I certainly was a believer in that concept, as was just about everyone I knew. In my limited experience, I thought that most people would be more likely to think that there was something wrong with an Irishman who didn't drink than there was with one who drank too much. As I soon learned, I was wrong about that. Alcoholism was, and is, a serious problem in Ireland. It was no laughing matter, though people, Irish people that is, laugh about it all the time.

My brother Kevin, who has a bit of a problem with it, was fond of saying things like, "A drinking problem? I don't have one . . . I drink, I get drunk, I fall down, then I get up . . . no problem!" Everyone would laugh when he said it. He even had a shirt with that saying on the front.

Most of the time, a person would be picked up by the local Garda for drunk and disorderly conduct. That would usually be the result of a fight or some sort of public disturbance. "Happy" drunks were never a bother. The "not-so-happy" drunks would be taken into custody, awaiting a determination by the local constabulary as to what should be done with the offender.

There were many times when I would meet someone referred to us who was still in a drunken condition. Talking to people like that was a waste of time, really, because it was hard to make much sense out of what they were saying or to believe all that we were being told. We always tried to make sure that the person had sobered up before we even went out to meet them.

Probably the most important thing that I learned in school was that there were three conditions necessary for a clinical psychologist, or any mental health professional, to have any chance at success with a client. First, a person had to be able to admit that they had a problem. If a person denied or refused to recognize that he or she had a problem, then they weren't ready to deal with it.

Secondly, the person had to have the cognitive abilities or the physical and mental capabilities to deal with whatever the problem was. In other words, they had to have the ability to work with us. There couldn't be some medical or physical condition that would prevent them from working toward a solution to whatever problems that person was having. If there was, that condition would, or at least could, prevent us from having success.

And thirdly, the person had to "want" to deal with the problem, and that was, in many instances, the biggest problem of all. If the person didn't want to address the problem for whatever reason, then there was no way anyone could make that person do whatever it was that needed to be done. The person had to fully invest in the plan of rehabilitation or else it wouldn't work.

That didn't mean that a person who recognized that they had a problem and had both the ability and the desire to deal with the problem was going to be successful. There would always be setbacks and roadblocks. Plus, the road to recovery, from whatever the problems were, was almost always a long, hard one. There were never any "easy" fixes.

The problems which our clients were dealing with hadn't developed overnight. Sometimes, it was a situation that had existed for a lifetime but never addressed before. It was never the result of a single incident involving something like poor impulse control.

It takes time to develop a habit and time to change habits, especially bad ones. Again, most of the problems were, in one way or another, related to alcohol, and many times a crime or criminal offense was involved, too, compounding the problem. It's not easy to make anyone, most of all an Irishman, stop drinking.

In 1994, Ireland passed a Criminal Justice Act which allowed a Garda to simply impose a fine and let the drunk person go home after they sobered up. In some cases where the officer suspected that there was more to the problem than just the occasion of having too much to drink, he or she could do something different like press criminal charges. In most cases, because the fine is fairly hefty, the fine itself was enough to deter people from repeating the unacceptable conduct. That didn't work for everyone. In fact, it didn't work for most people.

A person would have to have what is called a "dual diagnosis" to be taken someplace to be treated for a mental health problem. Alcoholism alone was not enough. There had to be schizophrenia, bipolar disorder, depression, or some other recognizable disorder before the professionals get involved.

Drug usage was another matter entirely. Ireland is quite strict in that regard, even for marijuana, which is handled differently from other drugs. People with addictions to opiates, such as oxycontin, are treated as criminals. Marijuana users are, too, but they usually receive fines, extremely large ones, for a first offense and an even larger fine for a second offense. After that, it's prison.

When people were put in the criminal justice system, we weren't involved. I never saw anyone in a prison. We weren't allowed in there.

In the prison system, there were rehabilitation facilities and programs. Those are separate and apart from what is offered at the mental hospitals. Actually, the Irish Prison Service is a big employer in Ireland and I probably would have taken a job with it if I hadn't been hired by St. Stephen's.

Sometimes, we would see people in the local gaols. Usually, that was shortly after a person was arrested. That was always exciting for me. I had never been in trouble with the law in my whole life, so it was a new experience every time I went into one.

Many times, the person was a well-known and chronic offender. The main problem with such people, whether it was alcohol or drugs, was that they had to be "clean" before they could be admitted to any of our programs. Not all were able to meet that standard. It made no sense to me, really, because it was almost as if the person had to solve the problem by themselves before the authorities agreed to help them with their problem.

Other times, I would see people in local hospitals or treatment centers. The local doctors or counselors might call upon us and ask us to take a look at someone. Most of the time, a person had already entered a facility on what was called a "voluntary" basis, which means that they "agreed" to go in, but doing that didn't necessarily mean that they could leave whenever they wanted to.

Problems would arise when voluntary patients wanted to leave but the medical professionals didn't think that was such a good idea. Most were allowed to leave when they wanted to because the medical staff had agreed that it would be okay for them to do so. Other times, when the staff would want them to stay longer and the person didn't want to, that's where we would come in. Small towns and villages didn't have the capacity to handle long-term care or short-term care either for that matter. St. Stephen's was one of the hospitals in Ireland that did.

Basically, a person could be put into a mental institution against their will if they had a recognizable and identifiable mental health illness, disease, or disorder and they were a danger to themselves or others because of it. I had learned in school that dementia, schizophrenia, and bipolar disorders were the most common types of problems I would likely see. It's one thing to read about it and quite another to actually meet people with those kinds of problems.

That was the biggest difference between clinical psychologists and other types of psychologists. We would be the ones to see the people and make the initial observations. I liked that part of the job. I was and I am a "people-person."

The thing about being told to go out to see a particular person or patient was, for the most part, that it could happen at any time of the day. The law requires that a person be seen as soon as possible, usually within twenty-four hours of being arrested or taken into custody if the Garda is involved and the person was charged with a crime. That's not the case with a person thought to have a mental health problem who hasn't committed a crime. Still, if the Garda and local medical personnel thought that a patient should be involuntarily hospitalized, someone had to see that person very quickly.

For me, every such experience was wildly exciting. I was meeting new people every time and I was always received with much courtesy. Because of my position, I was held in fairly high esteem wherever I went. People would be glad to see me, even the patients, and I would uniformly be treated extremely well. I wasn't used to that.

Most of the time I followed the recommendations of the local professionals, all of whom were more seasoned than I. They knew what they were doing and, usually, they were dead-on in their analysis. There wasn't a single instance when I questioned their judgment. I confirmed it, copying their analysis word for word for the most part.

About four months after beginning work, I was starting to settle in and feeling a bit of confidence in myself and what I was doing. Late one Thursday afternoon, Colin came into my office, which was actually a cubicle I shared with three other fellow employees, and asked me if I was willing to take a drive to Sneem. There was a man at the Garda station who needed to be seen, and he didn't have the time to do it. I immediately agreed to do that for him.

When I asked, he said that the man's name was Martin McDuffy. Although I didn't know the name, I figured that I'd probably recognize him when I saw him. Sneem is a small village where everyone knows everyone else. I was fairly certain that I'd know his family if I didn't know him, and that I must have seen him in church at Mass, if nowhere else, as the whole town was usually there on Sundays.

Just as I was ready to leave, he came running up to me and told me that the man was being held in Kenmare, not in Sneem, and I was to see him at the Garda station there. That wasn't a problem because Kenmare was on the way to Sneem, and I'd likely be back home much sooner.

Colin and the others were planning to be at the pub after work, as they usually did on Thursdays, and I was invited to join him when I got back. I was anxious to get there and get back as quickly as I could. I didn't want to miss that. A dart league had started and every now and again, someone wouldn't show up and I could fill in. I wasn't too good, but I loved to play.

CHAPTER THREE

Dr. Martin Michael McDuffy

Kenmare is a small town not far from Sneem, less than thirty kilometers away. It's situated right on the shores of Kenmare Bay. I had passed through it a thousand times on my way to and from Cork. I knew it well.

The drive to it was pleasant enough and I had no trouble finding the Garda station where Mr. McDuffy was being detained. As I opened the door and walked inside, I saw a man sitting in a chair in what was the lobby of a two-story building, which looked more like a house than a gaol. The man was reading a magazine. He looked up, momentarily, as I walked past him. I walked up to the counter, introduced myself to the woman behind it, and told her why I was there.

"That would be Mr. McDuffy right there," she said, pointing to the man behind me. Then she turned to the man and said, "Mr. McDuffy, this gentleman is here to see you. What did you say your name was again, sir?"

"Sullivan . . . Brendan Sullivan," I told her as I handed her a business card.

"Yes, Mr. Sullivan is here to see you, Mr. McDuffy," she said. "The two of you can have a chat in a room just down the hall. Give me a minute and I'll show you where it is," she continued.

At that, Mr. McDuffy stood, approached me, extended his hand, and said, "Nice to meet you, Mr. Sullivan. I appreciate anything you can do to help me. I'd like to go home as quickly as possible."

The Garda officer responded by saying, "I'll be taking him back to his house in a little while, but before I do that, he is to see someone, and we're waiting for that person to arrive. Mr. McDuffy is getting a little impatient with me."

"I've been here for well over an hour. I want to go home now, thank you very much, Officer," Mr. McDuffy replied.

"He's upset, which is understandable, but he's just going to have to wait. He was lost when I found him walking along the side of the road earlier today," she told me. "And a bit confused as to where he was, weren't you, Mr. McDuffy?" she asked.

"I wasn't lost! I was just taking a different road, one that I'd never been on before, that's all," he replied. "I could see the village from where I was standing, for goodness sake! I wasn't lost! I don't understand all the commotion you're making over this," he told her.

"But this isn't the first time this has happened, is it, Mr. McDuffy?" she responded.

He turned to me and said, "I thought she was bringing me back to my house, as she has on a couple of other occasions, but she brought me here instead. I don't know why she did that. I hope you can help me get out of here and back to my house. Can you do that for me?"

I was listening but not understanding what was going on. Why was he here? Why was I here? He was, after all, being held here in this Garda station apparently against his will, though he wasn't behind bars or restrained in any way. It didn't sound as if he had committed a crime. What was wrong with him? Was it safe for me to be with him?

I guess she could see my concern by the expression on my face because she said, "He's as gentle as a lamb. You have nothing to worry about. He's just having a bad day today, aren't you, Mr. McDuffy?"

"Yes, I am, thanks to you," he responded, "and I don't understand why I'm being treated this way. I just want you to take me home . . . now!"

"I'll take you home, but I can't do that at the moment. I'm the only one here, as you know," she told him. "You just need to be a little more patient with me, please."

At that point, I really had no idea what was going on.

I stood there as she finished what she was doing, and then she said, "Follow me, Mr. Sullivan. You, too, Mr. McDuffy," as she walked out from behind her desk, opened a door using a key, and held it open until we were in a hallway.

She then led us down the hall, opened a door, and said, "You two can talk in here for as long as you'd like. Just come out and find me when you're ready to leave, Mr. Sullivan. I'll check in on you every so often to make sure everything is alright."

I looked around and saw a small table in the middle of a room that couldn't have been much more than a few meters long and wide. Four metal chairs surrounded the table. There was nothing on any of the walls, which were white and as plain as could be.

"I can put you in a different room if this one's not big enough for you," she said, apparently noticing my reaction.

"This will be fine," I told her as I sat down on one of the chairs.

Though he was much taller than me, I didn't feel threatened by the man. He wasn't the least bit physically aggressive toward me. Besides, he looked to be at least fifty years older than me. Mr. McDuffy sat down at the other end of the table.

"Splendid!" she said. "Let me know if there's anything I can do for you. My name is Mollie," she added as she closed the door behind her.

My mind was processing all that I was seeing and hearing. My initial thought was that there must be some kind of serious mental health problem going on that wasn't like schizophrenia or a bipolar personality. Otherwise, why was he here? And why was I here? I didn't smell anything unusual on his breath or person, so it didn't seem to be alcohol-related, so I ruled that out.

I began thinking of what I would put in a report, though I didn't start writing things down. We're told not to do that. I was to do my best to put the person at ease and establish some sort of relationship before taking any notes.

He was an old man and looked to be well into his seventies, maybe even his eighties. He was dressed nicely, with a plaid jacket, tan trousers, and a stylish cap on his head, though his white shirt was wrinkled, and I noticed a stain on the collar. He was wearing a thin, black tie and was carrying a cane, or walking stick, in his hand.

I had noticed that he walked with a slow and steady gait in a dignified, stately manner. His speech wasn't slurred and he wasn't behaving abnormally at all, as best I could tell. I wasn't seeing anything out of the ordinary, so far, except for the fact that he was clearly unhappy about his circumstances.

I'm about a hundred and seventy centimeters tall, and I weigh about a hundred and eighty kilograms, which is about average for my height. He was much slimmer than me . . . gaunt, in fact, but he towered over me. I guessed that he stood almost two hundred centimeters high.

He stared intently into my eyes as we sat there, looking at each other, each waiting for the other to speak, probably. Though he didn't say anything about it, I was sure that he was thinking that I was an awfully young man to be coming to see him. I always thought that, though, no matter who I was meeting. It seemed as if everyone was older than me.

He looked to be old enough to be my grandfather who'd been dead for ten years. I hesitated before saying anything because I wasn't sure what to tell him about who I was and why I was there. So, after a few awkward moments, he asked me in a nice way who I was and why was I there.

From everything I had heard, so far, I got the impression that he truly had no idea that I had been sent there to see him because people had questions about his mental stability. I didn't want to alarm him, so I didn't say anything about that. Instead, I told him that I wasn't in law enforcement and that I was there to help.

"Can you give me a ride home?" he asked.

"Maybe," I answered. "I need to find out a little more about what's going on here before I can do that, though," I told him. "So, tell me, what's this all about?"

That seemed to puzzle him a bit, but he responded by saying, "Well, I have to admit that this isn't the first time the Garda has picked me up, never for a crime, mind you, but I wasn't lost like she said I was. I really was just taking a different route. I wasn't sure where the road I was on was going to end up, but I knew where I was. I was half-way up the mountain . . . I could see where I was, like I said before! Besides, even if I was lost, which I wasn't, it's not a crime to get lost, is it?"

"Of course not," I responded, "but is there anything else you can think of as to why the officer might have picked you up?" I asked. "You weren't in any danger, were you?"

"No! Not at all," he responded. "I was fine. I still am. I thought she was doing me a favor."

"You can't think of any other reason why the Garda would have picked you up?' I asked as nicely as I could.

"No, I can't"—but then he hesitated and said—"The only thing I can think of is that it might have something to do with those children."

"What children? What's going on with children? Were there children around?" I asked. That alarmed me.

"No, there were no children around, but . . . I don't know," he said, shaking his head back and forth. "Every now and then, when I walk by them, they look at me funny, and sometimes, they point at me and say unkind things. I think they're afraid of me."

"I don't know why they would be. I've never done anything to harm any of them, but some of the younger ones run away every now and then when they see me coming. Today, one of the older boys called me a name, and I didn't like that."

"What did you do when he did that?" I asked.

"I shook this stick at him," he told me, lifting up what was more like a walking stick than a cane. "I shouldn't have done that," he acknowledged, "but I did. Other than that, I really don't know, but that's all I can think of."

"You didn't hit him, did you?" I asked.

"No, of course not!" he answered. "I would never do that! Besides, he was a good fifty meters away. He ran to the other side of the playground where all of the others were."

"Then what happened?" I asked.

"I kept walking and then, about an hour later, several kilometers past there, that's when the Garda woman came along and picked me up. I was out on a dirt road just off the old Butter Road about half-way up the hill, as I said, on my way to the top when she found me and brought me here."

"What name did he call you?" I asked.

He lowered his eyes and said, "Amadon."

"Amadon," I repeated. "That wasn't very nice, was it?" I asked.

"No, it wasn't, but I shouldn't have raised my stick as I did," he said, again. "I wasn't trying to scare him. I was just letting him know that I didn't appreciate his remark, that's all."

I was beginning to get an idea of what was going on, but it was still a bit confusing. Was he being charged with a crime of some sort for that incident with the child? Or was there a serious mental health problem? I wasn't hearing or seeing anything that made me all that suspicious.

I told him that I was born in Sneem and had many relatives here. I asked where he lived and how long he'd lived there.

"I have a home out on Sea View Road, not too far out of town. My wife and I bought the house twenty years ago, but that was when I was still working, so we'd only come over for weekends until I retired. When I did, we moved here full time," he told me. Then he looked down, then back up, and added, "She died a few years back and now I live there by myself."

"How long ago was that?" I asked. "When you retired, that is?"

He looked at me with a somewhat blank look on his face, and said, "About ten years ago, I guess. I lose track of time these days. It isn't quite as important as it once was. The days run together now, it seems."

I told him that he looked familiar and asked if he and his wife attended Mass at St. Michael's, since ninety-nine percent of the people in town were Catholic and did. There is another church in the village, called, somewhat ironically, the Church of Ireland, which the few Protestants who live in Sneem attend. He told me that he did when his wife was alive, but not so much anymore since she was gone.

Actually, I couldn't recall ever seeing him before, but it seemed to be a good way to gain his trust by saying what I did. I was asking gentle but probing questions like if he knew so-and-so, who lived not far from where he lived just to make conversation, hoping that he'd say something that would indicate what the problems were, but I wasn't having much luck with any of that. He seemed as fit as a fiddle to me. I hadn't written down a single word though I had a pad and pencil in hand.

At that point, Mollie stuck her head in and asked how things were going. I thanked her and told her everything was fine. I assured her that I was having no problems at all. Then, as she was closing the door, she said, "Be sure to tell him about your home, Mr. McDuffy."

Neither one of us spoke for several moments, and then I asked, "What is it that you're supposed to tell me about your home, Mr. McDuffy?"

"That has nothing to do with any of this. I don't know why she said what she did. I have a fine home, thank you very much. It just needs a little work, that's all," he responded.

"Needs a little work?" I repeated.

"That's right. The roof needs to be replaced and I'm having trouble finding someone to do the work. Other than that, there's nothing wrong with my home," he said. Clearly, he didn't want to talk about any of that but I persisted.

"The roof needs to be replaced?" I asked. "That sounds like a pretty big problem to me, and it costs a lot of money to fix, doesn't it? Is that one of the problems you're having?" I asked. "Is money the problem?"

He bristled a bit, obviously not wanting to talk about his roof, and said, "No, money is not the problem. As I just told you, I haven't been able to find anyone to do the work, but I really don't want to talk about any of that, Mr. . . ."

"Oh! I'm sorry. I haven't properly introduced myself to you, have I? I'm Brendan Sullivan. Nice to meet you, Mr. McDuffy," I said, extending my hand to shake his. I wasn't about to give him one of my cards, and I didn't.

He shook my hand and asked, "But if you would tell me again . . . who are you? And why are you here to see me?"

"You have no idea?" I asked.

"No, I don't," he responded, firmly. "Who are you and why are you here?" he repeated.

At that point, I felt as if I had an ethical obligation to tell him who I was, but I didn't want to tell him too much. "I'm Brendan Sullivan and I'm a student from Cork," I told him.

That seemed to confuse him even more. "A student? A student of what? And you're from Cork? How are you going to help me?" he asked.

"I'm not sure, Mr. McDuffy. Maybe I'm supposed to give you a ride home, like I said before. I don't know. I was told to come down here and meet you," I responded.

"Well, you tell whoever it is you're working with that I'm fine and I don't need any help unless you can give me a ride home. If you can do that, I would be most appreciative," he said.

I had talked to dozens and dozens of people over the last four months, most of whom were truly in need of our assistance and most of them obviously so, but I wasn't quite sure what to make of him. He was nothing like any of the other clients I had ever met. I could see nothing wrong with the man.

His eyes were the most startling characteristic about him. They were a clear blue. He had a head full of white hair, although it appeared as if he could use a trim, but he was clean-shaven and otherwise quite respectable looking. He sat erect in his chair and gave no indication whatsoever that he had a clue as to why I was there.

My purpose in being there was to observe him and report my observations. Others would decide if he was a proper candidate to be involuntarily hospitalized in a mental institution. I wasn't about to tell him any of that or to ask him if he understood that, but I wanted to be able to report what he knew.

Did he know that he had a problem? Did he understand what was going on? Was he lost, as Mollie told me? Was dementia an issue? It didn't seem to be. I was confused, quite possibly as much as he was, if not more.

Instinctively, I asked, "And what about that roof? What's going on with that again? You can't find someone to fix it? Fix what? The whole thing? What happened to it?" There must have been a reason Mollie told me to ask about that.

Reluctantly, and somewhat sheepishly, he told me, "That was my fault. A few months ago, I left something on the stove and it caused a little fire. I admitted all of that to the authorities. It was an accident, that's all. I know that I need to get it fixed, and I will, but that's my problem, and it's nobody else's business. It doesn't bother me all that much. I don't know why people are making such a fuss over it or why that woman mentioned it to you just now. That has nothing to do with why I am here or why she won't take me back to my house."

At that point, I didn't know what to do or what to ask next. I wasn't able to discern an illness of any kind, and he seemed so self-assured and confident in himself that I just didn't know what to make of him. He was obviously an intelligent, well-educated man who was probably much smarter than I was. I had no idea what crime he was accused of committing, if any. I decided that it would be best to take a little break and see what else Mollie had to say about him.

"Mr. McDuffy, would you mind if I go out and talk to Mollie for a moment? I'll be right back. I need to ask her a few questions. Would that be alright?" I asked.

"Of course," he responded. "And would you be so kind as to bring me a cup of water? I've been here for well over an hour now and I'm a bit parched," he said.

"Not at all," I answered. "I'll be right back."

Mollie was at the front desk, with her head down, busily working on something. It seemed as if we were the only three people in the building.

"No one else working today, Mollie?" I asked.

"Willie and Timothy are out making their rounds if they're not sittin' someplace having a bite to eat, which is most likely the case," she answered. "What is it I can do for you?" she asked.

"I'd like to see some of the paperwork on Mr. McDuffy. Has he been charged with a crime?" I asked.

"He's committed no crimes," she answered. "He's as fine a gentleman as you'll ever meet. I brought him here to have Dr. Doherty take a look at him."

"He's the one who must have called you," she continued. "I didn't, but I called him before going out to pick the man up after I received a call from one of the locals. We've never done this sort of thing before," she told me.

"What? What do you mean?" I asked. Clearly, they picked people up and made arrests every day. What was so different about this? I wondered. "You've never done what sort of thing before?"

"Well, we received a call from a woman about a strange man walking around her home, and from her description, I knew who it was. So that's when I called Dr. Doherty and explained what was going on. He agreed to take a look at him, so that's why I went out and found the man and brought him here. Dr. Doherty was supposed to be here already, but he got tied up with other matters, apparently, so that's why this is taking so long. We wanted him to be seen by a mental health professional, and he's not that, but he's the closest thing we have to that anywhere around here."

"Dr. Doherty is a medical doctor?" I asked. "He's not a psychologist or a psychiatrist?"

"No, he's not. He sees people who are sick. That was my idea, actually, to have him see Mr. McDuffy. I didn't know what else to do. This isn't the first time something like this has happened with the man. That's why I called Dr. Doherty. I spoke to him myself. He agreed to come see him and he assured me that he'd be here by now. He must have been the one to call you and you just happened to get here before he did," she told me. "That's what's going on," she added. "I thought you might have worked in his office when you first came in, but you don't, do you?" she asked.

"No, I don't. I have no idea who Dr. Doherty is," I told her. Then I asked, "So he's not going to be put in gaol for any crime?"

"Good heavens, no! He's a brilliant man . . . taught at Trinity College in Dublin for years," she said.

"He's a professor? From Trinity College?" I asked.

"That he is . . . or he was. He's just getting old, that's all, and that's really what this is all about, I think," she said, "and he started that fire in his home last year, and . . ."

"Last year?" I asked. "He said it was just a few months ago."

"No, it was last year, maybe even the year before, and he hasn't done anything about it! It's a mess, and that's not all of it . . . there's more," she said.

"More?" I asked. "More of what?"

"He keeps getting lost and doing abnormal things, that's all. He forgets things, loses things, and does things that make people think he's lost his marbles. As I said, I think he's just getting old, that's all," she responded, "but we keep getting calls about him, so I had to do something."

When I didn't say anything in response, she continued, "And he has no one to take care of him. That's a big part of the problem, really . . . or that's what I think. He needs someone to take care of him, watch after him a bit."

"Abnormal things? What does that mean?" I asked. "What sort of things has he done that are abnormal?"

"Well, he lost his wallet the other day with all his money and identification in it. That was just last week. Someone found it and turned it in. He was lucky to get it back. And we've found him out walking late at night several times when it was dark outside, seemingly lost, though he wouldn't admit it. We thought it was dangerous for him to be out by himself like that, and there's more, a lot more, really, but I shouldn't say too much. I'm not an expert. I'm just a law enforcement officer trying to do my job, that's all."

"I think I've said too much as it is. That's for others to decide. That's why you're here and that's why Dr. Doherty is coming to see him sometime this afternoon," she told me. "But that's only part of the problem," she added.

"What else is there?" I asked.

"Well, his behavior has caused a little alarm for some of the local parents. He walks by the playground where all the children play and they're afraid he might do something, the parents are, that is. It's silly, really. He's never hurt a fly to our knowledge, but you know how parents can be these days, what with all the awful things going on that we read about in the papers and all," she said. "In fact, I received a call about something happening out there earlier today, but I haven't had the time to look into the matter," she added.

"Also, that business of his house is part of the problem, too. The father of one of the boys is a building inspector for the village and he has filed the papers and done all that he can to have the place where Mr. McDuffy lives condemned. He wants it torn down. He says it's an eye-sore and a nuisance. I think Mr. McDuffy has been given a couple of months to get things sorted out or else they're going to do something about it. They might be trying to have the place demolished, but I'm not sure about that. That's my understanding of the situation. We're not involved in that at all . . . the Garda, that is . . . but that's what I've been told," she said.

"It's my understanding that he's not supposed to be living there until he gets it fixed up, but he's been told that a hundred times and has done nothing about it. He just ignores the warnings. It's a bit of a problem for us because we hear the complaints. As I say, some of the parents are concerned, and then there's that inspector fellow. He called me today just before that woman did, complaining about him, again. So, it's a combination of things . . . that's why he's here . . . we had to do something, but as I told you a minute ago, he's done nothing wrong. He's committed no crimes. He's a fine man," she said.

I didn't say anything in response, still processing what she had told me, and then she added again somewhat defensively, "We had no choice, really. We had to do something, so today, when that woman called about him, I decided to bring him here. I'm the one who did that, and that's why he's here. So, you can blame me if you want."

"But where's the mental problem?" I asked. "There has to be a mental illness or disorder to put somebody in a mental institution. That's the sort of thing the people I work with are concerned about. What's wrong with him?"

"I don't know what's wrong with him. As far as I'm concerned, he's a nice, old man, like I said, but he's become a bit of a loo-lah. He's all the time forgettin' stuff . . . leavin' his front door wide open when he's off on one of his walks . . . all sorts of things. He lost his license to drive a while back. The government did that. I think that was mostly because of his eyesight, though. He doesn't see too well. And he was all the time parkin' the wrong way in places or locking himself out of his car, forgetting where he put his keys . . . all kinds of stuff. We've put up with him for years because he's such a nice man," she said, "but there's more . . ."

She leaned over the desk and whispered, "He talks to angels!"

I talked to angels, too. Most Catholics I know do, so I didn't think too much of that and said so.

"No! I mean he really talks to them! . . . walkin' down the road and all . . . having a conversation with them . . . people who don't know him and see him do those kinds of things think he's mad! But as long as he wasn't hurting anyone and no one was hurting him, what was the problem?" she asked, raising her hands in the air. "There was none! Or at least nothin' too much to worry about . . . nothin' for the Garda to do. Now we have a problem. The children are becoming afraid of him, but that's because of the parents, I'd say, but they've started to complain more frequently, with the house and all, as I was saying," she repeated.

Again, she lowered her voice and whispered though no one was there to hear what we were saying to each other, "There's another little problem, too. You see . . . Officer Ahern is related to one of the boys."

"Oh! I see," I said, not really knowing what to make of it. Everybody knows everybody else and we're all related to everyone else in one way or another. I knew Officer Ahern. He went to school with Siobhan.

"You know how that can be, right?" she asked.

"I grew up in Sneem and I know Officer Ahern. I probably know the family of the boys and everyone else involved in this, except for Mr. McDuffy," I told her.

"That's Dr. McDuffy, actually. We should be calling him that. As I said, he's a retired professor," she told me again.

"That's impressive," I said. "I could tell that he was an intelligent man."

"A lot smarter than you or me, I'd say," she responded. "No offense, of course," she added.

"None taken," I answered. "But Sneem is a small village where everyone knows everybody else and knows all about their business, right?" I asked.

"That's true," she replied, and then she said, "So, if you know all of those people, then you know what I'm talking about."

"I do now. I don't live around here anymore and I never heard about any of this. I couldn't figure out what was going on until you told me the things you just did. Now, I have a much better understanding of what's going on here. Thank you for that explanation."

"You're welcome," she responded. "But don't tell anyone that I told you any of that other stuff, about the inspector, Officer Ahern, and the rest, okay?" she added. "We're all wanting to see what Dr. Doherty has to say as I told you before."

"Well, I don't know how I can be of assistance here until we hear from Dr. Doherty . . . I mean, really . . . the man hasn't been arrested, and he's never hurt anyone, has he?" I asked.

"No . . . never!" she answered.

"And he hasn't ever hurt himself, has he?" I asked.

"Oh, he's fallen down once or twice and we had to administer first aid a time or two, but nothin' serious," she told me.

"So, there's not much I can do," I told her. "We'll just have to wait and see what Dr. Doherty has to say, I guess, just like you."

"I guess so," she acknowledged.

I looked at my watch and saw that it was already past five o'clock. I was thinking about being at the pub with Colin and the others. I really didn't want to have to wait around until Dr. Doherty saw the man. Who knew how long that would take? I was ready to leave.

"Well, I think I might as well go back to Cork and see what happens," I told her. "You've got my card. Can you send me a copy of his report?" I asked.

"I'm not sure if I can or not. I'll see what I can do, but you know how things are, with privacy laws and all," she answered, and then she added, "Sorry to bother you with all of this, but as I said, it must have been Dr. Doherty who called you. I didn't. Maybe he can give you a copy of his report. I called his office once you arrived and was told that he should be here any time now. He had a few more patients to see, but I have no idea when that will be. I thought for sure he'd be here by now."

"No worries. It's not your fault. I'll go back and say goodbye to Mr. McDuffy—Dr. McDuffy—I should say, and then I'll leave if you don't mind," I told her.

"I don't mind at all," she said. "Thank you for being here. Nice to meet you, Mr. Sullivan. Have a nice trip back to Cork. Thanks for coming."

She and I then walked together back to see Dr. McDuffy. I gave him the cup of water he'd asked for and said goodbye to him. The three of us then walked back up to the front where I first met the two of them. I wished him well and said that I was sorry not to be able to help. As I drove home, I thought to myself that would be the last I would hear about the man, but I was wrong.

CHAPTER FOUR

Dr. Doherty

It was late in the day by the time I made it back to Cork. The employee parking lot was nearly empty and I was able to park not far from the entrance, which was a rare occurrence since it was usually jam-packed. It was well after normal business hours.

The hospital stays open twenty-four hours a day, three hundred and sixty-five days a year, so there is no closing time for it, and most employees worked eight-hour shifts. Doctors could come and go as they pleased. The three shift changes were at 8:00 in the morning, 4:00 in the afternoon, and midnight. That was for most of the regular employees, such as the nurses, aides, maintenance personnel, and the administrative staff. Security guards were on duty at all times, but they were stationed at the entrances after 4:00 in the afternoon until 8:00 in the morning.

In the Clinical Psychology unit, there were many people who performed administrative functions, such as secretarial or record-keeping. Then, there were clinical psychologists and their assistants, which included people like Colin and me. General Psychology and Psychiatry were entirely different units, but the three were lumped together as one department.

We had little to do with the medical unit, which was a separate department, and was, by far, the largest department in the hospital. There might only have been a hundred people in my unit, all told. There were thousands of people employed by the hospital in one capacity or another, so we were a small part of the total package.

Every day at 8:00 and 4:00, there would be a mass entrance into and an exodus from the hospital as most of the people who worked at the hospital, in whatever capacity, would be coming or going. There were much fewer people on the evening shift, which worked from 4:00 to 12:00 than there were on the day shift, and then even fewer on the night shift, which worked from midnight to 8:00 in the morning. There were probably three times as many people on the day shift than the evening and night shifts combined, but that's just a guess.

Even though we, the trainees, were considered "professionals," we were required to punch in and out every day and follow the clock as rigorously as the rest of the staff did. However, we were expected to work longer hours and we weren't paid any overtime. We were "salaried" employees, not paid by the hour, but we still had to punch in and out.

It was normally at least 5:00 before any of the trainees, like me, left. The doctors and staff psychologists usually stayed even later than that. It was nearly 6:00 by the time I got back, so I had to go through security and then punch back in. I was surprised to see that Colin and several others were still there.

As clinical psychologists, since our job was, for the most part, to assess the problems at the outset, we were usually in a rush to get things done. We participated in the care and treatment of the patients after that, but we were more concerned with "intake." We were the ones who met people before they were hospitalized.

The "general" psychologists provided for most of the mental health care and treatment once the people were admitted to the hospital. They rarely, if ever, met with patients outside of the hospital setting. We almost always did.

There was a "team" approach to every patient, which included medical personnel, such as the doctors and nurses, and there were all kinds of doctors—internists, cardiologists, rheumatologists, orthopedics—everything, and then there were the therapists specializing in physical therapy, occupational therapy, and other things, plus there were sociologists and many other units, as well. Again, we were a part of the St. Stephen's team, but we were a small part of it. So far, I'd had little to do with anyone outside of our unit.

With cases such as Dr. McDuffy's, since he wasn't an admitted patient nor was he a "patient" at all yet, he was in the category of "intake." Dr. Delaney, who probably wasn't more than fifteen or twenty years older than me, was the head of the "clinical psychology" unit, but he wasn't over the entire department. When I walked in, he peered out of his office to see who it was. He didn't say anything to me, though, as I walked by.

I had met him on one or two occasions where all staff members were present, but I hadn't had much to do with him, so far. I was sure that he didn't know my name and had no idea who I was, but I knew that he was going to be reviewing my report, and I was a bit nervous about that prospect. I wasn't too sure that I'd done all that I was supposed to do, leaving as I did.

Since Colin was still there, I prepared my report as fast as I could and handed it to him within a few minutes. There wasn't much to it, but the timing was critical in these matters as there was a clock running, and those were our orders—to get those things completed as quickly as possible. After that, the higher-ups would be able to make a decision.

I certainly didn't make such decisions, and neither did Colin. We prepared reports. This was an easy one. I really didn't give it too much thought. I was a little worried about the fact that I left early before the man was seen by the doctor who called us, but what was I to do? I couldn't wait there forever, and I didn't see much of anything wrong with the man.

The first thing I said to Colin upon handing it to him was that the man hadn't been seen by a mental health professional, psychologist, or psychiatrist yet, though he was supposed to be seeing a medical doctor later after I left. I told him about how a Garda officer had started the whole thing without someone in the medical profession having done so, and I asked him about it. He explained to me that though it was unusual, it was permissible under the law.

"A family member or friend can initiate the process, too," he explained, "and that's how it usually starts, in my experience. From what you've told me, it was the doctor who called us in, not the Garda, so he's the one who started this one even though he hadn't seen the man first."

When I asked if I should have stayed and waited for the doctor to see the man, he told me, "You did what you could . . . you gathered information and talked to the man at length, and left it up to the doctor. I wouldn't have waited around all afternoon for the doctor to arrive, either. There's no problem with this one." He assured me, "You did nothing wrong."

My next comment was about how Dr. McDuffy had been a professor at Trinity College, Dublin, the most prestigious academic institution in the country. He, too, was impressed by that. He said it was rare for a man of that stature to be the subject of such proceedings. He'd never seen a case like it.

"Not here at St. Stephen's, as far as I know. Not since I've been here," he told me. "Those types of cases are handled privately, not here, not like this. It's a rare case, indeed."

I was jabbering on and on about how this man had been taken into custody and held in a Garda station even though no crime had been committed. I told him how it seemed to me to be a relatively insignificant matter involving a man who was getting older and becoming a bit forgetful; that was all. I thought the whole thing was strange and told him so.

Colin was busy preparing a report of his own on another patient, but he'd say something like, "I see what you mean," or "Is that so," every now and then, or he'd grunt some response I couldn't understand. He didn't seem to care too much about anything I was saying.

Due to the late hour, he had to get his report and mine to Dr. Delaney, our top boss, before he could leave. He wasn't a medical doctor, but he had obtained his Ph.D. and he insisted on being called a doctor. I didn't know his first name. Everyone called him Dr. Delaney.

Colin signed off on my report, though I'm not sure that he ever finished reading it. After he finished his and as he was rushing down the hall to get in to see Dr. Delaney, he told me that he would see me at Molly Malone's in a few minutes and we could talk more about it then.

Since we worked in a hospital, I was required to wear a white, long-sleeved shirt with a badge identifying me and my position.

Mine said "Clinical Psychologist in Training." I could wear whatever pants and shoes I wanted, but the shirt was mandatory. They gave me a supply of them when I started.

It was more like a light jacket, actually, and I usually wore a regular collared shirt underneath. I wore the badge around my neck with a string attached, but I could clip it on if I wanted to. Before going to the pub, I went home to change out of that uniform.

By the time I left my apartment, after changing clothes, it was half-past 6:00 when I arrived at the pub. I was thinking I'd be late, but I was the first one there. I chose a table in the back corner big enough to hold a dozen people. It was where the group normally sat and that's about how many usually came.

It was fairly close to the dartboards where the games would begin in an hour or so. Some people were already playing, getting ready for the competition. I was glad to see Saoirse walk through the door not long after I did. She was the next to arrive.

We sat there for a good fifteen minutes or more, sipping pints of Guinness and talking about what we'd done that day. She'd been sent out to Glenbeigh, another small village, a little further away than Sneem, on the other side of the Ring, to meet someone. The man she met was tied to a stretcher hands and feet when she got there, swearing that there was nothing wrong with him even though he had tried to stab his mother with a knife hours earlier.

The man had told her that it was only a butter knife, not a butcher knife, and he never meant to hurt her. The issue there was whether or not the Garda was going to charge him with a crime and put him in a hospital for criminals or have him put in an institution like ours without charging him with a crime. Depending upon what the medical professionals determined about the man's competency, two completely separate procedures were to be followed—one civil in nature and the other a criminal matter.

Although her case was definitely unusual, she was much more interested to hear all about my case than to tell me about hers. Her father had attended Trinity College, too, as she had, and she couldn't wait to get home and ask him if he knew Dr. McDuffy. We weren't supposed to discuss any of our cases with people outside of our department, and I told her so, but it was okay for us to talk about those things amongst ourselves. I asked her not to tell anyone, including her father about him, and she agreed not to.

To her, the most interesting part of the case wasn't about the Garda picking the man up, or the children, the roof, or any of the rest—it was about how advanced dementia had to be to qualify as a mental illness. For me, he was just a nice old man who was getting older. I called it "old-timers'" condition. I didn't think that it was an illness at all. That was just a part of getting old.

"It's true, dementia isn't a disease, Brendan, but it's a 'condition.' We both know that, but when it gets to a point where it's severe enough to reduce a person's ability to do normal, everyday activities, then it becomes something worse, like Alzheimer's . . . that's a disease. Most of the cases we deal with involve patients who have dementia, not Alzheimer's. People with Alzheimer's end up in a hospital like ours unless they have a family to take care of them," she told me.

"I know that," I told her, "and I understand that dementia is a symptom, not a disease, but my point is that it's normal for people to start forgetting things as they get older, isn't it? Once people stop working, and they don't have to be on time to be anywhere or do anything, they don't have as much to think about, and they forget stuff, right? I think that's just what happens as you get older. He's just old, that's all. That doesn't make him a mental case, does it?"

She laughed and said, "A mental case . . . you're funny! I don't think I've ever seen that term used in any of our textbooks, Brendan. What does that mean?"

"You know what I mean," I responded, regretting what I said. I was trying to impress her, and not doing too well at it.

Then she said, "I'm only kidding, but we can't talk like that anymore, can we . . . but seriously, I agree with you. I think it's normal for a person's memory to decline as they get older. I think it goes without saying that an older person's memory isn't going to be as good as it once was. It isn't going to get better, is it? Of course not. To me, that only makes sense."

"That's what I'm trying to say . . . I guess the real question is one of degree . . . how far does a declining mind or brain have to go before someone makes a diagnosis of dementia? And then, how bad does it have to be before someone else says it's actually Alzheimer's, and they put the person in a hospital or something? Just because someone is forgetful doesn't make him mentally ill, does it?" I asked. "The man's not mentally ill, he's just a bit forgetful, that's what I think. I didn't think he was demented at all."

"Maybe you're right, but I don't know. You met him, I didn't, Brendan. At the very least, it sounds like he's forgetful, and I'm taking a class about things like that and we . . . and I mean psychologists, not me . . . say that becoming forgetful is abnormal. Our profession says that it's not a normal part of aging to start forgetting things. We say that any decline in the thought processes of an individual is an indication of a problem—a symptom of a bigger problem," she said.

"I know . . . I've read that in our textbooks, too, but come on! We both know older people and they all start forgetting things at some point, don't they? I don't know of any older people I've ever met who don't forget things, like names of their grandchildren every now and then . . . things like that . . . do you?"

"That's true. My granny used to forget my name all the time before she died," she acknowledged. "She kept calling me Sheila, but that's different. That's not what I'm talking about. You don't think he was showing any signs of dementia, Brendan, after all that Garda lady told you?" she asked.

"Not that I saw, but I could be wrong," I responded. "But we're supposed to report what we see, not just what others tell us, right? I agree that he's got some problems going on in his life, and people have to keep an eye on things to make sure it doesn't get too bad. My point is that it's got to get really bad before it becomes an illness or a disease before we step in, doesn't it?" I asked.

"When a person becomes like that man who I saw today where he or she becomes a danger to himself or others, that's when it becomes a serious problem . . . that's where we come in . . . that's when the law comes into play," she said.

"Now that guy was crazy! That's different," I responded.

"My point is that the law gets involved when things get bad and when a person is a danger to himself or others. So, I guess that's it . . . how bad is too bad?" she said. "How bad was your man?" she asked.

"As I said, he didn't seem bad at all, to me, but the Garda woman said he'd done a whole bunch of unusual things, like get lost a few times and other stuff," I told her, "but he's no danger to anyone else. The Garda lady said he was as gentle as a lamb."

"He wasn't a danger to himself in any way?" she asked.

"Well, he set his house on fire a while back, does that count?" I asked.

"It might. I'd have to know more about him," she responded.

"Oh, come on! This man's a former professor! He's brilliant! He's not so bad that we have to get involved, is he? He's never hurt anyone and he's never hurt himself. I think we should just leave him alone. You know as well as I do that sometimes we meet older people who are as sharp as a tack, and other times, we meet older people who aren't. They can't remember names, facts, figures . . . they say things like, 'Oh, I can't remember his name right now' . . . . 'you know, what's his name?' . . . or 'I forget what I was talking about,' . . . things like that. I hear that all the time, don't you?" I asked.

"Of course, I do, but that's different," she said.

"No, I don't think it is . . . I think that's normal . . . and we can't be putting all the people who start forgetting things in hospitals now, can we?" I asked.

She laughed and said, "No . . . we can't do that, so it depends, I guess, on a lot of things, but we can agree that when it gets too bad, something has to be done, right?"

"There's no doubt about that, and some people are just a whole lot smarter than other people, to begin with, right? Take Dr. McDuffy . . . he's probably forgotten more than I will ever know. That doesn't mean that his brain is diseased or that he's mentally ill, does it? He's probably twice as smart as I am right now no matter how much he's forgotten, right?"

We both laughed at that, and then she said, "Of course not, and I agree with you . . . I'm sure that he's a lot smarter than you are right now!" We laughed again.

"But seriously, some people, and, apparently, it's a growing number of people in Sneem, are saying that Dr. McDuffy 'has' dementia and they want something done about it. That's what this is all about. The Garda lady told me that she didn't want to do what she did, but she felt like she had to because it had been going on for a while and people were complaining about him," I told her.

When I told her that, she lit up, grabbed my arm, and said, "You know what, Brendan, that could be a great project to work on! That would make a great thesis, wouldn't it?"

"A thesis?" I said, repeating her words.

"Yes, for a doctorate. You're planning to go on to get a Master's degree, and then a Doctorate, aren't you?" she asked.

I laughed and said, "At the moment, my plans don't go much past tomorrow. I plan to have a few beers tonight, listen to whatever Colin and his friends have to say, them being third-year students and so much smarter than we are and all, and then wake up tomorrow morning, go to work, and get ready to enjoy the weekend, it being pay-day and all. I'm not thinking much past that, are you?"

She smiled and said, "I am. I could change my mind, but that's what I want to do with my life even though it's going to take a while, and I think that McDuffy case of yours could be a really great topic. That's an interesting case you have there, for sure. I can't wait to hear what Dr. Delaney has to say about it."

Then she added, "I'd love to be able to work on it with you."

She was a really good-looking girl and the thought of doing anything with her was quite inviting. I was more interested in working with children, though, and I wasn't all that interested in senior citizens, like Dr. McDuffy. However, if she was, I was all in.

I smiled back at her, looking into her beautiful green eyes, thinking of what to say, and just as I was about to respond, Colin and two of his friends showed up, breaking the spell. When they did, Saoirse greeted them, stood up, and said, "I'll be right back. I'm off to the jacks!"

When she was out of earshot, Colin asked, "Havin' a nice chit-chat with Saoirse, are ya, Top Shillin'?"

"As a matter of fact, we were . . . 'til you showed up," I responded.

"She's out of your league, Sully. She's a stunner and you're a bleedin' tick!" he said, which made his two friends who I'd never met before laugh. I just smiled back and laughed with them.

The waitress came walking up to the table and he said, "Three Smithwicks, please, Luv." Then he turned to me and said, "Dr. Delaney wants to see the two of us first thing in the mornin', Sully."

"Dr. Delaney! What for?" I asked.

"That McDuffy case, of course. What else, ya sap!" he responded.

"Am I in trouble, Colin?" I asked.

"No trouble. He just wants to talk about it, that's all," he told me.

More people began to arrive and the conversation turned from work to other things, like the big football game in Dublin this Saturday—the Kerry team versus Dublin's finest. I knew all about it, of course, and would, without a doubt, be watching.

Several of the men were planning to go. A big music event was to take place in town that weekend, too. I had no plans to go to either. All of that cost a pretty penny and I wasn't able to afford the price of admission. Besides, tickets to the game were hard to find. Croke Park would be jammed without a doubt.

When Saoirse returned, she sat down just long enough to finish her drink, and then she was off. Before she left, I told her about how I would be seeing Dr. Delaney in the morning to discuss the McDuffy case. She seemed excited to hear it and asked me to let her know how it went.

After having two pints, I stood to leave. As I was walking out, Colin told me that I was a "slagger" and that he'd see me in the morning. He also warned me not to be late. "Delaney's always the first one in," he told me.

CHAPTER FIVE

Dr. Delaney

I was at work bright and early the next morning, anxious about meeting with Dr. Delaney. I was kind of dreading it, actually, like I had done something wrong, that I should have stayed until Dr. Doherty saw the man. I didn't sleep all that well because of it.

I was more than a bit apprehensive, though I couldn't quite understand what the fuss was about. To me, it was a rather simple matter. The man may have been a bit eccentric, but he wasn't crazy, and he wasn't a danger to himself or anyone else as far as I could see.

Colin was in the office when I walked in. "Good afternoon, Mr. Sullivan," he said.

"Afternoon? I'm ten minutes early!" I protested.

"As I told you last night, Dr. Delaney is always the first one in. He's been by twice askin' for ya. Let's go."

With that, the two of us walked down to the end of the hall and into what was the largest office in our wing of the hospital. His secretary told us to go right in, that he was expecting us.

Dr. Delaney was seated at his desk, facing us as we walked in. A large window, which looked out over a lot where hundreds of cars were parked, was behind him. There were some trees and a little park off to one side, and the bigger buildings of the city of Cork were behind all of that. He stood as we walked in.

"Come in! Come in! Thank you for taking the time to see me," he said with a smile. He extended his hand toward me and said, "I don't believe that I have met you before, Mr. Sullivan, so it's nice to meet you. I hope you're enjoying your work here with us so far."

We had met twice before, although I was in a group with many others at the time, but I thanked him and told him that I was very pleased with how things were going and happy to be there as we shook hands.

He was dressed in a suit and tie, not as I normally saw him, which was much the way the rest of us dressed, and he looked more like a barrister than a doctor. "I have to go to a meeting in town with some of the local businessmen," he explained, "but I needed to address this situation before I left. Please sit down. Mr. O'Riordan speaks well of you, Mr. Sullivan, and I want to assure you that you've done nothing wrong here, but I needed to get some additional information from you before making a decision on this case."

"I received a report from a Dr. Doherty late yesterday afternoon, shortly after the both of you had left for the day," he explained, "and Dr. Doherty seems quite insistent that a more thorough examination than he is able to provide is in order. He's not necessarily saying that involuntary hospitalization is appropriate in this case, but he wants us to look into the situation more carefully than he is able to do. He is, after all, a general practitioner. He has a family-oriented practice. He's not a psychologist or psychiatrist. This isn't his field."

I was about to tell him that I hadn't seen that report when he went on to say, "I know that you haven't seen this report, and I want you to take a look at it and let me know what you think before I make a decision."

As he was handing us a copy of the report, he said, "I'm sure that there is more to this story than meets the eye, so I am hoping you can provide me with a few more details. What am I missing? It's like two people are describing two entirely different men."

"What I'm trying to decide is whether Dr. McDuffy should be admitted for a short-term . . . seventy-two hours, if that . . . to allow further observation and evaluation, or not. I'm familiar with Dr. McDuffy by reputation alone. He was still on the faculty at Trinity College while I was there, but I didn't take any of the classes he taught. He's quite well-thought-of, you know. What did you make of him, aside from that business of the youngsters and their parents?" he asked.

"He was pleasant enough, Dr. Delaney, although he wasn't too happy about his circumstances when we met. I don't think he had any idea that people were suggesting he's mentally ill. I think that would have really set him off if he did. He didn't understand why the Garda picked him up and wouldn't take him home. It wasn't the first time that had happened, though. Apparently, he's gotten lost more than a few times on his daily walks in the recent past," I answered.

"Well, you didn't mention much of that in your report, but I surmised that might be part of his problem, yes? Not knowing or recognizing that a problem exists can be an indicator, correct? In fact, the very first step toward recovery in most of our cases is taken when the patient acknowledges that a problem exists. Is that the situation here? Is Dr. McDuffy oblivious to the problems he is having?" he asked.

"I think he's aware of the fact that he's done a few unusual things, but I seriously doubt that he thinks he has a mental health problem," I responded. "He just wanted to go home and couldn't understand why he wasn't allowed to do so. To me, it was more of a 'handbags' situation, as far as I could tell. He hadn't done anything wrong and they had no reason to be holding him."

"To be honest, I agreed with him. I don't think that they had a right to pick him up and hold him against his will as they did. He'd committed no crime, yet they, in effect, arrested him. I didn't tell the officer any of that, of course, but that's what I thought."

He laughed and said, "Handbags, you say . . . is that a term of art they're using in the universities these days, Mr. Sullivan? I know what you mean, but you're becoming a professional. I wouldn't want to see that word appear in any of your reports, understood?"

"Yes, sir," I answered apologetically. "But no one was hurt and no criminal charges had been filed against him, nor would there be any. I thought that they were going to let him go home shortly after Dr. Doherty saw him and that would be the end of it. I guess that didn't happen or did it?" I asked.

"Not right away, but they did take him home after he was seen by Dr. Doherty. There was no place else for him to go, except here, and I wasn't ready to allow that to happen until I heard more from you. I should be back before noon and I'd like to meet with the two of you then. Mr. O'Riordan, you'll help Mr. Sullivan with this, will you?"

"Of course, sir," Colin answered.

"Splendid. I'll see the two of you in an hour or two," he said, as he stood. He shook our hands and walked out of the door ahead of us, picking up his umbrella as he did. "I really have to run. Sorry!"

He was a tall, thin man with curly, black hair, and he seemed to cover about twice the distance with each step as I could. With his black-rimmed spectacles and gaunt face, he looked much older than his years. He was a friendly but comical-looking fellow, actually. We watched as he bounded down the hall and out of sight in no time.

Colin and I walked down the hall back toward our cubicles and stopped for a cup of coffee at the little snack area along the way.

"I need a little of this," Colin said as he poured himself a cup. "I stayed a little longer than I should have last night . . . again," he added.

I laughed and said "I was up worryin' about this meeting for a while. I had a hard time falling off to sleep. I don't know why. It's not like he's a walkin' menace, terrorizing the community."

"It's nothin' to worry about, Sullivan . . . just another patient. You can't take this stuff too much to heart or it will get to ya. Do the best you can and leave it up to the boys who make the big bucks, like Delaney. That's not us," he told me.

"Let's sit in here and take a look at this report. It's quieter and we won't be bothered," he said as he opened a door to what was a small conference room.

Saoirse happened to be walking in as we were about to enter and she asked, "So how did it go?"

"It's not over yet. Dr. Delaney had to go to a meeting. We're to talk about it some more later this morning. Colin and I are about to read a report from that doctor in Kenmare and figure out what to tell him when he gets back," I told her.

"Can I sit in?" she asked.

"I don't see why not," Colin responded. "It must be a pretty interesting case for Delaney to get involved. Sure, come join us."

Just as we were about to sit down, Colin said, "I'll make two copies of this report here, so we can all three read at the same time," and he walked over to the photocopier in the far corner of the room to make the copies.

"So, how's the form today, boys? Did you have a good night after I left?" she asked.

"I'm grand! Couldn't be better, except for this meeting, of course. I left not long after you did, but I had a little trouble getting to sleep, worried that I messed somethin' up," I answered a bit sheepishly, "I'm not so sure about Colin, here."

"Me head is bangin'," he said, "but we'll be alright. Nothin' too much out of the ordinary."

He handed us the copies as he sat down and said, "Let's see what the fuss is all about here."

The three of us sat there quietly reading for several minutes without any of us saying a word. Then Colin said, "This is nothin' to worry yourself about, Brendan, but this Dr. Doherty seems to think the man is a lot worse off than you do."

"He makes the man sound like he's a real loo-lah alright, but I didn't think that at all. He's never done anything to hurt the youngsters or anyone else," I answered, "and no charges had been lodged against him, ever, in his entire life, but there are things in here that I knew nothin' about."

"I talked to me Da about him last night," Saoirse said, "without telling him about any of this, of course. I was just asking if he knew the man, and he did. He spoke well of him . . . had him as a teacher in a few classes when he was there at Trinity, but that was years and years ago."

"This Dr. Doherty, who's a medical doctor not one of us, thinks the man's gone batty . . . forgettin' things and talkin' to angels and stuff," Colin observed. "That's a large part of his report, actually."

"And he makes quite the point about the house where he lives not being safe and all," Saoirse added. "He makes it sound as if he's a danger to himself if left to live alone because of the condition of his house."

"I think that there's probably a whole lot more to this than what's in this report. The Garda woman hinted that there might be some neighbors who want him off his property, maybe it's so they can get it from him, or at least that's what I thought she was suggesting. She didn't come right out and say that, and I could be wrong about that, which is why none of that is in my report," I said.

"That's the kind of stuff Delaney wants to hear about . . . he needs a bit more facts, I think, Sully. What else can you tell him?" Colin asked.

"Well, if I understood her correctly, it's the parents of those kids, and I don't know how old they are . . . the kids, that is . . . who are a bit skiddish about him. It's not so much what he's done but what they're afraid he might do. Then, there is the business of having the old man's house torn down, which is another issue. It's as if they're lookin' for a reason to get the man out of the neighborhood. They want to have somethin' done about the man.

"Remember, he's an outsider, and everyone who lives there is related to everyone else in one way or another," I added. "He's only lived there for fifteen or twenty years, I think, and that was only for part of the time, until recently, after he retired. So, he's an outsider. That was somebody else's land before he bought it. Maybe they want it back."

"That's no surprise there, is it?" Saoirse asked. "That's the way it is all over Ireland, in all of the villages, right? Even if you've been there for a hundred years, you're still an outsider, right?"

"That's the way it is in Sneem," I responded. "I didn't know the man, and I'm from there."

"Sneem, is it? Is that where you're from, Sully?" Colin asked.

"I was born there. Me father, brothers, sisters, uncles, aunts, cousins, and the rest of his side of the family all live there, but me Ma and her people are from here in Cork," I told him.

"I knew you were a bit of a bogger. I could tell that right off," he said. We all laughed when he said that.

"Seriously, though," he began. "There's nothin' wrong with your report here, Sully. Dr. Doherty provides a lot more facts and from what he says in there, it looks as if the man has dementia. At the very least, there are strong indications of it, but while that may well be true, it's all a matter of degree, right? How far along the disease has progressed? That's the question."

"If it's a disease at all," Saoirse interjected.

"That's right . . . if it's bad enough to be a disease at all," Colin agreed. "Dementia isn't called a disease until it has progressed to the point that it becomes seriously problematic. That's true, Saoirse. It's a gray area, to be sure."

"Delaney knows good and well who Professor McDuffy is and he knows if he was put in a hospital and the press got wind of it, they'd put it in the papers. I don't think he wants to see that happen, but he can't just ignore Dr. Doherty, so I think he wants us to give him a good reason to tell the doctor why we won't get involved. I think that's what this is all about," he added.

"It's got to be pretty bad before they lock you up, right?" I asked.

Before I could say another word, Colin interjected, ". . . 'before they lock you up' . . . is that what you just said?" He smiled and said, "You're studyin' to be a professional here, ya little shite! Don't talk like that in front of Delaney or you might be the one to get yourself in trouble here!" We all laughed.

He looked over at Saoirse and said, "He told Delaney that this was all just a 'handbags' thing! Can you believe that?" he asked.

We all laughed again and then I said, "But he didn't seem that bad to me at all as I told him. We had a nice little chat and I didn't think there was anythin' wrong with the man."

"I really didn't spend all that much time with him, partly because it seemed a bit silly, really. The Garda woman liked the man . . . she let him walk all over the place and do whatever he wanted . . . no cuffs or nothin'. She told me that after he was seen by Dr. Doherty, she'd take him home. She didn't think he'd be coming here. Of that, I was quite sure," I said, "or else I would have stayed. She probably would have insisted that I stay, but she didn't."

"He was seen by Dr. Doherty at half-past five yesterday afternoon and he spent at least an hour with the man, it seems. You arrived back here somewhere around that time," Colin confirmed. "No way you should have stayed around any longer than you did, Sullivan. You're fine with that."

"I agree," Saoirse added, "I wouldn't have, but it sounds like Dr. McDuffy is slipping a bit. Think about it . . . as brilliant a man as he is, or was . . . once he stopped teaching, studying, writing, or whatever it is that he did, there's no doubt that he wouldn't be as sharp as he once was, is there? People don't get smarter as they get older, do they?"

Colin looked over at her and said, "You're as bad as he is . . . you're a professional now! Or becoming one! You've got to talk like one . . . older people get dumber . . . don't say something like that to Delaney. I'm serious now! I mean that! You both want him to think you're brilliant. You only have one chance to make a first impression . . . you want to make a good one, so don't mess it up!"

"Now, listen to me, you two grasshoppers. While it's true, without any doubt whatsoever, really, that people like McDuffy or anyone else might not think as clearly as they once did. We in the medical profession . . . clinical psychology, that is . . . say that it is not part of the normal aging process for a person to become forgetful. That is a symptom of a more serious problem and when it gets too serious, it becomes a disease . . . like Alzheimer's."

"I know that, Colin! I told Brendan here that very same thing yesterday," Saoirse responded.

"You did, did you? Well, that's good, because that's what Dr. Doherty is saying here . . . that Professor McDuffy is clearly showing signs of advancing dementia and according to him, it's to the point where the medical profession needs to step in."

"Top Shillin' here doesn't think it's that bad," he added, pointing at me. "Dr. Delaney hopes that you're right, Sullivan. We just have to give him a good reason why he can say you're right and the good doctor is wrong. He has to say it in a nice way, so as not to offend the man."

He then stood and said, "That's it in a nutshell. When Delaney comes back, just answer his questions. He'll figure this thing out. I'd best be off. We have other things to do here this morning, haven't we?"

"Do you think Dr. Delaney would mind if I sat in?" Saoirse asked.

"You're here to learn like the rest of us. I think he'd be okay with that. I'll ask him," he told her. "You two snappers can go back to work now."

Two hours later, as I was immersed in preparing a report about another patient, Colin walked up and said, "Delaney is ready to see us. Let's go."

We walked down the hall and as we passed by her cubicle, Colin stopped, knocked on the glass partition, and said, "Come along, Saoirse. Delaney said you're welcome to sit in on this." She jumped out of her chair and joined us.

The three of us eagerly marched into Dr. Delaney's office, anxious to hear what he'd have to tell us. However, we were disappointed when before we sat down, he said, "I've talked to Dr. Doherty and he's agreed to withdraw the formal petition for involuntary hospitalization for the time being, but he did that as a courtesy to me because I've agreed to personally look into the matter."

"I'm going to want you, Colin, to go back down there to Kenmare and talk to Dr. McDuffy. You can take Mr. Sullivan with you if you want. I'll leave that up to you, and . . ."

At that point, Saoirse blurted out, "Can I go along, too, Dr. Delaney? I've familiarized myself with the case and would very much like to participate."

Dr. Delaney looked over at her, a bit surprised by her request, it seemed, and said, "I can't have all three of you out of the office at the same time. I really can't spare two of you during the week. We have too much work to do . . . you know that, unless you were to do it on your time . . . on a weekend."

I immediately responded by saying, "That's fine with me, Dr. Delaney." Saoirse chimed in, saying that she was fine with that, too.

Colin then spoke up and said, somewhat reluctantly, it seemed, "If it's something that's important to you, Dr. Delaney, I'd be willing to help out with that."

"You would? Well, in that case, I don't see why we couldn't do that then. I don't want this to be threatening to Dr. McDuffy and invade his privacy any more than we have to, though. I have met the man on several occasions, although that was years ago. As I said before, he has an excellent reputation in the academic community and I truly don't wish to mar that, unless it's absolutely necessary. Is that understood?"

He looked over at Colin when he said that.

"Understood, Dr. Delaney. I'll be mindful of that at all times," Colin replied.

"And I want to receive regular reports. I don't expect this to be done in a jiffy, but it's not to be a forever thing, either. I want to get a clear understanding of what's going on with the man and make the best decision possible under the circumstances, understood?"

"Yes, sir. Clear as a bell," Colin answered.

"Thank you, Mr. O'Riordan, and I thank you Mr. Sullivan, and you, Ms. O'Connor, as well. When do you think you'll find the time to begin?" he asked.

The three of us looked at each other, and then I spoke up, saying "This weekend is fine with me."

"Fine with me, too," Saoirse said.

The three of us looked over at Colin who said, "This weekend it is then."

"That's grand. I'll look forward to receiving a report on Monday. I'm in a bit of a push for time, so that will be all for now. Enjoy your trip to Kenmare. It's a beautiful village, quite historic, as I'm sure you are aware."

"Actually, he lives in Sneem, Dr. Delaney," I interjected.

"Sneem, is it? Well, that's a beautiful village, too, not quite as big as Kenmare, and a little bit farther up the road. It's a beautiful drive on the Ring of Kerry. Enjoy your weekend. That will be all for now."

At that, he pushed a button on his phone and said, "Shannon, if you would, please get Dr. Doherty on the line for me."

The three of us were still standing there, awaiting some further instructions or maybe to hear his conversation with the doctor, and he said, again, "That will be all for now, thanks." He obviously didn't want us to hear the conversation.

We then left somewhat hurriedly. Once we were out of his office, Colin turned to us and said, somewhat mockingly, in a higher-than-normal voice, "This weekend will be fine with me," repeating my words.

"And what about the game and the tickets I have to the concert this Saturday . . . cost me forty euro! What about that, Top Shillin'?" he asked. "If we don't make it back on time, you'll be payin' for them . . . I guarantee that, ya maggot!"

"Sorry, mate," I offered apologetically. "I didn't know."

"Yes, you did. I told you about that just last night," he told me.

"I didn't remember," I stammered.

"You didn't remember," he repeated mockingly.

Saoirse started to say something, but he cut her off and said, "Not a word from you, O'Connor! You were no help in there, either. 'Fine with me!'" he scoffed, "You're lucky to be going along. Not another word from either one of yas. Christ almighty . . . I've got better things to do with my weekends."

I could tell that he was serious, but not in a really bad way. He was unhappy, but not angry. Then he said, "We'll be getting an early start tomorrow, and I don't want any complaints from either of ya about that."

Then, I had a stroke of pure genius though I can't really say that I thought it through all that well. I blurted out, "How about we take two cars? That way you can leave when you have to, and you won't be late getting back."

He thought about it for a few moments and then responded, "Now that's the first good idea you've had in a while, Sullivan. We'll take two cars, and that's that."

I started to say something else, but he cut me off and said, "Stop it, will ya? You're starting to annoy me now. Plan to meet me here at 8:00 sharp tomorrow morning."

He turned and walked away, leaving the two of us standing there, watching him go back down the hallway to his office. I turned to her and she asked, "Shall we take your car or mine?"

"Whichever you prefer," I answered.

"I prefer to drive if it's all the same to you," she said.

"Grand. I'll meet you in the main parking lot out front at 8:00. I just live a few minutes from here," I told her. "I won't be late."

"8:00 it is. See you then."

I couldn't have been more delighted with the way things all worked out . . . except for the business about meeting with Dr. McDuffy. I wasn't quite sure how we were going to go about that. He might not want to talk to us, and I knew that we couldn't make him talk to us if he didn't want to. Colin would have to figure that out. All we could do was try . . . and I'd be riding with Saoirse.

CHAPTER SIX

Sneem

I didn't even call my father or any of my brothers and sisters to let them know I was coming. I was more excited about spending the day with Saoirse than I was about anything else. Meeting with Dr. McDuffy would be interesting from a professional point of view, but being with her was special. I was really looking forward to that.

I was in the parking lot fifteen minutes ahead of schedule waiting for her arrival. It was early September but the weather was changing. Cooler temperatures were upon us. I had a jumper on over my shirt and a wool stocking cap on my head. It was overcast, threatening rain, and I was chilly, wishing I had brought my mittens.

I watched as a bright red Ford Mustang convertible came driving in and stopped twenty meters away from where I sat. The window went down and I saw that it was Saoirse. "Want a ride?" she asked.

Once inside, I said, "Nice car! Too bad the weather's not better. It would be fun to drive with the top down."

"I know. I don't get to do it as often as I'd like, but I enjoy it when I do," she responded. "If it clears up a bit, down it comes."

"You like American cars?" I asked.

"My great grandfather worked for Henry Ford when he first began making cars and we've owned nothing but Fords ever since," she told me.

"In America?" I asked.

"No, here in Ireland. He opened a factory over a hundred years ago here in Cork and my great-grandfather was one of the first to go to work there. That was in 1917. You didn't know that?" she asked.

When I told her that I didn't, she said, "It closed before you and I were born, in 1984, which was sad for thousands of people, but my grandfather and even me Da for a short time worked there, too, for a spell, so we're a one hundred percent Ford family, and I like this one a lot."

"It's a beautiful car," I said. "I'll bet you get a lot of attention from the Garda."

She laughed and said, "I do. They stop me all the time, but I've never been given a ticket! I go a little too fast now and again, and they pull me over for it. They ask for me driver's license and then for me phone number and when I give it to them, they let me go. I always give them the wrong one!" She laughed as she told me that part.

"I love driving the country roads in this thing. That's one of the reasons I wanted to drive," she added. "I'm looking forward to today. It's going to be fun."

As she was about to exit the parking lot, I asked, "Aren't we supposed to meet Colin here?"

"Just as I was leaving yesterday, he told me that he'd meet us at Kelly's Bakery there in Sneem. He said he was sure you'd know where it is," she said.

"I do. It's right in the center of the village, and there's really only one road through town," I told her. "You can't miss it."

"He said he'd be there around ten o'clock. We'll be there before he is, so we're fine," she said, and then she asked, "So how are you today?"

"Frozen!" I told her. "It's a bit nasty out, but it's supposed to clear up before too long. How about you?" I asked.

"Top form! I'm looking forward to meeting Dr. McDuffy. I told me Da that we were going to Sneem, but I didn't tell him why. He was a bit curious, but I just said it was work-related and I couldn't talk about it. We've got a ways to go to get there. What's the best road to take, Sullivan?" she asked.

"Brendan, please. Colin calls me that all the time when it's not 'Top Shillin', Maggot, Bogger, Spanner, or somethin' else," I responded.

She laughed and said, "That's true. He's all the time messin' with me, too, but not nearly as much as he does with you. So, what's the best way to go?"

"There's only one way, really. We take the N-72 through Ballincollig and Macroom, past Ballyvourney, until we catch the N-78 and take it to Kenmare and then on to Sneem. It'll take us about two hours to get there, but there's some pretty scenery to see along the way, once we get to Kenmare," I told her.

"Two hours, you say? I think we might get there a little quicker than that," she said with a smile. Then she asked, "Have you had your coffee yet?" as she took a sip of hers. When I told her I hadn't, she stopped at one of the shops nearby to let me out and said, "Get me a scone while you're there . . . with some light butter on it, please."

Minutes later, we were zooming down the road. Her Mustang had a standard transmission, so she was busily shifting gears and moving in and out of traffic until we were outside of town, on the N-72, traveling at a much faster rate of speed than we would have been if I was driving. That was for sure.

Along the way, we didn't talk much about our work. Instead, she told me all about her family and I told her all about mine. She was the fourth youngest of five children and, from what she told me, didn't lack for much as a child. She was quite the tennis player in school but said she wasn't good enough to play as a professional and had pretty much given it up for the time being.

"I just don't have the time, and tennis isn't nearly as popular in Cork as it is in Dublin. There are hardly any courts at all, and the ones that are here aren't very good. Plus, there's no one to play," she told me.

I didn't know anybody who played tennis . . . no one. We considered that an "English" sport. It was way down below soccer, somewhere near cricket, and nobody I knew played cricket, either. I didn't tell her any of that, though. It certainly wasn't approved by the GAA. That was for sure.

She had lived in Dublin all of her life before taking the job at St. Stephen's in Cork, and she had never been to Sneem before, so all of this was new to her. An hour later, the fog lifted a bit and the sun began to peek through. She pulled off the road wanting to take the top down, but it was still misty, so she decided against it.

We arrived in Sneem in about an hour and forty-five minutes, well before we were supposed to meet Colin. "Not too bad," she said. "I could have gone faster if the weather was better . . . maybe on the way back."

Colin wasn't due for another fifteen minutes, so we went inside the bakery to get more coffee and something to eat. Then, we walked down the road a few meters, past a park, to where a metal bridge passed over the Sneem River, which was roaring. Inside the park was a statue of one of its most famous citizens, a man who had been a world-champion wrestler about a hundred years earlier.

"This is a beautiful little village," she said. "I love how all the buildings are painted different colors the way they are. That's such an Irish thing. I don't think any other countries do like we do in that regard, do they?"

"Not that I know of," I responded. Of course, I hadn't traveled anywhere outside of Ireland in my life, yet, but I didn't tell her that.

"And there are more bars and restaurants than anything else," she added. "Look at them all! There must be two dozen of them! That's another thing we Irish are good at, aren't we?"

"It's a tradition that we're quite proud of, as you know. I've read where other countries have community centers, and so do we . . . we call them bars, that's all," I answered.

She laughed and then I asked, "Did you know that Ireland has the oldest bar in all the world?"

"No! You're makin' that up, Sullivan. That's not true, is it?" she asked.

"It is! You can look it up. Sean's Bar, in Athlone, is said to have opened sometime in the ninth or tenth century. That's an historical fact!" I told her.

"An hysterical fact, you mean!" she answered.

We laughed and I agreed. We stood on the bridge, which shook as cars drove by, admiring the beauty of the river and the countryside until it was time to find Colin. When he arrived about ten minutes late, he was in no mood to chit-chat. "Let's get this over with," he said after getting some coffee and a pastry.

"I don't want to miss one minute of that game today. Do you know where this old codger lives?" he asked. When I told him that I did, he said, "Let's go then! We can all three ride together. I'll drive."

He was about to get in his car until he saw what Saoirse was driving, and then he turned to Saoirse and asked, "This *is* your car?" When she told him that it was, he said, "Nice car, Saoirse! Let's take it. In fact, how about I drive!"

"No chance of that, Colin!" she replied as she got in the driver's side.

"Snapper, you get in the back," he told me as he got in the front passenger side.

Then he added, "They must pay you a lot more than they do me."

"Not quite. I have me Da to thank for this," she told him.

"Can you put the top down on this thing easy enough?" he asked.

"Sure," she answered.

"Then let's do it!" he said.

Minutes later, we were on our way out of town headed to meet Mr. McDuffy . . . Dr. McDuffy that is, with the top down.

"So where am I going?" she asked.

"Take your first left over the bridge," I told her. "That's Sea View Road."

"Isn't this a nice, little village, Colin?" Saoirse asked as we crossed over the bridge. "Look at all these beautiful buildings . . . so colorful. I love that about Ireland."

"Looks a bit lively for such a small place," he replied. "Look at all the bars! Maybe we'll have time to stop for a pint before we head back if we get through with this old geezer fast enough," Colin said.

"Now, when we get here, let me do all the talking," he told us. "You two squids just listen. Don't be taking any notes or anythin'. We don't want to scare the man."

"What are you going to tell him about why we're here, Colin?" I asked.

"I don't know yet. I'll figure that out once we get there," he told me.

"I don't see any street signs," Saoirse said. "Is this where I turn?" she asked once we passed over the bridge. There was a small road just wide enough for one vehicle to make it through, which looked more like an alley. Cars were parked on both sides of it.

I told her that it was and that none of the streets had signs. There weren't that many and everyone who lived there knew what they were. "The houses don't have numbers on them, either," I told them.

They couldn't believe that, but I assured them that it was true. "That's what it's like when you live in a small town," I added. They laughed at that.

"Like the song by U-2 . . . about the town where the streets have no names," Colin added.

"So, I just drive down this road until we come to his house, is that it?" she asked.

"That's it," I told her. "No turns, but I'm not exactly sure which house is his. I don't know the man. I was born here, but I was a small child when my parents divorced and I moved with me Mum to Cork. I'm sure my father knows him and where he lives, but I don't," I added.

"You told me you knew where he lives, Sully . . . do ya or don't ya?" Colin asked.

"I'll find it easy enough, I guarantee it," I assured him. "But I don't know exactly which one it is," I admitted.

"But you'll recognize him when you see him, right?" Colin asked.

"Of course!" I responded. "I met him just the other day. I'll remember him, and he should remember me, too, but maybe not. I'm dressed differently. We'll see," I said.

"So, give me the name of somebody you know who lives on this road, Top Shillin'," Colin said. "That's how we'll approach this fellow . . . lookin' for directions."

I had to think for a minute, and then I said, "Kevin Mulligan. He was a classmate of one of my brothers and his family lives out here someplace, not far from where we are."

"Alright then. Now, all we have to do is find the man," he responded. "I hope this doesn't take too long."

Then, he said, "Slow down, there, Saoirse! You're takin' these turns like we're in a race car!"

"I thought you were in a hurry to get out of here, Colin," she responded as she downshifted into a lower gear.

"We're here now . . . we can enjoy ourselves a little. Besides, I almost spilled me coffee all over meself back there. Thank you for slowin' down a bit."

Then, he added, "This is a fine man we're about to meet. Last night, I talked to one of the old farts at the bar who went to Trinity," as he glanced over at Saoirse. "And he had nothin' but good things to say about the man. I'm actually looking forward to this," he acknowledged.

Hearing him say that made me feel better. I was still thinking that I had ruined his weekend by doing what we were doing. He was really a nice guy, just a little gruff with me at times, that's all.

A few minutes later, after we passed the Sneem Rowing Center, Colin said, "Look at this! They have a rowing club in this place! Where do they go? Up and down the river?"

"No, this river leads to Kenmare Bay and then on out into the Atlantic," I told him. "That's why they call it 'Sea View Road,' although you can't really see the sea."

"That's a good one," he responded. "You can't see the sea but it's called the 'Sea View Road.' I like this place," he said, laughing. "That's Ireland for you. No signs to tell you the name of the road, no numbers on the houses, and the names of the roads make no sense. Ah, the Irish! We're a lovable bunch, aren't we?"

"Slow down, Saoirse," I told her, "I think this may be it over here on the left," as we passed the Sneem Bed and Breakfast and several large two-story houses with manicured lawns and iron fences around them, off to the right.

"Here?" Saoirse asked as she slowed down and came to a stop at a driveway off to our left. We could see a beautiful two-story brick home a hundred meters down a gravel path with a view of the river.

"No, that's not it. Maybe it's the next one, up there on the right," I told her. "I know the family that lives in that house you're looking at. We could ask them if we can't find the place."

"Is it on the left or the right, ya maggot! You said you knew where the man lives!" Colin said, raising his voice as he spoke.

"See that gate up ahead on your right?" I said, pointing. "Turn in there. I think that's it."

There was a metal gate, the kind used to keep cattle in, that was open with weeds all around it. A raggedy, broken down, wooden fence was on both sides. She drove about a hundred meters along a dirt path that led up. Ahead, we saw a small shed that wasn't in very good condition.

We drove another hundred meters further up what had become a fairly steep incline to the crest where we saw a house. It was more like a cottage, actually . . . a small, single-story, block building painted white with a thatched roof that was in extremely bad condition. Two large windows were on either side of a dark blue door, which sat in the middle of the house. A man was standing in the doorway, looking at us.

"That would be Dr. McDuffy himself," I said.

"And that would be as traditional an Irish house as you will ever find, isn't it?" Saoirse added. "There must be thousands of houses just like this all over Ireland."

"But look at that roof," Colin said. "It looks like there's been a major fire here not too long ago."

"I put that in my report. He left something on the stove and started the fire," I responded, "and it's been that way for over a year. That's part of the problem."

"Well, let's meet the man," he said, "and remember, let me do the talking."

Dr. McDuffy stayed in the doorway as we all got out of the car at the same time and began walking toward him. He was dressed like a country squire with a dark brown, tweed jacket over a white shirt, with light brown trousers, and a somewhat stylish felt hat on. It looked like the same outfit I'd seen him in two days ago. He had what looked to be the same walking stick in his hand, too.

"Top o' the mornin' to you!" Colin said as we approached him.

"And the rest of the day to you," he responded. "And what is it I can do for you?" he asked.

"We're looking for a man named Kevin Mulligan. Would you happen to know where he lives?" Colin asked.

"I do. He lives just down the road a short way," he told us, pointing, "but I don't think anyone is there at the moment," he told us. "There were no cars in the driveway earlier this morning when I walked by."

"He has a son who's a friend of mine from school," I interjected. "I haven't seen him in years. I was hoping that I might be able to say hello."

Colin looked over at me as if to say "I told you to let me do the talking," but Dr. McDuffy responded and said, "So are you from around here?" he asked.

"Yes, my father is the headmaster at the school," I told him.

"You're Patrick Sullivan's son?" he asked.

"I am," I told him. "The youngest in the family.

"I've met your father on many occasions. He's a fine man," he said. "And what's your name?" he asked.

"I'm Brendan . . . Brendan Sullivan," I said, and I extended my hand to shake his. I looked intently to see if he had any recognition of me, but it didn't seem as if he did. "And these are my friends . . . this is Colin, and this is Saoirse," I said, pointing to each.

We all shook hands with the man and he said, "Well, I'm back from my morning walk, and I just now fixed a pot of tea. Would you like to come in for a cup?"

We gladly accepted his invitation. I was quite proud of myself for my part in getting us into his home. Colin looked over at me with an approving smile.

Once inside, he said, "Have a seat."

Saoirse offered to help, but he dismissed her, saying, "It will only take a minute and I'll join you. Sit down and make yourselves comfortable."

Colin and Saoirse sat down on a couch in front of a large fireplace, off to the left, next to a wall, which had a turf fire burning brightly. There was a large, leather chair in the middle of the room, which was obviously where Dr. McDuffy would sit, directly in front of the fire. A small table with some chairs around it was off to the right.

He could see that I hesitated before sitting down in what was "his" chair and said, "Go ahead! Sit there! Make yourselves at home. I'll be right there. You're welcome here."

Somewhat reluctantly, I sat down in "his" chair. There was little doubt that he didn't remember me from the other day. I was dressed differently, and the circumstances were entirely different, so I wasn't sure if that was such a bad thing or not. I wasn't going to mention it. I was sure that we were all thinking the same thing.

We sat there, closely observing what he was doing, how he was acting, and examining his living conditions. The gaping hole in the roof over his head, which was covered up with plastic, was, quite obviously, the "gorilla" in the room.

"Don't mind the mess," he said. "I had a little fire in here a while back and I'm having trouble finding someone who can put the roof back on the way it's supposed to be. No one seems to know how to properly do thatched roofs anymore," he told us.

We grunted a response but didn't say anything.

Saoirse changed the subject and said, "This is a lovely view you have here, sir." I was glad to hear her not calling him by name or addressing him as a "Doctor." How would we know? She didn't let on that we knew anything about him at all. That was smart of her.

The view out of the large, plate-glass window was a magnificent one. It looked out into the water. I wasn't sure if that was still Kenmare Bay or if it was the Atlantic, so I asked.

"Somewhere out there, it becomes the Atlantic. I don't think there is a specific dividing line," he responded with a chuckle. "That's why they call this road 'Sea View' even though you can't see the sea from the road, only from up here on top, as we are."

"So, you can see both sides from up here. That's grand! It's a spectacular view you have here, sir," Saoirse added.

He turned and said, "Michael . . . my name is Michael McDuffy. Call me Michael, please."

"And this fire is perfect, Michael," Colin told him. "Thanks for inviting us in. It was a rainy, nasty day in Cork earlier this morning. I had a bit of a chill. This is brilliant!"

"You all came from Cork this morning, did you?" he asked. I thought he might be sensing something was out of the ordinary when he asked the question, but I wasn't sure.

"We did. Just out for a nice drive, actually. That car of Saoirse's is fun to drive," Colin responded, "and Brendan here wanted to show us where he was born and all."

"I see," he said as he placed a small tray with four cups on it. There was some sugar, honey, and a few sliced lemons on a plate, off to the side. "Come over and fix yourselves a cup the way you want it, if you don't mind. I think that would be the easiest way," he said as he sat down on a chair he pulled from the end of the table a few meters away.

We all got up to fix ourselves a cup, chatting about how the sun was now shining and the temperature outside was actually quite pleasant, whereas it had been cold and rainy an hour or so earlier.

"That's Ireland for you, isn't it?" he said, "four seasons in every day."

We laughed and agreed. It was true. That was Ireland's weather. It had been chilly and rainy, and now it was warming up and the sun was out.

As we were sitting there, enjoying the fire and the tea, talking about anything and everything other than the real reason we were there, Colin asked, "So what happened with the fire, Michael? It looks like you were lucky it didn't burn the whole house down!"

"I was fortunate in that regard, I guess, though I don't feel that way. It was all my fault, so I have no one to blame but myself," he responded. "I was cooking something, and I don't remember what it was, and I left a newspaper a little too close to a burner . . . I still read the Irish Times several days a week . . . and it caught fire. By the time I noticed it, there were flames going up the walls and into the ceiling."

"Actually, I was extremely lucky. One of my neighbors is a volunteer fireman and he happened to be passing by at the time and saw the smoke. He called it in and went back to his house where he had some of his equipment. One of the smaller fire engines arrived in no time."

"He and this other man were able to put most of it out by themselves. The others arrived not too long after and finished it up. It took me a long time to get the smell of smoke out of the house. You three don't smell smoke now, do you? Other than what's coming from the fireplace, of course," he asked.

We all agreed that there was only the pleasant smell of a turf fire in the house, nothing else.

"I was very fortunate, indeed," he added, "but you'd think I was a menace to the community. People made a big commotion over the whole thing and now they're after me to get this thing fixed. They won't leave me alone! I'm the one who has to live here . . . what business is it of theirs?" he asked.

"That's true," Colin responded. "They don't have to put up with it, you do, but how long ago was that?" he asked.

Dr. McDuffy gave him a somewhat quizzical look and answered, "I don't know . . . it happened a few months back . . . maybe three or four months ago. I'm not sure. Now that I'm retired, the days of the week, the month, or even what year it is aren't nearly so important as they once were. I always knew when Sunday came along, but now I don't even go to Mass on Sundays too often anymore, so it really doesn't matter much what day of the week it is, now does it?"

"Just so you'll know, today's Saturday," Colin told him, "in case anyone asks."

We all laughed at that, too.

"I need to get that roof fixed, though. They just keep pestering me about it. I don't know what I'm going to do," he said, shaking his head.

"One of my brothers is a carpenter. He lives on the other side of town near the old Butter Road. He might be able to help," I offered. The thought just popped into my head. I hadn't thought of it before that moment. Maybe Rory could help. "I think he works on thatched roofs, too," I added.

He brightened noticeably when I said that. "Really?" he exclaimed. "That would be wonderful if he could. I can pay him . . . there's no problem with that," he assured me, "I just can't find anyone who knows how to do it properly. I won't let just anyone on my roof. It's important to me that it's done right," he said.

"His name is Rory. He's my oldest brother, and I'll ask him," I told him.

At that, he stood and said, "Well, I certainly hope that he can. That would be a godsend, indeed! Would anyone like any more tea?"

None of us did, and there was an awkward lull in the conversation after we said so. After all, we had told him that we just stopped to ask for directions. I stood and said, "Well, we should be leaving. We'll stop by and see if my friend is home or not. Thank you for your hospitality. It was nice meeting you, Michael," extending my hand to shake his.

"It was my pleasure," he responded. "I am so glad that the three of you stopped here. If you can help me with my roof, it would be a miracle . . . truly, a miraculous thing. I'm at a total loss and have been for months."

The other two stood, thanked him for the tea and the directions, and we all ambled toward the door. He was right behind us, following us out. For some reason, he picked up his walking stick as he did.

"You use that to fend off the snakes, do you?" Colin asked.

Dr. McDuffy chuckled and said, "I still have a hard time believing that Saint Patrick didn't miss a few."

We all laughed at his response. There are no snakes in Ireland and everyone knew it. Whether or not Patrick should get all of the credit is another issue. Then he added, "I have a little problem with my balance every now and again. This helps me with that."

He turned to me and said, "I will look forward to hearing from you, Mr. Sullivan. That would be an enormous help if your brother is able to fix my roof. Say hello to your father for me. I think he'll remember who I am."

I assured him that I would do that and told him I would talk to Rory as soon as possible. I promised to be in touch with him after I did, one way or the other. He gave me a piece of paper with his number on it and asked me to call when I found out something. He waved to us as we drove off.

"Good job, Snapper!" Colin said. "That was a stroke of genius on your part with your brother and all. Was any of that true?" he asked.

I assured him that it was.

"Well, I'd say that we had an extremely successful meeting, and maybe your brother can help the man with his roof. That would be perfect, absolutely perfect," he said. "That man was as right as rain, I'd say," he added. "At least, he was today. That much we can tell Delaney on Monday, right?"

"Is that what are we going to tell him?" Saoirse asked. "That there's nothing wrong with the man and Dr. Doherty is all wrong? We can't do that, can we? We've got to do better than that, don't we?"

"You're right about that, Saoirse. We've got to do better than that. Delaney will be expecting more than that from the three of us. Maybe we should try to talk to some of the locals about him before we leave. Brendan knows people here. Who should we talk to?" he asked me.

"I'll talk to my father," I responded. "He'll be able to tell us a few things and don't forget, he didn't recognize me at all, it seemed, and it's been over a year, supposedly, not a few months, since that fire occurred. So, there are a few red flags we can mention, right?"

"Good points, Brendan, but he couldn't have been nicer to us, could he? He was a real gentleman . . . every bit a country squire with the hat and jacket and all, I'd say," Saoirse said.

"Oh! That's another thing . . . those were the same clothes he had on the other day," I added.

"That's not a good sign, but I liked him, and I hope your brother can help," she said.

"We'll see. He works in construction. I'll ask. I don't know about him fixing a thatched roof. That part I made up," I acknowledged.

"Well done, Sullivan! That was quick thinking on your part. I give you that. So, let's see if that Dr. Doherty is working today, and if not, we can stop in at one of those bars in town and see if it has some Guinness on tap, shall we?" he said, "and then I'll be on my way back to Cork to get there before the game starts."

CHAPTER SEVEN

Dan Murphy's Bar

Since it was a Saturday, the Garda station was closed, and Dr. Doherty's office was in Kenmare, there was no one for us to talk to. "Let's have a pint for the long drive home," Colin suggested. Saoirse and I quite willingly agreed.

Murphy's Bar was right across the street less than fifty meters away. Colin pointed to it and said, "That one will do." It was a three-story, bright red building, which sat right next to Riney's Bar, painted a light blue, and was next to the Sneem Tavern, which was a mustard yellow. There were others, but Murphy's was the closest by a few centimeters, so in we went.

The bar was jammed even though the game between the home team, Kerry, representing Munster province, and the team from Dublin, which represented Leinster, wouldn't begin for a few hours. Dublin was trying to win its fifth title in a row, which would be a first in the 132-year history of the event. The pre-game hype had begun and people were already glued to their seats where they would probably be for the rest of the day. We went upstairs and found a booth in a far corner where we could be near a TV and still talk.

The teams had played to a draw two weeks earlier, so this was a replay, and all of Ireland would be watching, even in the north. This was sponsored by the GAA and although teams from Ulster province compete, all the players had to be Catholics, not Protestants. This event and the All-Ireland Hurling Championships were the two biggest days of the year for the true Irish sports fans, like me.

I was now rabid for the Kerry team even though I had been rooting for Cork when the two teams played earlier in the year. One of the players, Gavin White, was from Sneem and I would have gone to school with him, though he was two years older. That is if I'd gone to school there, which I didn't. I knew him, but not too well. To my surprise, Saoirse told us that she was mad about the Dublin team.

"My father has been taking me to the games for years," she told us. "I so badly wanted to play, but it interfered with my tennis, and he wouldn't let me. He was afraid I'd get hurt."

"Why aren't you at the game?" I asked.

"I gave my ticket to me younger sis. I've gone to each of the last four and she's never been. Besides, we're going to win easily today! No doubt about it," she said.

"You gave a ticket to the game to your sister?" Colin asked, incredulously.

"I did," she acknowledged. "I'd rather be here. This is more important to me," she added.

"You're a bit of an amlog, too, aren't you?" he asked.

She laughed but didn't respond, except to say, "If you say so, Colin," or something like that.

Colin was pulling for the Kerry team, too, even though he was a huge fan of the Cork team as I was. It had been defeated by Kerry in the final round of the Munster bracket. "We beat Limerick the week before, and Tipperary the week before that, but we didn't play well that day against Kerry . . . it just wasn't our day. I was there, though," he told us, "rooting them on."

"Kerry had little trouble making it through to get where they are," I added. "First, they beat Clare handily, then they beat Waterford without much difficulty as well, and then they slaughtered us in the final," I said. "They had chances to beat Dublin two weeks ago, so they're a good team. This is anyone's game. I've heard it's even money with the bookies."

"I'm rooting for the Kerry team today," he responded, "but I'm Cork all the way, for sure. Let there be no doubt about that. I can't wait for next year, but I'll be at the bar in time to watch the whole game today, no thanks to the two of you, cheering them on, and then I'm off to the concert. My chums will save me a fine seat, I'm sure."

"I'd be at the game if it weren't for the concert. Who knew that they'd play to a draw? I bought my tickets a month ago," he told us.

"Who's playing?" Saoirse asked.

"A group called Thumper. They're new, but they're gonna be really good. One of my buddies knows some of the guys in the band, but if it was Cork playing, I'd be in Dublin right now without a doubt," he said.

"My whole family is for Kerry and has been forever, so I'm totally rooting for them today," I said. "I want them to win, but I'll not be betting any money on them."

"Me neither," Colin chimed in. "Dublin has the experience and they're still the favorites, I think."

"Speaking of family, do you really think your brother will be able to help Dr. McDuffy?" Saoirse asked.

"I dunno, but I'll definitely ask him," I answered. "If he can't, he should know someone who can."

"Do you want to call him or go see him today before we leave?" she asked.

"Not today. He's undoubtedly banjoed by now. He might even be in Dublin at the game. I'll call him tomorrow," I told her. "I promise you that."

Just then, a woman walked by who I recognized as the Garda lady I had met in Kenmare. She was dressed like a normal person, not in uniform, but I was sure it was her.

"Excuse me!" I yelled to be heard over the noise in the room and the television, and then I tapped her on the shoulder as she passed by. She turned and gave me a look like she had no idea who I was.

"Your name is Mollie and you're a Garda officer, right?" I asked.

"I am," she answered.

"I met you in Kenmare a few days ago. Don't you remember?" I asked.

Clearly, she had no recollection of who I was, but she responded, "Yes, my name is Mollie, and I'm a Garda officer, but I don't recognize you. Who are you again?"

When I told her, she said, "Oh yes. Now I remember. What can I do for you?" The expression on her face changed a bit from being one of the revelers to being more like the professional woman I'd met the other day.

I told her how we had just met with Dr. McDuffy at his home and asked if she wouldn't mind talking to us for a minute or two. I introduced her to Colin and Saoirse and explained who they were.

"I was just going to the jacks, so give me a minute and I'll be right back," she said as she proceeded on her way to the bathroom.

"That was a stroke of luck, wasn't it?" Saoirse commented.

I agreed and said, "She told me a few other things the other day that I think you should hear, that I didn't put in my report. "Hopefully, she can tell us a little more."

"Delaney's going to like that," Colin added. "Good job, Sullivan."

When she returned, I told her about how we had come to see Dr. McDuffy and follow up on the concerns she and others had about the man. She was pleased to hear that, but not surprised.

"He's a very nice man, as I told you, but there are concerns as you now know," she responded. "I'm glad to hear that someone is taking it seriously."

I told her that he was fine today and that he couldn't have been any nicer to us, and then I asked her to tell us what happened after I left and if there was anything more she could tell us about him.

She moved a little closer to our table, lowered her voice, and said, "Well, I know that you are who you say you are, and I don't think I'm violating any rules by telling you what I know. I like the man, but he's slippin', there's no doubt about it, as I told you before."

"After you left, Dr. Doherty showed up about half an hour later. Dr. McDuffy wasn't in a very good mood by the time he got there . . . much worse than when you saw him. They talked for quite a while—well past the time I was to have closed the office and gone home, to tell you the truth. I wasn't happy about that because I had to drive the man home first, as you will remember."

"What did he say to you? The doctor that is?" I asked. "We've seen his report."

"I haven't seen it and I don't have a clue what's in it. You may know more than I do. I put them in the same room as the one you were in, but I didn't hear a word of their conversation. When they were done, he said he was going to write his report straight away, though, and that he was going back to his office to do just that before he went home for the night himself," she told me.

"I put him in my car and drove the man home. That was it. I haven't heard another word about it 'til now," she added.

"He agreed with you, Mollie. He thinks that the problem is getting to the point where some sort of professional help is necessary. He's a medical doctor, though, not so much with the mind as the body, if you know what I mean," I said.

"I do, but I had no one else to call," she responded.

"I know. That's why we've come all the way from Cork to handle this . . . there is no one else around who can help the man, but it's not up to us, the three of us, that is, but we're to report back to others about what we see. I was hoping that there might be something else you can tell us about him that you haven't already told me? Can you think of anything?" I asked.

"I told you about the fire, didn't I?" she asked, and we immediately told her that we saw the damage and what he told us about that. "How long ago was that, Mollie?" I asked. "Do you remember?"

"That was well over a year ago, and he still hasn't done a thing about it," she said.

"He said it was only a few months ago," Colin offered.

"That's not correct. I know that it was at least a year, maybe even two, because I came down here two years ago and I think that happened not long after I arrived, so although I'm not sure exactly when that was, I'm certain that it's been well over a year. Of that, there is no doubt, and it's closer to two years ago, I'd say."

"I'm from Galway, meself, but me chara lives here, so I came to be with him. He knows more about the man than I do, actually. I'm afraid I can't think of what more there is to tell you about the man other than what I told you the other day . . . let me think," she said as she cocked her head to one side and put her hand to her chin.

"Did I tell you about the woman who came into the office here in Sneem a few days before you came and she had found his wallet and . . ."

"Yes, you told me about that one," I interjected.

She looked at me and said, "I did? Well, there was another time before that when the exact same thing happened, but that was a few months ago. Did I tell you about that?"

"You did," I told her.

"Well, there's more . . . a lot more," she said. "The woman at the post office thinks he's as batty as can be. He stops in there once a week, if not more, as he has done for ages apparently, and he still doesn't know her name! He gets it wrong every time. She thinks it's funny."

"He's all the time forgettin' the key to his box, plus he does silly things like droppin' his mail on the floor, or forgettin' to put stamps on things. She laughs about it, but she tells me those things every so often. She's one of the ones who think we should be keeping a closer eye on him. She's not supposed to give out mail to people who forget their keys or do some of the other things she does for him, but she does it because he's such a nice man."

"That business of losin' his wallet is pretty serious stuff, though. It had all of his identification and credit cards in it, not to mention money! He had dropped it somewhere along the Sea View road, which he walks every day, so the person who found it knew exactly who it belonged to."

"She was an honest person, and gave it all back, but she brought it to us, not back to him, because she, too, is concerned about him. She wanted us to know. It had a lot of money in it at the time, and he'd have had a hard time replacin' all of the other stuff that was in there. It had his banking information, his medical information, and everything else in it . . . everything!" she told us with a look of incredulity on her face.

We nodded our heads in agreement but didn't say anything. She went on, saying, "Then, there was the time when someone found him walking down Church Street on the opposite side of the river, not knowin' where he was. The man who picked him up knew him and where he lived, so he took him home that day, but he came in and told us about it the next day. He was worried about him, too. He knew Dr. McDuffy, but Dr. McDuffy didn't know him. That was a few weeks ago, maybe three or four."

"Then there was the time when he had dinner at the Sacre Coeur restaurant and walked out without paying! I don't know what he was thinking that day. They told us about it, but didn't want to press charges, of course."

"He paid the bill the next time he came in, and was all apologetic and all, but he's all the time doin' silly stuff like that, and there's more . . . much more, not to mention that business with the children!" she said, "but that's nothin', really. I wouldn't pay any attention to any of that! He wouldn't do those children any harm, but I can understand the parents' concern. That's not his fault."

I reminded Colin and Saoirse about how the incident with the children occurred a few hours before Mollie went to pick him up and have him seen by Dr. Doherty that day when I saw him. They both remembered that story. It was in my report.

"I didn't want to do it . . . I truly didn't," she told us, "but something had to be done. There's more, I'm sure, because I'm only here in Sneem about two days a week. Normally, I'm in Kenmare where we have cells to put people in when we have to arrest someone."

"We send one officer here to Sneem every day, except for weekends, but we rotate. As you probably know, there's no place to put a person we arrest here in Sneem, so we have to take offenders to Kenmare. This is like an outpost. It's called a sub-station, actually."

"The other officers have stories to tell, too. Every one of us knows who he is and how well-respected he is, him being a professor and all. He's a nice old man . . . he really is . . . he's just getting old, that's all there is to it," she said, "but he's slippin'. It's sad, really, but listen, it's nice to see you again, Mr. . . . ."

"Sullivan," I told her, "but you can call me Brendan."

"Brendan, and it's nice to meet the two of you as well, but my food is getting cold over there and I need to get back to me boyfriend. I can talk to you more about it next week if you'd like when I'm at work. That would be better," she said.

We thanked her for talking to us and I told her that I'd be back in touch sometime soon to keep her up to date with what was going on with the man. As soon as she left, Colin took a last swallow of beer, stood, and said, "Well, that was helpful, but it's time for me to go! I don't want to miss a minute of the game."

"You two write the report today or tomorrow so that I can see it bright and early on Monday morning. I'll make whatever changes need to be made and put it on Dr. Delaney's desk first thing. Safe home, you two . . . and go, Kerry!"

He left twenty euros on the table and said, "You two can buy the next round . . . each of you, that is," and off he went.

Saoirse and I sat there, watching him until he was out of sight, and then she said, "I'd like to see at least some of the game today. How about you?"

I told her that I would, too, and that I could write the report up tomorrow. We'd done enough for today with the McDuffy case.

Actually, if it wasn't for her, I'd have been watching every minute just like Colin would be, but I didn't tell her that, of course. I would much prefer to be with her. Instead, I asked her where she was planning to watch.

"I'm not sure," she answered. "If I wasn't here, I'd probably watch it at home with my family, but it's such a beautiful day I wouldn't mind taking a drive along this Ring of Kerry thing. I probably won't have too many more days like this where I can leave the top down before next spring."

I tried to hide my enthusiasm for that suggestion, and said, "Well, we could go all the way around, ending up in Killarney in a few hours if you want, but you've probably done it many times before, so you know all about it . . . you probably don't want to do that now, do you?"

"Actually, I've never done it before . . . at least not with me doin' the driving. I think my parents took me around a time or two, but that was when I was little, not paying all that much attention," she said. "It's been a while since I did that, and I don't remember all that much about it, though I've heard all about it my whole life."

I jumped at that and said, "Well, if you've never done it before, you won't find too many days better than this one to do it, and you're right, the cold weather will be upon us before you know it."

"You wouldn't mind?" she asked.

"Not at all," I answered. "It's fun for me to be riding with the top down like we are. I've never done that before," I told her, which was true. I never owned a car before starting work at St. Stephen's and no one I knew had a convertible, let alone a sporty Ford Mustang as she had.

"Well then, let's do that. You know the way, yes?" she asked.

"There's only one way and the views are spectacular. You'll probably want to stop and admire them every few kilometers." Then, I added, "If you want, I can drive. That way, you can be looking out and not having to mind the traffic and all."

"No chance of that, Top Shillin'!" she said, sounding very much like Colin. "That's part of the fun!" she added. "We won't have any trouble finding a place to watch the game along the way. The whole of Ireland will be watching in every home and bar across the entire island, I'm sure. Let's go then!"

CHAPTER EIGHT

The Ring of Kerry

From Sneem, the road ran along the coastline to Cahirdaniel, home of the great Liberator, Daniel O'Connell, then out to Waterville, Cahirsiveen, and Glenbeigh. From there, we would head back, taking a road through the Black Valley and Dunloe Gap, over the MacGillycuddy's Reeks, the highest mountain range in Ireland, and on to Killarney, completing the circle. It was a little over an hour from there to Cork.

It would be a long drive, maybe three or four hours, depending upon how many times we stopped along the way but for me, it was going to be a great day. I was hoping that someone I knew would see me riding with this gorgeous girl in this fabulous car as we passed through town, but no luck there. We left Dan Murphy's Bar a little before noon. The game wouldn't start for another two hours.

The sun was shining brightly as we left Sneem, heading due west along the Ring. It's a peninsula, so we'd have Kenmare Bay on our left for a short while, and then it would become the Atlantic Ocean—once we rounded the tip—and headed back east. From there, we would be able to see the waters of Dingle Bay on our left most of the way, in between the two peninsulas.

The only problem with driving with the top down was that we couldn't talk to each other too easily. We'd have to scream to be heard. The only times we could hear each other was when she pulled off the road to stop and take a picture of the view, which she did fairly often.

"This is marvelous!" she said. "I've seen plenty of pictures, but they don't do it justice. This is much more spectacular than I imagined."

I agreed. Spending as much time in Sneem as I had, I knew most of this area quite well. There wasn't much to see in Cahirdaniel, which wasn't as big as Sneem, and the best pub in town, the Blind Piper, was packed, so we zoomed past without stopping. She drove a lot faster than I would on that narrow road, zipping around and through the curves in the road as if there was nothing to it.

Waterville was next and it's the biggest attraction in the area for most people because of a spectacular beach where people can swim. Less than a thousand people live there, so it's still small, but it has much more commerce than Sneem or anyplace else on the Ring. There were plenty of pubs in the town, and tourists were the main source of money for the locals. We got there in about forty-five minutes after leaving Murphy's and we still had plenty of time before the game was to start.

"Of all the little towns on this route, I like Portmagee the best," I told her. "That's where the boats leave for Skellig Michael, and . . ."

"Skellig Michael!" she interjected. "If we have the time, I'd really like to see it," she said. "I know all about it."

"We have time. We can do that, and you can see the two islands off in the distance from the tip of the island. It takes about an hour to get to them by boat, but we won't be able to do that today. The boats will probably be gone by the time we get there, and even if they haven't, I expect they'll be full," I told her. "People book those trips months in advance."

"My father's done it, and so have several of my older brothers and sisters. I'd like to get out there someday soon, too," I agreed. "On a day like this, we should be able to get a good view of them, though," I told her. "I've been there before, to Portmagee that is, just never to the island on one of the boats."

"If it's okay with you, I'd like to do that," she said. "It would be grand just to see them if we can."

"We won't have any problem finding a good place to watch the game there, too," I said. "Even though there aren't but about a hundred people who live in that little village, there are several pubs to choose from. It's quite popular in the summer, especially because of the Skelligs. They have a chocolate factory as well, and that attracts some visitors, too," I told her.

"A chocolate factory?" she asked. "Really? That's unusual."

"It's true! They make chocolate and send it all over the world. I doubt it would be open now because of the game, but it might be. People either work on the boats, the men that is, or they work at the chocolate place, but the boats only go from the beginning of April to the end of September. Other than that, there's not much there," I told her.

"I like that idea. Let's go," she said.

"Where? You mean the chocolate factory?" I asked. "It'll probably be closed as I said."

"No, Portmagee, to see Skellig Michael!" she responded as if to say I was a dunce or something, thinking she wanted to eat some chocolates.

We passed through Waterville without stopping, and then went on for another twenty kilometers or so until we reached Cahirsiveen, which is a lively, little town of over a thousand people. Again, I told her that here, too, tourism was the main source of income for the locals. Two of my sisters had worked there at one of the restaurants years ago. The only road to take goes right through the center of town and everything that's there to see is on it.

We arrived in Portmagee about forty-five minutes before the game was to begin, so we drove out to the place where we could get the best view of the Skelligs. There was an area for cars to park and a small path that led to an observation point where we could see them the best. There were about a dozen other cars there, so we weren't the only ones doing what we were.

As we were walking along the way, we came to a place that had some signs and markers all around it. We read that it was the spot where the first trans-Atlantic cable from North America had come to a hundred years ago. That was a bit hard to imagine, but there it was, etched in a stone marker.

It was no longer in use, of course, but that was a big thing back then. It was hard to believe that a cable ran underwater all the way from North America to where we were standing, but it did. I wondered how many kilometers of cable it took, but it didn't say. That was an amazing accomplishment.

Fifteen minutes later, when we got to the place where we could get the best view of the two islands, which were still a good distance off, she asked, "So are those both called Skellig Michael, or do they have separate names?"

I didn't know, but we found a sign that explained that the larger island was Skellig Michael, and that's where the monks had lived. The smaller one was called Skellig Bheag, and that's where birds lived, like a hundred thousand of them at times during the year. We read that there were several different kinds of birds living there, like gannets, puffins, terns, and cormorants. Most were seasonal but some lived there year-round.

"How those monks lived out there for over six hundred years is beyond me. It's unimaginable," she said. "I'd like to go there and see for myself where they lived and how they did it someday. I can't comprehend it."

"It's not inexpensive," I told her. "It costs over a hundred euro to get on one of those boats, and they only land in good weather, so it's a bit tricky."

"I'm going to do it, but not today. It's time for us to go watch that game," she said. "Dublin's going to win easily!" she teased.

"We'll see," I told her. "I'm hopin' they don't!"

About a third of the people in all of Ireland live in Dublin, so it had about ten times as many people to choose from than we had in county Kerry, and they had won the last four years, so she was probably right, but since the two teams had played to a draw two weeks earlier, it figured to be a close game.

"Want to wager a pint on it?" I asked. It was a bet I would gladly lose, though I would prefer to win it, of course.

"Certainly! You're on!" she responded.

Finding a place to park was a bit of a challenge as there were cars parked everywhere. Everyone was there to watch the game just as we planned to do. We found a spot at the church, which was two blocks away. Finding a place to watch the game was going to be a bit trickier.

All of the pubs were full, so we went to the Landings Restaurant, which was the biggest place in town, besides the church. It had television sets in every room, it seemed. It was standing room only, but we found a spot off in a corner of one of the rooms where we were able to see the game. It took a few minutes to get our beers, but we settled in just as the game was getting started. Our timing was perfect.

It was a loud and boisterous crowd, entirely favoring the boys in green and white. Dublin's colors were blue—dark blue bottoms and light blue tops. We couldn't hear what the announcers were saying over the noise of the crowd, but we were able to see what was going on well enough.

The Dublin team scored early in the contest and were way ahead within the first ten minutes of the game. Kerry was competitive, and they were starting to make a comeback when Saoirse said, "Let's go. We can listen to it on the radio. This is a mob scene in here and I'd rather be driving." We finished our beers and off we went.

I had never driven on the north side of the peninsula past Cahirsiveen, and I was looking forward to that part of the drive the most. Again, we couldn't talk, except for when she stopped to take pictures, which she continued to do frequently. Since she was driving, I was able to take in the views without worrying about the traffic.

However, there weren't many cars on the road to worry about. Undoubtedly, that was because most people were watching the game, so driving wasn't a problem at all. She took that as an opportunity to go faster than normal, and that's exactly what she did. On most Saturday afternoons, if the weather was good as it was today, the roads would be littered with cars, but not today.

The next day, I read that three out of every four people in Ireland watched that game. The rest were undoubtedly listening to it on their radios as we were. Kerry was making a game of it, but they hadn't recovered from that disastrous start as of yet.

Saoirse drove that Mustang faster than any car I'd ever been in. She must have figured that the Garda would be watching the game, too. With a red scarf around her neck, dark sunglasses covering her eyes, and a black cap on her head, she was quite the sight. If there were any Garda out and about, they would have stopped her, for sure, just to get her name and telephone number, if nothing else, as she said they often did.

As we were leaving Glencar, after passing through Glenbeigh, dark clouds began to appear on the horizon, so Saoirse stopped and put the top back on. It started to mist as we entered the Black Valley. As we were passing by the Gap of Dunloe, it started to rain fairly hard. That made her slow down just a little.

We listened to the end of the game on our way from Killarney to Cork. Kerry was trounced and I owed her a pint. We didn't get back until late in the afternoon, and we were both tired at the end when she dropped me off at my apartment.

"I'll get in early Monday morning and look over your report, if you'd like, Brendan. This is your case, and you're the one who has to do it between now and then, but I'm glad to help if you want . . . whatever you say. Do you want me to?" she asked.

I agreed, of course, and told her I'd see her then. I waved to her as she started to drive off. Then, she stopped, rolled down her window, and said, "Don't forget to call your brother!" and then she was gone.

I had forgotten all about that. I would do that tomorrow. I was absolutely certain that he'd be in no condition to talk this afternoon.

I was up early the next morning, writing a report about our meeting with Dr. McDuffy. I wasn't going to call my brother until much later in the day. I was sure that he was langered after what happened yesterday, although I was also certain that he would be up and at Mass as it was Sunday. His wife would make sure of that, and it was required by the school that the kids go, so he'd be there. The school took attendance at mass on Sundays seriously, more so than regular days of the week, actually.

As for the report, I wasn't quite sure what to make of it all. It was as if there were two different men being talked about. I was determined to keep my opinions out of it and just report exactly what was said and done as well as I could remember.

I also tried to put down word for word what the Garda woman told us. I left out the part about my brother fixing the roof. I needed to see if that was likely to happen before saying anything about it.

Later that morning, I went to visit my mother. She was just returning from a Druid ceremony. This one had been held in the Killarney National Park, in the woods, next to the big waterfall not far from Mucross Castle, in the National Park. She said that they had caused quite a stir, dressed as they were in all-white robes. I was sure the tourists got a big bang out of it. The park is quite a popular destination for people coming to visit Ireland and today was another lovely day, though it was a bit on the chilly side.

She was quite proud of it all. She told me that over a hundred people attended the event. For whatever reasons, and she had no idea why, their numbers were growing. She wanted them to continue to expand so that they would become more widely accepted as a serious religion, and not just a novelty act about the history of our country before St. Patrick arrived.

I had little interest in the theology of Druidism, but I did like the fact that it was part of restoring Irish culture. The Celts and the Druids were here over two thousand years ago, well before Patrick set foot on our island. They were a part of Ireland's history, too.

I was one who truly liked learning how to speak Gaelic. My father was proud of me for that. It was now a required class in all the schools. Furthermore, all over the Republic of Ireland, signs on the streets and roads had the names in Gaelic, right below the English. I liked that. I preferred that, actually.

I don't know how she knew it, but she could tell that something was different about me. "So, do you have a girdle now, Brendan?" she asked. I avoided answering the question as best I could, which made it all the more obvious. Then I had to tell her all about Saoirse and our day yesterday. She was happy for me.

When I told her about why we were in Sneem, though I didn't tell her too much, she said that she knew of Dr. McDuffy, but didn't know much about the man. "Your father knows him much better than I do. While I was there, he was still a professor and spending most of his time in Dublin, as I recall. I believe he and his wife . . . and I can't remember her name at the moment . . . had moved there on a permanent basis a few years after I left your father. They kept to themselves. We'd see them in church every Sunday when they were in town, but they sat way in the front, up by the altar. We always sat in the back because of all you children forever making noise. She was a lovely woman. I never heard a bad word about either one of them."

When I asked if she thought Rory would help the man, she said, "Of course, he will! That's what neighbors are for! I'll call him myself, I will," and she picked up the phone and did just that.

My mother really was a nice woman and I loved her very much. I had no knowledge of why she and my father grew apart as they did and never asked. It bothered me, though, and I always wondered why, even to this day. Two people say they love each other, raise a family together, and then go their separate ways . . . why?

Rory was still a bit under the weather, but he was glad to hear from her and quite willingly agreed to help. I'm not so sure that he would have been anywhere near as accommodating if I had been the one to ask, but I was glad she did it for me. I was to call him at work the next day so he could check his schedule and maybe go out to take a look at the job. I told him that I would meet him there whenever he would be able to make it.

I was in the office at half seven, way early, the next morning. In fact, I was there, coming out of the stairway just as Dr. Delaney was getting off the elevator. We were on the third floor of an eight-story building. He had an inside parking space, in the basement, whereas scrubs like me parked outside, a fair distance away. The closest spots were left for the patients, their families, and visitors. I, of course, was able to walk to work.

He greeted me, calling me by name, and asked if we had met with Dr. McDuffy. When I told him that we had, he said that he was looking forward to hearing all about it. He told me to come see him first thing, once Colin arrived.

Saoirse was in not long after me, and she made a few suggestions for changes to the report I'd drafted. Colin came buzzing in just as the clock ticked eight, looking like he was in top form. Without even saying good morning, he asked, "Do you have that McDuffy report for me to look at?"

I handed it to him and he stood there for a few seconds, scanning it. Then he asked Saoirse if she had seen it. When she told him that she had, he said, "Well, it looks good to me. I'll let you know if Delaney wants to see us about this or not."

He was surprised when I told him that I was here when he came in and that he'd told me that he was looking forward to meeting with us and seeing the report first thing. "You're a real goer, you are, Sullivan. That will impress him, for sure. I don't think I've ever been here before he was. I'll go down and check with his secretary right now."

I spent the whole morning anxiously awaiting Colin to summon me to the meeting, but it never happened. It wasn't until late in the afternoon, just before I was about to leave, when Colin popped his head in the door and said, "Delaney will see us now. Get Saoirse and meet me in his office."

— ◆ —

Chapter Nine

The Diagnosis

The first question Dr. Delaney asked was whether or not my brother was going to fix his roof. It startled me because I hadn't put any of that in my report. I looked over at Colin who said, "I told him about that part of our conversation."

"He agreed to go look at the roof and see what he could do," I replied. "He's going to call me and let me know when he'll be able to go meet the man and see what needs to be done. I'll try to be there when he does."

"Well, I hope he can help," Dr. Delaney replied. "If Dr. Doherty is correct, and I'm saddened to say that I believe he is . . . it would be enormously important to keep Dr. McDuffy in his own home, in surroundings with which he is familiar, but first things first. Let's see what your brother can do for the man. Regardless, it sounds as if you are establishing a good rapport with Dr. McDuffy, Mr. Sullivan, and I like that. I hold him in high esteem and would like to help him in every way possible if we can. He has a wonderful reputation in all of Ireland's academic community, and across the globe, actually. I would hate to see it tarnished," he added.

"Saoirse and Colin are part of that, too, Dr. Delaney. I think all three of us did well in that regard on Saturday, sir," I said.

"Well, I can't have all three of you out of the office on this one case as I told you before, so I'm going to put you in charge. Colin will continue to supervise, but I will expect further reports from you, Mr. Sullivan," he responded.

"Can Ms. O'Connor continue to work on this with me?" I blurted out. "He definitely took a liking to her," I added, "just in case I can't make it out there every time."

He looked a little surprised by my question, but answered, "If she has the time, that will be alright, but that's up to her, and I don't want that to be during regular working hours. Again, we're too busy to spare the three of you, or even two of you, on this one case.

"I am going to let Dr. Doherty know of what took place this weekend and that we are going to continue to monitor the situation. It appears fairly obvious that he is suffering from dementia, but I am encouraged by how he interacted with the three of you."

"As you will discover as we go along, Dr. McDuffy will have moments of lucidity. He will continue to be his brilliant self, at times. However, he will have more and more incidents where he is not himself . . . where he is the victim of this dreaded disease."

"I'm hoping that if your brother can get his roof fixed, that will alleviate some of the concerns that the locals, the Garda, and Dr. Doherty have about him, and it will keep him in his home."

"I thank you all for going out of your way, on your own time, to look into this for me. I think you did a fine job. I have a meeting out of the office in fifteen minutes and really have to run. That will be all for now," he said. "Have a nice night," he added as he picked up his briefcase and walked past us down the hallway.

When he was gone, Colin turned to me and said, "Well done, Top Shillin', you've made a good first impression. You, too, Saoirse, but I'm a wee bit thirsty at the moment. Can we talk more about this over at Molly's? You can buy me that pint you owe me . . . both of you, that is . . . two separate ones."

"I have a report I have to finish up before I leave," Saoirse said. "I'll meet you there. It won't take me more than a few minutes," she added as she rushed back to her cubicle.

Once she was out of earshot, Colin turned to me and said, "She's a stunner, Sullivan, and she's way out of your league . . . you know that, right? You're in the minors with her."

"Oh, I know . . . we're just friends," I responded. I might have blushed.

Several of Colin's friends were already there by the time we arrived and all they could talk about was the game on Saturday. That's all that most of Ireland was talking about. The whole country was either watching or listening on Saturday, I think.

When Saoirse arrived, she said, "I'll have just the one. I've got class tonight."

Colin raised his empty glass, piped up, and told the waitress, "Be sure to put this next one on her bill before she leaves, Luv!"

Then he turned to me and said, "You'll be gettin' me the one after that, Sullivan!"

She stayed for about half an hour, but we never did get a chance to talk about Dr. McDuffy's case. There were too many other people around and none of them had any interest in talking about anything related to work. There were several fans of the Dublin team in the bar and they were lording it over all the rest of us.

"The 'drive for five!' We told ya! Next year we'll be going for six!" they hollered. Truth was, they'd be hard to beat, but we'd hear none of it. It was quite noisy, but that's the way it usually is whenever alcohol gets involved.

She left after the one pint and I left shortly after she did. I was quite proud of myself because of the things Dr. Delaney had said to me. I was hoping that Rory would be able to fix the roof. When I got home, I called him to ask if he could schedule the meeting at Dr. McDuffy's house for as late in the day as possible, hoping that maybe Saoirse could join me.

He said he'd let me know in the morning after he made the arrangements. He knew a man who did the thatching, but he hadn't talked to him yet. He'd made the call and left a message, though.

"I can't do that sort of thing, Brendan, and there aren't many who can. I'm hoping he's willing to do this for me. Unless he's willing to help, there's not much I can do. It sounds like this is something really important to you. Why so?" he asked.

I didn't want to tell him too much and said, "He's a personal friend of the head man here where I'm working and I'm wanting to make a good impression."

"By fixin' a man's roof? I thought you were becoming a psychiatrist or something?" he responded.

"A clinical psychologist, Rory, not a psychiatrist. I'll never be one of them. It's a bit complicated, and I'll tell you more when I see you. It is important to me, though, for sure. I'm going to make it a point to be there, if I can, no matter what time it is," I told him.

"Okay. If you say so, baby brother. Once I talk to the man, I'll let you know. As I told you, there's no way I can do it. I don't have the patience," he said. "He's the only man I know of in the whole area who does it, and he'll be coming from Killarney. He'll be doing me a big favor if he agrees to do it."

I thanked him and said that I needed about two-hours notice and I'd be there. I had dozens of other cases to work on, but the McDuffy case had become the most important one for me. Without a doubt, that was, in large part, because my work was being overseen by Dr. Delaney, and it brought me back to Sneem, too.

That was where I was born and nearly all of my family lived. I'd spent many a weekend and most of the holidays there as a child. I'd be lying, though, if I didn't acknowledge that working with Saoirse on the case was the topper. That was massive.

The next day, I was tipping along, doing all that was needed to be done, anxiously awaiting the call from Rory all the while. It was late in the evening when the phone finally rang. I was still up, studying Abnormal Psychology, one of my least favorite subjects.

"The earliest he can make it is half-past five on Friday, Bear," he told me. I guess I reminded him of a little teddy bear when I was a baby because that's what he always called me ever since I can remember. "He's doing me a big favor. I had to talk him into it, and he won't do it on the cheap, either, just so you'll know."

I assured him that money would be no problem. I didn't know that for certain, but I couldn't imagine that a retired professor from Trinity College Dublin wouldn't have a sizeable fortune saved up over the years.

"Make sure your man is there," he told me. "I wouldn't want to waste a trip. If he's not, my man might never come back."

"He'll be there, Rory. I'll make sure of it. That's one of the reasons I'm comin' over, to make sure things don't go wrong," I told him.

"You can come over to the house for dinner after," he said. "You haven't seen any of your nephews and nieces in quite a while. Sean is taller than you are now."

It was true. Rory had married young, not long after graduating from Secondary School. Sean was only two years younger than me and I didn't doubt that he was taller than me by now. He was pretty close to me the last time I saw him, and he's still growing. I'm not getting any taller. I was growing out, not up.

"That'll be grand! Thanks, Rory. See you then!"

I told Saoirse and the others of the latest development the next day. Colin had no interest in going and, much to my disappointment, Saoirse had other plans. Dr. Delaney was pleased to get the update, but we didn't meet with him. Colin did, and he told us both what he'd said.

I called Dr. McDuffy later that afternoon to give him the news. I was glad that he remembered who I was. He even knew my name. He was delighted. "That's wonderful, Mr. Sullivan. I will look forward to seeing you on Friday afternoon," he told me.

That night, I called my father. I remembered that my mother had told me how he knew Dr. McDuffy fairly well. When I asked, he said, "I can't say that we're the best of friends, Brendan, but I've met the man on many occasions and I know a lot about him."

"He's quite well-thought-of in academic circles. He's a large part of the reason why the country has put our language back in the schools. He's got or he had that much clout. That was years ago, though.

"He taught a somewhat rare topic . . . with an unusual name . . . what was it now . . . Antiquities . . . that's what it was," he told me.

"Antiquities? What's that, Da?" I asked.

"It's the study of the ancient past . . . all the great civilizations of the world. His specialty was Greece, as I recall. He's quite the intellectual, Brendan, though I've heard some stories around town here lately that are a bit worrisome. Some people are concerned about his health, his mental health, that is," he told me.

"That's why I'm doing this, Da, but don't mention it to anyone, please. It's supposed to be kept quiet, privacy and all, don't you know?" I told him.

"Oh, I know quite a bit about privacy concerns, Brendan. You can believe that. Well, if you're coming to Sneem to see Dr. McDuffy, you can stop by and see your old man every now and again, now can't you?" he asked.

I promised him that I would. He was an "empty nester" now and probably needed some company. He was still a bit disappointed I hadn't become a teacher. Diedre and Maura had, but none of his boys.

The rest of the week flew by. I was up to my ears in work, and the night classes required time and effort, too. It wasn't as if I could just show up and sit there. I had to prepare. My fellow classmates were, for the most part, a lot better students than I was, it seemed. I sat in the back and didn't participate in classroom discussions all that much, but I managed to keep up.

Friday finally arrived and I left work a little early to make the drive to Sneem in order to be there on time. I called ahead and reminded Dr. McDuffy that we were coming. Fortunately, he remembered and said he was looking forward to seeing us.

I had to get there before Rory or that other fellow did to make the introductions. After all, Rory didn't know the man. I was the middleman in all of this. I made it there in a little less than two hours with no trouble at all. There wasn't much traffic on the road because I left well before most people would be getting off work for the weekend.

When I arrived, Dr. McDuffy was nowhere around and I had a bit of a panic attack. I immediately went looking for him, hoping that he was out on one of his walks. I drove on up the road a few kilometers past his house and saw him coming down the road toward me.

As I was rounding a curve, probably going a little too fast, I came upon him as he was walking right in the middle of the road. I slammed on my brakes, coming to a stop a few meters away. There was no danger, and he ambled up to my car, seemingly unphased.

At first, it seemed as if he didn't recognize me, which was understandable. I had sunglasses on, I was in a different car, and I was wearing my favorite hat, a flat cap, plus a black jumper. I didn't look anything like what I had the other two times we had met, so I was relieved when he called me by name and said, "You're early! Is your brother here already, too?"

"Good afternoon, Dr. McDuffy, and yes, I am a few minutes early, but no, Rory isn't here yet. He'll be here shortly, I'm sure, and he's bringing with him a man who can fix your roof, if anyone can," I told him.

"Well, I certainly hope that he can," he said. Then he asked, "Why are you here? I thought you lived in Cork. Are you a carpenter, too?"

That was a good question. I didn't want to tell him the real reason why I was there, so I just said that I wanted to be there to introduce the two of them and do whatever I could to help.

"That's very kind of you, Mr. Sullivan. I appreciate that. If it weren't for you, I'd have never known of your brother or this other fellow. I'll meet you back at the house," he said as he turned to continue his walk.

When I offered him a ride, he refused. "I enjoy my walks. I need the exercise. I'll be back soon enough. The door's open and they're welcome to go in and start without me. That will be alright with me," he said with a chuckle.

When I turned in the driveway, Rory was there standing outside his car, talking on his phone. He was by himself.

"My man missed a turn and is on his way here now. He'll be here any minute. Where is this fellow we're to meet?" he asked.

Before I had time to answer, Dr. McDuffy strode into the driveway, and I made the introduction. As we were standing there, talking, an old, white pick-up truck pulled in several minutes later. An old man, seemingly about the same age as Dr. McDuffy, exited the truck and the two old men exchanged some words, shook hands, and were laughing about something as if they were long, lost friends.

"Do you two know each other?" I asked.

"Never met the man before in my life," the old man replied, "but I've never met a stranger, either, and now we're the best of friends!" The two men laughed again.

Rory introduced me to Seamus O'Reilly, a short man with a balding head and a reddish complexion who looked like about a thousand other Irishmen I'd met in my life. He had a twinkle in his eye and a smile on his face.

He took a look at the roof and said, "Holy Mary, Mother of God! What happened here?" he asked.

Dr. McDuffy told him about the fire, saying, "I'm embarrassed to tell you, but I have no one to blame but myself, Mr. O'Reilly."

"Seamus, please. Me father was Mr. O'Reilly and he's no longer with us, God rest his soul, and don't you worry about a thing. I can fix that for you so that it will be as good as new!" he said, and then he added, "but it's gonna cost you more than a few quid," as he held up his hand and moved his thumb across his fingers.

Ireland had converted to the euro before I was born. I had never heard anyone refer to our currency as anything other than euros, but I knew that it was the Irish pound before that, and that was decades ago. We all knew what he meant.

He laughed when he said it, as did Dr. McDuffy. Rory and I remained silent. These two men were having their own conversation.

When they stopped for a moment, Rory said, "There aren't many men around who can properly fix a thatched roof, Dr. McDuffy. I'm glad to have been able to find one for you, and you've got the best man for the job here in all of county Kerry."

"I am, indeed, most grateful to you, sir, for your help," Dr. McDuffy responded. "And for your brother's help as well," he said, gesturing toward me.

I muttered some response and then Seamus said, "That's kind of you to say, Rory, and it's him you have to thank for me being here, Michael. I've known him since before he was a twinkle in his father's eye." Seamus added, "I've not met his brother here before today. Their father taught a few of my wife's nieces and nephews here in Sneem years and years ago, and I met him way back then. I'm here because of Rory, here. I'm pleased to meet you, Mr. McGuire is it?"

"McDuffy," he replied, "but call me Michael, please. Hardly anyone does anymore." He added, "Like you, I'm older than most people I meet these days."

"Well, Michael, let me take a look and see exactly what needs to be done here," Seamus said as he grabbed a ladder from the back of his truck and headed toward the side of the house. We all followed him as he did.

After looking at the roof from on top of his ladder, lifting up the black plastic that was covering most of it though he didn't get on it, he came down off the ladder without saying anything about his observations and went inside. The rest of us had been standing there, several feet away, in a semi-circle, watching, not saying a word. We followed him inside, waiting for him to give us a clue as to what he was seeing.

He began tearing down some of the make-shift plastic that was covering the holes in the ceiling, making a huge mess as he did.

"Sorry about that," he said. "But I've got to see what needs to be done," he explained.

"Don't mind the mess. I'll clean it up when you're gone," Dr. McDuffy told him.

Several minutes later, he said, "I'll need to figure up all that I'll need and what it will cost you. Rory, here, can take care of the inside, right, Rory? I don't usually fool with that part of the job. I'm strictly a thatcher."

"No worries there, Seamus. The thatching is the hard part. I can't help you there. You're on your own with that," he responded. "I can do the rest."

He turned to Dr. McDuffy and said, "I'll draw up a contract and give it to Rory here. He'll let you know what his part will cost. If it's all the same for you, I'd like for you to pay me separately. I'll need a third down, a third when I'm half-way finished, and a third when the job is complete. Does that sound fair to you, Michael?"

"It does indeed!" Dr. McDuffy responded. "Cost is no object. I just want it properly done, that's all. Do you have an idea when you might be able to begin?" he asked.

"I'm as busy as a one-armed paper-hanger at the moment," he replied, "but this job needs to be done as soon as possible. It's rotten up there and it has a foul smell about it. If something isn't done soon, you could lose the whole roof as it is. I'll get started on this just as soon as Rory finishes up his part with the rafters and joists. I don't want it getting any worse than it is, but that has to be done before I can begin."

Then, he turned to look at Dr. McDuffy, squinted a bit, and said, "It looks as if it's been this way for quite a while now, Michael. Why has it taken you so long to get around to fixin' it?"

"I couldn't find anyone to do it!" he responded, throwing up his hands. I knew that was only part of the problem. There were other reasons for the delay, but I wasn't going to mention any of that.

"There's truth to that," Seamus acknowledged, "and when I'm gone, there will be one less person who knows how to do this sort of thing. I don't know of anyone else around who does this anymore, and no one seems to want to learn. It's a sad thing, it is . . . sad, indeed."

"I won't let the grass grow on this, what with winter coming on before we know it," he told us. "But I can't do anything until Rory here replaces all of the rafters, and from the look of things, most of the joists as well. Can you get to that fairly quickly, Rory?" he asked.

Rory assured him that he could and would.

"And you'll take care of gettin' rid of all the debris? I don't have the ability to do any of that. I work by meself these days," he told us, "and all I've got is this old truck of mine. I can't be doin' that sort of thing."

Again, Rory said that he could do that. "I live just down the road, on the other side of the river, and I have a crew of five men. We can get that part done in no time," he said. Then the two of them talked between themselves as to how the roof should be left before Seamus got on it.

I didn't hear much of what they were saying, and I probably couldn't have understood it, even if I did. I chatted with Dr. McDuffy as they were talking. He was clearly quite pleased with what was going on.

"That shouldn't take me but a week or two," Rory said, and then he added, putting his hand on my shoulder, "This here is the youngest in the family, Seamus, my youngest brother. I'll be putting him to work on this, too. He's the one that got me into this."

Mr. O'Reilly turned to me, studying my face, and said, "Yes, I can see some of your mother in you. I know her as well," and then he turned back to Rory and said, "and you look a little like an old boyfriend of hers!" and then he slapped his knee and bent over with laughter at his own joke. We all laughed at that. I wasn't sure that he knew my parents were divorced. I didn't ask and I didn't tell.

"Alright then," Seamus said. "My work for today is done here, and I have a powerful thirst. I'm off to Dan Murphy's place for a pint of the Holy Water. Who'll join me?" he asked.

"I can't, Seamus. I'm sorry," Rory said, "My youngest is home sick and my wife is expecting me half an hour ago." Then, he turned to me and said, "This isn't a good night for you to come visit, either, Brendan. Let's plan on doing that next time."

"I'll join you," Dr. McDuffy said, "if Brendan here will give me a ride home. I don't like walking in the dark down this road by myself late at night, and they won't let me drive anymore."

He turned to me, awaiting my reply. I couldn't refuse, so off we went. Dr. McDuffy rode with Mr. O'Reilly.

For the next two hours, I sat in a booth at Dan Murphy's Bar with the two men, listening to them as they traded stories and told tales of the old days. Clearly, the year 1949 was one of the most significant for both men. That was when Ireland officially broke away from the Commonwealth and became a Republic—no longer a "free state" and a territory belonging to England.

Most importantly, that was when we were no longer required to swear an oath of loyalty to the Crown. That had been one of the sticking points in 1922 when we became a "free state," though still under the dominion of Great Britain. Many Irishmen died over that issue, refusing to take the oath.

Both men were now in their 80s, it seemed, from the things they said. Both were too young to have fought in WWII, but both had vivid recollections of those times. I barely spoke at all. I was completely enraptured by the conversation, and I laughed at all of their jokes.

"So three men walk into a bar, sit down, and order pints of Guinness. One's an Englishman, the other's a Scot, and the third an Irishman. Flies get into the pints of all three men. The Englishman says, 'Take this back! There's a fly in my beer!' The Scot takes a spoon, scoops out the fly, and takes a sip of his beer. The Irishman grabs the fly by both wings and says, 'Spit it out, ya bastard!'"

All of us laughed uproariously. Not to be outdone, Dr. McDuffy says, "A man is running late for church, and he's searching for a parking place all over, unable to find one. At wit's end, he says 'Lord, if you find me a spot, I swear I'll go to mass every Sunday for the next year!' He turns a corner and finds the perfect spot, and says, 'Never mind, Lord. I've found one by me-self!'" Again, we all laughed.

Some of the jokes weren't all that funny, but I laughed all the same. Just watching these two old men carry on the way they were was enough to make me laugh, no matter what they said. After four or five pints, I was scuttered, but both of them were still going strong.

Fortunately, Seamus—and he insisted that I call him that— said that he was going to "head off."

When I asked, he assured me that he would be fine. "I think the car drives itself from this point on. Besides, all the Garda know me and they'll take care of me as long as I don't hit the stray sheep," he added.

I was happy to make it back to Dr. McDuffy's place. I just had to drive a few kilometers down a deserted road to get there, and I was able to do it without any problem, or at least none that I was aware of. I was very careful as I did. I wasn't much of a drinker.

As I let him out, I asked, "I might come back on Sunday after church, and if you don't mind, Dr. McDuffy, I might stop by to say hello. Would that be alright?" I was thinking of coming back to visit Rory and his family, and if I did, maybe have another conversation with him and see how he was doing.

"You're welcome to come over to the house on Sunday," he responded, "and it can be any time. I haven't been to church in quite a few years, so the morning is fine, as well."

"No church in the morning? Really?" I asked, surprised by his answer.

"Not so much since my wife left me," he answered. "She always made sure we were there, on time, every Sunday, and then some . . . the holy days of obligation . . . first Fridays of the month and all the rest."

I didn't know much about his wife, other than she had died a few years ago, and didn't ask about that, but I said, "I know . . . that business of the pedophile priests and all have turned me away, too."

"That's an outrage, it is, but that has little to do with it, as far as I'm concerned," he responded, solemnly. "There is a God," he said, "and I believe that there is only one God . . . many religions, but just one God . . . and the question is how to define the term. Each religion defines it differently. The Catholic church doesn't have a monopoly on God, but I choose to be a Catholic.

"I've struggled with those questions all of my life, Mr. Sullivan. How to reconcile the differences between religions, that is. Father O'Flanagan doesn't have the answers, and I've heard him speak so many times that I know what he's going to say before he opens his mouth, so I've stopped going to listen to him altogether. So, if you want to do so, you're welcome to come by on Sunday at any time of the day."

With that, as he was closing the door, he said, "Good night, Mr. Sullivan, and thank you for finding Mr. O'Reilly for me."

I drove slowly back to the main road and pulled into the parking lot of my father's school. I was in no condition to drive back to Cork. I woke up several hours later, feeling somewhat bollixed, but better, glad to know that I wouldn't have to get up in the morning and go to work. I planned to spend the weekend studying. All in all, it had been a grand day, and the weekend was here. I was much relieved to arrive home safely at whatever hour it was.

CHAPTER TEN

Recognition of the Problem

Saturday was a blur, and when I woke up on Sunday, I was still out of sorts, not feeling much like going back out there, so I called Dr. McDuffy and told him that I wouldn't be coming to see him. I didn't make it to Mass that morning, which wasn't all that unusual, though I did try to go every Sunday, just not all that hard and any excuse would do. Today, my excuse was that I didn't feel well.

I was wandering around my apartment, still feeling kind of knackered, and for some reason, I kept thinking about what he had said to me about him struggling to define the term God. I'd never thought much about it before. It was always "God the Father, God the Son, and God the Holy Spirit," and man was made in the likeness of God.

God was always depicted as having a long, white beard and sitting on a cloud. He made everything, knew everything, and was omnipotent and omnipresent. What was to define? What else was there to know?

As kids, we never questioned the teachings of our church. We didn't dare. We'd have been smacked silly by the priests, and then even worse by our parents if we did.

My mother probably wouldn't have hit me because she was a Druid and she was my mother. My father handled the corporal punishment side of child-rearing, but I never understood the theology of Druidism anyway. They worshipped nature and all the natural wonders of the world. I never quite got their concept of who or what created all of what exists.

From my understanding of things, the Druids believed that there were many gods, not just one. That was what most religions believed back then before Abraham. The Jews were thought to be the first to believe that there was only one God, as best I knew, but I didn't know that, for sure. To my knowledge, the gods of the Druids were nothing like the gods of Greece and Rome or any of the others.

Then again, I knew nothing about Druid gods. There weren't any books or plays about them for me to read like there were from the Greek and Roman days, but I didn't know all that much about those civilizations, either. Druids worshipped trees, stones, plants—things like that—and the red stags. I figured that if there was a head god, it was probably in the body of one of Ireland's red deer.

I never gave it much thought before as to why, but for some reason, one of my favorite topics when I was younger was mythology. Even though it wasn't offered in school, I read the Iliad and the Odyssey over and over. My father encouraged me to do that. In fact, he rewarded me when I did so.

Come to think of it, the Harry Potter books and movies that all the youngsters were now mad about, including me, were like them in some ways—magical, mystical creatures and beings you couldn't see or hear, only imagine. Maybe that was the allure. Maybe it was the imagination part, and the innocence of being a young, impressionable child who believed in Santy and the rest was what made those books so attractive to me and others like me.

I knew all the Roman gods—Neptune, Mars, Apollo, Vulcan, Mercury—all of them, and I knew their Greek counterparts—Zeus, Athena, Poseidon, Ares, Hades, Aphrodite, Hermes, Triton—all of them, too.

I guess it was kind of weird, but it absolutely fascinated me. The Druids had no gods who were anything like them that I knew of, but ancient Ireland was nothing like the Greek or the Roman empires, either. I knew little about the Celts, but I knew that Druids were said to be Celtic priests. So, all Druids were Celts, but not all Celts were Druids, as best I understood it. I just lumped them together.

The Greek and Roman societies were the most amazing to me, though, more so than the Egyptians, Babylonians or any of the others. For whatever reason, the Greek philosophers—Plato,

Aristotle and Socrates, in particular, seemed to have fared better in history than any of the Roman philosophers. Even though the Roman Empire lasted much longer and is considered by most people to be the greatest civilization ever, I couldn't think of a single Roman philosopher who had met the test of time as those three Greeks did.

There must have been some, but I couldn't think of any right at that moment. The Caesars weren't philosophers, they were ruthless men who ruled with iron fists, as best I knew. Many had odd, almost strange, personalities and behaviors, like Nero who played his violin while Rome burned, plus they often killed each other to gain power, even fellow family members. Cicero, maybe? But I didn't know much of anything about him.

Plus, the Romans had those barbaric events in the Coliseum where lions ate Christians and gladiators fought to the death for the amusement of the people and the Caesars. "Hail Caesar! We who are about to die salute you!" I remembered that expression and repeated it many times over the years. It always puzzled me . . . shook me to the core, actually. They didn't really mean that, did they?

The Greeks didn't have any of that, although I did remember stories of Spartan parents leaving babies who were less than perfect out to die. The Greek civilization was more like a bunch of city-states, not one cohesive unit, unlike the Romans. Plus, they didn't take prisoners as the Romans did and make slaves of them, to my knowledge.

I also liked the story of Spartacus, the slave who fought Rome and won, for a while. Every now and then, when asked my name, I'd say, "I am Spartacus!" The American actor, Kirk Douglas, said that in the movie. Nobody ever thought it was all that funny when I did, except for my father. He was the only one to laugh whenever I did.

One of my favorite characters in all of history was Socrates, although I couldn't remember ever reading a single thing that he wrote. I first learned of him when my mother took me to the Irish Botanical Gardens, just outside of Dublin, where we saw a statue of him. That's not why she took me there, but I always seemed to end up standing next to it, wondering who he was. I knew that he was called the father of western philosophy, but I didn't understand exactly why.

I had no idea why the Irish honored him that way, and still don't. She took me there because of all of the trees, plants, flowers, and things, which was part of her Druidic bent, I'm sure. For me, if the Irish put a statue of him there as it did, that was good enough for me even though I didn't understand why they did that. It was a beautiful place, especially during the spring when the flowers were blooming.

The one thing I knew about him . . . and he was famous for saying something like this . . . was that he said that the more he learned, the more he realized how little he knew. I could relate to that.

He was one of my heroes. That saying became my motto in life. I was no genius. I knew how little I knew, but it had the effect of bringing down the more brilliant ones around me a notch or two. I was in good company.

Religion is one of those things no one ever talks about, especially in Ireland. Most people are Catholic, so they all believed the same thing, and there was no need to talk about those things. When they did, there was no argument, no discussion, and no debate—everyone knew the doctrine and the rules. No one questioned them, ever.

As for the Protestants, that was a totally different story. The only real difference was over the Pope, so it was more of a political and historical thing. So much bad blood had been shed over the years it was hard to imagine that a true reconciliation would ever be possible. It had nothing to do with theology, as best I could tell. They, too, were followers of Jesus Christ, and their church services were nearly identical to ours.

But no one who was Catholic talked to anyone who was a Protestant about theology or anything else. If they did, it was sure to cause a disturbance. After the Treaty in 1922, and then when we became a Republic in 1949, most Protestants went to Northern Ireland or England.

There was never any disagreement over religious beliefs in my world . . . ever . . . but occasionally, probably because of my mother's influence, I'd hear this little voice in my head that questioned such things. I'd never actually talked about any of that to anyone, though;

I'd just think some doubting thoughts. This was one of those times where I was hearing that voice, and I wasn't getting anywhere with it.

As the day went on, I began to snap out of the doolally state of mind I was in and I changed my mind. I decided to go have dinner with Rory, if it was alright with him, and maybe pay a visit to Dr. McDuffy while there, after all. It was still early enough for me to do that.

"We eat early, Brendan, so be here around half five, if not before, alright?" he told me. Then I called Dr. McDuffy and made plans to see him later that afternoon. It was early September and it would still be light around that time. I didn't want to get there too late.

I was glad to see Rory and his family. He was now in his late thirties and had been married for almost twenty years to Marlene who had been his girdle since they were young pups. They had six children, ranging in ages from Sean, who was now eighteen, all the way down to the youngest, Ella Grace, who had just turned three, with one on the way—a typical Irish Catholic family.

It was pure chaos in the home, though, and I was glad to be able to walk away unscathed not long after dinner ended. I offered to help clean up, but they would hear none of it. They wanted to get the kids into bed early, what with school the next day and all. I told him how much I appreciated what he was doing for Dr. McDuffy, but not too much about why. I'm sure he was curious, but he didn't press me on it.

My plan was to take Dr. McDuffy back to Murphy's bar and have a few pints. I really enjoyed seeing him laughing and telling jokes. I had given some thought to why I hadn't been able to think of any jokes at all while Seamus and he were swapping stories back and forth. I felt a bit inadequate. I made it a point to have a few at the ready and was determined to do better this time.

However, when I arrived at his house, those plans changed. He was in no mood to go to a bar. "I haven't had that much to drink in years," he explained. "And I can't remember much of the conversation, to be honest," he said apologetically. "I hope I didn't embarrass myself too much. I have felt poorly ever since."

I assured him that he hadn't behaved badly at all and told him how much I enjoyed being with the two of them. "Well, come in . . .

come in. Have a seat," he said as he put another log on the fire. I took a seat on the couch, and he sat in his favorite chair right in front of the fire. The thought occurred to me that he needed a dog. I could visualize one sitting right next to him, on the floor, close enough for him to pet her.

Then, he asked, "So what brings you here this evening, Mr. Sullivan?"

"It was a good question—why was I there? The best explanation I could come up with was that I had just been to see my brother, Rory, and I wanted to make sure that there was no misunderstanding about all of what was going on.

"I just came from having dinner at my brother's house and I wanted to talk to you and make sure that you are okay with what's going to happen here. I don't want you to feel like I'm forcing you to hire my brother to do the work on your house, that's all," I told him. "If you want to get a second opinion, he told me that he can give you the names of some others who do the same kind of work that he does. There are several other men in and around Sneem who would be able to help you."

"No, no, no! Not at all," he responded. "I've had no luck whatsoever finding anyone to help. You were a godsend. I thank God for you."

"But it's always good to get a second opinion, isn't it?" I asked.

"That's probably true," he acknowledged, "but I liked Seamus and I like the fact that your brother is the son of Patrick Sullivan. I'm very comfortable with using the two of them. I don't want to try to find someone else who might give me a better price, but that's a nice thought. I appreciate that."

"Oh, it's no bother. There are those who are said to take advantage of our senior citizens, and I didn't want to do that," I told him.

"Thank you for that, but it's not necessary. I haven't received the contract yet, but I trust that they'll be fair. No matter what the cost, I doubt that I'll be wanting the names of anyone else," he said.

Then he peered into my eyes and asked, "How did we meet again? I don't remember when I first met you or how." He said in a soft, barely audible voice, "But you look familiar to me."

I didn't want to tell him that it was in a Garda Station barely over two weeks ago, and I certainly wasn't going to tell him that it was because I was part of a team trying to decide if he should be involuntarily hospitalized due to dementia. I hesitated before responding.

Then I said, "My friends and I were driving down this road . . . lost, sort of . . . and we stopped here to ask directions. That was a couple of weeks or so ago. Remember?"

"I remember that day, but I was thinking that we might have met before that, but I can't recall when that would have been," he said.

I wasn't about to remind him of the day in Kenmare, so I dodged the question and said, "Maybe, but I think that was probably the first time. I was with a man named Colin and a girl named Saoirse, and we were in a flashy red Ford Mustang convertible, and . . ."

"Yes, yes . . . I remember that well. I guess that must have been it, then. Pure luck, was it?" he asked.

"I guess so, and we thank God for it, right?" I responded.

"Yes, indeed . . . thank God," he whispered. Then he said, "You know, I used to be a professor at Trinity College Dublin, but that was a few years ago, and I . . ."

"I know . . . my father told me all about that, Michael, and I couldn't be more impressed. He had nothing but good things to say about you," I told him.

"Well, that's nice to hear. Be sure to tell him that I said hello," he said.

"I will," I told him. "I expect that he might be by to say hello one of these days, especially when Rory gets to working on your house."

"That would be wonderful," he said. "I haven't seen him in a few years. Ever since my wife died, I've kind of kept to myself. I don't socialize so much anymore."

"You probably read quite a bit and write an article or two every now and again, yes?" I asked.

"No, I don't do any of that, as a matter of fact," he responded. "I used to, but that's been years ago. Those days are gone. Now, it's all I can do to read the Sunday paper. Back then, I thought of myself as being quite the intellectual, and I did all of those things," he said somewhat wistfully.

"I thought I knew so much and I was so impressed with how people held me in such high regard . . ." Then he paused, looked over at the fire that was burning brightly, then back at me, and continued, "Yes, those days are gone. Look at me now."

"There aren't many people around anymore who knew me back then, or what I was like, certainly not around here. Now, I have neighbors who aren't my friends, who think I'm a crazy person. Apparently, I scare children. They run away when they see me . . . say unkind things to me sometimes. I was never that way, and it bothers me greatly," he told me.

"Even my own children, and I have a wonderful, and highly successful son and daughter who I love very much, who now have little to do with me, and that saddens me, too," he acknowledged, almost mournfully. "And then there are the grand-children who I rarely see," he added. "I haven't seen them in years. For all I know, I might even be a great-grandfather by now."

He spoke very slowly in a low voice, deeper than I'd ever heard him speak. For the most part, he looked into the fire, not at me, as he spoke. It was almost as if he was talking to himself.

The thought occurred to me that I might have an ethical obligation to tell him who I really was and why I was really there, but I thought better of it. I couldn't do that. This man was having an introspective moment, and I was fortunate enough to be there. I could only listen. I wasn't going to pry.

When he paused, gathering his thoughts as to what to say next, I interjected, "Where are your children, Michael? Where do they live? What do they do?"

He looked over at me, brightened a bit, and said, "They live in the United States. Both are professors—one teaches Art History, and the other is a law professor."

"They took after you, it seems. I'm sure you're quite proud of them," I said.

"Their mother had a lot to do with that. I don't know that I deserve any of the credit at all. I was always too busy with my head stuck in my books. I'm afraid I wasn't quite the father I should have been. Ever since my wife died, I . . ." and his voice trailed off, and he lowered his head, unable to finish the sentence. I sat silently until he did.

"I just don't hear from them as often as I'd like. She would always make sure that we spoke to them regularly, at least once a week. She made me travel to see them every year. I haven't been back since she passed," he said, looking back to the fire. "I could call them, I guess, but I don't . . . or they could call me, but they don't," he added.

"Do they come back to see you?" I asked.

"They both have been back many times, but it's been a while since they were last here. Now, I have trouble remembering all of their names . . . the grandchildren, that is . . . or their ages. My wife kept track of those things—birthdays, graduations, what sports they were playing—all of that."

"I keep calling my grandson, whose name is Edward, Andrew, and I can never remember my daughter's youngest child's name. It's Keira or Kylie or something like that, not a family name. I don't know where she got that one. Whenever I get it wrong, she gets mad at me. I don't like that," he said.

"Maybe that's why I don't call too often or maybe that's why they don't call me so much anymore. I don't know what it is, and I don't know what to do about it, either. It saddens me," he acknowledged.

For a moment, I thought he was going to cry, but he didn't. Instead, he stiffened and said, "Can I offer you a drink? I have some Bailey's in the refrigerator. It's been there for a while, but it should still be good, or something to eat?" he offered.

"No, thank you. I just came from my brother's house, as I said, and I had supper there with him and his family. Thank you, though," I responded. "But I'll join you if you're going to have some of the Bailey's," I offered.

"Not unless you do," he responded. "As I said, I don't drink much these days and the other night with Seamus and you was a rarity. I'm sorry if I'm not too conversant tonight. I'm just not feeling that well. I didn't get out for a walk today, and I always feel better when I do," he said. "I usually go out twice a day, morning and night, for that reason," he added.

"Have you ever thought of getting a dog?" I asked. "I've never had one myself, but I've always wanted one, though."

"A dog . . ." he said, repeating my words. "That's just what I need . . . something else to take care of. I can hardly take care of myself, Mr. Sullivan. I don't think it would be such a good idea for me to take on that responsibility, especially a puppy."

"My wife always had a dog in the house. She wouldn't allow being without one. She loved Golden Retrievers the best. I preferred the Irish Setters, but they require more attention and more exercise. Ours died not long after she did. I have thought about it, though, but no . . . I don't think that's such a good idea, but thank you for the thought," he said.

Then he asked, "What was the name of that girl who was with you again?"

"Saoirse," I told him.

"Saoirse," he repeated. "A fine name for an Irish girl. We named our daughter Caitlin. The priest said, 'that's not a name . . . Cathleen . . . that's a good Irish name.' My wife stuck to her guns and kept it." He laughed when he said that.

"What was your son's name? Or what is it, I should say?" I asked.

"Patrick, what else?" he responded. "I think it's mandatory that every Irish family has at least one son named Patrick, right?" he asked with a snicker. I agreed.

"That's my father's name, and I have a brother named Patrick," I told him.

"I rest my case, as a barrister would say," he answered.

"And I have another brother named Kevin, plus sisters named Siobhan, Deidre, and Maura, and then there's Rory, of course, who you know."

"Those are all fine Irish names, they are," he said. "Yes, indeed. I have trouble remembering names these days. My memory just isn't what it used to be. I have to write things down or I'll forget them!" he said. "It's not easy getting old, Mr. Sullivan, but it beats the alternative, doesn't it?" he asked.

"Brendan, please, Michael," I responded, "and yes, it does. Some people don't have that luxury," I responded.

"It's no luxury, Brendan. It was for a while, but that was when my wife was with me and we had nothing to do but enjoy each other's company in what they said would be the 'golden years' of our lives . . . and they were right, for a while. Not so anymore, I'm afraid," he said solemnly.

"Have you ever thought about moving back to Dublin where there are more people you know and who know you?" I asked.

He looked back into the fire, hesitated for a moment, and said, "I could never do that, Mr. Sullivan."

"Why not?" I asked.

He looked up, stared at me, heaved a deep sigh, and said, "She's still here."

There wasn't much to say in response to that comment, but I mustered, "You miss her quite a bit, don't you, Michael?"

"That I do, Brendan . . . that I do," he responded in a voice I could barely hear.

With that, I realized that I had pried enough into this good man's private life, but I had been given an insight into the man that explained a few things. I didn't doubt for a moment that he carried on conversations with her while walking down the road, just as the Garda lady had told me. Yes, she was still there with him that night, just as sure as I was. He needed to be kept in that house at all costs, just as Dr. Delaney had suggested. He would be lost without her, that was clear. He could never be moved.

Clinical psychologists are supposed to obtain information and assist in making a clinical judgment about a client's mental state. I had done that. I had peered deep into his soul. I had done enough. It was time for me to leave.

I stood, extended my hand, and said, "It's been a pleasure getting to know you a little better, Michael. I'm glad to have been able to help you some, as I have. I'll be back when my brother and Mr. O'Reilly, or Seamus, start working on your house. I look forward to helping out with that."

He stood and walked me to the door, saying "I'm anxious to have them get started. I thank you for your concern, Brendan, and I look forward to seeing you again in the very near future. I hope to be in better spirits next time. I trust I didn't bore you to death with my sad story."

"Not at all, but it certainly was different from our time at Murphy's Bar the other night with Seamus! That was fun! I look forward to having another pint with you when you're up to it," I said with a smile.

"As will I, Brendan. Have a safe drive home."

On the ride home, I thought about all that I had to tell Dr. Delaney and the others. I definitely felt good about what I had been able to do to help Dr. McDuffy, so far. It was all because of my brother, of course, but I could take some of the credit.

After all is said and done, being a clinical psychologist was about helping people who have problems. That was what I had decided to do with my life. I was still more interested in working with young children and teenagers, but this was part of my education, too, and I was learning a lot about working with senior citizens.

I felt sorry for this great man and I was going to do whatever I could to help him. It wasn't all about Saoirse anymore, as it was at first. I was developing some strong feelings for him. I felt good about what I was doing.

The next day, when the three of us met with Dr. Delaney, he told us that he was delighted to hear what had been accomplished. So was Saoirse. She said that she wished she could have been there for both meetings. I wished she could have been there, as well. Colin could have cared less, I think.

Dr. Delaney told me to stay in touch with Dr. McDuffy and keep him posted on all developments, especially about the roof and all of that. Keeping him in his home was critical, he stressed. I assured him that I would do so.

When I asked what else I could be doing since I couldn't provide counseling or much of anything else, really, he said, "We have a unit that specializes in these types of cases. I'll ask Dr. O'Brien to have a look at this and see what she has to say. Depending upon her schedule, she'll probably be by to see you sometime today."

"Now that our unit has diagnosed the problem, another unit will take over with the care and treatment part of it. I don't normally do this but, in this case, I am going to continue to be personally involved with this particular patient. I promised Dr. Doherty that I would, and I will."

"As a general rule, I leave that to others. I'm so busy with the administrative requirements of this job that I don't get to treat patients at all. It's not what I wanted when I was your age just starting out, but that's how things have worked out," he told me.

"I'm going to recommend to Dr. O'Brien that she keep you on this case, Mr. Sullivan," and he turned to Saoirse and said, "and you, too, Ms. O'Connor, if you want, on your own time that is. Mr. O'Riordan, I'd like for you to continue to supervise their work, please."

"Of course, sir," he responded.

"I'd like that, Dr. Delaney," Saoirse answered. "I have a keen interest in this area, and I thank you for allowing me to do so," she told him.

"This is a teaching hospital and the two of you are just beginning your work here. Clinical psychology offers many options for you to choose between, and you may find that this is the path you might want to follow. Regardless, it should be beneficial to your overall career growth, and it is obvious that you, Mr. Sullivan, have developed an excellent rapport with our new patient."

Then his phone rang and he said, "I've got to take this call. Thank you all, again, for what you've done on this case, especially since you have done so much of it on your own time. I appreciate it. That will be all for now."

Once we were out of his office, Colin congratulated me and said, "You're in like Flynn, Sully! Keep me in the loop." Saoirse said again how sorry she was that she couldn't make it either time over the weekend, wishing she had been there. She asked that I give her a little more notice before going back the next time. I assured her that I would.

CHAPTER ELEVEN

Kathleen O'Brien

Later that afternoon, a well-dressed, older woman walked into the room which I shared with three other "trainees" as we were called, and asked, "Is there a Brendan Sullivan here?"

"That's me," I responded as I stood to greet her.

"I'm pleased to meet you, Mr. Sullivan," she told me with a warm smile on her face, and then she extended her hand and said, "I'm Kathleen. I've heard nothing but good things about you. Let's go gather up Ms. O'Connor and find a place to have a little chat, shall we?"

We walked down the hall to Saoirse's cubicle, interrupting a phone call she was on and waited outside her room until it ended. Then the three of us walked down the hallway into an elaborately furnished room by hospital standards and took seats at the end of what was a long table.

"We'll be fine here. This is where we meet with some of our larger families and important guests. No one will be using it at this hour," she began.

I didn't know quite what to expect, her being the head of a department and all, but she spoke in a soft voice and put me at ease immediately. She was an attractive woman with reddish hair, of average height and weight, who was elegant in her mannerisms. She didn't act like any other doctor I'd ever met, and she wasn't wearing a name tag like everyone else did. I wasn't sure what to make of her, but I was favorably impressed.

Once we were seated and settled, she began by saying, "I'm the head of our Caregivers Unit here at St. Stephen's, and I want you to know that it took me years to get the administration to allow me to use that term, so it makes me feel good every time I do."

"I dislike using the 'D' words, like 'dementia, disease, disorder, or death,' or the words 'hospice' and 'Alzheimer's' . . . all those have such negative connotations, don't they?" she asked, not expecting an answer.

"My unit provides care to those types of patients, however, and that's why I'm here. We try to make the last few years of life for a person who has those kinds of problems as pleasant as possible. We 'care' about people. That sounds much better, doesn't it?" she asked with a smile.

We agreed.

"Dr. Delaney sent the McDuffy case over to me earlier today, thinking that I would assign it to one of the newly-hired employees, much like either of the two of you, to work on, I'm sure, but I know Dr. McDuffy personally, and I want to be involved in his care and treatment," she told us, "so I am going to keep it and I'll be working with the two of you on his case for now and we'll see where it goes. I consider him to be a friend."

Her eyes were an unusually dark shade of green that seemed to match the green dress she was wearing. She looked quite stylish. She didn't have any airs about her, though. There was a smile on her face and her eyes sparkled as she spoke.

She went on, "I have known Dr. McDuffy since he was a young man, back when he was just starting out at Trinity College. He taught one of the courses I was required to take as a first-year student and I developed a crush on him, as young, impressionable students often do with their professors.

"I hasten to add that he was married by then and had young children, so there was nothing of a romantic nature between us, but I was absolutely enthralled by him and totally enamored with him. From then on, I took every course he taught. I was an enthusiastic student, eager to learn all that there was to learn, a few years younger than the two of you, and I hung on every word he spoke.

"To be honest, I was in love with the man, though he had no idea I existed, I'm sure, at least not at first." She actually giggled when she said that, which made the two of us laugh. We knew what she meant.

"He was a strikingly handsome young man, too, which made things even worse, with a true passion for his work. He was an inspiration for me then, and he remained so long after I graduated. I daresay that he was one of the most influential people in my life."

"I have followed his career and met him several times at social events over the years, but it's been a while since I last saw him. The last time was at the ceremony given for him at the College upon his retirement, some ten or fifteen years ago. I have the utmost admiration for the man. I have a vivid memory of him, and it's entirely favorable.

"Even though I chose a completely different career after I graduated, I learned so very much from him about the history of the world we live in, from a societal point of view, that I will never forget him or what he taught me. That's what a liberal arts education does for you, isn't it?" she asked, again not expecting an answer.

"They teach you things like philosophy, art, literature, music, political science, the social sciences . . . and you come away with your head full of thoughts and ideas but nothing of much commercial value, right?" she asked. "Nothing you can actually 'do' with all the knowledge you've gained. There aren't many jobs out there for people like that, except at colleges, universities, and some of the better secondary schools, right?" This time she paused, awaiting a response.

"I did the same thing, Dr. . . ." Saoirse began.

"Kathleen, please. Dr. O'Brien is much too formal for me. I insist," she told us.

"I did the same thing, Kathleen, but I decided fairly early on that I wanted to study psychology. I began taking the proper courses during my second year. I might want to become a psychiatrist, but I'm not so sure of that just yet," Saoirse told her. "That takes quite a few more years of schooling, as you know."

"Good for you, Saoirse," she said, and then she turned toward me, awaiting what I had to say for myself.

"I went to school here in Cork, and the main reason I decided to do this was and is that I want to help young children who are the victims of divorce, as I was," I told her. "I'm from Sneem, originally, so Dr. McDuffy's case was kind of right up my alley, so to speak, but it was just a coincidence that I was assigned to his case."

"I noticed that in the notes," she said. "Well, for whatever your reasons, you both are to be commended for being here at St. Stephen's, and for your work on this case, so far."

At that point, she extended one hand to me and the other to Saoirse and said, "So, let's go to work, together, and see what we can do to help this man, shall we?"

She squeezed our hands as we smiled at each other and said, "Let's make the last years of Dr. Martin Michael McDuffy's life as good as they can be, okay?" We held that thought for several seconds, and then she added, "But it won't be easy."

When she said that, the expression on her face changed. The twinkle in her eye faded and the smile on her lips disappeared. Her brow furrowed and the wrinkles on her face, covered by make-up, became visible.

"Dr. McDuffy has a death sentence, as we know, and all we can do is do our best to make his last years as painless as possible," she said grimly. "There is no cure."

It looked as if some moisture formed in her eyes and that she might cry when she said those words. Then she stiffened, her smile came back, her eyes brightened, and she said, "But that's our job . . . that is our profession. It is the one you two have chosen, and it's our solemn responsibility to provide the best care and treatment needed to make that happen."

"Do either of you have much experience in this area?" she asked.

"I'm taking a class on geriatrics at the moment," Saoirse replied.

"Geriatrics . . . that's another term I'm not particularly fond of. It means senior citizens with special needs, as I take it. I prefer to refer to our patients as 'seasoned adults.' That has a much more pleasant connotation, doesn't it?" she asked.

We both chuckled and agreed.

"How about you, Mr. Sullivan?" she asked.

"Well, to be honest, I am more interested in the youngsters, especially the teenagers, as I said, but I haven't had too many opportunities to work with them just yet here at St. Stephen's. I just happened to get assigned to Dr. McDuffy's case and now, I'm totally involved. I was at his house last night for a social call. I really like the old man," I admitted. "He's a funny guy once you get to know him."

"I'm sure he is," she responded, "and it seems as if you have become a bit of a chum. I read, with delight, your summary of that night you spent with him at Murphy's Bar together with that Seamus O'Reilly fellow."

"Those two men were hysterical," I told her. "I enjoyed them immensely. I had as much fun that night as any I've ever had in my entire life."

"I laughed when I read your summary of that meeting. I wish I could have been there," she said with a smile.

"If you're lucky, you'll see that man a few more times before the end comes. Unfortunately, you'll be seeing an entirely different man as we go along," she added glumly.

"But the three of us, and some others, will do all that we can to be of assistance to dear old Dr. McDuffy," she continued, "and as I said, that's the best that we can do." Her cheerful countenance darkened and her eyes fell to the floor as she added, "until the bitter end."

When Saoirse asked what was to be expected of the two of us, she said, "Before we get into that, I'm going to give the two of you an assignment and, if it's not too inconvenient, I ask that you complete it at your earliest opportunity, preferably within the next week or two, if you can. Will you do that for me?" she asked. "Can you do that? Do you have the time for it, given your other responsibilities? It will take you several hours, I'm sure."

"Of course!" we responded enthusiastically. "We can find some time, I'm sure. What is it?" Saoirse asked.

"For now, I ask that you both read two books," she told us. "One is the *Thirty-Six Hour Day*, and the other is entitled the *Loss of Self*. They are both in my office and if you give me a minute, I'll go and get them now. These are my personal copies, which I never give out because whenever I do, I never get them back. I have no doubt that the two of you will return them, right?" she asked. We assured her that we would.

With that, she stood and said, "I'll be right back," and left us sitting there, wondering what we were in for. "I'll bet she was a beautiful woman in her day," I said.

"She's a beautiful woman now, Brendan," Saoirse replied.

"I know . . . but you know what I mean," I stammered.

"She's a beautiful older woman. She reminds me of Maureen O'Hara. I think she looks a lot like her," she said.

"I've seen that movie with her and John Wayne, *The Quiet Man*, a few times myself," I told her, "and she's probably the most famous actress we've ever had."

"Or actor, too. Who else is there?" she asked.

I thought about it and said, "Maybe Pierce Brosnan, Liam Neeson . . . or Gabriel Byrne? Peter O'Toole?"

"Pfff!" she scoffed. "They can't hold a candle to her. I'm a bit partial to Saoirse Ronan these days, for obvious reasons, but she has a long way to go to get to Maureen O'Hara's status, that's for sure."

Dr. O'Brien returned to the room as we were finishing the conversation and she said, "I like Saoirse Ronan, too. I loved her in *Brooklyn* and *Lady Bird*, but not so much in *Mary, Queen of Scots*. She has a bright future ahead of her, for sure."

She handed each of us a book and said, "These will provide you with an excellent primer for what we are about to do. I find them much more informative and useful than the traditional texts you'll be required to read, and they're directly on point with what you can expect to be doing. They're not textbooks, so they shouldn't be as laborious as those are."

Then she stood and said, "I'm sorry, but I've got to be off. I'm late for a meeting. It's been a pleasure meeting the two of you, although I wish it weren't under these circumstances, and I look forward to working with both of you."

"Let's plan on meeting again next week in this room, at this same time, shall we?" she asked with a smile. That wasn't a question, and we both readily agreed. Then she stood, shook our hands, and gracefully exited the room, saying "See you then."

When she was out of earshot, Saoirse said, "She's one of the big muckety-mucks in the whole hospital! This Dr. McDuffy is a special man indeed!"

I took the *Thirty-Six Hour Day* book and Saoirse the *Loss of Self*. Our plan was to read both books within the week. I began reading mine that night.

I didn't get a chance to talk to Saoirse for the next few days, though we passed each other in the hallways several times. We were busy at work and there really wasn't much time to chat. We were given half an hour to eat lunch and that was only if time permitted. I often didn't eat lunch at all.

We both had night classes, but not together. It wasn't until noon on that Friday, when I saw her sitting at a table by herself in the snack room, that we had a chance to talk and compare notes. She was finishing up as I sat down.

"Mine is dreadfully boring," she told me. "It's so sad that it makes me want to cry. It's all about how older people with dementia lose their personalities and their identities, forgetting who they're married to or who their children are—things like that."

"Mine is no better," I told her. "It's about how the days pass so slowly that you would swear there were thirty-six, not twenty-four, hours in each day. It sounds absolutely gruesome for the families and those who take care of those people."

"Have you finished it yet?" she asked. I told her that I hadn't and was only about half-way through. "Me, neither," she said. "But we've got to finish at least the one by Monday, don't we?" she asked.

I agreed. We both wanted to make a good impression on Dr. O'Brien. "There goes my weekend," she said. "I had other plans, but those will have to wait. Me boyfriend's not going to be too happy about that. He had other plans for us."

I was devastated when she said that. I had no idea that she had a boyfriend. I didn't say anything about it, though.

"And I was planning on going down to see Dr. McDuffy, but that might have to wait, too," I told her. "This is more important. I don't want to disappoint Dr. O'Brien."

"What about fixing the roof and all that?" she asked. "I think that's more important than reading these books," she said.

I told her that I had spoken to Rory and he had told me that he hadn't been able to start work on the place this week, but that he was hoping to get over there first thing Monday morning, for sure.

"Seamus can't do anythin' until Rory's men get the joists and the rafters in place, so there won't be anything to see or do this weekend," I told her. "Rory said that his part shouldn't take too long, though. He hoped to finish within a few weeks. The thatching part is what's going to take some time. I'll let you know how it goes, and I'll keep a close eye on things," I assured her.

So I spent the weekend in Cork, reading that book and studying. On Monday, when we met with Dr. O'Brien, we had each finished one book, but that was it. Neither of us had been able to read more than that. We exchanged books and would have another week to read the second one. Dr. O'Brien wasn't upset with us.

"That's fine," she told us. "Thank you for what you've done. You're busy people, I'm sure, what with your classes and all, and now you both have a better idea of what's in store for us, yes?" she asked.

"Dr. McDuffy's not anywhere near as bad as what I'm reading, Dr. O'Brien," I responded but before I could complete the sentence, she interrupted me and said, "Kathleen, please."

"He's nothing like what I read about, either," Saoirse agreed.

"But he will be," she told us. "And sooner than you might think," she added. "It's usually a rapidly progressive disease which runs its course in a few years after a diagnosis is made. There are seven stages to it and my guess is that he's in stage four, which is where a 'moderate decline' is evident. In this stage, he recognizes that he is having some problems, but he's able to cope with them. He may be four or five years into the disease by now."

"In stage five, it becomes 'moderately severe' where he is unable to cope with some of the problems, which continue to worsen, and, at that point, he will be in need of assistance. We don't have an onset date, so it's hard to say exactly where the good doctor is on that chart, but that's my best estimate, from what I've read."

"Isn't there something that can be done to slow down the process?" Saoirse asked. "Some drugs or something?"

"Or surgeries or procedures to cure the problem?" I chimed in. "It's about blood flow to the brain, right? Arteries or veins getting tangled, maybe? Isn't that it?" I asked.

She looked at us with a grim, humorless face and said matter-of-factly, "No, there isn't . . . no drugs, no procedures, not yet."

She lowered her eyes, paused for a few seconds, and then continued, "All we can do is provide palliative care and do our best to prevent our patients from suffering. It's a death sentence, I'm sad to say, as I've told you before." It was clear that she meant it.

"It is a death sentence," she repeated. "You must accept that as a fact. It is what it is. There is no hope of recovery or improvement," she added.

"Really?" I asked somewhat incredulously. "No medicines or therapies whatsoever?"

"I'm afraid not," she answered. "I wish there were. Though we're spending millions on research trying to find a cure, we have little to show for it. Every so often, we think we have a breakthrough, only to discover that it was just a flash in the pan.

"When you finish reading the two books that I've given you, there are a few others for you to read. There are studies being performed. It's a global problem and the world is throwing money at the issues, to no avail, so far.

"It's important for the two of you to know the medical issues involved with the disease because you're students and this is a learning process. You're correct, Brendan, this pernicious disease involves a tangling of neurons, or ganglia, to be more precise, but we don't need to get into all of that for now. We, as clinical psychologists, have nothing to do with any of that, though. That's for the researchers.

"For years, the diagnosis of Alzheimer's Disease was only made upon an autopsy, but about thirty or forty years ago, a scan was developed called the PET scan, or Positron Emission Tomography, which takes a picture of the brain. There is no need to get Dr. McDuffy in here and make him undergo all of that. There's little doubt about the diagnosis, unfortunately," she said.

"And there's nothing to be done to correct any of that?" I asked. "No drugs, no nothing?" I asked, again. "That's hard to believe."

She looked at me and said somewhat more firmly this time, again, "No, Brendan, there isn't. I wish there was, but there isn't. Trust me, if there was, I would know about it, I assure you."

I apologized and said something like, "I'm sure you would."

She went on, saying "That doesn't mean that there isn't anything that we, the clinical psychologists, can do to be of assistance. We aren't the researchers or the brainiacs who figure these things out . . . we're the ones who must deal with the patients. We are the caregivers. Hence, the name of our department."

"I understand," I said meekly. "It's sad, very sad, indeed."

"Yes, it is, and this job doesn't get easier just because a diagnosis has been made. Things are going to become more difficult. We never win, but that's what we do."

Then she asked, "So where are we with Dr. McDuffy? When are you to see him next?"

I told her how my brother was to have started with the debris removal today, and that he planned to have the joists and rafters in place within the next couple of weeks so that Mr. O'Reilly could begin with the thatching process.

"And when do you plan to go down to see him next?" she asked.

I told her how I had planned to go back this past weekend, but since nothing had been done on the house, I stayed at home to finish reading the book. "I'll make plans to go back this weekend, for sure," I told her, "but what are we to do when we see him, Dr. O'Brien?"

"Brendan, please call me Kathleen. I insist," she said somewhat sternly. "We're going to be the best of friends by the time all of this is over. Let's get the formalities out of the way as quickly as possible," she said with a smile. She always seemed to have a smile on her face, except when she had something really serious to tell us.

"You two are to be his friends, that's all. Don't let on that you're working on his case or tell him anything about this hospital, or me. That would only make things worse. It would confuse him.

"Your connection is through your brother and Mr. O'Reilly. You've helped a lot in that regard, more than you realize, and you're to be commended for that. I mean that sincerely," she told me.

"Ask him about his wife, his career and his family. He has two brilliant children and some grandchildren. Ask him about the 'old days,' get him to talk about what it was like when he was your age, but don't try to counsel him or try to use any psychological theories you might be reading about on him, okay? You're not psychologists. Not yet. Understood?"

We agreed.

"And get some information about his family members. You aren't to try and make contact with them, though. Let me do that. This is, as you can appreciate, having read those books, a delicate subject."

"It can be particularly hard on family members. In this case, Dr. McDuffy really doesn't have many family members here in Ireland, not any with whom he's close, that is, and that's a problem, which makes what we do for him all the more important."

"The children will remember me, I expect. I have met them on many, many occasions over the years, even though that was before they moved to the States, thirty years ago. Find out where they work and I'll find them."

"Would you like to join us in Sneem sometime?" I asked.

"Do you want us to ask if he remembers you?" Saoirse chimed in.

She didn't respond for a few seconds, giving the questions some thought, and then said, "No, I don't think so. Maybe later, but not now. We'll see. I want to remember him as I have known him. It is going to be extremely painful for me to see him decline as he most surely will."

"Besides, if you tell him too much, he'll figure out why I'm involved and why you're involved, and I don't want that just yet. You are his 'friends,' as far as he is concerned, not clinical psychologists."

"That's so sad. He was so charming when I met him," Saoirse said.

"And he sure was lively that night with Seamus," I told her. "I couldn't get a word in edge-wise."

"I would have absolutely loved to have been there for both of those occasions. I remember how he could light up a room with that smile of his, and his laugh was infectious," she told us. "That's the way I want to remember him, but we'll see how it goes. It may become necessary for me to meet with him or with his family. We'll see."

Then she sighed, stiffened, stood, and said, "Alright then! Let's plan to meet again next week, same time, same place, and see how things are progressing. I'm off to another meeting. That's all I do these days—go to meetings, it seems. To be honest, I look forward to meeting with the two of you as much, if not more, than any of the others. The two of you are quite fortunate to have this opportunity at this early stage of your careers to meet this man and to witness this wicked disease from both a personal and a professional point of view. I hope you appreciate it. Enjoy the man for what he still is. He won't be this way for too much longer, as I've told you." The corners of her mouth turned down as she spoke.

Saoirse and I made plans to go see him on Saturday if the weather was good. If not, we'd go on Sunday. Either way, she would drive and I was delighted with the prospects of that, even more so than with seeing Dr. McDuffy, despite the fact that she had herself a fella. I shouldn't have been surprised that she did, as pretty as she was, but I have to admit, I was sorely disappointed to learn that.

CHAPTER TWELVE

Marjorie Sullivan McDuffy

The week flew by and, because my skills were beginning to improve, I was being given more and more responsibilities, which required more time. Taking classes at night while also working full-time at my job during the day was time-consuming as well. Actually, I think I needed thirty-six hours every day to do everything I had to do, just like the book I'd read said. I finished the other book, too, during the week, at night before going to sleep.

One good thing about the night classes I was taking was that they helped me to actually put some of the things I was reading about and studying into practice. The McDuffy case was really helpful for Saoirse since she had that class on geriatrics. I planned to take that class the next time it was offered.

When Saturday came along, the weather was perfect and we were on the road bright and early with the top down. By the time we reached Kenmare, though, we had to stop to put it up. We also put our jumpers on. It had turned a bit too chilly, and a soft but steady mist was coming down. "Typical Irish weather," she said. "Four seasons in a day."

When we arrived at his house, he wasn't there, though the front door was wide open.

"He must have just stepped out," I offered.

"You let him know we were coming, right?" she asked.

I assured her that I had done so and said that he was probably out for one of his walks. "He does those a couple of times every day," I told her.

We looked inside but didn't dare enter. The house was a mess with ladders, extension cords, and saw-horses scattered around. It was total chaos, but it was obvious that work was being done.

Then we walked around to the back of the house, going up to the top of the hill to get a better view of the roof. There was a black plastic covering up most of it, so we couldn't see much of anything, except for the view of all that was around us. The wind was gusting and was causing some of the plastic to flap up and down.

"He's got quite the view from here, doesn't he?" Saoirse said. "He can see Kenmare Bay off to the left and the Atlantic to the right, just like he told us. It doesn't look like much from the road, but it really is a beautiful place, isn't it?" she asked.

"That it is," I agreed. We stood there in silence for a few moments, admiring the view. The rain stopped and the sun began to peep out. Just then, we noticed that he was walking into the driveway. When he saw us, he greeted us warmly.

"Good morning!" he said as he walked up to where we were standing. "What brings you two here today?" he asked.

"I came to see how my brother is doing," I told him.

"We're well underway and I'm delighted. Your brother says he hopes to be finished this week and then Mr. O'Reilly can begin. It should be all done before winter arrives. I couldn't be happier with the progress being made," he said. "And I have you to thank for it."

"Oh, it's not me, it's my brother," I said. "He's the one to get all the credit." Then I extended my hand and said, "Brendan Sullivan, nice to see you again, Dr. McDuffy. You remember Saoirse, yes?"

"Of course I do, Brendan, and how could I forget a face like hers. Nice to see you, again, Saoirse," he responded, shaking her hand as well. "But, please, call me Michael," he added. "It makes me feel younger, not like the old, aging, retired professor that I am."

I wasn't sure if he was going to remember our names or who we were, which is why I introduced ourselves to him, again. I thought to myself that was part of the problem with cases like his—once a doubt enters a person's mind, like mine, about someone else's mental state, it clouds everything. It was a little like the old saying, "you can't un-ring a bell." The bell had been rung and I was doubting Dr. McDuffy's mind and memory. I couldn't help it. I was.

It didn't seem to bother him, though, and he said, "Let's go inside and get something warm to drink. It's turned a bit chilly all of a sudden."

He noticed that the door was ajar and said, "The wind must have pushed this open while I was gone. No worries, there's nothing inside for anyone to steal anyway. It's in a sad state at the moment, but that's a good thing. I'm happy about that!"

"This is a beautiful place you have here," she told him, "and you have a fantastic view from up here."

"That I do, and my wife deserves all the credit. She's the one who found it and fixed it up the way it is, or was, and will be again. She loved this house so much.

"She fell in love with it at first sight. That's why it's so important to me to get it back to exactly the way she had it, and then keep it that way. That's what she wants me to do, and that's what we're doing. She's happy about all of this, very happy," he told us.

"How long has she been gone?" I asked, wishing I hadn't once the words were out of my mouth.

He turned to me, hesitated, and said, "She's still here, Brendan. That's why I'm so happy to be getting this house fixed up the way we are, and why I can't leave."

I couldn't think of anything to say in response to that but fortunately, Saoirse said, "I'd love to see a picture of her if you don't mind."

When she did, it was as if the drawbridge to an old castle was lowered. He said, "You would? Well, I'll be glad to show you. You two sit right over there by the fire and I'll be right back." Moments later, he returned with two large photo albums and handed one to each of us. "You can look through these while I fix us something to drink. Coffee or tea? Which will it be?" he asked.

We both asked for coffee and sat down on the couch, side by side, each with a book of photos in hand as he walked over to the kitchen area, which was a mess and seemingly unusable. He had set up a small table off in the corner where he was able to use what was a coffee machine to heat the water and make us some coffee, while he had some tea. We were slowly turning pages, mumbling things about how beautiful she was and all.

When he returned with a tray and three cups, he pulled his chair over as close as he could to us and began to explain what each photo was all about. Then, a few minutes later, he asked Saoirse to scoot over, so he could sit in between us and see the pictures better. We squeezed in quite easily.

It occurred to me that he was a lonely old man who probably didn't have many people to talk to. From his comments, it seemed as if he hadn't viewed either of these albums in quite some time. I thought of Dr. O'Brien and how she would undoubtedly love to be sitting there with us. He was as delighted to be telling us about each one as we were to be having him do so.

"That's our wedding day," he said. "That was the happiest day of my life, at the time. I had just accepted a position as a graduate assistant at Trinity and she was in her last year of graduate school. We had found a house to rent not far from the campus and were in love."

"That was such a wonderful time of life, possibly the best time of my life," he added, as he heaved a large sigh.

Then, he looked over at the two of us and asked, "Are you two engaged?"

The question startled the both of us, and we both responded at the same time and in much the same way, saying, "No, no. We're just friends," or something like that.

"I see," he responded, though he clearly didn't. He had no idea why the two of us were together or why we there, except that I was Rory's brother. I told him that Saoirse and I went to school together at the university in Cork.

"Cork University, is it? That's a fine school there," said. "One of the best."

Saoirse then said, "We're in graduate school there. I went to Trinity College Dublin, Dr. McDuffy, and so did my father."

"Did you now? Well, good for you. That's the best school in all of Ireland, I'd say, but I'm a bit prejudiced, as you may know, because I worked there all of my adult life after being a student there for years," he told us.

"We know," she responded. "My father took several classes from you and he speaks very highly of you," she said. When she did, I was a bit fearful that he might wonder about that comment and catch on to why we were really there, but he didn't. He thanked her for the compliment and let that thought pass, going back to looking at the next photo.

"That one there is when young Patrick was born. That was probably the next happiest day of my life," he told us. "He came along about nine months to the day after we married." He laughed when he said it. "We were good Catholics, don't you know? We waited until we were married to consummate our love affair. That's what the church wants us to do, right? Multiply, so that eventually, we'll outnumber them!"

Then he added, "That's not the way you young people do things anymore, though, is it?" he asked not expecting an answer, I'm sure, and we didn't give one. I hadn't lost my virginity yet, but I wasn't so sure about Saoirse.

At one point, about halfway through, while looking at a photo of the family when the children were maybe ten and twelve and he would have been in his early to mid-thirties, in the prime of his life, he said, "That's when I wish time would have stood still, but time and tide wait for no man."

"Chaucer," Saoirse immediately responded.

"That's correct, Ms. O'Connor. Very good!" he said. "You get a star for class participation today," he added with a chuckle.

Saoirse smiled, somewhat proudly, and thanked him. Then he said, "If one neglects education, he or she walks lame to the end of life."

Neither of us responded to that.

"Plato said that. He was a student of Socrates who is said to be the father of western philosophy," he added. "That was a momentous time in the history of the world. Obviously, you two are among those who realize the value of an education and are taking advantage of the opportunities you have been given. Good for you. Good for both of you."

We turned our attention back to the picture and said that it was, indeed, a beautiful photograph of a picture-perfect family. Nothing more could be said. We "oohed" and "aahed" appropriately.

Then he turned to Saoirse and said, "Saoirse . . . that's a beautiful name . . . and Irish . . . you could only be Irish with a name like that."

She had obviously impressed him, and he was, it appeared, letting her into his life on a more personal level.

"And Brendan's a fine name as well. He was, and is, known as the navigator to the Irish, even if the rest of the world doesn't give him the credit he deserves, but you knew that, I'm sure. I'll bet that you didn't know that Christopher Columbus is said to have studied the book written about St. Brendan's voyage to the new lands before he, Columbus that is, set sail for the Americas. Did you know that, Brendan?" he asked.

When I told him that I didn't, he said, "Now you do. Navigatio Santi Brendani Abbatis is the name of it. Some people think St. Brendan wrote it, but he didn't. It was written several centuries later by monks at the Abbey in Galway, which is named after him. He is the patron saint of seafarers and travelers."

"There's so much to learn but no matter how hard you try, there is only so much knowledge you can acquire over a lifetime. The sad part is that, in the end, you're left wondering what it is that you've learned because the answers change over time as we make more and more scientific and archeological discoveries."

He paused for several seconds, and then added, "And the more you learn, and the more knowledge you obtain, the more you realize how little you know. Socrates said that or something to that effect. Actually, what he said was that he knew that he knew nothing. He was famous for that expression, among many others."

"I've seen the statue of Socrates in that park in Dublin," I told him. "He's one of my favorite people in history and that's one of my favorite expressions."

"Is he now? Well, he's a good one to use as a model, that's for sure. One of my favorites, too."

Then he shook his head, smiled, and said, "And then, to top that off, after a lifetime of study and effort, you forget most of what you've learned! There was a time when I thought I knew everything . . . it's true. I thought I knew so much, not everything, but quite a lot . . . but I was wrong. I knew a lot about a little slice of life, that's all. Life is a puzzle, isn't it? It's a great, big puzzle, one that we can never quite figure out."

"I'd say that you solved it, yes, Dr. McDuffy?" Saoirse asked. "At the very least, you figured out the answers as best you could, didn't you? You certainly did more than just about anyone in all of Ireland, I'd say, and an unexamined life is not worth living, right?"

He took her hand in his and said, "Yeats . . . very good, Saoirse . . . but no, not by a long shot, my dear. Not by a long shot. Looking at these photos helps me to realize just how lucky a man I was, though. I was very fortunate, indeed. I have much to be thankful for."

"Where are your children now, Dr. McDuffy? You told us that they're both professors, but where are they?" I asked.

"Michael, please . . . call me Michael, the both of you . . . they're both in the United States, and you are correct, both have become professors," he responded.

"And where, in the United States, are they?" Saoirse asked.

"One is at Stanford and the other at the University of California in Berkeley, not too far from one another," he answered. "They see each other quite frequently."

"And what do they teach?" she asked. He had told me that before but Saoirse wasn't with me when he did.

"Caitlin teaches Art History and Patrick is a law professor," he told us.

"Art History?" Saoirse asked. "How did that happen?"

"Her mother was an artist. That's what she studied in school," he told us.

"Well, they followed in your footsteps, didn't they?" she asked. I had said the same thing two weeks earlier.

"That they did, but why they had to go clear across the globe, ten thousand kilometers away, I'll never know. That wasn't our plan for them. It broke my wife's heart not to be able to see her grandchildren every day. She wanted to move to the US to be with them, but I wouldn't allow it. I couldn't leave Ireland . . . I just couldn't."

Then he added, "Maybe I should have. I don't know, but I didn't."

We spent the next two hours poring over the albums. He was energetic and enthusiastic about telling us details surrounding each and every picture, it seemed. I couldn't help thinking of Dr. O'Brien as he did, remembering what she had told us about him and what we should do when we visited with him.

Saoirse didn't seem to tire at all from hearing him tell the stories as he was. I was enjoying being with the both of them, though I was ready to move on long before she was. She was most interested in hearing about his wife.

"She was a Sullivan, and this is where the Sullivan clan lived for centuries until they were conquered by the Vikings, and then the Normans, and then the Anglo-Saxons from Brittany, but never the Romans!"

"The 'golden age' of Ireland came from the time after Patrick converted the island to Catholicism up to the time the Vikings invaded us. It was a peaceful, loving community of like-minded souls. Everyone was a follower of Jesus, all worshiping God, writing books, living in monasteries, abbeys, and other such places in communal living arrangements."

"But no, the Romans came to the shores of our island, saw us standing there with spears and swords, faces painted blue, ready to fight, and they turned around and left us alone. They must have thought of us as savages, not worth conquering. I don't know why, but they never came back."

Then he turned to me, and said, "That's right . . . you're a Sullivan, too," as if the thought had just occurred to him, and added, "I didn't put that together until just now. Maybe you're related to her in some distant way."

"There are a lot of Sullivans in County Kerry, that's for sure, Michael," I agreed. "So, it's definitely possible. In fact, there's probably no doubt about it. I'd say that she and I are related in some fashion if you go back far enough, right?"

"That's true. That's a large part of why she chose this place. I would have gone anywhere on the island with her, wherever she wanted, except the north. I stay away from there, even now," he said. "She didn't know exactly where her people hailed from, but it was here in Kerry, to be sure, and she considered Sneem to be her ancestral home, whether it actually was or not. She has family still living here, but I'm not too close to them."

"She was a beautiful woman," Saoirse said as she studied a picture of her in her later years.

"She still is," he replied as if she was sitting there with the three of us. "A man, or woman, isn't dead until the last person on earth who knew them is no longer alive. Then they cease to exist. She's still here," he said matter-of-factly as he sat looking at pictures of her and the children they'd had together.

Again, we said nothing in response to that statement. I was relieved when we turned the last page of the second album. It took quite a while to go through them all. I snuck a peek at my cellphone every so often, keeping an eye on the time. I was tired of sitting there all that time, but sitting there with Saoirse as I was, I wasn't about to complain.

I was pleased that we had been able to have him go through the photos with us as he'd done, telling us all about his past. We had done exactly what Kathleen had told us to do. I kept thinking about how happy she would be when we told her of our day with him.

He had told us all about himself and his life, his wife, and his family. He came alive as he did. It was clear that he was still in love with her and she was still very much in his thoughts. It was also clear that when he told us that she was still there, he meant it. I took it to mean that she was there in spirit, not in bodily form, but didn't push the issue. I wasn't sure exactly what form she was in, as far as he was concerned, and didn't ask.

For me, it was a golden opportunity to see the real man. I was sure that Saoirse knew that we were doing what Dr. O'Brien had told us to do, just as I did. She was much more animated than I was. She interacted with him more than I did, asking questions at every opportunity.

The two of them were having a grand conversation. I'd chime in every now and again, but it was mostly between the two of them. After he sat down with us, he held the albums in his lap and we both looked on over a shoulder.

We said our goodbyes not long after turning the last page and thanked him for sharing the photos with us. We promised to return to see how the work was progressing. "I'll keep after that brother of mine, I will," I assured him. He thanked me and waived to us as we drove away.

"That was special, wasn't it?" Saoirse said.

I agreed and said, "I can't wait to tell Dr. O'Brien."

She corrected me and said, "Kathleen."

I asked about stopping for a pint at the Dan Murphy's Bar, but she wasn't hungry or thirsty. Then I suggested a visit to the Killarney National Park for a little hike to get some exercise, which wasn't too much out of the way, but she wasn't interested in that, either. She said she had too much work to do. "I haven't finished that second book we were to read and I want to get that done by Monday when we meet with Kathleen," she told me.

I was disappointed. I thought to myself that she was probably going to be with her boyfriend, too, but I didn't say anything about that. She was, as Colin so delicately pointed out to me, "out of my league," so I needed to get over that. I was happy just to be with her.

Clearly, she was determined to make it back to Cork as quickly as possible. I had no say in the matter. The weather improved and she stopped to take the top down right before we crossed over the river and left Sneem.

We didn't talk much on the way home. We were both deep in our own thoughts. I think we both knew that we might never see the man we saw today again from what Dr. O'Brien had told us to expect. Plenty of other thoughts were running through my head as well.

That Monday, Saoirse and I could hardly wait to meet with Kathleen and tell her of our visit with him. However, when we did, she wasn't nearly as excited to hear about it as we had hoped. She smiled and said how much she would have liked to have been there, and how good it was for us to have witnessed all that we did, but then she told us of a phone call she had received earlier in the day.

"He had a bad day yesterday," she said glumly. "I received a call today . . . actually, Dr. Delaney received the call, and he told me about it . . . from a Garda officer. She found him walking down a remote, dirt road, after dark. He was lost, disoriented, and confused. She thought about bringing him here but, instead, took him home and then waited until this morning to let us know about what had happened."

Saoirse and I were shocked. "That's unbelievable!" she said. "He was as right as rain when we saw him. I didn't notice a thing out of the ordinary. He was brilliant, quoting Plato and Socrates."

"That's the nature of the disease," Dr. O'Brien said. "Maybe some of the things you talked about and him looking at all of those photos as you did brought up some old ghosts . . . stirred up his mind a bit. As I think about it, that's probably what happened. Maybe he got depressed, suicidal, even. Who knows?"

"As you learn more about it, you'll find that a person's memory of events years and years ago is much better than that of just a few days or weeks earlier. We don't quite understand why that is, but it's a commonly-reported and widely-accepted fact. Regardless, and whatever the reason for it, he had a bad day yesterday . . . a regrettable day. I'm afraid he may be moving into the next stage of this dreadful disease."

Neither of us could believe our ears. We were in absolute shock and said so, repeating ourselves over and over again. We couldn't believe it.

Then she brightened and said, "I would have loved to have been there with you, though. I'm so glad that the two of you had that opportunity to see the man as he was. That truly was remarkable. Make sure you document it well. It is an extremely important part of the history we will develop in this case."

We assured her that we would.

Then she asked, "Did he recognize the two of you and remember who you were?"

"I re-introduced ourselves to him when we arrived, but he seemed to recognize us, and he acted like he remembered Saoirse, too, but I wasn't totally sure about that. Should I have done what I did, or wait to see if he recognized us?" I asked.

"Next time, see if he recognizes you and if he knows your names. It's important for our file," she answered.

"He always had excellent social skills, so he's probably still able to hide things like that quite well," she added.

"I thought he remembered me right off," Saoirse said. "We got on amazingly well as the day went on," she added. "It was a thrill and an honor to be with him as I was."

"I'm so glad to hear you say that. I can just imagine what that must have been like for you . . . and for him," she said.

"I think it's fair to say that we've established a wonderful relationship with the man, just as you and Dr. Delaney told us to do," I told her. "I like the man. I do."

"He couldn't have been nicer to us," Saoirse told her, "and he said something about my name being such a good Irish name. He told Brendan here all sorts of things about St. Brendan that he didn't know. I didn't either. He's obviously a brilliant man . . . simply astounding, actually."

"That's why it's so hard to figure out what happened yesterday. It's like *Dr. Jekyll and Mr. Hyde*, isn't it?" I asked.

"It's a perfect example of what I was telling the two of you last week. This disease is diabolical. It gives hope and snatches it away. It allows you moments of lucidity and then replaces them with moments of a total loss of memory and function. It's a horrid experience for all concerned. You were able to witness a bright spot, an extremely bright moment, and I'm glad that you were," she said.

"However, don't lose sight of the path he is on and what our goals and objectives are. I think it would be a good idea for you to pay him another visit as soon as possible, especially after what happened yesterday. He's not stupid. He knows that bad things are happening to him . . . no one needs to tell him that what happened yesterday is extremely disturbing to everyone involved. No one knows that better than he does."

"Besides, it seems as if the two of you may be becoming two of his closest confidantes. The more you see him, the better the chances are that you will continue to be such. He will be much more likely to remember you if you do."

"The sooner that roof is finished, the better, too. As I told you before, keeping a person in a familiar environment is especially important. It must be quite disorienting for him to have all of the work being done there at the moment. It sounds as if the house was a complete mess. Did you sense that?"

We told her that the house was, indeed, a mess, but that we didn't think it bothered him so much. He had told us how happy his wife was about all that was going on.

"His wife?" Kathleen asked.

"She's still there," Saoirse told her. "To him, that is."

"I see," she said. Then she turned to me and asked, "Do you think that's a problem?"

"I don't know," I responded. "He told us he could never leave the place because his wife was still there, just like Saoirse said."

"How long has she been gone?" she asked.

"It's been years, but I don't know how many," I answered. "He hasn't given us a clear answer, and when he has, about other things like the roof, it's been wrong."

"We need to find that out. It's an important fact. I'd like to know how long he's been living alone. That's important for us to know," she told us. "We need to be good historians. That's part of our job in these cases."

Then she asked if we had found out anything about his children. When we told her what he had told us, she said that she would contact them. "I expect that they might have some suspicions, at this point, but they need to be involved. They need to know what's happening. I'll take care of that."

The mood was somewhat somber. I was disappointed, and I was sure that Saoirse was, too. We had expected that it would be jubilant.

When our meeting ended and Kathleen had left the room, Saoirse and I looked at each other and wondered aloud what would happen next. This wasn't a *Dr. Jekyll and Mr. Hyde* type of case . . . that case involved a man with a severe bi-polar condition . . . but it was as if we were dealing with two completely different men.

To Saoirse, that was an extremely important topic for discussion in her class on geriatrics or maybe the paper she was working on. For me, it was just sad. I wasn't thinking of writing a thesis on the subject as she obviously was.

I returned to Sneem on Friday because Seamus was supposed to be there and Rory had told me that his part would be mostly finished by then. Saoirse wasn't able to make it. I was late in arriving because I couldn't get out of Cork until after 5:00, and by the time I arrived, neither Rory nor Seamus were there and Dr. McDuffy was home alone. He didn't come to the door for several minutes after I knocked, and when he did, he had a blank look on his face.

He was disheveled and it looked like he hadn't shaved in a few days. When I tried to engage him in a conversation, he answered my questions with monosyllabic responses. He told me that he wasn't feeling well and asked me to come back another time. He actually closed the door in my face somewhat abruptly. It was disturbing.

When I called Rory, he told me that he was nearly finished, but neither he nor Seamus had been out there today. I thought to myself that I should have called him before I left Cork, but that it was a good thing . . . a really good thing that neither of them was there that day. I wouldn't have wanted for either of the two of them to see him as I just did. They would both be there first thing in the morning.

He told me that Seamus was now going to be able to start working since he was finished with the rafters and had begun working on the inside of the house. I didn't mention anything to him about how Dr. McDuffy was acting when I saw him earlier. I hoped to keep any mention of those issues from either of the two of them. They didn't need to know.

I was more than a bit concerned about the situation, and I was glad that I came and saw it for myself with my own two eyes. I'd made plans to stay the night in Sneem at my father's house and be there first thing in the morning when the two of them arrived. I called my father to let him know that I'd be seeing him earlier than expected because of what just happened and asked about his plans for dinner. I'd spoken to him several times over the past month or so, but we hadn't spent much time together. He was available and delighted to do so.

We met at one of his favorite places, the Stone House Restaurant, where they had a salmon special for ten euros. Siobhan and Deidre, who were married and still living in Sneem, came to join us. They left their husbands at home minding the kids.

It was a fun evening. I didn't tell them too much about why I was there other than the business of Rory fixing a house up for one of my clients. We talked about old times, new times, and all sorts of things, and shared many a good laugh.

They were impressed just to know that I had any clients at all. To them, I was becoming a bonafide clinical psychologist and they were proud of me. They still thought of me as the baby brother who was snatched away from them, so to speak, by our mother.

I don't think that any of them ever quite understood the business of her being a Druid. It was something we never discussed. They were all pretty estranged from her after the divorce. I was really the only one who had much to do with her. I spent the night in his house, in the same room I lived in as a child. It hadn't been changed a bit.

CHAPTER THIRTEEN

The Druids and the Celts

I was the first one to arrive the next morning after a stop for coffee and a scone at Kelly's Bakery. Dr. McDuffy was just returning from his morning walk. He was a completely different man.

He apologized for his behavior the night before and explained that he wasn't feeling well and thought it must have been something he ate. I wanted to ask about him getting lost a few nights earlier, but I didn't, because he might have wondered how I knew about it. He brought it up, though, and told me that some strange things were happening to him lately.

That was a good sign. It showed me that he knew he was slipping. It bothered him, as it would me or anyone else. He knew that his faculties were diminishing. I didn't need to tell him that. No one did.

That was the first step in the recovery process for a person with a mental difficulty. As I had learned, many people don't recognize or admit a problem, such as most of the alcoholics I had met. Until they did, little could be done to help them.

There was no doubt that he "wanted" to deal with the problem, which was another of the steps. The problem for Dr. McDuffy was, of course, the fact that he didn't have the mental faculties to deal with his problem. Those were being taken from him by this deadly disease, and without that cognitive ability, nothing could be done. There was nothing he or anyone else could do about it, unfortunately.

"I've walked that road a thousand times," he told me. "But I lost track of time and it got dark sooner than I thought it would. When it did, I became disoriented. I didn't know where I was. It was quite unnerving," he acknowledged. "It wasn't the first time, either," he added. "I just don't understand what's happening to me."

When he told me that, I wondered if it was a good idea for psychologists to tell patients, such as Dr. McDuffy, what was going on and really explain things to them. He was an extremely intelligent man and one would think might have done some research on the subject, but I wasn't sure of that. Shouldn't he know? Shouldn't he be told?

Wouldn't all medical doctors tell their patients of medical problems, like cancer? Of course, they would. What about psychologists? What was our responsibility in that regard?

Hearing him talk made me doubt that he understood what was going on and what was going to happen to him. I wasn't going to tell him. In fact, I was told not to tell him. I wasn't qualified to counsel our clients. I made a note to ask Kathleen. She would know what to do.

He was delighted to learn that Rory and Seamus would be coming over shortly and invited me inside while he put on a pot of water for coffee or tea for them and for us. We chit-chatted about the weather, Brexit, and other things. He was most concerned about how the outcome would affect the border between the Republic of Ireland and Northern Ireland.

"I don't want to see any more troubles erupt," he told me. "I don't really care too much about what they do as long as they don't hurt this country of ours. They've done enough to us over the centuries." He wasn't a fan of Boris Johnson, but he didn't much care for Leo Varadkar, either.

"He isn't really speaking up too much these days. He's hardly ever heard from, but that's one of the big sticking points—what to do with the border between a European Economic Union country and a non-EEU country," he said. "That's where many of the most serious situations arose in the past—at the borders. That's where the guns came across, and that's where most of the killings took place."

"They could always give us back the six," I said.

He laughed and responded, "That will be the same day that the United States gives back the land it took from the Native American Indians. I wish that would happen, but I doubt that it ever will, unfortunately . . . not while I'm alive. I'm fairly certain of that. I've just about given up on all that 'one Ireland once again' chatter. It sounds wonderful, but it's not going to happen, I'm afraid. I wish it would, but it won't."

We heard a vehicle pull into the driveway and walked outside to see Rory getting out of his Ford F-150 pick-up truck. The bed was loaded with lumber. The first thing he said was "I'm going to put you to work, little brother! I can use an extra pair of hands. I'm by myself today."

I told him that I was glad to oblige. I wasn't much use with a hammer, and he knew that, but I could carry things and be a go-fer.

"I'm going to be putting up the trim here on the inside. I'm done with the framing stuff. These are the finishing touches."

"When I leave here today, my part of the work will be pretty much done. I don't know how much time it will take Seamus to do what he has to do, but it's taking shape, isn't it?" he asked. We both agreed. Clearly, it was much improved already.

"We'll have this place looking as good as new in no time, Dr. McDuffy," he said, and he turned to me and whispered in a lower voice so Michael couldn't hear, "and I want you to know that I did this as a 'rush' job just for you, baby brother!" slapping me on the shoulder as he did.

"You've done a marvelous job. I can't thank you enough," Michael told him.

"Ah, wait 'til it's finished. I'll be dressing it up here later on today, putting on the first coat of varnish. You'll think you're in a showroom, you will," Rory told him. "I use only natural oils. You'll be delighted with it, just wait. I guarantee it!"

Then he whispered, "Be sure to tell your Ma about all of this and how well it's turning out."

He really was doing a masterful job. I was very much impressed with his work. I'd never seen anything he'd ever done before. I just knew that he was a carpenter who opened his own business a while back. Now, he was a general contractor.

I assured him that I would. "I still miss her, and so do the rest of the kids, and the grandkids as well. We don't see her as much as we'd like to, I'm sad to say."

"I wish things weren't the way they are, but that's the way it is. Maybe you can help out with that a bit, Bear. Maybe bring her here with you one of these times. Can you do that?" he asked.

I told him that I would try and thanked him, again, for all that he had done and was doing. He really had done it fast, too, in just a few weeks, actually. "I made this my top priority, I did," he repeated, "just for you."

A few minutes later, Seamus pulled into the driveway. He exited his vehicle and said with a laugh, "Sorry I'm late, lads. The problem with Saturday mornings is that they always come too soon after Friday nights."

At first, he didn't notice me, and when he did, he said, "Brendan! Good to see you again. You've come to help? Or are you here for some more of the Holy Water?"

I laughed and said, "Both!"

After some tea and more laughter, he said, "It's time to go to work and . . . keep this in mind . . . the sooner we finish, the sooner we'll be at the bar!"

I offered to help him, but he told me that he always worked alone. "There aren't many who know how to do this, lad, and it's best that I do it by myself," he told me.

Dr. McDuffy walked back and forth, inside and out, watching all that was going on, joining in the conversation every so often. Once he started to work, Seamus was all business. There was little conversation with him.

Rory, on the other hand, was as chatty as he could be. As I was handing him things or holding the end of a tape measure or a board, he kept asking questions about this woman who I was seeing. Dr. McDuffy had asked about her and if she would be joining us and that's all it took to get him started.

I hadn't told Rory or any of the rest of the family about Saoirse. There was nothing to tell, really. I wished that there was more to tell. I told him that we worked together and were just friends.

He wouldn't take no for an answer, though. He kept asking and asking. Dr. McDuffy was no help as he told him how beautiful she was. It got to the point where I had to stop answering his questions. I didn't want to reveal anything about her to him because Rory didn't have any idea that she was a fellow student and we were there for business purposes, which was the real reason why we were there, but he kept prying.

Finally, he gave up and said, "I guess I'll just have to meet her for myself, and tell her all the bad stuff about you, bein' a Druid and all."

When he heard that, Dr. McDuffy piped up. "Are you a Druid, Brendan?" he asked.

I assured him that I wasn't a Druid, but I acknowledged that my mother was. "That's a fact," I said, "and there's no denying it."

"That's interesting," he said. "The Druids certainly played a large part in how St. Patrick brought Christianity to the Celts and all of the Emerald Isle."

I was vaguely aware of that and told him so. "I should know more about them, I guess, but I don't," I admitted.

"I'll explain it to you over a beer someday," he said, "but not now . . . not while there's work to be done."

I told him that I would enjoy that and thought to myself that I'd like to have Saoirse there with me when we had that conversation. I was sure that she would enjoy hearing about them, too.

Rory was working feverishly to get the trim up. He didn't like working on Saturdays, but made an exception for me, in this case. When it was time for lunch, he stopped long enough to eat a sandwich his wife had prepared for him, and then went right back to work.

When we asked, Seamus told us that he didn't want to stop for lunch. He wanted to keep working and get as much done as he could today. "That's an hour more we can have in the bar, the way I figure it," he said with a laugh.

Dr. McDuffy and I had a little something to eat together. We planned to eat with Rory, but he had already devoured his sandwich and was back at work by the time it took us to fix what we ate. He was no slouch. I had a hard time keeping up with him. As quiet as

Seamus was, Rory was just the opposite. He talked non-stop, but he kept working all the while.

He told me all about his children, his wife, his life, and everything else that came to his mind. He told me things about all of our brothers and sisters that I never knew of before, being as I was so much younger than the rest. I was his full blood-brother, but I don't think I ever talked to him as much, just me and him, in my life, and I enjoyed every minute.

Dr. McDuffy walked back and forth, around and around, trying not to get in the way, adding a word here and there in the conversation, but mostly, it was between Rory and me. He'd walk out and watch to see what Seamus was doing, too. He was happy to see all the work that was being done. I'm sure that he liked having company, as well. If we weren't there, he'd have been all alone, for sure. I wondered what he did with his time when we weren't there. He didn't have many friends, it seemed.

He thanked us repeatedly for doing what was being done. "I'm glad to do it for you, Dr. McDuffy. It's grand to be doing this with my youngest brother, Brendan, too. It's good to get to know him better," Rory told him.

Then he turned to me and said, "You should come down more often, watch the kids play soccer and all. They'd love to see you, and so would the wife, I'm sure."

"Soccer?" I asked. "I thought that was forbidden in your house."

"It is, by the GAA that is, but Sean has played since he was a wee lad, and once he got old enough, he switched over to hurling."

Then he stopped what he was doing, looked over at me, shook his head, and said, "I'm glad those days are over. Watching him runnin' around with a stick was much more than I could handle. I'm glad he and the others gave it up, the hurling, that is. I was barely able to watch."

"Holy Mary Mother of God! It scares me just to think back on those days! Now they all play football, the boys that is, none of them cared that much for soccer. It scares me just to think back on those days!"

We laughed when he said it and then he added, "And the funny part is how much I luved playing it meself, when I was their age."

"That was before you got hit in the head, though, right? I heard all about that, though I was too young to know anything about it. Da never would let me play because of what happened to you," I told him.

"That wasn't me, it was Kevin, but that changed things some for me, too. I loved playin' it all the same. So, all the girls are all playin' soccer now. It's the sports children play the most these days, believe it or not, all over Ireland! They're all doin' somethin' or other, except for the baby, of course, but Sean has a strong passion for the game, Gaelic football, that is, and he's pretty good at it."

"He's mad about the Kerry team, juniors, and all the rest. I take him to the games every chance I get. There's a game this afternoon I'll be going to. He's friends with all the guys and hopes to make the team next year. The whole family goes, except Marlene. She likes the time to herself. She'll go every now and then, though, but she can't make it today."

I asked when Sean's next game was and promised him that I'd come watch first chance. "Shannon's pretty good herself, so you'll have to see her play, too, and the others. I watch them all play and I go to as many of the games as I can, but I can't make them all. I do the best I can," he said, and then he turned his attention back to what he was doing.

About mid-afternoon, Seamus, who was standing at the highest point on the roof, stood up with one foot on each side, stretched, and said, "I think that's enough for today. I've got a powerful thirst and it's time for some of Mother's Milk!"

Rory responded by saying, "That sounds good to me. I've done all that I can do for now, as well. If it's alright with you, Dr. McDuffy, we'll call it a day."

"That's fine with me!" he responded. "It looks like you're almost finished as it is, aren't you?" he asked.

"I am," he confirmed, "just one more coat of the varnish, and a few more boards here and there, but I have to let the wood dry, so I'll be back another day, probably next Saturday. There's not much left to do, though, and it won't take me but a few hours to do it. We're getting close. I'll send some boys over on Monday to clean up the mess Seamus and I have been making."

"Other than that, it's all about the roof, and I'm thinking that this whole job will be done pretty soon, right, Seamus?" he asked.

"I've got one more layer to add and I'll be finished as well, but that will have to wait. I'll be back next Saturday, too, and with some luck, I might be able to finish then, too, although I doubt it. This was a fine mess you made here, Michael, but it's coming along just fine."

"I've got a full week of work ahead of me, and I can't be here before then," he told us. "I don't usually work on Saturdays, but this needed to be done, so I'm here."

"Next Saturday it is, then," Rory said. "I thank you for squeezin' us in as you did, Seamus."

"I'm glad to do it for you, Rory. Be sure to tell your Da that I send my best," he responded.

"That's my Da, too," I reminded him.

"That's right! I keep forgetting that you two are brothers. You say hello to him for me, too, then," he said. Then he added, "You're Patrick's youngest . . . a bit of a mistake, I'm guessing!" With that, he slapped his knee and laughed and laughed. Rory was, after all, eighteen years older than me, and we didn't look all that much alike. I have the flamin' red hair and he is all black.

"Will you join me for a pint, Michael?" Seamus asked.

"I can't very well refuse, now can I?" he answered. "If Brendan here will give me a ride home, that is." I readily agreed.

"If he won't, I will. Let's be off!" Seamus said.

Just as we were about to leave, Rory looked at his watch and said, "I really can't join you, boys, much as I'd like to. I've got to take me children to the game. I'm sorry, I am. Have one for me." So, the three of us headed to town. Michael rode with Seamus.

When we arrived in town, Seamus said, "Let's go to Riney's Bar today."

"I like to spread the wealth, so to speak, little as it is," he added with a laugh.

I was expecting another rollicking good time, like the one we'd had weeks before, but as soon as we sat down, Seamus said, "I've only got time for one or two today. The Missus wants me to take her to a Church social tonight and made me promise not to come home jarred."

After having a couple of pints and many good laughs, he said, "I'd best be off. It's been a pleasure, gentleman. I'll see you again next Saturday," and off he went, leaving the good doctor and me there by ourselves.

He turned to me and asked, "So, would you like for me to tell you a little about the Druids and how they influenced St. Patrick?"

"I would," I responded.

At that, he pulled a necklace out from underneath his shirt and said, "You've seen this a million times in your life, but did you ever wonder why the Celtic cross is different from most of the other crosses in the world?"

When I told him that I hadn't ever given it much thought, he said, "It was because of the Druids and the Celts. Patrick was trying to convert the natives here in Ireland to Christianity and was having trouble doing so. The Druids were actually recognized as being the priests, or the religious leaders, if you will, of the Celts, and one of the gods they worshipped was Belanus, their sun god. So, Patrick devised a plan to combine the cross with the sun and, thereby, join the two religions together."

"The Druids, as I'm sure you know, worship all things in nature, most particularly trees, plants, animals, the moon, mountains, stones, and, of course, the sun. So, he put this circle," he said, demonstrating, "around the cross and told them, 'Whenever you look at the cross, from now on, you'll see the sun, and whenever you look at the sun, you'll see the cross,' and it worked."

"I had no idea," I responded.

"And that's not all. The Druids and their beliefs are responsible for many of the holidays we Catholics and all other Christians now observe," he added. "It wasn't just Ireland that he affected, it was Rome, too." Again, I was unaware of any of that.

"It's true," he told me. "Take All-Saints Day. As you know, it's a Holy Day of Obligation for Catholics and as you also know, it is the day after All-Souls Day or what most people call Halloween. What you probably don't know is that Halloween, though it wasn't called that back then, was a Druid day of enormous significance."

"November first, which wasn't designated as All-Saints Day until the eighth or ninth century, was the first day of the Celtic calendar long before Christ came into the world. Before then, it was recognized by the Celts and the Druids as a day to honor the dead. They called it 'All Hallows Day.'"

"The church . . . the Roman Catholic Church that is . . . also began calling it 'All Hallows Day' after St. Patrick converted the Celts since the word 'Hallows' also meant 'holy person,' or 'saint,' apparently. The church deemed it a day to celebrate all of the 'good' spirits in the world and all of the saints. It did that to recognize the Celtic or Druid tradition.

"The last day of October was, therefore, the last day of the Celtic year and it was called 'All Hallows Eve.' The term Halloween came from that expression. One of the popes officially designated it as 'All Souls Day' many years later."

"One of the chief deities of the Druids was a god named Samhain. He was said to be the god of the dead and a very powerful figure. He has much to do with this whole discussion."

"Back then, the Druids believed in reincarnation, and I assume that they still do. You'll have to ask your mother about that. I don't know."

"So, when a person died, it was believed that they would be reincarnated. Depending upon the life they led, they either came back as a human if they were good or as an animal if they weren't so good. It was their 'judgment day.'"

"So, it was their belief that on the last day of October, every year, Samhain allowed all souls who had died within the preceding year to roam the earth. After that, they would begin their next lives, whatever that was to be. It was on that day, the first day of November, that he decided what would become of those who had died."

"And all Celts and Druids feared All Hallow's Eve because of all the evil spirits, witches, and ghosts who would be in their presence, so . . ."

"But weren't the good spirits roaming the earth, too, Michael? They weren't afraid of them, were they?" I asked, interrupting him.

"Yes, they were there, too, and yes, the people weren't afraid of them. You're right about that. So, as I was saying, because they were afraid of the evil spirits, they built huge bonfires to keep them away. Evil spirits and witches were said to be afraid of fire."

"People would walk through the villages and towns carrying lighted torches to scare them away. The evil spirits were said to be mischievous and play tricks on the living. The townspeople took all of that very seriously, not at all like what the day or night, actually, has become. From what my children tell me, it's especially important in the United States, but there are no 'tricks' played on people, especially the children. It's all good fun.

"That's where what has become the traditional use of pumpkins to make jack o' lanterns came from, too. Back then, the Irish, who were mostly Celts, even after they became Catholics, would hollow out potatoes, turnips, rutabagas, beets, and pumpkins, among other things, and put candles in them to ward off the evil spirits on All Hallow's Eve. When the Irish emigrated en masse to America, they took that custom with them, and it spread. The use of pumpkins continues to this day."

"And there's more to the Druid story, much more . . . take the celebration of Christmas . . . from what I have learned, it was begun by the Vatican to appease the Celts, too, although not everyone agrees with me on that," he said. "They were a large group of people located in many other parts of Europe, like what is now Germany, France, and Spain. The Roman armies defeated them everywhere they were found, driving them westward with many of the Celts ending up here in Ireland."

"Christmas, you say? Really? What did the Druids have to do with Christmas?" I asked. "I had never heard of anything like that."

"Again, the Celts and the Druids . . . remember, Druids were essentially the priests, scholars, and the ruling class, if you will, of the Celts . . . celebrated that time of year as the beginning of the winter solstice. It signified a 'return to life.' It was said to be 'the' shortest day of the year when, after that, the days would begin to get longer."

"For the Druids, it was a big event in their calendar. They burned evergreen trees, which lit up the sky, danced, played music, and made it something special. Some people still do that with their Christmas trees in America, I'm told, when the trees are dead not long after Christmas Day. We still do that here in Ireland, too, as you know, but that's where the tradition began."

"The people of Rome celebrated the day, too, but they did so independently from the Irish. Rome never conquered Ireland, but Roman armies had fought and defeated the Celts many times over the years in many locations. The Celts were brave, and they resisted the Roman aggression everywhere, but they were no match for Rome . . . not many were. The Romans were very good about merging their civilization with that of the people they conquered and that was, apparently, a tradition they took from the Celts many years after Constantine embraced Christianity."

"The holidays weren't connected necessarily, but they were very similar. So, people of Celtic origins in what is now France, Spain, Germany, and Ireland, among other places, were already celebrating that day for different reasons, as I explained. Because of that, the church made it a holy day of obligation for Catholics, and that was done to appease the Celts and the Druids and attach them more closely to the church."

"After all, who really knows what day Jesus was born on? Nobody does! The church just picked that day and that's the reason they did it . . . and it was because of the Celts and the Druids, see?" he asked.

"I had no idea," I answered.

"And it was the Druids who added mistletoe to the occasion. They believed it was an all-powerful product of the sacred oak tree. It was, and it still is, a sign of peace, and love, of course."

"I don't know why they chose the twenty-fifth day of December, though, because that's not the shortest day of the year. The true 'winter solstice' is the day when one of the earth's poles is the furthest away from the sun, and that's on the twenty-first. But the point is that the twenty-fifth day of December was chosen as the day to honor him because of those pagan traditions. Those were the traditions of the Druids for hundreds of years before St. Patrick had anything to do with them, so he gets no credit for that."

Then he took a sip of his beer, looked around to make sure that no one was listening to our conversation, and said, "Don't tell anyone this, Brendan, but I like much of what they have to say, especially the part about reincarnation."

"Druids believe that souls are immortal. They think that there is life after death. I agree with that. They believe that there is a place where souls go, awaiting their next life. They call it 'Summerland' or the 'other world.' I picture it as a magical island in the Atlantic not far from here, just off the coast of Ireland. That's where I will go to meet Marjorie when my time comes."

He drew a deep breath, sighed, and said, "There's more, Brendan, but that's enough for now, and I think it's important for you to know some of these things. If your mother is a Druid, she should be proud of her heritage, not ashamed of it, and you should be proud of her, not ashamed of her."

"I'm not a Druid, Michael, and I don't pretend to know much about what they believe or don't believe, but she did take me to some of their ceremonies when I was a child. I don't remember much of what I heard since I was so young, but I'm a Catholic, though I don't go to church as often as I should these days," I told him.

Then, although I don't know what compelled me to do so, I asked in a lower voice, making sure no one could hear me, "Are you a devout Catholic, Michael?"

He looked at me with a somewhat stoic look on his face and said, "We'll save that discussion for another day, Brendan. Let's finish our beers and be on our way. I didn't sleep well last night, and I've had a long day, but it's been a grand day . . . my house is nearly finished, and I have you to thank for that."

"Here's to you! Slainte'!" he said as he hoisted his glass and finished off the last drop of the 'Holy Water,' as Seamus likes to call it.

After I dropped him off back at his house, he stood for a few moments at the doorway, admired what had been done that day, and said, "Marjorie is happy with what's being done here. She thanks you, too, Brendan."

Then he added, "Safe home," and closed the door behind him.

C H A P T E R   F O U R T E E N

Advanced Directives

Kathleen was delighted to hear about the progress being made on the house, and so was Dr. Delaney. However, when I mentioned the part about being at the bar with him and him telling me all about the Druids and the Celts, she lowered her eyes, shook her head, and said, "Yes, he's always had somewhat different views of reincarnation, heaven, and a few other things from what the church tells us to believe. His wife, Marjorie, was the true believer in the family."

"I'm not surprised to hear that he doesn't go to Mass anymore. I think he attended Mass as faithfully as he did because of her. Actually, that would probably be a good idea for him to do. It will give him some social interaction. You might suggest it to him."

"I'm sure that he came to those opinions as a result of his enormous fondness for the Greek and Roman civilizations because they had similar beliefs. Both believed in an after-life and thought the soul was immortal."

"Their religious beliefs are intertwined with the mythology of their gods—Zeus and Jupiter, and all of the female goddesses like Hera, Juno, Venus, Aphrodite, Athena, Minerva, and all the rest. He taught me all of that. I loved learning all about them from him. He had such passion for the topic."

"The next time you're with him, see if you can do that again . . . have another conversation with him like that, that is. Once he gets started, it might take him back to his days of being the professor, preaching to adoring students, like I was. It was spell-binding to hear him talk," she told us. "It will be for you, too, I'm sure, if you can pull that out of him."

"But I digress. You have done well. I thank you and I congratulate you both. We are now able to create a plan of treatment for Dr. McDuffy that will satisfy everyone, and most importantly, that will include Dr. McDuffy. We hope that he will be happy with this, too."

"Thanks to what you've done, I'm confident that we're going to be able to keep him in his home, and that's extremely important. I don't think that anyone, like Dr. Doherty or any of the others, will want to have him taken out of his home, as we initially feared, thanks to your brother and Mr. O'Reilly who sound like quite a humorous fellow, I must say."

"He is that, indeed," I confirmed. "It's a joy just to hear him laugh, as he does quite frequently."

"If I ever need a thatcher, I'll know who to call. So, while you were doing all of that, I was busy locating his children, which I was able to do. I spoke to them both over the weekend and made them aware of the situation. As you might imagine, they were devastated to hear the news. At first, they were resistant, unwilling to accept our diagnosis, and they were asking a lot of questions."

"However, after I provided them with further information and a copy of Dr. Doherty's report, they became more understanding. They are both extremely bright individuals. I was able to get them on a video-conference call and talk to them at the same time."

"We were able to see each other, and I think that helped a great deal. Today's technology is absolutely amazing, isn't it? So easy and not all that expensive. It was wonderful . . . made things so much better."

At that point, Saoirse interrupted her and asked, "Has that diagnosis been made, Kathleen? Have you determined that his condition has advanced to the point where he is to be classified as an 'Alzheimer's' patient?"

Kathleen looked at her and said, "No, it has not. The records will reflect a diagnosis of dementia, not Alzheimer's disease, although they will reflect our expectation that his condition will continue to deteriorate. That's an extremely important distinction to make."

"In fact, that brings me to my next point, which is that Dr. McDuffy needs to prepare his advanced directives, and that needs to be done as soon as possible," she told us.

"Advanced directives?" I asked. "What are they?"

Saoirse turned to me and said, "His Last Will and Testament, a Living Will, Power of Attorney . . . things like that."

"Very good, Saoirse," Kathleen said.

"We covered that in our geriatrics class just last week," she told us.

"That's wonderful and, as I'm sure you know then, only a solicitor can help us with that. We have some forms and all that we use for many of our patients, but that wouldn't be appropriate for this situation. So, I looked and found that there's a solicitor in Sneem, and I think his name is Curran if I'm not mistaken. Do you know the man, Brendan?"

"I know who he is, and he'll know who I am, but that's about it. I think he's a second or third cousin. I've met him at family gatherings a time or two," I told her, "He's as old as my father is."

"Well, I'll ask you to contact him and see if he's willing to meet with Dr. McDuffy to get those things done sometime in the next week or two. His daughter, Caitlin, who's now married to an American man named Golding, is coming as soon as she can and she wants us to help her get those things done while she's here."

"Don't mention any of that to Dr. McDuffy, of course. Let her do that. I told her that we would make the arrangements with the solicitor so he would be expecting her call. Again, her name is Caitlin Golding . . . Caitlin McDuffy Golding, and she will be calling him sometime soon. So, you'll call Mr. Curran, yes?" she asked. I assured her that I would.

"Now, Dr. McDuffy may already have a Will, but if he can't find it, that won't be of any use. Even if he can find it, it probably needs to be changed. Most likely, he would have left everything to his wife, but since she died before he did, it will probably need to be changed, but maybe not."

"Caitlin didn't have a clue about where that might be, nor did her brother, but she's going to ask. I should hear from her sometime this week. She was to call him and then let me know."

"Are they both going to come see him?" I asked.

"For now, she'll be the only one coming over, not Patrick. He can't get away at the moment, but he'll come as soon as he can," she answered. "They're both busy people and both are in the middle of their Fall classes. They can't just get up and leave. It will be difficult for her, but she now knows how important and time-sensitive all of this is."

"We're not at a critical stage just yet because he can be quite lucid, at times, as you saw just a couple of days ago, but things could change quickly. I told them it's an urgent matter and asked them both to call more regularly from now on. They need to pay more attention to their father. He needs them now."

"They're quite willing to help, though, and they made it clear that money is no object. They've both done well for themselves, but money isn't what he needs, and money can't buy what he needs, nothing can."

"He's fortunate to have the money, though, or access to it. Most people don't. People without money and without a family to provide support end up in hospitals like this one, or worse . . . much worse, like gaols or prisons, as we know."

"That won't be the case with Dr. McDuffy because he can afford the best care money can buy, even though that won't be enough to save him, as I said," she told us solemnly.

Then, the expression on her face changed back to the professional that she was, and she went on, saying, "It's possible that he'll have the other documents, and Caitlin will ask. Even if he's done them in the past, he might not know where they are, as I said, but we'll see. If we can't find them, they're no good to us, or him, and they'll need to be done again."

"He may be quite resistant to this whole idea, but it's critical that we get this done as soon as possible. I can't stress that enough," she told us. "That's why having his daughter here to help with that is so important. She'll be able to convince him to do these things."

When I asked why it was so urgent, Saoirse turned toward me and said, "Because he must be of sound mind when he executes those documents, Brendan."

"Very good, Saoirse. I'm sure you do quite well in school, don't you?" she asked.

"I'm near the top," Saoirse responded modestly.

"Well, that's exactly why it is so urgent, and at least two people must swear that he is of sound mind when he does so. I don't want it to be either of you two, so if you're asked, you must decline, and it can't be his daughter, either, because she's a likely beneficiary. Maybe your brother and that Seamus fellow can do that, but it must be done quickly, understood?" she asked.

We both responded affirmatively.

"Also, we're going to have to find someone who can be in the home with the good doctor at least part of the time," she said. "That's my job, so I'll take care of that, but it could be a major problem for us. He's probably not going to like that too much. He's such a proud, dignified man. That's not going to sit well with him, I expect."

"But he should welcome the help, shouldn't he? Someone to drive him places, cook for him, clean for him, run errands . . . all of that should make his life easier, don't you think?" I asked.

"Maybe, but I doubt it. You don't know the man as I do. I expect that it will take a while to convince him of it. We'll see. First things first, let's get that house of his buttoned-up, get the advanced directives done, and we'll go from there. That's our plan."

When she finished speaking, she looked at us as if to say our meeting was over, and she asked, "Any questions?"

I asked, "I just don't understand how he can go from being so incredibly bright and entertaining to losing his mind altogether so quickly . . . and I mean from one day to the next ... how is that possible?"

"That's the disease, Brendan," she said softly. "That's how it works. The brain gets tangled . . . strangled, if you want to think of it like that . . . and it doesn't work correctly after a while . . . like when a person is being strangled and can't breathe."

"Actually, that's a very good way to think of it . . . his brain is being strangled and it's gasping for air . . . awful, really, but it makes the point. We can all imagine how it must be even if we haven't actually experienced it, not to be able to breathe, that is . . . air pipes getting squeezed and struggling to get a breath of air. That's sort of like what's happening to Dr. McDuffy's brain. Does that help you understand it a little better?" she asked.

"You can't strangle a brain, can you?" I asked.

"It cuts off the supply of blood to the brain, Brendan," Saoirse responded. "And bodily functions stop working correctly, too, because the brain doesn't give the necessary commands, right, Kathleen?" Saoirse asked.

"That's correct, Saoirse. The mind or the brain, if you will, stops functioning properly, and that includes sending the proper signals to various parts of the body. Many of those things happen somewhat automatically, and we don't even think about them, but as the disease advances, those messages aren't sent properly, and the body begins to shut down . . . the brain is no longer in control," she said. "The brain is dying, and the body follows suit," she added grimly.

Then she brightened a bit, and said, "But we're not there yet. We're still in stage four of this process, so take nothing for granted here. Changes could occur sooner than we want. You might not have too many more days like the ones you've had with him, Brendan, and you, too, Saoirse, so enjoy those days when they occur."

It really was befuddling how he could be so alert and so intelligent on some occasions, and so lost on others. I'd seen him in both conditions, but never on a really bad day. I wasn't looking forward to those days, but I didn't say anything more about it in response.

"Anything else from you, Saoirse?" she asked.

"No, ma'am," she answered. "I haven't spent as much time with Dr. McDuffy as Brendan has, but I intend to spend more time there over the next few weeks. As I believe I told you before, I've been thinking more and more that this issue . . . that being the line where a person goes from being able to handle his own affairs to being unable to do so . . . would be a good one for a thesis. It's hard to put a finger on it, yet we, the medical profession that is, must do so."

"I think that would be an excellent thesis, Saoirse, and this will be the perfect case to work on . . . you'd be hard-pressed to find a better one. This could be a 'textbook' case, although that's the last thing in the world Dr. McDuffy would want."

"He's such a brilliant man. He would absolutely hate to see that happen, and you couldn't make it too personal without permission. All of this is to be kept private as you know. It's a shame, really, but that's part of life, and that's part of the job the three of us have chosen to do."

"I wish there was more that we could do, but there isn't . . . yet . . . so we'll do the best we can for the man, with love," she said, "and I do love the man. I do."

With that, she stood and said, "See you two next week, unless I hear from his daughter before then. If I do, I'll let you know. Thanks for all you are doing."

After she was gone, Saoirse and I sat there for a few moments, not saying much of anything, and she asked, "So when are we going back out there?"

"Saturday, unless something changes. Seamus is supposed to finish up then. Rory said his men were to be out there cleanin' up the place today. His part of it should be totally done by then. It looked awfully good last weekend and I'm looking forward to seeing what it looks like when he's completely done. Can you make it?" I asked.

"I'll have to change my plans a bit, but I will. I think it's important. I hope I can be there when he has another lucid moment. I enjoyed going through the pictures with him the other day. I'd love to hear him talk about the Greeks and the Romans. That would be somethin' to hear, wouldn't it?" she asked.

I agreed and said, "And I hope we can go to the bar with Seamus and him, too. It will be fun if we do. I guarantee it!"

She laughed when I said that and said, "It sounds like fun alright, but I'd be worryin' about the drive home. I never drive after having more than a pint or two. I'd be deathly afraid to wreck that car of mine."

"You'll learn some new jokes, I can promise you that much," I told her. "I couldn't get a word in edge-wise with the two of them," which was true.

"We'll just have to see what sort of shape he's in on Saturday and hope for the best. See you then, if not before," she told me as she stood and left. "I've got class tonight. Gotta run. Bye for now. Remember to call that solicitor," she reminded me.

CHAPTER FIFTEEN

The Antiquities

That Saturday, I made arrangements to meet with Saoirse even earlier than before. I wanted to make sure that we were there before my brother and Seamus arrived, not after they started to work, so we could have a little time to talk to Michael about some things. She agreed and showed up right on time. I was sitting on the bench, waiting for her.

"I don't usually get up this early, Brendan. I'm a mess. I'll tidy up a bit later," she said as she greeted me.

She was a little grumpier than normal, no doubt attributable to the early hour. After coffee and a scone, she gradually began to act like her normal self. Still, there wasn't much conversation on the way over.

Despite our best efforts, we arrived in Sneem just as Rory was turning down Sea View Road ahead of us and we followed him to Dr. McDuffy's house. There was some unexpected traffic on the road in Kenmare and a light drizzle most of the way, so Saoirse wasn't able to drive as fast as she wanted to or I expected her to. Seamus was already there and the two men were having an animated discussion, laughing about something or other.

We interrupted their conversation and Seamus said, "Well, good afternoon, lads. Glad you could make it, and I'm delighted to see that you've brought a beautiful lassie with you."

"This is Saoirse O'Connor," I told him.

"Pleased to meet you," he said, shaking her hand. "Your presence has greatly improved the general appearance of this group of spuds, that's for sure," he told her with a twinkle in his eyes.

"Ah, another Irishman with the gift of gab. I've heard all about you there, Seamus O'Reilly! Nice to finally meet you," she responded.

"You have, have you? Well, only half those lies are true," he said, slapping his knee and laughing all the more.

"I'd love to spend the day talking to you, young lady, but I have work to do. If you happen to still be around later in the day, maybe we'll break bread and share a pint or two," he said.

"I'll do that if we're still here when you're finished," she told him.

"The thought of that will get me workin' all the faster," he said, and up the ladder he went, leaving the four of us standing there, watching him.

Then I turned to Rory and said, "This is Saoirse."

The two of them exchanged pleasantries and when she went inside to freshen up, he said, "Good God almighty! How did you find her? She's a stunner, she is!"

I told him, again, that we were just friends and that that we were nothing more than fellow students, but he'd hear none of it. "Just friends indeed!" Clearly, he was impressed. I think his opinion of me went up considerably, even though there was no truth to what he was imagining.

When we walked inside, I was amazed. The house looked unbelievably good. When I said as much, Rory responded by saying, "Nothin' like a fresh coat of lacquer to brighten up a place, right? Much better than a coat of white paint, I'd say. We finished a job earlier than expected yesterday afternoon so I came by with some of my men and we knocked out all that was left to be done."

"I think it turned out rather well if I do say so meself," he added. "What do you think, Bear? Is it satisfactory?" he asked.

"Oh, it's fantastic, Rory! The woodwork is top shelf. It's a fine job you've done here . . . a fine job indeed! Don't you agree, Michael?" I asked.

"It never looked better . . . never. We bought it from an older couple who had lived in it for ten years or more, and we fixed it up some . . . my wife did all of that . . . but it never looked this good . . . never. I couldn't be happier with how it turned out," he said.

"And the roof, too!" Rory said. "How about the job Seamus is doing with the roof?" he asked.

"There, too, it never looked better . . . never. I can't thank you all enough," he said.

With that, he handed Rory a check and said, "This is payment in full, I believe, and the job you did was worth twice the price!"

"Well, I'll be happy to accept that as a bonus if you're willing to pay it!" Rory responded with a laugh, and then he said, "I'm glad that you're happy with my work and I hope you'll let your friends know about me. My best source of future customers is my past customers."

"I'll be sure to do that," Dr. McDuffy responded. "And I might be making my last payment to Seamus, too. He might be finished today from what he told me."

"It looks that way, but Seamus is a perfectionist. Until it's perfect, it's not done. I'll leave that up to him, but I'll come back when he's finished and gather up the odds and ends that are left around your yard once the job is totally completed. I promise you that, Dr. McDuffy," he said.

"Michael, please . . . and please stop by anytime you're in the neighborhood and say hello. I don't get much company these days."

Saoirse joined in with all the congratulatory conversation about how the entire house had been cleaned up, the floors swept, and the rest since she was there a week ago, and it had been. It absolutely shined. "I did the best I could," Rory said with some humility, "I'm glad you all like what I've done."

Rory didn't stay long since all of his work was finished. "I just wanted to come by and make sure everything was to your satisfaction," he said. "And to pick up this," he added, holding up the check. "My wife likes this part the best. It goes straight to her. She handles the books."

He said his goodbyes and was gone within half an hour, leaving the three of us sitting by the fire. Saoirse and I were on the couch, side by side, and he was sitting in his favorite chair, a few feet away. Seamus was on the roof, busily working away.

As we sat there, sipping our coffee and tea, Saoirse asked, "So, Professor McDuffy, it's been an absolute pleasure to meet you, and I've heard so much about you since we first met. I was hoping that you might tell us a little more about yourself and the things you did at Trinity . . . the courses you taught . . . if you don't mind, that is. You were long gone by the time I got there, but my father took a class from you and he's told me a thing or two about you, as have some others. Would you be willing to do that for us?"

That was exactly what Kathleen had told us to do and she was spot on with that question. I was hoping that he would agree.

"Well, I hope your father and the others spoke well of me," he responded.

"That they did," she assured him. "It's an honor to be meeting you as we are. 'Tis, indeed."

"I don't mind telling you a few things about those days if you really want to know," he responded, "although some people find it somewhat boring, but I'll agree to do so only on one condition."

"And what is that?" she asked.

"That you call me Michael. I am no longer Professor McDuffy as I was for most of my life. Those days are gone. Will you do that for me?" he asked.

"I will," she answered.

"And that goes for you, too, Brendan. You slip up every now and again, but I insist. Can you agree to that?" he asked.

I also agreed.

"Well, that's not something I can summarize for you in a few, short sentences. It's going to take a little while for me to explain all of that to the two of you and I sometimes get carried away when I do. Are you sure you want me to?"

We assured him that we did. After all, it was still early morning and Seamus would undoubtedly be working until well into the afternoon.

"Just a short summary, Michael," I said. "I'll not be takin' any notes, but I'd love to hear about those things."

"I'm most interested in hearing about you and what you learned from all of that more than anything else. We could read the other stuff in a book," Saoirse told him. "In fact, let me ask . . . did you write any books, Michael?"

"Well, there's the one textbook entitled *The Antiquities*, and I believe it's still in use today, but I'm not sure about that. It's intended for first-year students, more of an overview, actually, and it was written decades ago, early on in my career. I wrote plenty of articles that were published in various magazines, but that's the only book I ever wrote. I was encouraged to write a few more on many occasions, but I never did, just the one," he told us.

"Maybe you should do that now, Michael," I suggested.

"That ship has sailed, Brendan. No chance of that happening. Marjorie was all the time telling me to do just that, but I never got around to it. Maybe I'll do that in my next lifetime," he responded with a chuckle.

Then he sighed, took a sip of his tea, and said, "Alright then, here goes . . . as you know, I believe, I was the chairman of the Antiquities Department within University College Dublin for many years. As such, I had the opportunity to study the greatest of what are now called the 'ancient' civilizations, which included both the Greek and Roman empires, and many more. Generally speaking, the term 'antiquities' refers to the time before the Middle Ages, which covers thousands of years."

"During that time, I learned about all of the greatest civilizations in the history of the world—from the time when humans first began to live together in a community setting and formed societies. The earliest of those 'great' civilizations is said to have been in Mesopotamia, which is in modern-day Syria, Turkey, and Iran, near the Tigris and Euphrates rivers.

"Incidentally, that is where the Biblical 'Garden of Eden' is thought to have been located, though there is much debate about that, as you are undoubtedly aware . . . Adam and Eve and all of that. Not everyone believes those biblical stories to be true. Most of the world does, however, as about two-thirds of the people in the world are either Christians, Muslims, or Jews, and all three of those religions believe all of what is in the Bible, or they profess that they do."

"Sumeria is generally regarded as the earliest of the 'great' civilizations, and it came into being about four thousand years before Christ. Some say that may have been only thirty-five hundred years before Jesus was born. In either event, humans, or homo sapiens, have lived together in large, successful communities for approximately five or six thousand years . . . not a very long time when you consider that planet earth is thought to have been formed some five billion years ago and dinosaurs roamed the earth for over a hundred and fifty million of those years until they became extinct sixty-five million years ago."

"Great civilizations have sprung up from all across the globe . . . Egypt, the Mayans in Central America, the Chinese, the Incas in South America, the Aztecs in Mexico, and yes, the Greeks and Romans are definitely considered by all historians to be among the greatest of all civilizations. Those two came into existence at about the same time. Greece was first, about eight hundred years before Christ, and it was the more dominant of the two for centuries. That ended when it was militarily defeated by Rome a few hundred years before Christ was born."

"The Roman Empire lasted well into the fifteenth century, A.D., if you consider the eastern part, as most do. That was when Constantinople fell into the hands of the Ottoman Empire. Rome, which was the capitol of the Western Empire, was defeated by Attila the Hun in the middle of the Fifth Century, and it was effectively destroyed a few years later by some barbarians from what is now Germany."

"The Roman Empire is generally considered to be the greatest of all civilizations because of the length of time it dominated this part of the world as well as for its enduring legacies. Those of us who live in Europe are, understandably, partial to that point of view. Others, like the Chinese and people from Mexico, will debate that issue."

"The height of Greek power in terms of world dominance, though much of the world was undiscovered at the time, as you know, came when Alexander the Great conquered most of the known world three hundred and some years before Christ was born. That's when he rode off into oblivion, conquering the people living in what is now Iran and Afghanistan. He is said to have died in Babylon in the palace of Nebuchadnezzar II in the third century B.C."

"That was located south of Baghdad, in what is now Iraq, a long distance from Pella, his home. Most say that was a foolhardy expedition, the result of his youth and his overly zealous ambition to conquer the entire world. He was only thirty-three when he died."

"Some argue, quite convincingly, actually, that the Mayan Empire, which lasted for some twenty-five hundred years in what is now the Yucatan Peninsula of Mexico and Guatemala, is the greatest of all civilizations. They disappeared off the face of the earth under mysterious circumstances, still not fully understood, about 1000 A.D. We are still, even now, and I mean to this very day, discovering spectacular ruins from those days."

"Not enough is known of them because records were destroyed . . . by the Roman Catholic Church, I'm sad to say . . . but from what we know, they were extremely advanced, though their propensity for human sacrifice is certainly not admired. They made advances in the fields of astronomy and mathematics that are astounding. It's a pity that so much of their heritage was destroyed by the Spanish conquistadores and the priests who accompanied them. Their beliefs were considered heresy, and therefore, their writings were burned."

"Egypt, with its pyramids and all was without any doubt whatsoever one of the most advanced civilizations the world had ever seen before. Unlike the Mayans, its history is quite well-documented. They recorded everything, but archeologists are still uncovering secrets from those days, too."

"It makes one wonder just how far the human mind has evolved over the centuries, doesn't it? Incredible discoveries are being made in the material world these days, what with space travel and all, but the human mind with its propensity for wars and strife doesn't seem to have changed all that much as far as I can tell. What do you think?" he asked.

I just shrugged my shoulders, shook my head, and said that I really hadn't thought too much about that before. Saoirse agreed with him, and said, "When I read some of what those people said, like Socrates, Plato, or Aristotle, it makes me think it could have been written by someone from this generation."

He looked at her approvingly, saying, "I agree with you, Saoirse. Those men were brilliant without a doubt," and then he went on.

"China is an ancient civilization and I confess, I don't know as much about it as I would like. The language is such a barrier, and not that much of what has been written about it over the centuries has been translated into English, in comparison to other civilizations. I learned a great deal about the Chinese people over the years, but I do not consider myself to be an expert on China or the Far East, though others say that I am. I guess I know more than most, but there is much I don't know about them."

"Theirs was, and is, one of the great civilizations of the world though, without any doubt whatsoever. The first dynasty in China dates from about two thousand years before Christ, which is roughly about the same time as the Mayans were in what is now Mexico and Central America. The last dynasty ended at the beginning of the twentieth century around 1911 or 1912, so that's about four thousand years all total."

"Other civilizations, such as the Aborigines in Australia and the indigenous peoples of North America, or the tribes of Africa, to name just a few, are known to have been in existence for tens of thousands of years. That would place them well before Sumeria, but there isn't much physical evidence of what knowledge those peoples generated or what those societies were like. Their histories have been passed down by word of mouth from one generation to the next, so little is known of them and there isn't much physical evidence of what life was like for them, either."

"I could go on and on, but I won't," he said. "That gives you an idea of what I did with my life . . . I endeavored to learn about the ancient past and share with my students all that I had learned. It was a fascinating topic and I thoroughly enjoyed doing what I did. I was fortunate to have been able to find a job that paid me to do what I loved doing."

"Despite my best efforts to be objective and impartial as a student and social scientist, if you will, I confess to having an affinity for the Greeks for various reasons. That was my favorite period in history . . .

the ancient Greek civilization, even more so than the Romans or any of the rest. It must have been an absolutely magnificent time to be alive. They were the first, as I'm sure you know, to attempt to form a democratic union . . . not one ruled by the theory of 'might makes right,' as has always been the norm."

"Their leaders and rulers strived to be egalitarian. They thought of all people as being equal. They wanted all people to have equal rights . . . such concepts never existed before. The Romans never did that . . . no society did. They were the first to do that and I admire them so very much because of it."

"If I had the opportunity to go back in time, that's where I would go. I would want to have been there when Socrates was in his later years of life, with Plato there with him as a student. Plato then taught Aristotle. The three of them weren't alive at the exact same moment in time, but they lived in the same century. That was quite a remarkable period in the history of the world, and it is called the 'Golden Age of Greece.'"

Then he paused and leaned back in his chair. We didn't say a word. He took a sip of his tea, and went on, "I haven't talked about any of these things in years. It's interesting to reflect back, as I have just done, but I'll tell you what I have been thinking about lately, which might surprise you."

"All civilizations came into being for much the same reasons . . . first and foremost, it was for security . . . to protect against invaders, whether they be beasts, as they were in the beginning, or enemies. Secondly, it was to collectively provide food for people to eat and survive. Next, it would be, as it continues to be now, for people to prosper and make money. That's why people leave places like Sneem and move to the big cities like Dublin or to the United States . . . to make more money."

"But from the very beginning, when men first looked up into the sky, all wondered how any of this came into being. Who created all that is? And why?"

"Human beings, through these great societies, and that includes each and every one, created their own belief systems, which we call 'religions' to answer those questions. Not surprisingly, they didn't all come up with the same answers. What is surprising, at least to me, is that to this very day, we continue to have much the same answers to those questions. There hasn't been much change in religious thought since the days of Mohammad and the advent of Islam.

"The five religions recognized as being the predominant ones are Christianity, Islam, Judaism, Hinduism, and Buddhism, though there are dozens more. Like the two of you, I was raised Catholic in this overwhelmingly Catholic country, and I have led my entire life as a follower of Jesus Christ. People in this part of the world had little knowledge of China or the Far East back then, around the time when Christ walked the earth, and they had absolutely no knowledge whatsoever about the peoples of North, South or Central America."

"Jesus was born during the era of Roman rule but as we now know, unbeknownst to them, both the Chinese and Mayan civilizations were flourishing at that time. Also, the Buddha lived six hundred years before Christ was born, so Buddhism and Hinduism were well-established by that time, though little was known about any of that. People who lived in India and Southeast Asia had developed their cultures and belief systems long before Jesus Christ came to earth."

"Catholics and all other Christians follow Jesus' teachings and we have been taught to believe that God created all that is, just as the Bible tells us. There is no consideration whatsoever given to the beliefs of any of those other civilizations. I think it's fair to say that all religions begin with the same basic proposition . . . there is a God or a creator . . . of that there is no doubt . . . and the rub is in defining the term."

"I'm wrestling with all of that here lately, and it surprises me. You'd think I'd have all of that figured out by now, but I don't. I guess I'm having these thoughts because I'm getting closer and closer to the end, maybe. I've got to know what to say when I meet St. Peter, don't I?" he asked.

Saoirse and I sat there spellbound as he spoke and neither of us responded to what was a rhetorical question. His voice deepened and he spoke with authority on subjects he had spent a lifetime studying. We didn't dare interrupt him, but then he stopped for a moment, looked at us intently, and whispered, "Christians constitute roughly one-third of the people on earth. One-fourth of earth's population are Muslims. The Hindus are a fifth of the people on earth, and one in ten people in the world are Buddhists. We can't say that we are the only ones who are right and all others are wrong, can we? If we insist that they must conform their beliefs to ours, how will we ever resolve our differences? Can you answer that?"

We didn't respond, though I think he was expecting some sort of answer to that question.

When we didn't, he went on and said, "I can't . . . I can't say to my fellow scholars in India, most of whom are Hindu, that the Hindus are wrong, can I?"

"And I can't say to my friends in China that Confucius or Lao-Tzu was wrong, can I? Of course not. Nor can I tell scholars from Southeast Asia that Siddhartha Gautama, the Buddha, was mistaken in his teachings, could I?"

"My goodness! When you think about it, we Christians can't even agree on some of the most basic things, can we? And we will fight to death over such things, won't we? No one in Ireland can deny that, now can we? Look at us! It's shameful, really, isn't it?"

"And I assure you, with the utmost confidence, that I can't tell my Jewish colleagues that the Jews are wrong, that Jesus was and is the Messiah. After all, Jesus was a Jew from the day he was born until the day he took his last breath on earth. As we know, the history of Judaism and Christianity is extremely closely intertwined, but that history includes Islam, too . . . all three claim Abraham as a common ancestor. All three are, as Mohammad said, 'people of the book.'"

"So, when you think about it, we . . . and I mean the entire world . . . are completely confused by the concept of God, or gods, and there is no end to the debate in sight. What would it take to unite the world? What are the answers to those age-old questions?"

"In that regard, I am much like Socrates . . . I can't tell you after a lifetime of study that I have learned anything which can help to solve the issues that divide mankind. I can't say that I know anything more now than I did when I was your age! I have learned many facts and formed many opinions, but I can't say that I know anything more to answer the most basic questions that all of humanity wants answers to."

He paused again, looking at us questioningly. When we didn't respond, he continued, "I can't! I don't know what I could tell you, even now, about such things. I have spent my life gathering facts, facts, and more facts. I've read what most of the greatest thinkers in the history of the world have written or said, but to what end?"

His voice trailed off and he turned to gaze into the fire when he finished. "What have I learned?"

He didn't say a word for several moments, and neither did we. We knew he wasn't finished. He had more to say.

Moments later, he continued, "So, you ask me to tell you about my life and what I've learned as a result of decades of study, and there's my response . . . that's what I've done and that's what I've learned."

"Now, if you were to persist and say 'we want answers, not more questions,' then I'm afraid I can't be more helpful. I don't have answers to the questions about how we came to be, and why. I wish I did, but I don't."

"So where does that leave me? I come back to where I began, actually, and that is with my admiration for the ancient Greeks. Of all the civilizations in the world that I have learned of, I like the things they said and did better than any of the others. I choose to believe what they believed about the concepts of an after-life and reincarnation."

"So, you believe in reincarnation, Michael? That's not what the Church teaches us, is it?" Saoirse asked.

He turned to her, looked her in the eye, and said, "I realize that what I have just told you might surprise you, and that some might consider that to be heresy. I'm sure that you would have expected to hear me say that I ascribe to the teachings of our church, as most here in Ireland do, but I can't say that I do, not entirely, at least."

"I can't do that," he repeated. "I'm sorry, but I can't, and it bothers me. I wish I knew, but I don't and I don't think I ever will, nor will anyone else, I expect."

Then he hesitated again and went on, "The Greeks and the Romans, too, believed in an after-life, as did the Druids, the Egyptians, and many others, as I said before, though they used different names and had different descriptions of the place people go after they die. No one knows what heaven is like. The Greeks and Romans both believed in the immortality of the soul, as did the Celts and Druids, as I told Brendan last week. They didn't believe that the human body went into the ground and that was the end of it."

"One more thing . . . they didn't believe that 'heaven' was the stopping point, like we Catholics do . . . it was more like a 'resting' point or an in-between spot. It was a place where one's soul went before moving into another human body. It wasn't like you went to heaven and that was it . . . no, they didn't think that was our final destination."

"I think it's important to keep that distinction in mind. That's what Hindus, Buddhists, and others believe, too. They believe that the soul continues to evolve until it reaches the point, which they call 'nirvana' when it can evolve no further."

"We Catholics are taught to believe that when St. Peter meets us at the pearly gates on judgment day, and if he allows us into heaven, that we will live in eternal bliss ever after. I don't believe that. I'm sorry, but I don't."

"When you think about it, and I have given the matter a considerable amount of thought over the years, that is the most basic of all questions that mankind asks itself . . . 'what is going to happen to me when I die?' If there is no after-life . . . no reward for leading a good and worthy life, what is the point of being good? Or, to put it differently, what is the risk of not living a worthy and admirable life? Is there one?"

"Why be good? Why not just kill, steal, cheat, and do whatever is necessary to survive? Might makes right! That was, and it remains to this very day, the over-riding object of all societies, for the most part."

"Go back as far as you want . . . conquer, capture, enrich, enlarge . . . grow into being a great civilization through the use of military force. Now, it's the United States of America with the biggest and best military and the most deadly and lethal bombs. Russia, and now China, are their chief competitors in what is called the 'arms race.' The object is to be the most powerful country on earth, just like the Egyptians, the Greeks under Alexander, the Romans, the Ottomans, and so many others sought to do."

"But in my lifetime, before the rise of the United States of America, it was Germany, and before them, the Turks and the Ottoman Empire, and before that, it was Great Britain, Spain, France, and the other colonial powers from Europe. There were others before all of them, but you get my point. That's been the history of all societies and of mankind."

"Now, it's important to note that religion has played a major role in all of that, but it was really all about power and military power at that. Who was the strongest—not the best and the brightest. More than anyone else, the Greeks sought to do just that . . . be the best by being the brightest . . . and that's why I admire them so much more than the others."

"Jesus, the Buddha, Lao-Tzu, Sri Krishna, Moses, who is credited for writing the first five books of the Bible a thousand years after Abraham died, Mohammad, among others, all tell us that there is an after-life. Their message is different, but in many ways, it's the same . . . what you do on earth determines what will happen to you when you die, so be good."

"All religions are the same in that regard . . . all say 'be good! If you are, you'll be rewarded! If you don't, something really bad is going to happen to you!' But who knows, for sure, if any of that is true? I wonder about all of that sometimes."

"But since you ask what it is I believe, I'll tell you . . . I believe that there is a God. I believe that with all my heart. All that exists didn't come into being by accident. There must be some purpose for us to be here and I believe that we must be good human beings, not ignorant savages. We must evolve. We must get better. We must improve ourselves. That only makes sense."

"That said, I believe that Charles Darwin and those who believe in evolution are, to a large extent, correct. The scientific proof is undeniable, but that doesn't explain the origins. The story begins well before a single-celled, water-born amoeba is, somehow, found here on planet earth when evolution is said to have begun."

"Besides, who created the thing that went bang?" he asked. "And how did matter come into existence in the first place? How did something come from nothing? No one knows the answers to those questions, and I don't think that anyone ever will."

Then he looked at his watch, which he pulled from his pants pocket. It was round and hung on a chain from his belt. I thought to myself that it was probably given to him at his retirement ceremony.

"I've been talking for quite a while now. Let me finish this thought and then we'll go out and see how Seamus is doing. So, as I was saying, I believe that there is a 'higher power,' as it is now the politically correct way of describing what you and I call God, that has had something to do with all that exists."

"And I believe that there is a 'reward,' if you will, for those of us who lead worthwhile lives. I believe that there is a 'purpose' for us to be here. I also believe that there is a place where people who have fulfilled their 'purpose' and are to receive their 'reward' go upon their death. I call that place Elysium, just as the Greeks and Romans did, and I hope to go there and be with Marjorie," he told us, "and I hope to be going there soon."

"The Greeks and Romans describe in some detail what they thought 'heaven' was like, but I have a different idea of what that place will be like. I think we Irish have our own 'Elysium' and that it's somewhere not far from here," he added.

"I am just like Socrates in that regard . . . I don't really know that any of what I've just told you is true, but that's what I choose to believe, so there you have it! That's what I have come to believe after all of my years on earth!"

Then he leaned back in his chair, heaved a deep sigh, and said, "I hope that I haven't offended you by some of the things I have said, and I know that Father O'Flanagan would have me ex-communicated if he were to hear me say what I have just said to you, but that's the truth. So, you're sworn to secrecy, agreed?" he asked.

We both said, "Agreed," but nothing else. The silence was deafening.

"So, what do the two of you make of all that?" he asked.

After a few moments, I responded and said, "I'm going to have to think about all that you've told us for a while, Michael. I've never looked at things that way."

Then Saoirse asked, "So how do you define God, Michael? Who is he? What is he, if he's not who we have been taught to believe that he is?"

He looked at her and asked, "I've spent a lifetime thinking about these things, Ms. O'Connor, knowing all the while that it is heresy to think such things, let alone say such things out loud as I have. I think it's best for you and Brendan here to figure those things out for yourselves."

"I will, eventually, or we will, I should say," she responded. "And I understand that everyone has to make up his or her own mind about that, but I want to hear what you have to say . . . you're the most brilliant man I've ever met. Who and what do you say God is?" she asked.

He didn't respond right away. Instead, he heaved another big sigh, stood, and said, "Who would like a little more coffee or tea? My tea is now cold as I've been talking so much."

We both stood, walked over into what was now a clean, well-organized kitchen area, and refreshed our cups.

"It really looks fantastic in here now, doesn't it, Michael?" Saoirse asked.

He agreed and thanked me once again for my part in making all of that happen, and then said, "Let's walk outside and see how Seamus is doing."

The three of us walked outside to the top of the hill, maybe fifty meters away, and looked down to see Seamus working away. We yelled to him, and he waived, saying, "I'm fine, thanks! I've got another hour or two to go here," or something like that. He didn't stop working, though, and we walked back inside and sat back down.

Then he turned to her and asked, "Are you sure you want to hear what I have to say about that?"

"I am," she answered.

"Me, too, Michael. I'd like to know as well," I told him.

"Well, if you insist . . . I owe you that much for what you've done for me, and I guess I might have to be answering those very same questions when I get in front of St. Peter before too long, so I'd better get my answers straight, hadn't I?" he asked with a laugh.

"Here goes . . . no one knows and no one will ever know the answers to these questions. Socrates was right . . . I know how little I know, but that's not good enough. It's like being in school. I have to put down an answer, even if it's wrong."

"I don't believe that God is a human being . . . we might be made in the image and likeness of God, but I doubt it. He doesn't sit on a cloud above us with a great white beard as he is so often depicted. I think we can all agree on that."

"And 'he' is not a 'he, she, or it.' I don't believe that there is a physical presence to whatever it is that created all that is. Keep in mind that the 'Big Bang' is said to have occurred nearly fourteen billion years ago, and the universe has been expanding at an incredibly high rate of speed ever since. It still is, at this very moment, with no end in sight."

"I try not to think about it too much because it truly causes a headache when I do, but we are traveling at over sixteen hundred kilometers an hour as the earth revolves around its axis every day. That's a circular motion, mind you. The earth is over forty thousand kilometers in circumference, and it is traveling forward at over a hundred thousand kilometers per hour as it revolves around the sun once every year, through space."

"And that doesn't include our forward motion through space, as we, our universe that is, which is called the 'Milky Way,' hurtles through space away from the place where the 'Big Bang' occurred at who knows what rate of speed. I don't! It makes me dizzy to think of it. Can you imagine that? Just imagine it!" he said. "You can't! No one can," he added.

Neither Saoirse nor I responded and he went on, saying, "That's the point, really . . . no one can explain any of this, though they try, and no one really knows how it all started. It's silly to say it, but we haven't really advanced too far from the question of what comes first, the chicken or the egg, have we?"

"And the greatest minds on the planet, Stephen Hawking, though he just left us not long ago, Carl Sagan, Lisa Randall, Lawrence Krauss, Neil DeGrasse Tyson . . . Einstein, Werner von Braun, Copernicus, DaVinci . . . or anyone else in the history of the world . . . no one you can think of knows . . . no one knows and no one ever will."

"Scientists have recently discovered 'black holes,' and now that is the rage. Einstein speculated that something like them existed, but he didn't know. He was guessing, or theorizing. They are making discoveries, but it is all an enormous mystery. All of that's been in the last fifteen or twenty years."

"Other scientists, located in Switzerland are working, thousands of meters underground, on a project to discover what they are calling the 'God particle.' They have spent billions of dollars and countless hours on that project. They are trying to find a scientific answer to the question of who and what is 'God,' but that is a question that is and will always be unanswerable, in my humble opinion."

"No one will ever know the answers to the questions surrounding the origins of matter, let alone life. How did matter come into existence? . . . how is it that we look as we do? . . . with fingers, toes, eyes, ears, a heart, digestive system, and a brain . . . a brain . . . to think as we do. Is that an accident of nature? I think not," he said.

"There is a higher power . . . there is a creator, an entity of some kind which caused all of this to happen, and I'm not just talking about planet earth . . . there are millions if not billions of so-called universes, some of which are, I'm sure, similar to ours."

"Did you know that the outer limits of space are expanding faster than where we are here on earth? Soon, not in our lifetimes, but soon, humans, if we still exist, won't be able to see the stars that we now see with our normal vision . . . they will have gone out of sight. It's hard to imagine, yet we act as if the answers are just out of reach, soon to be attained. That's nonsense."

"Again, it is as Socrates says, we know nothing and to pretend that we do is pure folly."

"That's not your answer, Michael, and you know it," Saoirse said. I was surprised to hear her confront him that way, but she did.

He turned to her and said, "You're right, my dear. That is not my answer, but my answer may not please you. Are you sure you want to hear it?"

"I don't want you to tell me what I want to hear, I want to hear what you have to say," she told him, almost demanding an answer. Then she added, "Please."

He heaved another deep sigh, chuckled to himself, and said, "You're having to drag this out of me, aren't you, my girl," as he patted her on her knee. "Just like my daughter, Caitlin. She wouldn't let me rest, always wanting to know more."

"Alright, here is what I really think is the most logical explanation of how we human beings got here and how we have become what we are . . . and this doesn't begin to explain things from the moment in time when a 'Big Bang' took place, if such a thing actually occurred, it only explains what has happened since."

"I think that another species of life, quite possibly other human beings, much like us, who existed billions of years ago, perhaps, although it doesn't have to be that long ago, found this blue planet, orbiting around a relatively small sun in a distant universe and they came here. I think that they planted seeds. I think that another species, perhaps homo sapiens, like us, created what we have here."

"And I think that explains, in part, why there is so much chaos and tragedy in the world with cyclones, hurricanes, earthquakes, plagues, pandemics, sickness, death, and the rest . . . they are still experimenting. They don't know, either. To me, that makes sense . . . how can there be a devil in the world if our God is omnipotent and all-powerful? How? I think that's nonsense."

"Please, understand . . . I don't know that anything of what I am telling you is the truth. This is just my explanation of all that I have seen in the few short years, relatively speaking, that I have lived. I would not pretend to tell you that this is what you should believe. You must decide that for yourself, and I don't believe it with a fervor such as to say that I am right and whatever you believe is wrong. That's not correct, either."

"And this . . . this is the most important thing I can tell the two of you, I think," he said as he took my hand in his left hand and Saoirse's hand in his right, ". . . no one is wrong!"

"Do you hear? No one is wrong! If no one is right, how can anyone be wrong?"

"Think about it . . . Jesus, the Buddha, Mohammad, Sri Krishna, Confucius . . . they all are saying essentially the same thing . . . be good! Lead an honorable life, and there will be an afterlife that awaits you."

"They all say that. It just takes a while longer for the Hindus and the Buddhists to get there. We Christians like to think it happens immediately upon death. I am not so sure of that, but I hope to be going to Elysium when I die, to be with Marjorie. That is what I choose to believe."

"Even the atheists, the agnostics, and all of the evolutionists aren't wrong . . . they just haven't answered the questions completely. There may be no 'god,' who knows? Those who doubt, the agnostics, that is, they're not wrong, either. They have good reason to doubt, as I have just explained. We all have doubts! We must!"

"The evolutionists aren't wrong, either. They just haven't answered the question of who created the thing that exploded and the things that were created as a result, as I said a minute ago . . . the atoms, the molecules, the gases, and all the rest. They're not wrong."

"So, as my life comes to an end, I choose to believe that which I have learned from the Greeks. This world is a mysterious, miraculous place, regarding which I have only a limited amount of knowledge, but I will be a good, virtuous person, and I hope to arrive at Elysium, and be with my Kathleen forevermore."

"Kathleen? You mean Marjorie," Saoirse said.

"What? Did I say Kathleen? I'm sorry. Of course, I meant Marjorie. Forgive me," he said. "I don't know what I was thinking."

Then he stood, clapped his hands together as if to break the spell that he had put us under, and said, "That's it. There is no more. I have told you two all that I have to say."

We stood. Saoirse hugged him and thanked him profusely. I went to shake his hand and he put both arms around me and hugged me, too.

Saoirse looked at her watch and said, "Oh my! Look what time it's getting to be. I really should be going."

I was disappointed to hear her say that, and said, "I guess it's time for us to leave you be, for now, Michael. I've enjoyed being with you here today, but Saoirse has things to do back in Cork, so we'd best be off until another day."

"It's been a pleasure being with you this morning," Saoirse told him. "And if you don't mind, I'll come back and visit with you every so often, Michael. Would that be alright?" she asked.

"You will both be welcome anytime at all, and I hope to see both of you again sometime soon," he told us.

We walked outside, yelled our goodbyes to Seamus, who yelled back, "Not coming to the bar with me?"

Saoirse told him that she had to get back to Cork. He responded by saying, "Ah, you're just all the others . . . just makin' an old man feel good. I was so looking forward to that. Maybe another time."

She laughed and said, "I hope so, Seamus, I do."

I agreed and told him we'd definitely want to do it another day, and off we went, waving to the two of them as we drove away.

I was mentally exhausted from all that I had heard. My brain hurt and I didn't feel much like talking. Saoirse didn't have much of anything to say, either, as we drove back down Sea View Road toward Sneem. We did what we were told to do, but we got more than we bargained for in that conversation with Michael . . . much more, and I wasn't sure what to make of it all.

CHAPTER SIXTEEN

Stage Four

It was still early by the time we left Dr. McDuffy's house, not quite noon, and it was a beautiful day. I was in a bit of a fog, but I was with Saoirse, and we had the whole rest of the day to do something with, so I was hopeful that something good would happen now that we had completed our business in Sneem. I was trying to think of something we could do together, so the day with her would continue.

"That was amazing, wasn't it?" Saoirse asked.

When I agreed, she said, "I think I learned more about religion and world history just then than I did in all my years in school."

Again, I agreed and said that I'd never heard anything like it before. "Nobody says those kinds of things here in Ireland, not in the schools, and certainly not in the churches. It's heresy, really," I told her. "But it made sense to me," I admitted.

"I didn't know any of that about Socrates," Saoirse responded. "The only thing he claimed to know was that he didn't know anything? That's funny, really, but it must be true if Dr. McDuffy said so . . . he's an expert."

"And, he's right, when you think about it . . . we don't really know all that much about how all of this came into being, except for the 'Big Bang' theory and what the Bible tells us. Those are the only two explanations that I know of, and it makes you wonder, doesn't it?" she asked.

I mumbled some kind of response, basically saying that I didn't know and I would have to give it more thought. Then I asked her what she felt like doing for the rest of the day, expecting her to say that she had to get back to Cork to do something. Instead, she told me that she wanted to get a little exercise.

"All that talking and thinking makes me want to be outside and in nature . . . maybe go for a little walk," she said.

That sounded great to me, and I said, "How about the Killarney National Park? It's not much more than an hour away and it's not too far off the way back. Me Mum and her Druid friends had a big celebration of some sort there last weekend and she told me all about it. There's a huge waterfall there that's a sight to see, she says."

I was delighted when she agreed. We didn't talk all that much on the way there. The top was down and we really had a hard time hearing each other when it was. Plus, I think we were both still contemplating some of the things that Michael had told us. I know I was. There was a lot to think about.

Although it was a Saturday, and there were tons of visitors, we had no problem finding a place to park in one of the many lots surrounding the main attraction, Mucross Castle. There was a large cafeteria, a bakery and some novelty shops, too. Some people were going to take a ride on boats around the Lakes of Killarney, which are famous. Others had rented bikes and were riding the roads in the park. Still, others were sitting in horse-drawn carriages, being driven all around the place. Most were there to walk, like we were going to do.

Our plan was to walk on a manicured, well-traveled path to see the Torc Waterfall about two and a half kilometers from the entrance. We walked past the castle, along the side of one of the lakes, together with dozens of other people—some coming, some going on a well-marked trail.

Neither of us had on walking shoes, but it wasn't a difficult hike, at least not at first. It was flat, level ground with beautiful fields and trees all around us, with the lakes off to our right. It was no problem at all for either of us.

"Look there!" she said, pointing off to her left. I turned and saw a herd of the red deer Ireland is famous for. "I've only read about them. I've never seen them before," she told me.

"We've got the spotted deer in the Phoenix Park Zoo, and they're rare, too, but not these. They're the largest mammals in all of Ireland, and would you look at the one over there . . . the one with the big antlers . . . he's lookin' right at us! Do you see him?" she asked.

I looked and saw, among the dozens of red deer in the herd, this one large male with huge antlers, standing off to the side, looking straight at us.

"He's got the face of a human, doesn't he?" she asked. "Look at him!"

His face did seem to look like that of a man, in some ways, and I agreed.

"Maybe the Druid gods made him become a red deer in this life, like Michael said . . . maybe that's why," she said.

"That wouldn't be all that bad, would it?" I asked. "They're protected here in Ireland. No one can kill them," I said, "and people like us love to see them."

"I think it's best to come back as a human," she answered, "so he must not have been all that good."

I laughed and said, "That's if the Druids got that right. We Catholics don't believe in reincarnation, remember. It's either heaven or hell, there's no in-between. Come to think of it, whatever happened to purgatory? That was like a half-way house. What was wrong with that idea, I wonder?"

Saoirse laughed and said, "I have no idea, but it's like what Michael told us, who knows? I know that deer has the face of a man, that's for sure," she said. "He doesn't look like any deer I've ever seen."

We stood there looking at it, with it looking back at us for several minutes, and then we moved on. It was a sight to see, though. I hadn't seen many of them in my life, either, but here in the park, they were plentiful. Ireland was working hard to grow the herds and restore their numbers to what they once were. They had been hunted to near extinction for years.

Once we got into the woods, the path changed dramatically. It became a dirt trail with rocks and the roots of trees on it, and it was an uphill climb the rest of the way. The path to the waterfall was well marked, and it was well maintained, too, but it was a difficult climb. We stopped to admire the views several times and to catch our breath.

It took us an hour to get there and when we did, we saw the huge waterfall we came to see. Hundreds of people were milling about, going up, down, and around the rocks, trying to get the best view of it. There were no guards or security around, so people were free to walk anywhere they pleased at their own peril. Some went as high up as they could, and others went down into the woods to where the river or stream came out below.

We found a rock not far off the path where we could sit and take some photos. I was tired and glad for the rest. I didn't admit that to Saoirse, though. She looked to be as fresh as a daisy.

It was definitely worth the walk, and I was glad we did it. Being with Saoirse was a massive part of that, but when she asked if I wanted to walk any further, I told her that I'd had enough. I was enjoying just being there with her. I was happy to sit and stay where we were for a while and said so.

"Me, too," she said, "but I'm really glad we did this. It's a beautiful place here. It must have been somethin' to see last weekend when your mother and her friends were here."

"Me Mum said that there were hundreds of Druids here last Sunday, all dressed in their white robes, who caused quite the scene," I told her.

"I imagine that they did," she responded. "What do they do anyway? Do they say prayers and sing songs, as we do?" she asked.

I told her that I hadn't been to one of their ceremonies since I was a little boy, but that's what I remembered—just songs and prayers, nothing much else—no sermons or anything.

"No animal sacrifices?" she asked.

I laughed and said, "None that I can recall."

We sat there, side by side, enjoying the beauty of our surroundings, not saying much. The roar of the water cascading down the mountainside would have made talking difficult in any event. I was still thinking about some of the things Michael had said to us.

It was true. All that I knew came from the Bible, my parents, and the priests. God made everything and that was it. The business of Charles Darwin was just a bunch of his wild theories . . . man evolving from apes and all of that. I didn't give much credence to it, but I couldn't prove that any of it was wrong. Some of the scientific evidence seemed irrefutable, but that didn't explain how it all started.

After what seemed like an hour, though I'm sure it was nowhere near that, we decided to head back. Once the sounds of the water faded, as we were walking along, I said, "You know, Dr. McDuffy never did tell us who or what he thought God was. He told us who he thought might have created this planet and all that is on it, but he never said how it all started, did he?"

She looked at me and said, "No, he didn't. I asked him, but he didn't tell us. He doesn't know, but I wanted to know what he thought. He wanted us to figure that out for ourselves."

"I'm not sure that even he has an answer for that. How does anythin' come from nothin'?" she asked. "No one has a clue about that. Where do atoms, molecules, and the rest come from? Nobody knows."

I shook my head and didn't respond, other than to say, "Not me, that's for sure," I acknowledged. I had no better answer for any of that.

"That's God. That's what I say, just like the church tells us. That's what I think," she said. I didn't respond.

"The walk back was a lot easier than the walk there. It was all downhill. The deer were still in the fields as we walked by, but the big stag was nowhere to be seen.

We arrived back in Cork an hour later, and by then, it was late in the day, nearing sunset. She dropped me off at my apartment, saying that I'd found a good place to live so close to where we worked. As we were saying our goodbyes, she said, "It's sad to think that we may never again see the Dr. McDuffy we saw today, isn't it?"

"It is, and I hope that's not the last time we'll see him that way, but we'll just have to wait and see. Kathleen will be happy to hear all that we have to tell her, won't she?" I asked.

"We did exactly what she told us to do, but I'm not so sure that she's going to be too happy about some of the things he told us," she responded. "I think she truly loves the man and this has got to be bittersweet for her. She knows what awaits him. We'll find out soon enough. See you then. Enjoy your day tomorrow."

I went to church on Sunday and listened carefully to the sermon, still thinking of things Michael had said. On Monday, I had plenty of other things to distract me during the day, as my workload was increasing and other cases required much time and effort, but I found myself looking at the clock every so often, awaiting the time when Kathleen would come knock on my door for our meeting. When she did, she had Colin with her as well. "He wanted to join us today and see how things are going," she told us. "We just came from a meeting with Dr. Delaney."

They both sat silently as Saoirse and I prattled on about all of the things Dr. McDuffy had told us and how well the work on his house had progressed. When we finished telling them all that we had seen and heard, she asked us not to put so much personal information in the report as we had.

"If you don't mind, next time, and in future reports, I would ask you to keep some of his personal beliefs and his thoughts about religion and all, out of there. That's not what is important. What's important is how his brain is functioning."

"You've done well, Sully. You, too, Saoirse. It sounds as if you've been able to help him dramatically," Colin commented. "I'm sure he enjoyed telling you all of that just as much, if not more, than the two of you enjoyed hearin' it. Good for you! Well done!"

Kathleen turned to him and said, solemnly, "They have helped him, and we are helping him. There's no doubt about that whatsoever. We are preparing ourselves, and him, for the next stage of this dreaded illness, whenever that arrives, and we all know it's coming. It's just a matter of when."

Then she brightened and said, "I have news, too, and it's good. I spoke to his daughter over the weekend and she has made arrangements to come see him later this week." Then she turned to me and asked if I had contacted my cousin, the solicitor. I told her that I had called and left a message, but I hadn't spoken to him yet.

"Be sure to follow up on that right away. That's one of the things she wants to get done while she's here, and she'll only be here a week, so we won't have much time. She's also going to want to interview some people who might be able to provide in-home assistance. I'm working on that unless you know of anyone in Sneem who might be able to help," she asked, turning to me.

"Are we there yet, Dr. O'Brien?" Colin asked. "It sounds to me as if the man is still hangin' in there fairly well, though he's a bit jammy now and again, for sure."

Kathleen turned to him, and in a firm but kindly way, said, "This disease is a killer, Colin. It can take a turn for the worse at any time, and once it does, there's no turning back. This is an urgent matter. It can't wait. We must treat it that way. This is the fourth stage, but the next one can begin at any time, and it will be worse, much worse, than this one. Yes, now is the time to do this. I'm sure about that."

Clearly, Colin had overstepped his bounds a bit. He clammed up after that, and Kathleen went on. She had put him in his place.

"She'll be staying at the Westin in Dublin, and I'll drive over to see her there. It's a classic, older hotel that's been fixed up quite nicely . . . a bit on the high side, but that's not of much concern to her. It's near Trinity College where she spent most of her life as a child and as a young adult, so she'll be comfortable there. I have plans to meet her there for dinner when she arrives."

"She might spend a day there and after that, she'll go to Sneem where she'll need to find a place to stay, although she'd like to stay with her Da, if possible, I expect. Is there room for her in the house?" she asked.

I turned to Saoirse who had a blank look on her face. She responded by saying, "I really don't know. We never looked in the bedrooms, so I can't say for sure. I think so. There are two bathrooms, that I know, and there's another room, but I don't know what's in it. It's probably another bedroom, but I can't say for certain about that."

"Well, she'll figure that out. In any event, we must get his Last Will and Testament taken care of and prepare ourselves and the good doctor for what lies ahead. From my conversations with Dr. Delaney, it seems as if Dr. Doherty, the Garda, and the others are relatively satisfied with what's been going on, but again, that could change at any moment. There haven't been any recent incidents or complaints."

"I've told her about the two of you," she said, turning toward Saoirse and me, "and she will want to meet you. If you can, I'd like for you to make arrangements to meet her at least once, either here in Cork or in Sneem, while she's here in Ireland. I think that it's important for her to know who you are."

"Will you be coming down with her?" Saoirse asked.

"I might, but probably not. I'm a bit busy these days," she answered, "and it might confuse him if I did."

I was surprised by her response. I thought that she would want to see the man and the house, as much as we'd talked about him and it. The thought occurred to me, for the first time, that she really didn't want to see Dr. McDuffy for some reason, though that was just a hunch.

With that, she stood and said, "Well, as usual, I'm a little late for my next meeting, so I'm going to have to leave now, but I expect that I will be seeing you later in the week once Caitlin's travel plans are a bit clearer," as she made a quick exit, leaving the three of us sitting there.

Colin turned to us and said, "Is the man fadin' that fast? He was fantastic the day I was there and it sounds as if he's still doin' well. What's the fuss? Dr. O'Brien is takin' quite an interest in this case, isn't she? The man must be a personal friend or somethin' . . . is that it?"

Saoirse answered, saying, "She's known him since her college days when he was one of her professors, so I'm sure that has something to do with it. He's in stage four of the disease at the moment, and things start to get really bad once stage five gets here, Colin. She's telling us to be prepared for what is to come."

"Stage five is it? What's that all about?" he asked.

I answered and said, "She's had the two of us reading books about Alzheimer's, and from what I've gathered, that's when they require assistance with daily living. People aren't able to prepare meals, wash clothes, and they don't take care of their personal hygiene as well as they should—things like that."

"You mean like you? Of course, I know what that means, you clod!" he responded. "And they get more forgetful . . . forgetting things like their address, phone numbers, and personal information . . .

things like that. Things are going to get worse. I know that," he said. "But I was askin' what our response is going to be to all of that? What's the plan?" he asked.

"In-home care, for one thing, Colin. I guess that's what's next. Other than that, there's not much we can do for the man except help him as best we can," Saoirse told him.

"Is he needin' all that help right away, do you think?" he asked. "I thought getting the house fixed would solve most of the problems and then they'd leave him alone. Was I wrong?" he asked.

"He's done some pretty strange things lately, Colin, and I've seen him when he's in some of those troublesome conditions a couple of times since you've been there when all this started, so it's not all smooth sailing these days, by any stretch, though it has been for us most of the time. I'm not sure why she thinks it's that urgent, but she does. She's the expert," I answered.

"Well, from what he was able to tell the two of you on Saturday, it seems to me that he's still pretty sharp," he said. "We've got lots of cases a whole lot more worrisome than this one, that's for sure," he responded.

"Kathleen says that things can change quickly. She says it's not unusual for people to be able to remember things from years ago better than they do things that happened more recently, like last week," she told him.

"I know that, too, Saoirse," he responded. "I was teaching your class on geriatrics a while back, remember?"

"I remember, but it's one thing to read it in a book, and quite another to actually see it happening," she responded.

"And they have good days where they are fairly lucid, and bad days when they're not too coherent," I added. "That's a common thing, too, Colin, so yesterday was one of his lucid days. Maybe he's having a really bad day today. That's what happened the last time we talked to him. I hope not, but we don't know."

"It's called 'Moderately Severe Cognitive Decline,'" Saoirse added.

"You two seem to forget . . . I'm the third-year student here! I've handled quite a few of these cases over the years, thank you very much. I'm just sayin' that this man is a whole lot better than any other patient I've seen since I've been here, okay? That's all, but it seems as if you're takin' quite an interest in the man and his case, and you're learning a lot about geriatric patients, which is good," he said. "Maybe that's what you'll do when you get out of this place."

"Remember, we're only here for a few years and then we move on. Keep your eyes on the target. What are you gonna do when you get out of here? Have you figured that out?" he asked. "Is this the kind of stuff you want to be doing?"

"Not likely," I told him. "I'm still more interested in helpin' the kids, but I've enjoyed meeting this man, that's for sure."

"Me, neither," Saoirse said, "but this case is going to make a great thesis paper. He's an extremely interesting man . . . world-famous, in fact. It's been an honor to meet him. My Da can't believe it. He thought I'd be dealin' with nothin' but people who can't afford real professional help. He was shocked when I told him how I was meeting with Dr. Michael McDuffy."

"If I had any idea he was that was anywhere near as good as he is, I'd have stayed on the case and kept the two of you squids out of it completely. That's the kind of people I want to work with . . . the ones with money!"

His eyes lit up when he said that, and he rubbed his fingers together as he said it. We laughed, thinking that he didn't really mean what he said, but he might have. He couldn't wait to get out of St. Stephen's and he had no qualms about letting everyone know it. He had another six months or so before he'd be able to finish up and move on, and he was ready to leave now.

I think Saoirse and I were just happy to be getting some experience, and working with Dr. Delaney and Dr. O'Brien on a case as fascinating as this one was the cherry on top. Without a doubt, it was one of the most interesting cases to work on in the entire department. Others had gotten wind of it and were quite jealous of us, in fact.

Later that week, Kathleen stopped by and told me that Caitlin was hoping to meet with us in Sneem on Saturday morning. She wanted to know if we could be there then. I told her that I was planning on it, but Saoirse couldn't make it, much to my disappointment, and hers.

CHAPTER SEVENTEEN

Caitlin McDuffy Golding

I arrived in Sneem late Friday afternoon and met me Da, Rory, Siobhan, and Patrick at the Blue Bull restaurant for dinner. Kevin, Deidre and Maura couldn't make it. We had a lively conversation and a nice meal. For the first time, ever, I was the center of attention.

Although I hadn't moved too far, I was the one living furthest away from home. They asked lots of questions about Cork and what it was like to live in a big city as I did. They were all culchies, and quite happily so.

Cork is the second largest city in the Republic with over two-hundred thousand people in it. The next two, Limerick and Galway, didn't have half as many. There are only about a hundred and fifty thousand people in all of County Kerry. Dublin, of course, had over five times as many as we did in Cork, however, with well over a million people. With less than six hundred people in it, Sneem is a tiny, little village in comparison.

I spent the night with me Da and stopped in at Kelly's Bakery early the next morning for some coffee and a couple of scones, which was becoming an enjoyable habit, before heading out to Dr. McDuffy's place. I was in no hurry as I expected Caitlin to arrive much later on, coming from Dublin as I figured she was. I didn't get there until well past 10:00.

Seamus was on the roof, busily working away. It seemed to me as if he had completely finished repairing the damaged part and was now just touching things up, adding things here and there, to make the thatched roof look like it was one continuous thing, not an add-on. It looked perfect to me as it was, just like the typical Irish cottages I'd seen all over the island or in paintings and on postcards. Even the front of the house appeared to be a brighter shade of white.

When Dr. McDuffy greeted me, I asked him about that. "Did you have the place painted as well? Your house looks absolutely grand!"

"I did that meself," he told me, pointing to the front of the house. "I only got as far as the front here, where you're looking. It was a little too much for me. I didn't do all that well, but it does look better, doesn't it?"

I agreed.

"My daughter is here," he told me excitedly, "and she's very happy with what's been done. She arrived yesterday."

I was surprised to hear that and said something about it. I realized immediately that I said the wrong thing, because he gave me a look as if to say how did I know she was coming. Fortunately, he let it pass and didn't ask any questions about how I knew anything about that.

"She got here late yesterday morning, by train," he told me. "Actually, she took a train to Killarney and then she rented a car to get from there to here. She should be back any time now. She just went into town to buy a few things."

"She called me the night before last and told me she was coming. It was a bit of a shock, actually. We've been talking more lately, but I wasn't expecting a visit. It's been a few years since I've seen her, and that was when Marjorie and I went over there to see her and her brother and their families in California. She hasn't been here in several years, not since the funeral."

I still wasn't sure exactly when it was that Marjorie died, but I wasn't going to ask him. Caitlin would know. I'd ask her.

"I bought a few gallons of paint and some brushes to get started, but I made a huge mess of things. I'll not do that again," he added. "I'll get someone else to help me with that."

Then he turned to me and asked, "In fact, would you be willing to finish it for me, Brendan? I'll gladly pay you."

At first, I declined because I'm not all that handy of a fellow, but then, as I thought about it, I said to myself, "Why not?" I could paint. I wouldn't do as good a job as a professional, but I could do it. I didn't really care about the money, though I could certainly use it, and I knew that he would probably have a hard time finding someone to do the work for him, so I agreed.

"That's marvelous!" he said, "Let's get you to work!"

"Now?" I asked. I wasn't quite prepared for that.

"Why not? No time better than the present," he answered.

I couldn't think of a good reason not to, so I agreed to start right then and there. I had an old top and a pair of buffers in the back of my car, so I put them on and the two of us walked out to the shed to get what I needed to go to work. Within fifteen minutes of my arrival, I was putting paint on the walls. They definitely needed it. The walls soaked up the paint and it made an immediate difference.

Seamus saw what I was doing and yelled something to me, which I couldn't understand. He was way up at the top of the roof, at the pitch. It looked dangerous to me, but I was sure that he knew what he was doing. I just waved back at him and gave him a thumbs up.

Half an hour later as I was busily slapping white paint on the backside of the house, I heard a car pull in. I put down the brush, washed my hands as best I could, and walked out front to see who it was. I expected it to be Caitlin, but it could have been Rory, the mailman, or someone else. I didn't know.

I saw a tall, thin, elegantly dressed, older woman carrying several bags of groceries. For some reason, I was expecting her to be younger. Then I realized that since Dr. McDuffy was in his early to mid-eighties, that she was probably in her early sixties. She was quite attractive, though, however old she was.

She was surprised, if not shocked, to learn that I was the Brendan Sullivan of whom Kathleen had told her. "You're Brendan Sullivan?" she asked, dubiously.

"I am indeed," I told her. "I've just been enlisted to help your father paint his house. I don't claim to be much of a painter, but I'll do my best. This front part is your Da's handiwork."

"Yes, I know," she said with a grimace, looking at the partially completed front of the house, which still needed some work.

"I'm glad to help," I told her.

"Well, it's nice to meet you, Mr. Sullivan, and I thank you for what you've done to help my father," she said.

When I asked, she said, "Yes, I caught a train from Dublin to Killarney yesterday morning, which took a little over three hours, and then I rented a car there. I arrived late morning. I flew into Dublin on Thursday and had a nice visit with Kathleen there that night."

"I took my father to see your cousin yesterday afternoon," she continued, "and we took care of a few things that needed to be done. I thank you for making those arrangements for me as well."

I hadn't even spoken to my cousin, the solicitor, but my father must have. I didn't know, but I took the credit, saying that I was glad to help.

"And it was your brother who has done all the work fixing this place up, have I got that right?" she asked.

When I confirmed for her that she was correct, she said, "And I met Seamus earlier this morning, just as I was leaving for town. He's quite a character, that one."

I chuckled and agreed. "He's the best! It's hard to find anyone who can do thatched roofs anymore, but my brother knew Seamus, and that's how we found him," I told her. "I had never met him before, either. My brother gets all the credit for that."

"It looks absolutely marvelous," she said, "especially on the inside."

"Now my brother did all of that, and he does good work, too, if I do say so myself," I said somewhat proudly. "He was glad to help. The two of them get all the credit for what's been done. I'm just the go-between, so to speak."

"He's being modest, Caitlin," Michael interjected. "He's been a godsend," he told her.

"Well, I know who you are, Mr. Sullivan. Kathleen told me all about you and your lady friend. My brother and I thank you for all that you've done for our father, and we want to compensate you for that," she said.

When I told her that was all part of my job and that I didn't expect to receive any money for that, except for the painting I was doing, she whispered, so that her father couldn't hear her, "Your work is not yet done here, Mr. Sullivan, but we can talk about that later. Let's go inside and have a little chat if you don't mind."

I was truly a mess at that point with paint all over my hands, my arms, my clothes . . . everyplace . . . and she could sense my reluctance to go inside, so she added, "after you finish what you're doing and clean up a bit. We're in no hurry. I don't have to leave until tomorrow afternoon, so I'll be here all day."

I agreed and went back to work as she and Michael went inside to unload the groceries and other supplies she had purchased.

I wasn't doing a great job, by any means, but the contrast was so dramatic that it looked much, much better and I was being given the credit for that. Both she and Michael were delighted with what I had done. I had more to do, but when I ran out of paint, I was done for the day. Seamus was coming down the ladder as I was finishing up.

I still had another wall to do, plus I didn't do any of the trim work, like the wood around the windows or up near the top where the thatched roof joined up with the walls. I was glad to call it a day. I could come back to do that next weekend, and maybe bring Saoirse with me. There was no hurry with that, not like there was with the roof.

By that time, I saw Seamus on the ground loading his tools in his truck. I cleaned up the mess I'd made as fast as I could, washing the brushes and all. As I was putting the ladder I'd used to reach the higher up spots back in his shed, I thought to myself that it needed to be sorted out. It was a complete mess. That was something Saoirse could definitely help with, next time, while I was painting.

I walked up to where the three of them were standing, next to Seamus' truck. I watched as Caitlin paid him, in cash, the balance of what was owed now that the job was finished. I heard him say that US dollars were fine, though I couldn't see them or hear how much it was.

She and her father thanked him profusely for the work he had done, saying how good it looked. There was no doubt about that. It was as if an entirely new roof had been put on.

It was a shame, really, that no one had taken a picture of what it looked like before he began his work. It would have been quite a "before and after" shot, especially with the fresh coat of white paint. Seamus thanked them for the compliments but was disappointed when told that no one would be joining him for a pint in town, not even me.

I said that I'd go if the others did, but Caitlin told him that she was only there for one more day and had too many things to do around the house before she left. Dr. McDuffy apologized, explaining how his daughter had come from America to see him and he couldn't go if she didn't. He swore that he would join him any other time he happened to be in town and made him promise to call if he was ever in the neighborhood. The two men embraced, had a few laughs, and he drove off, leaving the three of us standing there watching as he did.

Caitlin looked at me as if to say that I was still in no condition to come inside without actually saying it. I took the cue and told her that I needed a few minutes to change clothes and would be joining them shortly.

"Take your time. I think I'll take a little walk down the road here with my father. We'll be back in a jiffy," she said as she took him by the arm and the two of them sauntered out to the road at a leisurely pace.

"You're welcome to go inside if you'd like, Brendan," he told me. I thanked him and said that wouldn't be necessary.

"The water hose and a towel are all I need. I'll be fine, thanks," I told him.

They weren't gone long, and by the time they returned, I was cleaned up as well as could be. I'd need a good shower for the rest of me, but that could wait. The three of us walked into the house toward the fireplace area.

It was now mid-October and a bit chilly. A fire was burning brightly. Caitlin had added some flowers, hung a few pictures and photographs, and otherwise spruced up the inside since I'd been there the week before.

"There's nothing like a turf fire," she said as she put her hands over the burning logs.

"They don't have the turves in America?" I asked.

"No, they don't," she answered.

"Not even the briquettes, as most do even here?" I continued. "That's what I've been told. Is that true?" I asked.

"Yes, it is," she answered. "I don't know why. I've tried to get them, without success. It would seem to me to be a good business for an enterprising Irishman to get involved with . . . no smoke, slow-burning, and more heat, but for whatever reason, it hasn't happened. I think it's because they're so heavy that the cost of shipping makes it too expensive."

"I can buy the little things Irish-Americans love to buy for gifts at Christmas and all, but they're quite costly and more of a novelty than anything else. So, this is grand for me to be standing in front of a turf fire with my father as I am. I have so many pleasant memories of doing so as a child, right, Da?" she asked as she put her arms around him.

Dr. McDuffy made an approving noise of some kind. He was mostly quiet, not as talkative as usual, but clearly pleased to have his daughter there with him. Caitlin was basically interviewing me, making sure that I was acceptable for what she had in mind for her father going forward.

"Your father has shown me pictures of you and your family from back in those days. You had a beautiful family," I told her, trying my best to favorably impress her.

"Still do, don't we Da?" she said as she squeezed him once again.

"That's right. We do," he responded with a tender look. "I just don't get to see them as much as I would like anymore."

"How long have you been in America?" I asked.

"My brother and I moved there over thirty years ago," she answered. "We don't get back as often as we used to, not since our mother died. We used to see each other at least once a year during all those years, and usually twice a year . . . once here and once there."

"How long ago was that when you were here last?" I asked.

She turned to me with a questioning look, as if to say, "why did you ask such a question," and answered, "It will be seven years ago next month. In fact, next Sunday, it will be exactly seven years, right Da?" she asked. "That was for my mother's funeral."

Again, he grunted a positive response, and then she added, "and we miss her every day, don't we, Da?"

"That we do," he agreed, looking stonily into the fire.

I didn't ask how long it had been since they had seen each other, but I got the feeling that Dr. McDuffy hadn't traveled to the United States since the funeral and they hadn't seen each other since then. I wondered if Caitlin could tell that there had been some substantial changes in him since she had last seen him, but that was none of my business. I wasn't going to ask about that. I'd let Kathleen handle those issues.

"Let's sit down and have a little chat, shall we?" Caitlin said as she took a seat on the couch, maneuvering her father so that he sat down next to her, "and you sit next to me here, Da, if you will." I sat in Michael's chair.

"I'll be flying back to California early Monday morning. The Fall semester has just begun and I really must get back, though I'd like to stay longer. I'm going to be staying in close contact with my father, though, and I'm going to come back and spend more time here once the opportunity presents itself. I'll be keeping a close eye on things until then.

"Dr. O'Brien speaks highly of you, Mr. Sullivan, and if you're agreeable, I'd like to stay in touch with you, if you don't mind," she said. "I'd like to be able to call you every now and then to see how things are going. Are you willing to do that for us?" she asked.

I was surprised to hear her mention Kathleen's name because neither Saoirse nor I had ever said anything about her to him before, so I asked somewhat gingerly, "Does your father know Dr. O'Brien?"

"He does, indeed," she responded, "She was one of his best students. I remember her from those days, too, though I am much younger than she is. We've seen each other every now and again over the years, but it'd been years since I'd last seen her. I still consider her to be a close friend of the family."

"My father had a tradition of inviting students . . . not all of them, mind you, only the best, or his favorites, over to our house around the holidays. She was there many, many times, for years. She stands out."

"There was a time there that my Mum was a bit jealous of her, wasn't she, Da?" she asked teasingly, looking over at him as she did. He didn't respond to that comment, other than a little snicker.

"Does he know that I know her, too?" I asked, wondering if he knew of her involvement in this case and how I came to meet her father.

She looked at me and said, "Yes, he does, Brendan. I hope you don't mind me calling you that. My children are older than you are. It seems more appropriate."

I assured her that I didn't mind. I preferred it. "Of course," I answered. "To be honest, I'm not quite used to being called Mr. Sullivan. I keep looking to see if my father is in the room whenever I hear someone say that name."

"So, are you agreeable to that?" she asked.

When I told her that I was, she said, "That's wonderful. My brother and I very much appreciate that." Then she paused for a few moments and then added, "My father is an extremely intelligent man, Brendan. He's still sharp as a tack, at times. He's just getting older, and living alone as he does doesn't help things, does it, Da?"

This time, he made no response whatsoever.

She continued, "He considers you to be his friend and he likes you, and I've had a candid conversation with him about all that is going on with him and why Kathleen is involved. It was necessary that we do that while we were with your cousin, the solicitor, when executing those documents yesterday. He asked my father a rather large number of pointed questions. My father didn't like that very much, did you, Da?"

This time, Dr. McDuffy responded by saying, "No, I didn't," but didn't elaborate, keeping his head turned away, looking toward the fire.

She went on, "He doesn't agree with everything we have planned for him, but he understands that he is having some problems with daily chores, getting around, things like that, and needs some assistance. That's where you and some others come in, right, Da?"

He was still looking at the fire, off to his left, and didn't respond. I wondered just how much of what was going on he really understood, but I didn't ask.

"He's just a stubborn, old Irishman, that's all. He wants to keep things just as they are, right, Da?" she asked again in a jocular tone of voice.

This time, he grunted a positive response and said, "That I am and that I do."

"I've discussed this with my brother and he, too, wants you to be our contact person on this here in Sneem," she continued. "He'll be calling you sometime before too long after I tell him about meeting you and of our conversation."

"That will be fine," I said.

"You'll be under Kathleen's supervision, of course, and you'll be paid for your services," she said.

I was reluctant to talk about St. Stephen's, Dr. O'Brien, or anything to do with why I was there, other than to help with getting the house fixed up as I did, and I was sure that she could sense that.

When I didn't respond immediately, she said, "Brendan, can we speak openly?"

"Of course," I responded, "if you think that's best."

"My father realizes that he has become a bit more forgetful as he gets older, and we discussed these things for hours last night. He accepts the fact that he can use a little help now and again, and he has agreed to allow us to provide that for him. That includes you."

"At first, he was totally against it, but now, after hours of debate, argument, and discussion, he's willing to give it a try. He has a better understanding of what's happening to him," she said. "He's not pleased with it, by any means, but he's got to accept the reality of the situation, and he does."

"He does?" I asked. "Really?" I knew that he was aware of the fact that he was having a few problems. He had admitted that to me, but I didn't think he understood that he had dementia. To my knowledge, he knew nothing about any of that. "Everything?" I asked.

It was an important question, but she gave me a strange look and said, somewhat firmly, "Yes, he does, Brendan, and so do my brother and I."

I still didn't know what that meant. I was as sure as I could be that he didn't fully understand what was going to happen to him before too long, and I was beginning to wonder if she did, but I wasn't about to mention the big "A" word. Instead, I said, hoping to get a laugh out of him, "He definitely needs some help with the painting, right, Michael?"

And then I added before he had time to answer, "Not to mention a ride to Dan Murphy's Bar every now and again!"

He looked over at me, smiled, and said, "That I do, lad . . . that I do."

Caitlin continued and said, "As I told you, we talked about a number of things when we met with the solicitor yesterday afternoon, and we talked for several hours last night about all of those things. We're here to help. He knows that."

"He's given me his Power of Attorney for some of these legal matters. He knows that my brother and I love him and that we will do everything we can to help. He understands that we're doing this for him, right, Da?"

He looked over at her and smiled, but said, "I appreciate that, Caitlin, but I don't need as much help as you think I do. Now that the house is fixed up, I still say that I'll be fine without any of that."

"Now let's not get into that again," she said in a kind but firm voice. "You can't drive and you need lots of help around the house and you know it!"

"Why can't he drive?" I asked. "Is it because of his age?" I knew he couldn't drive, but I didn't know why not.

"No, she responded. It's because of his eyes. He doesn't see too well anymore . . . glaucoma. They wouldn't re-issue his license the last time it came up for renewal. When was that, Da?"

"I don't remember. It's been a few years," he responded. "It was sometime after your mother died. I'm glad she wasn't around when that happened. I always did all of the driving."

"So, you know that you need help with getting around . . . you can't walk all over the place anymore, and there will be times when you will need to go to Cork or Dublin," she told him.

"I can take the bus," he responded.

"No, you can't . . . not everywhere, and let's not talk about the house or the fridge, Da. It was sheer mank in here when I arrived. It took me an hour to clean the fridge! You know that! You saw me do it!"

"And the food! It's lucky you're alive! There was no food fit for eating in there at all! But let's not go into any more of that, please. We agreed on all of that last night, didn't we?" she asked.

He grunted another response. It was clear that he was willing to go along with all that she had proposed, but he wasn't happy about it.

"So, he's agreed to allow us to have someone come into the house," she said. "And that's that. We'll have no more discussion about it, right Da?" she asked.

"Only to cook and clean," Dr. McDuffy responded, "and to drive me places every now and then."

"That's right . . . to cook and clean and look after things . . . like wash your clothes, make the bed, buy you groceries, take you to the doctor's office, when need be . . . things like that. Clearly, he's not happy about it, but he's agreed to go along with it . . . but . . . we must find the right person."

"I want it to be a beautiful, young, red-headed Irish girl!" he said. He chuckled as he said that.

"Yes, I know, Da," she responded with a laugh. "And if we can find such a girl who is willing to put up with you, that's exactly what you'll get."

Then she turned back to me and said, "And he's agreed to allow you to be a part of the process."

I looked over at him, and he glanced back at me with an approving look, without saying a word.

"If you're agreeable to that part, too, that is," she added. "There's more to this than just the painting and the occasional odd job around the house," she added.

"I'm fine with all of that," I responded. "But what did Dr. O'Brien say?" I asked without revealing that I was an employee of the hospital. She knew, but I was pretty sure that he didn't.

"She said that it was fine with her. She'll be talking to you about all of that next time you see her," she told me.

Then I thought of Saoirse and I said, "I know a beautiful, red-headed Irish girl who might be willing to help. She couldn't be here every day, but she would be part of the team, I think, if that's okay with you, Michael."

"You mean Saoirse?" he asked. When I told him that's exactly who I had in mind, he said with a smile, "I'll have no trouble with her. She's a keeper, Brendan. She'd be just fine."

I started to explain to Caitlin who she was and she said, "I know all about her as well, and that's fine with me, too. The two of you can work together, but I mean someone who can be here every day."

"Every couple of days," Dr. McDuffy interjected.

"Every day, Father! We talked about this . . . she doesn't have to stay all day, just come every day . . . she'll cook you your breakfast, fix lunch for you, clean up the house a bit, and then she'll be gone. On occasion, she'll take you places you'll need to go. You're going to be glad to have her. Just give this a chance. You agreed to all of this already!" she said.

He grumbled something I couldn't understand. It was obvious that he wasn't happy about any part of the plan Caitlin had devised. Even though it was obvious that he needed the help, he resisted it, but he was going to go along with it.

"She can even help you buy some presents for your great-grandchildren, Da . . . you have a few of them now, don't you know? I'll bet you don't even know their names . . . she can help with that, too," she told him.

Dr. McDuffy grumbled but didn't say anything. I piped up and said, "I'll be happy to help in any way that I can, especially that part about taking him to Murphy's pub every now and again. I think I might make that one of my regular chores. It's a dirty job, but someone has to do it, right?"

He grunted approvingly when I said that. Actually, it was almost a laugh, but not quite. This was a serious matter, and he knew it.

"That's wonderful," she responded as she handed me a hundred euro note. When I saw what it was, I said that it was too much, but she persisted, thrusting it back into my hands, "That's for the work you did today on the house. It's just a starter. We'll pay you more when you finish."

Then, she gave me another hundred euro note and said, "That's for your friend . . . what's her name?"

"Saoirse O'Connor," I told her.

"And tell Saoirse that I'm . . . we, I should say, that includes my brother . . . are looking forward to meeting her. He's planning to come over as soon as he can, but he can't break away for at least another month or so. I think he's planning to be here over what's called the Thanksgiving Holidays in America, and stay for a week or more. That's in late November and I'm going to try to be here when he comes. If not, I'll be back over the Christmas holidays."

With that, she extended her hand and said, "Do we have a deal?"

"I guess so," I answered. I was surprised by the whole conversation, but I was willing to stay on with the man, and I was absolutely delighted to know that Saoirse was approved to be working with me on this case as well. The fact that we would be paid for it was the cherry on top.

We shook hands, and then she stood as if to say that the conversation was over and it was time for me to leave. I stood, too, as did Dr. McDuffy.

"Thanks for all you've done for us, Brendan," she said. "We appreciate it."

"I thank you, too," Dr. McDuffy said. "You've been a godsend."

"It's been my pleasure," I told him, and that was the truth, "and you're welcome, Mrs. . . ."

"Caitlin," she said. "Caitlin McDuffy Golding, but please call me Caitlin." Then she added, "Kathleen is making all of the arrangements for finding us just the right people to be with him here in the house, and . . ."

Dr. McDuffy interrupted and said in a louder than normal voice, "Person, Caitlin . . . just one!"

"Yes, well . . . it will start out as just the one person, but there will be others, Da. She's got to have a day off every now and again, and she might get sick a time or two, so there will be more than one. You know that," she told him.

"Kathleen has all of your contact information, and I'll be dealing with her, primarily, but I'm sure that I'll be talking to you again in the very near future, Brendan. Again, thank you so much for what you've done for my father," she said as she shook my hand again and ushered me out the door.

"It's been my pleasure," I repeated.

When my feet were outside, the door closed behind me. She was a business-like person—very pretty but all business, and she had to get back to America and the life she had created for herself over there.

Clearly, money would be no object when it came to the kind of care her father would receive.

It was obvious that Dr. McDuffy would be cared for as much as humanly possible, but I thought to myself that neither one of them really knew what lay ahead. From what I had read and what I had been told, dark days . . . very dark days . . . were on the horizon.

Today had been another good one, however. I felt good about all that had been done and all that I was about to do for the man. Kathleen's game-plan was working well.

Dr. McDuffy had been on his best behavior, and he hadn't shown any signs of a diminishing brain in the conversation, but I hadn't given much thought to how he cooked, cleaned, or did all of those other daily activities. Clearly, he needed the help. There was no doubt about that and he should appreciate the assistance, though it might take some time for him to get used to it.

As I drove back to Cork, I thought about all that had transpired that morning and was confused by it all. It was as if there was a six-hundred-pound gorilla in the room, but nobody talked about it. We all knew that Alzheimer's disease was, quite likely, in his future, but those issues were basically ignored. Did he know? We certainly didn't talk about it while I was there, not in front of him.

Dr. McDuffy and his daughter were two extremely intelligent people, so wasn't it best for us to openly discuss the medical issues of dementia and Alzheimer's disease with them? Was it best to ignore the problem, as far as the patient was concerned? Is that what clinical psychologists thought was the best way to address the problem?

But what was the best way to deal with the problem? I thought to myself that many people would rather commit suicide than go through that. I sure wouldn't want to go through it. I didn't know what I would do if I were in his shoes.

Today, he was lucid, and he had successfully executed his Last Will and Testament and all of the other necessary documents. He'd given his daughter a Power of Attorney to handle some of his legal affairs. That, too, was a serious matter. I wondered if he fully understood all of the documents he had signed yesterday and the legal consequences of all of that.

My cousin, the solicitor, must have thought he was competent to sign those documents, or else he wouldn't have allowed them to be executed. I did, although there were undoubtedly times within the recent past when he wouldn't have been able to do so. Fortunately, all of that was now taken care of.

As I drove home, I reflected back on all that had been accomplished in the last week and felt as if the treatment plan orchestrated by Kathleen was going exactly as she wanted it to. The home was completely fixed up, his Last Will and Testament had been executed, and arrangements were being made for some help to keep him in his home. Plus, Saoirse and I were officially designated as liaisons between the family and him.

I was sure that Kathleen would be pleased, and so was I. I couldn't wait to tell Saoirse all about it. That was still the part that interested me the most in all of this, working with her, that is, . . . and now we were to be paid for it, but I cared for the man, I did.

I now considered him to be more of a friend than a client. In fact, I was proud to say that I was a friend of the great Dr. M. Michael McDuffy. I was. But what about him? What was going through his mind? Deep down, what was he thinking about all of this? I didn't know.

CHAPTER EIGHTEEN

The Professor Emeritus

That Monday, Kathleen was in a particularly good mood when we met. "I congratulate the two of you for a job well done," she began. "As you know, I met with Dr. McDuffy's daughter last week and I talked with her again this morning before she left. She couldn't be more delighted with what we have accomplished."

"Of course, it is a war that we will lose, and she understands that, but we have won several battles here recently, and I give the two of you much of the credit," she said.

Saoirse interjected that I was the one who deserved most of the credit, but Kathleen would hear none of it. "The two of you, together, deserve the credit . . . we're a team . . . but we're not done yet," she told us.

I hadn't had an opportunity to tell Saoirse that I had volunteered her to continue to work on Dr. McDuffy's case, but Caitlin had, quite obviously, told Kathleen all about that, because she went on to say, "I'm delighted to learn that the two of you, on your own time, totally independent from what we're doing here at St. Stephen's, will be providing further assistance to the man. I have discussed the situation with Dr. Delaney and he has no problem with your doing so. He will continue to be our patient, and you will be required to do various things in connection with that, as well, however."

Saoirse looked over at me with a puzzled look on her face, but Kathleen wasn't finished talking, so I couldn't explain things to her.

"Also, he has spoken to Dr. Doherty who is satisfied with all that has been done or is to be done, so there won't be any further proceedings in that regard, either. I am to meet with people at a couple of local agencies to find the best possible candidates to provide the in-home services that will be needed. That's the next important goal to accomplish, and I'll take care of that."

"Once I have selected the person, or persons, who will be providing those services, I will want the two of you to meet them at Dr. McDuffy's home. Again, you two will be my eyes and ears on this. I will want to continue to meet with you on a weekly basis, as we have been doing for some time now, and receive your reports. Please do your best to keep the time spent on things relating to our work here at the hospital separate from the time you spend on things that you will be doing that are more personal to Dr. McDuffy. He is, officially, still our patient."

"Dr. Delaney has no problem with you being paid for your time and efforts which are separate and apart from what you are required to do here at the hospital. When you go over to Sneem on weekends or holidays, on days when you're not to be here at the hospital, you have his permission to be compensated by the family for that time. That's only fair."

She paused for a moment to gather her thoughts, and then she said, "I think we've accomplished all of our short-term and mid-term goals, and I couldn't be happier about it. We are as prepared as we can be for what is to come."

"Of course, much of this was possible because of the support of his two children. As you no doubt observed, money will be no object when it comes to providing the best possible care for the man. That certainly isn't the situation for most of our clients, however, as you no doubt have learned by now."

She paused again and asked, "Now, before I go any further, to talk about what's next, do the two of you have any questions?"

I asked, "If you don't mind, Dr. O'Brien . . ."

"Kathleen, please, Brendan," she interjected. "I don't want to have to tell you again."

"If you don't mind, Kathleen, would you tell us just how well you know Caitlin McDuffy? I think it would help me, or us, to better understand the relationship between you and the family. I wasn't sure just how much I should share with her when I met with her on Saturday."

My question surprised her a bit, and she took a few seconds to respond. "That's a fair question," she began. "And you're right, I am having some rather frank discussions with her, and I don't think it's necessary for either of the two of you to know of those conversations or to have such conversations with her. Suffice it to say that we know each other well enough that it is not your typical doctor-patient-family member relationship.

"In fact, this case is unique in many ways, but Dr. McDuffy is a rare bird . . . he's a treasure, actually. We may never have seen a person of his ilk before here at the hospital. His kind of people, and by that, I mean those of his intellect and stature, are almost always dealt with by private physicians."

"I don't want you to think that he's being given preferential treatment because of my friendship with the man and his family, but there is, truly, no question but that he is being treated somewhat differently from others. It would be difficult to deny that, given all that we are doing in this case. Again, I think that's because of how his brain is functioning, and where he is in the disease process, more so than who he is."

"We try to provide the best possible care to all of our patients, though it's fairly obvious that he is being given more attention than most. There's no denying that. I can justify all of that as being the result of his intellect and his current situation, as I said."

"This is just such an unusual case. Look at the things he said to you this weekend! The man is absolutely brilliant when he is having lucid moments, as he did with the two of you last Saturday. This is an entirely different situation from any other that we have ever had to deal with here at the hospital, without any question whatsoever, so my relationship with the family is irrelevant, really."

Clearly, I had hit a nerve. I wished I hadn't asked the question, but the cat was out of the bag on that one.

She leaned back in her chair, took a deep breath, and said, "But, I guess that there's no harm in telling you a little more about how I know the man. I don't want to see any of this in a report, though, and it's to be kept private between the three of us, agreed?"

When we both responded affirmatively, she continued,

"As I may have told you, but I don't think so, he taught a course entitled the *History and Philosophy of Religion in the Western Civilization* that I took my first year at Trinity College. I was absolutely enthralled by the class and by the professor. From that point on, I took every course he taught."

"In fact, I chose it as my minor so that I could receive credit for doing so. Otherwise, those courses would have been 'electives,' and I would have had to spend much more time, and money, to graduate. I always planned to do what I now do, but I deviated from that, to some extent, during that period in my life, and it was because of him. I was totally captivated by the man and the topics he cared so much about."

"It sounds like you were in love with the man," Saoirse said with a grin. "Were you?" she asked.

Kathleen blushed and said, "I was, indeed. I admit it, but he was married by then and nothing ever came of it, although I carried a torch for him for quite a few years, it's true. I wasn't the only one, mind you! There were plenty of other young women just like me in that regard. He was absolutely the best professor I ever had. He was brilliant, and he was extraordinarily handsome, too."

"He would have students over to his house around the holidays, several times a year, and I was always in attendance. I knew the two children from the time they were young pups until they went away to America, and that was after they obtained their degrees from Trinity. I even baby-sat for Caitlin and Patrick on several occasions."

"So, I knew the two of them, all four of them, actually, quite well. I was sad when they left, and he was devastated to see them go, both at about the same time, too. I think that they wanted to get out from underneath his shadow . . . and he cast quite a large shadow over them, indeed."

"I lost touch with the family when that happened. I had obtained my doctorate in Clinical Psychology by then, just as the two of you might do, and began working in this field. I received a wonderful education at Trinity, and I have Dr. McDuffy to thank for much of that. Besides my father and my two grandfathers, he is, or was, the most influential man in my life, so there you have it," she told us.

"That's why I have taken such an interest in his case. I supervise a large staff of qualified professionals, as you know. This is the only case in which I am as personally involved as I am, and I'm glad to have the opportunity to be able to help the man as we are doing, to repay him, so to speak, in some small way for what he did for me."

"Even now, and I do mean to this very day, he is considered a Professor Emeritus at Trinity. If you mention his name at the College, people will remember him and speak well of him. He enjoyed and continues to enjoy, an excellent reputation. I don't want to see anything done to tarnish that," she said emphatically. "That is for certain."

"But you don't want to see him?" Saoirse asked. "Don't you think he'll remember you?"

"Caitlin and Patrick do, but I doubt that he does. It's been so long ago. He had many students who admired him as I did. I wasn't the only one, as I said before," she responded.

"Besides, I'd rather remember him as he was, and as I was, too," she said with a giggle. "I have nothing but pleasant memories from those days. It was silly, really, but I did admire him so very much, it's true," she told us with a somewhat rueful smile on her face.

"So, have I answered your question, Brendan?" she asked. "Does it help you understand the man, and who he is, or was, and my involvement in the case? I care for the man and I want the two of you to like him as a person, as well," she told us.

"I think it's important for the two of you, as budding clinical psychologists, to learn to care for your patients," she added, "not to get too emotionally involved, mind you, but to truly care for and empathize with your clients and what they're going through, and that includes their families."

"I wish I'd had a professor like that," Saoirse said.

I thanked her for sharing that with us and told her that it helped me understand things a little better, and then I said, "I remember meeting him for the first time in Kenmare, when I had no idea who or what he was. I thought that I would never see him again. I'm glad

I was wrong. It was a real treat to hear him tell us all about his days as a Professor of the Antiquities."

"It was fantastic," Saoirse added.

"I'm sure it was," she responded. "Again, I would have loved to have been there."

"I think you should come with us one day to see him," Saoirse said. "I think he would love to see you, and I'm pretty sure he'll remember you. He mentioned your name, by accident, the other day," she told her.

"He did?" she asked. "How did that happen?

When we told her how it came about, she said it was just a slip of the tongue and not to make anything of it.

"I was confident that Caitlin would remember me, but I wasn't sure just how well that would go. It had been so long since we had seen each other. I was pleased with how well that went," she told us.

"We had a nice visit talking about old times. It's been what . . . thirty years or more since she moved away? That's a lifetime, so much has changed since then.

"I met my husband not long after they left for the States and that was the end of my involvement with Dr. McDuffy and his family, except for occasionally seeing him out and about with his wife at various social functions, alumni events, or other things. We remained cordial, but I had children of my own by then, and I was busy with my family and my career."

"I hadn't thought about him for years until all of this came about. It's been a bit of a trip down memory lane for me, and I've enjoyed it, although I know full well what lies ahead and I'm not looking forward to that."

She leaned back and said, "So! Now you know . . . and now let's talk about what's next. As I said earlier, I want the two of you to meet the people who will be providing the in-home care to him on a daily basis, and that should happen quickly within the next week."

"After that, I will want you to stay in touch with him, with them, and with me, and monitor the situation. I heard that you're a painter, too, Brendan, and that you have some more work to do around the property. Is that true?"

"Well, I'm no painter, but I do have some more painting to do, and there's more work to be done on the outside. Saoirse can certainly find things to do on the inside, I'm sure. It's like he was living in a cave there, all by himself. He definitely can use the help, but so you'll know, from what I could gather, he wasn't too pleased with any of the assistance that's headed his way. He and his daughter argued over it, from what I could tell. I'm a bit surprised that he agreed to it," I told her.

"I'm aware of that," she responded, "Caitlin told me all about it and I expect that we may have some trouble down the road with that, but we'll see, and we'll do what needs to be done. This disease changes a person. It's like that book the two of you read, *Loss of Self.* He will change, and it won't be for the better, unfortunately."

Then she looked down at her watch, saw what time it was, stood, and said, "As usual, I'm late for another meeting and I must be off. Again, I congratulate and thank the two of you for all that you've done, so far. See you next week, if not before."

In a flash, she was gone. We sat there for several moments, not saying a word, and then Saoirse said, "She was absolutely bee's knees over the man, wasn't she?"

"Still is, I'd say," I responded.

"I think it's brilliant. She's definitely glad to be in a position to help the man the way she is . . . kind of like she's thanking him for all that he did for her. It's fantastic, really, being able to repay him for what he did to help her. I hope that I have as much passion for my work when I'm her age as she does. It's obvious that she loves what she does," she said.

"That's true," I acknowledged. "I'm still more interested in the children, and I want to get more involved with that area, but I've enjoyed meeting him and helping him as we have. It seems as if we've made ourselves a friend in the process, haven't we?" I asked.

"You mean Kathleen or Dr. McDuffy?" she asked.

"I meant Dr. McDuffy," I told her.

"That we have, for as long as he'll remember us, but we've made a friend in Kathleen, as well," she added. "I hope we can keep this relationship for quite a while. She's a treasure, too."

"And don't forget Dr. Delaney . . . he's aware of all of what's going on. He knows who we are. We've been quite fortunate to have this opportunity, haven't we?" I asked.

"We have, indeed, and I thank you for that, Brendan. You get most of the credit, and I very much appreciate the fact that you allowed me to be involved in this case," she said with a huge smile.

I didn't tell her that she was a big reason why I was doing so much of this. It was true. I truly don't know if I would have been anywhere near as willing to do all the things I had done if she weren't involved. When she said that, I might have blushed, and I blurted out, "We're not done yet, Saoirse. We still have a long way to go, it seems, maybe years, and there's that thesis to write, too."

"Maybe . . . and maybe not. We'll see," she responded. "Anyway, I've got a report due on another case and a test in one of my classes tonight, so I've got to run. What are you up to tomorrow? Maybe we can have a pint or two and talk about this a little more then."

I had a class that I probably shouldn't miss, but I told her that I'd meet her at the pub after work tomorrow whenever she was available. Just before she walked out of the room, I added, "And we'll be getting paid for it, too!"

Colin happened to be walking by at that very moment and he said, "Getting paid for what, Top Shillin'? What are you gettin' paid for?"

"Oh, nothin'," I answered.

"Nothin' indeed. What's goin' on here, squid?" he asked.

So I told him a little about what was going on, and he said, "And you're gettin' paid for paintin' a house and cleanin' up the yard, is that it? Well, better you than me, Sully. I want no part of it."

And I didn't want him to have any part of it, so that was good. All in all, it was a grand day and we were going to be paid for our time . . . grand, indeed.

CHAPTER NINETEEN

Stage Five

Late Friday afternoon, Colin, Saoirse, and I were summoned to Dr. Delaney's office. Once we were seated, he began, "I received a disturbing phone call from Dr. Doherty a few hours ago. Dr. McDuffy was involved in an incident that required intervention by the Garda.

"Dr. O'Brien is out of the office this afternoon, and I've been unable to reach her by phone, so I decided to discuss this with the three of you. She has been keeping me advised on how things have been going. We are both quite pleased with all of what has taken place over the last month or two, up until now."

"Apparently, Dr. McDuffy isn't taking too well to having someone in his house. The first person, a young female, resigned after just a few days. She told her supervisor that Dr. McDuffy refused to allow her to do her job and basically forced her out of his home on her last day there. She won't go back."

"The agency employed by the family, with the assistance of Dr. O'Brien, sent down another aide this morning, a male, and that didn't go well at all. In fact, it was much worse. The two men argued with each other and then, according to the man, Dr. McDuffy became physically violent, so he called the Garda."

"Fortunately, the officer who received the call and went to the scene was someone who was familiar with the situation and she contacted Dr. Doherty, who then contacted me. Somehow, she knows the three of you."

"Now, first of all, since Dr. McDuffy continues to be our patient or client, if you will, I want to make sure that the three of you are aware of what has happened and that you take the appropriate precautions. Colin, I don't think you're involved in this as much as these other two, but I wanted to keep you in the loop on this. I'm especially concerned about you, Ms. O'Connor . . . I don't want anyone getting hurt, so be careful."

"As for you, Mr. Sullivan, I would tell you to be careful, as well, and don't allow yourself to get involved in any physical confrontations with Dr. McDuffy. If a problem arises, I want you to get out of the house and let Dr. O'Brien and I deal with it. As you may have learned through your studies, that type of behavior . . . physical aggression, that is . . . isn't uncommon with this disease even when the person never showed any signs of such behavior ever before in his or her life."

"As the disease progresses, a person's personality changes. By all accounts, Dr. McDuffy has never been a violent man. There is nothing to suggest such propensities . . . no domestic violence, no criminal charges . . . nothing . . . ever, in his medical files, criminal records, or in his personnel files from Trinity College."

"You have all those?" I asked.

Dr. Delaney looked at me and answered, "Yes, we do, Mr. Sullivan. Dr. O'Brien is quite thorough with all of those details. So, as I was saying, there is nothing to suggest that he is, by nature, a violent man and we have no doubt that what happened earlier today is an aberration and an indication that the disease is advancing."

"Uncharacteristic irritability or anger is one of the signs in the progression of the disease," he told us. "Getting lost or misplacing possessions are two others."

"He's done both of those things before, many times," I said.

"Is it possible that the other man provoked him in some way?" Saoirse asked, somewhat meekly.

"That is a possibility, but we're not taking any chances. That man won't be going back there and from what I've been told, it was all Dr. O'Brien could do to make sure that someone else would. The agency is to send another woman, an older, more experienced one, tomorrow."

"Now, it's my understanding that the two of you will be going back there from time to time, on your own, to assist the man. Is that correct?" he asked.

When Saoirse and I affirmed that it was, he asked, "And were you planning to be there tomorrow?"

When we told him that we were, he said, "I'd like for you to get there before the attendant does. She is to arrive at 9:00. Can you do that?"

When we told him that we could, he said, "Be careful, but do all that you can to make sure that things go smoothly. If there is any problem . . . any problem whatsoever, get out, okay? Let Dr. O'Brien and me know about it and we'll decide what should be done. Understood?"

When we told him that we did, he said, "Terrific. This is my after-hours number," as he handed us business cards. "I expect that you have Dr. O'Brien's. If you don't, get it, please. I would rather that you get it from her, not me. We have your contact information on file and may be calling you over the weekend."

"Again, I thank you for all that you have done on this case, so far. Unfortunately, it seems as if we're moving into stage five of the disease."

Colin asked if Dr. McDuffy was arrested, and when told that he hadn't been, asked if we should call the Garda if an incident like that should occur.

"Not unless it's absolutely necessary," he replied. "This is, after all, a hospital and we are treating a patient with a known medical problem. We want to deal with the issue as a medical problem, not anything else if we can."

"And it's important to keep in mind that we're training all three of you to be the best clinical psychologists you can be. This may be your first experience with an Alzheimer's patient and you need to know what to expect and how to handle a situation like that. Good question, Mr. O'Riordan."

"Stage five . . . and there are said to be seven stages or progressions . . . involves, simply put, a worsening of things. It begins with a person needing more help with daily activities. He or she becomes more forgetful and disorganized. It's a matter of degree, really. From what I've been told, Dr. McDuffy needs help with managing his daily activities, and that is undoubtedly true, correct?" he asked, looking directly at me.

"I don't think that there's much doubt about that, Dr. Delaney," I responded. "From what I have been told, and what I have observed, he absolutely needs help with things like cooking, cleaning, buying groceries, washing his clothes, driving . . . just about everything, really."

"That's what Dr. O'Brien has told me as well. So, we're basically talking about a progression. Is the man having difficulties with managing his own affairs? Yes. There is little doubt about that. That's why we were called in the first place."

"Is additional care needed? Yes. That, too, is indisputable. Is his personality changing? Yes. This physical violence incident is proof of that. Is he going to become more irritable and difficult to deal with? More than likely."

"Will things continue to worsen? Yes. Is this disease advancing? Yes. Clearly, that is the case. Stage five is simply an advancement or worsening, of his condition, and some more, unpleasant characteristics appear, like anger and erratic behavior."

"So, we can expect that there is a potential for physical aggressiveness. What should you do if that happens? Avoid it entirely, if at all possible."

"To be clear . . . your instructions are to get out and call either Dr. O'Brien or me before calling the Garda or anyone else, unless there are physical injuries involved in which case medical personnel should be summoned, or there is an immediate threat of danger, requiring a law enforcement officer.

"Does that answer your question?" he asked.

"It does," Colin told him. "Thank you, Doctor."

"Alright then. Anything else? I'd like to receive your report first thing Monday morning, please. Any other questions?" he asked.

I blurted out, "I have one."

"And what is that, Mr. Sullivan?" he asked.

"Do you think Dr. McDuffy understands what is happening to him?" I asked.

The look on his face changed as he responded. "That's a good question, Mr. Sullivan. Not having seen the man, and not knowing him nearly as well as Dr. O'Brien does, I can't honestly say. I know him to be an extremely intelligent man, but that is by reputation alone. To answer your question, I don't know if he fully understands the implications of what he is about to go through. My guess is that he doesn't, but not knowing the man, I can't be sure of that."

"Do you think that we, as clinical psychologists, should tell him? Do we have an obligation to tell him?" I continued.

"Well, none of the three of you should do that, that's for certain. Leave that to Dr. O'Brien or to me. So, we're clear . . . none of the three of you are to engage in a conversation of that sort with Dr. McDuffy . . . is that understood?" he asked.

Before we had time to answer, he said, "You are not fully trained or qualified to do that. The three of you are students, under supervision, and until you are properly certified to make decisions like that, you cannot do so."

Again, he asked, "Is that understood?"

The three of us confirmed that we would not do so, but I persisted, "Do you think, as a general rule, that a patient has a right to know?"

He looked at me and hesitated before answering. "You ask another good question, Mr. Sullivan, and our profession, not just me, does not have a good answer for it. The best I can do is tell you that it depends . . . it depends upon a lot of things, especially upon how the patient is likely to respond. This disease is a death sentence, as you know," he told us.

"We have become aware of that," I responded. "But with Dr. McDuffy, who is, still, a brilliant man, this is a different case. What about him? Of all people, him being a college professor and all, other than a medical doctor, he should understand, don't you think?" I asked.

"Clearly, he still has the intellectual capabilities to understand what the disease involves. From what I've read and what I've been told, I think he's still in denial, which is normal. I'm not sure that he understands that he is dealing with Alzheimer's," he responded. "As I said a minute ago, I doubt that he does."

"So, the diagnosis of Alzheimer's has officially been made?" Saoirse asked.

"Yes. I'm afraid so. There is little doubt about that, unfortunately," he answered.

"But we've had such wonderful conversations with the man," Saoirse said. "I just don't understand how that can be. He's still a brilliant man."

"He will have lucid moments, and he will continue to wax eloquent, on occasion, as you have seen. When he does, pay close attention. He is, or he was, a great man. He will be especially good when talking about things in his past while not remembering much of what happened just a few days, or weeks, earlier. That's the nature of the disease, I'm sad to say," he told us.

"So, we're in stage five," Colin stated in a questioning sort of way. "And there's nothing that can be done to slow the process down?" he asked.

"Yes, he is, and no, there isn't, though there is much research being done all over the world about it. Through the use of new imaging technologies, researchers have identified a protein called amyloid-beta that is said to be one of the first objective signs of the disease. They are trying to find a way to block, reduce, or eliminate that, but they haven't had much success with that, just yet," he told us.

"Wouldn't Dr. McDuffy would be a good candidate for such testing?" Saoirse said.

"He might well be, Ms. O'Connor, but I'm not sure that it's reached the point where the testing is being done on humans. It's not being done here in Ireland, that I know of, and I would know. I think they're still working with mice and rats in the laboratories, but I could be wrong about that. Dr. O'Brien will know more about that than I do. She is, as you have learned, an expert on these matters. This is her specialty if you will," he said.

He then looked at his watch and asked, "Have I answered your questions? Is there anything else? I have somewhere else to be."

When none of us spoke, he said, "Well, thank you for coming to see me. I will look forward to seeing your reports on Monday. Again, contact me should an emergency arise. Otherwise, I'm sure you'll be seeing Dr. O'Brien and she will be keeping me advised."

"I hope all goes well this weekend for the two of you and for Dr. McDuffy. We want to keep him in his home for as long as possible, that is for certain, but we need his cooperation."

Once we were out of his office, Colin said, "I'll be needing a pint or two after that cac. That's no way to start off the weekend, now is it?" he asked. "I won't be joining you tomorrow," he added. "You're on your own with the man."

Neither Saoirse nor I could join him at the pub, though I would have done so if she was going. We made plans to meet even earlier than normal in the morning. Again, she would drive.

CHAPTER TWENTY

Bridey Maloney

Saoirse and I arrived at his house bright and early Saturday morning, and as usual, we were fairly uncommunicative on the ride over. As good as a convertible is on a warm, sunny day, it's equally as bad, if not worse, on a day when the temperature is down. The ragtop doesn't keep the cold air out too well.

When he opened the door, we saw a disheveled man with a fierce, hostile look on his face. When he recognized who we were, his face softened and he invited us in. We immediately walked toward the fire to warm ourselves.

"Can I fix you some tea?" he asked in a low, barely audible voice. We gladly accepted his offer. I sat down on the couch as Saoirse followed him over to the kitchen area to assist.

I overheard her asking him if he remembered the day when Colin, she, and I showed up on his doorstep, looking for directions to one of his neighbors. He grumbled a positive response. "Who knew that we would become such good friends from that chance meeting? That's fairly remarkable isn't it?" she offered.

He agreed and said, "Please excuse my appearance. I didn't sleep well last night. I'll be right back."

He went into his bedroom and returned a few minutes later with different clothes on, looking much better. He went back into the kitchen to finish fixing the tea. Saoirse followed behind him. I stayed by the fire.

I overheard the two of them chatting about how good the house looked. She did most of the talking. He mumbled responses. By the time the tea was ready, he became more intelligible.

It was obvious that some major cleaning had taken place. The carpet looked as if it had been thoroughly vacuumed since I was last there, and the furniture was brightly polished. The home had a fresh, clean smell about it, too, and Saoirse commented on it.

"Yes, well, the people my daughter sent to help me did a good job with that. I'll give them that, but otherwise, it's been an enormous bother. Someone doesn't need to be here every day. I don't want or need that much help! It's been upsetting to have them here and I wish it would stop," he told her.

"When you knocked on the door, I thought it was one of them, again," he told her. "I'm not sure, but I think someone will be here again today. I hope not."

"Do you have some milk for the tea?" she asked, changing the subject as she opened the refrigerator door to look in. "Oh my!" she exclaimed. "Look at your fridge! You've got enough in here to eat for a month, I'd say!" as she took out a container of milk.

"My daughter did most of that, but that man they sent here yesterday brought some, too. I told him I didn't need most of those things, but he wouldn't listen. Some of those things were for him. I'll never eat them."

"He was a most disagreeable fellow and I had to throw him out of here, I did. I called the Garda when he wouldn't leave," he told her.

"You called the Garda, did you?" she asked. "That must have been quite unpleasant." We had been told that it was the other way around, that the man had been the one to call the Garda.

"I did. He won't be back again . . . he'd better not be. I told him never to come back!" He raised his voice and was clearly agitated as he spoke, telling her a little more about what had happened the day before.

When they sat down, he asked me how he and I had met and I began to repeat what Saoirse had just told him, but he interrupted and said, "But I mean before that. I remember meeting you before that time, didn't I? I have a vague recollection of it, but I can't remember when that would have been."

I assured him that it must have been some other handsome, young fellow who looked like me. Saoirse laughed when I said that.

The answer satisfied him, but then he asked, "And how is it that the two of you know Kathleen O'Brien? According to my daughter, she is involved in all of this, and you two know her. How is that possible? I don't understand a lot of what's going on here."

"Well, let's see . . . let me ask you, how do you know Dr. O'Brien?" I asked, begging the question.

"Kathleen O'Brien? She was one of my best students and she became a dear friend to my wife and me. She watched our children when they were young. I haven't seen her in years, but I knew that she became a psychiatrist, or a psychologist, one of the two, and was quite successful in whatever it was she chose to do, but how do you know her?" he asked, again.

Before I had time to answer, Saoirse came to my aid and asked, "Would it be alright if I used your toilet?"

"Of course," he answered. "You know where it is," he told her.

Once she was out of sight, he said, "That's a fine lass you have there, lad. Easy on the eyes, she is."

"That's a fact, Michael," I agreed. "We're in school together," I told him, although I'd told him that before, I wasn't sure that he'd remember.

"Is that so?" he asked. "And where would that be?"

"Cork," I told him.

"The university? So, you're in your third level, are you? Well, good for the two of you. Education is the most powerful weapon you can use to change the world . . . Nelson Mandela said that," he told me.

"Develop a passion for learning and you will never cease to grow. I don't know who said that, but it's true. Get as much of it as you can," he said. "It will never fail you."

We sat quietly until Saoirse walked back into the room and then he asked, again, "So how is it that the two of you know Kathleen O'Brien?"

Before she could answer, I said, "She's one of our teachers."

"She's the best, really," Saoirse added. "We're fortunate to be able to have her."

"I don't doubt it," he responded. "She was an excellent student of mine, as I said, but then she went into the field of social work, as I recall. Is that what the two of you are studying? Social work?" he asked, looking at Saoirse.

"That's part of it," she responded. "And she thinks the world of you," she told him.

"Does she now?" he said with a smile. "That's nice to know. I have nothing but good things to say about her, but I'm flummoxed by all of this . . . how my daughter shows up out of the clear blue, as does Kathleen O'Brien, who I haven't seen in years and years, and now the two of you know her, and she's your teacher . . . I can't quite make sense of it all," he told us.

When we didn't respond immediately, he continued, "And my daughter was so insistent that I prepare my Last Will and Testament and other things . . . that was the first thing we had to do . . . right after she arrived! She barely had time to put down her bags and off we went, and now all of this business of people in and out of my home every day," he said as he waved his hands up in the air. "It's too much!"

"But it looks grand, doesn't it?" Saoirse said. "Not just the outside, which looks fantastic, but inside, too. So bright and clean . . . and it smells so good in here. You have to like all of that, don't you?" she asked.

"There's food in the fridge, it smells fine, it looks good . . . all of that is true, but I didn't need all of this," he responded, waving his hand around. "I was doing fine without it after the roof was fixed, that is, and I have you to thank for that, I do," he acknowledged, looking over at me. "I wholeheartedly agree that had to be done. I have no quarrel with any of that, but all the rest? That's not necessary!" he said firmly.

"It was me brother and Seamus O'Reilly you have to thank for the work, and we have nothin' to do with any of the rest of that stuff," I said, which was only partly true, but he didn't know that, at least not yet. He might figure it all out, eventually, but he hadn't done that yet.

"I just brought the three of you together, that's all, although I did do some painting for you, and I have more to do today," I told him. "That's why I'm here this morning, and Saoirse is here to help me with that and maybe help you clean out that shed of yours while we're at it."

Just then, there was a knock on the door and when he opened it, there stood a middle-aged, red-headed woman who introduced herself as Bridey Maloney. She had some cleaning utensils in both hands and stood there for several seconds until he invited her in, begrudgingly, undoubtedly because we were there. We introduced ourselves to her and she to us. Dr. McDuffy didn't say much of anything to her.

Without much further ado, she said, "Well, it's nice to meet the three of you, but I'd best be getting to work." She walked straight toward the bedroom area as if she knew her way around the place, though we knew she'd never been there before.

"I'll do my best to stay out of your way, Dr. McDuffy. I don't want any trouble here today," she told him. "I see you have your tea. I'll fix you somethin' to eat after a while."

He grunted a reply but said nothing.

When she was out of sight, and we heard the bedroom door close, Saoirse said, "She seems like a nice person."

"I don't need someone here to watch after me this way," he responded. "My bed doesn't have to be made every day. That's my daughter's doing, and somehow Dr. O'Brien . . . Kathleen, that is . . . has something to do with it, too, and now the two of you tell me that you are two of her students. Maybe it's all just a coincidence, but I don't quite understand how it all came about. I'm confused by all that's going on here lately," he told us, shaking his head. "There's more to it. I'm sure of it."

"Well, you have to admit that what's been done here is good for you, right? Nothing bad has happened, has it? Your home is spruced up, your house is clean, your refrigerator is well-stocked . . . what's not to like about all of that, Dr. McDuffy?" I asked.

"Michael, please . . . it's more than I need, that's all, and why is all of this happening all of a sudden as it is? My daughter arrives and my whole world is turned upside down. Why?" he asked.

"I don't know, Michael," I told him, "but I think you should be thankful. Your daughter loves you, and so does Kathleen O'Brien, that's for sure. They both want what's best for you."

"I have no doubt that they mean well, and I love them both, but I still don't get it. I'm glad to see the two of you here today, but why does this other woman have to be here? Every day this week, someone has been here. Why is that necessary?"

"The first one, a woman, cleaned the whole house, washed my sheets and all my clothes. That was just a few days ago. I sent her home because there was nothing else to do! How many times can she clean my house?" he asked. "Then that man arrived yesterday, and he was a dreadful sort. Now this woman . . . it's too much!"

"She's in there making your bed and tidying up the place as we speak," Saoirse assured him. "And she'll fix you something to eat after a while. She won't be here long, I'm sure. Now, what's wrong with that, Michael? I think you should be happy to have her," she told him.

"Happy indeed!" he said. "I'm not! Not at all, but enough of that. I'll take that up with my daughter the next time she calls. Let's go outside and get some fresh air. I don't want to be in the house while she's here."

"Oh, come on now, Michael? She's not that bad now, is she? She's not going to harm you, and she seems like a nice woman. Give her a chance," Saoirse said as the two of us stood and followed him toward the door.

"Let's go to work and let her do her job," I added. "That's why we're here."

"I had that first woman get a couple of gallons of paint so that you can finish the house," he told me. "That should be enough, don't you think?" he asked. I agreed.

"We can always put another coat on if it needs it," I told him. "It hasn't been painted in years."

"Not since we bought the place, it hasn't. That's true," he acknowledged.

We walked outside to the shed where the painting supplies were located. I was pleased with myself for how we had responded to his questions about his daughter and Dr. O'Brien, hoping that was the end of it. Clearly, he had questions about all that was going on in his life, but he hadn't figured out how the two of us were involved . . . yet.

When we opened the door, Saoirse exclaimed, "Bejaysus! Would you look at this! It's quite a mess you have here, Michael! When was the last time you cleaned this place?"

He replied sheepishly, "It's been a while. I'm not much of a handyman, I'll admit. I spent most of my life in a classroom, as you know."

"Well, it will keep me busy just gettin' stuff off the floor. Would you get me somethin' to throw the junk into as we go along? I'll do the best I can for you, Michael, but this place is in rag order, that's a fact," she said.

I took one of the gallons of paint, the ladder, some brushes, and whatever else I needed to finish up what painting remained to be done, and walked off, as he walked to the other side of the yard. Moments later, he returned with a wheelbarrow, telling her to put all the garbage in there. He stayed with her some thirty meters away from where I was, telling her what could be thrown away and what should be kept. I could hear their conversation, though I didn't participate.

Half an hour later, I heard the sound of the washing machine, and then I heard him say, "Jesus, Mary, and Joseph! How many times do they need to clean my clothes? They're going to be the death of me, I'm tellin' you," as he headed back toward the house. I dropped what I was doing and followed him in, as did Saoirse.

We arrived in time to hear her say, "I've got a list here, Dr. McDuffy," as she held up a sheet of paper, showing it to him, "And it says that your sheets are to be cleaned today."

"They were washed just the other day. That's not necessary!" he complained. "How many times do my sheets need to be cleaned?" he asked.

"I'm just following orders, sir," she told him. "Look here!" she said, pointing. It says, "Wash sheets on Saturday, and that's today. I'm just doing what I've been told to do."

He turned to us and said, "See what I mean? This is too much! Don't you agree? Tell her that I'm right!"

Saoirse and I looked at the list, together, and she said, "It looks pretty good to me, Michael. There's nothing wrong with being clean and organized. I'll bet your closets haven't been touched in years."

"Ugh! You're no help. Brendan, tell her to stop!" he said.

"Sorry, Michael. I've got to side with the women on this one. I think it'll do you good to have all this done for ya," I told him. "I wish they'd come do it for me at my place!"

"Christ almighty! You're no help, either. I'm doomed," he said.

"Michael, you've got to admit that everything that is being done for you is good! What's wrong with any of this?" I asked.

"I don't need it, that's all," he replied. "I want my life back the way it was before my daughter got here," he said.

Although I shouldn't have done it, and I regretted doing it just as soon as the words left my mouth, I said, "Do you? With all the mess, no food in the house, the roof half-burned, your sheets probably never cleaned in months . . . you want all of that back?"

He looked at me with a concerned look on his face, without answering, and then I said, "You told me yourself that you were having some difficulties with things, especially since you can't drive and all . . . things will be easier for you now, yes?" I asked. "You've got to admit that, don't you, Michael? Be honest," I told him.

"Maybe you're right, Brendan . . . maybe you're right," he acknowledged in a soft voice. "It seems as if everyone is against me," he added.

"No, everyone is with you, Michael," Saoirse assured him. "Everyone is here to help you," she told him, "including Brendan and me."

"Maybe so," he said, "but it doesn't seem that way to me."

"Let's go back outside and get back to what we were doing and leave Ms. Maloney here to do her job, okay?" Saoirse asked. I agreed. He didn't say anything, but he didn't protest, which was a good sign.

As the three of us turned to exit the house, I thanked Ms. Maloney, who whispered, "I'm glad the two of you are here. They had to talk me into coming here today. They had to pay me extra, too. It's a Saturday, after all, and I don't normally work on Saturdays. I wasn't too keen about doing it. I can tell you that."

Once we were back to doing what we had been doing, we didn't talk too much about that little dust-up. The back and forth chatter was all about an item here and there in the shed, whether to throw it away or keep it, and where to put it. Most of it was junked.

It was definitely a good thing that Saoirse and I were there that day, though. There was no telling what would have happened if we weren't. Ms. Maloney probably would have been sent home, never to return.

An hour or so later, she came outside and said, "It's time for the elevenses."

The three of us walked inside and saw where Ms. Maloney had set up tea and some snacks . . . little cheese rolls and things. We sat at the table where there were cups, silverware, napkins, and the rest. It was quite nice.

"There now," she said. "Enjoy!" and she went back to whatever she was doing. Moments later, I heard the sound of the dryer starting up.

"This is nice, isn't it, Michael? Very nice, indeed. I haven't had this in years. We don't do this at work, do we, Brendan?" she asked.

"Work?" Dr. McDuffy piped up. "I thought the two of you were in school . . . that's what Brendan told me. Which is it?" he asked.

"We're both," Saoirse responded, "It's a work-study kind of thing, so it's a little of both."

"And what is it you're studying?" he asked her.

Before I could say a thing, she answered, "Clinical Psychology."

"Clinical Psychology is it! Very good . . . very good, indeed," he said, and nothing more.

I knew that he was processing that information, but I decided not to try to explain it any further. Instead, I said something rather trite, like "Isn't this a nice snack? I'll bet she didn't have to do this. I'm guessing that it isn't on her list of things to do, and this cheese thing is quite tasty isn't it?"

Saoirse agreed. Michael had food in his mouth and couldn't respond as he was too busy eating.

A few minutes later, we were back outside and back to work. I had finished the last wall and was working on the windows and trim. There were only eight windows in the whole house, two on each of the four sides, and I was well on my way to finishing the last of them when, an hour or two later, Ms. Maloney called out, "It's time for your lunch."

Again, the three of us walked back inside to see empty plates with glasses of water at each setting. A plate full of sandwiches sat in the middle, with some crisps in a bowl off to the side.

"There's ham and cheese on some and some have turkey and cheese. I hope you'll like them," she said.

Saoirse and I thanked her profusely and she told us that we were welcome. "I'm only to work four hours today and I'll be off once I clean the dishes when you're done," she told us.

We told her that we could do that and she was free to leave if she wanted to, but she would hear none of it. "No, I'll leave when my time is up, and if it's alright with you, Dr. McDuffy, I'll be back again tomorrow. I've had no trouble with you today, and I'll come again, but only if that's alright with you, sir?" she asked.

"Of course, it is! Right, Michael?" Saoirse said.

"You don't have a problem with that, now do you?" I asked. "Look what she's done for us!" I said as I sat down and took a bite from one of the sandwiches.

Somewhat reluctantly, without looking at her, he said, "I guess that will be alright, but only for an hour or two. I appreciate what you've done here today, Ms. Maloney."

"You're quite welcome, Dr. McDuffy. I know of your reputation and it's an honor to serve you," she said.

"I thank you for saying so," he responded a bit more politely than he had been all morning.

I was delighted to hear that coming from the both of them . . . him and her. I was sure that Caitlin and Dr. Delaney would be as well, not to mention Kathleen. We chit-chatted amongst ourselves about the food, the house, and how much progress was being made on the shed as she was gathering her cleaning utensils and things, preparing to leave.

"We found things in there that are sheer relics, didn't we, Michael?" Saoirse asked.

He laughed for the first time that day when she said that. He had to agree. "As I told you before, I'm no handyman. I didn't know what half of those things were. They must have been here when we bought the place," he told us. "I don't remember seeing some of those things ever before in my life!"

"I should be finished with my painting in an hour or so," I told them, and I asked how much longer they figured to be in the shed.

"We won't finish today, Brendan. There's much more work to be done in there, right, Michael?" she asked. "And there's more work for Brendan to do around here, too, yes?"

He agreed and said that he'd like to paint the fence around the entrance to his driveway. I told him that the fence needed to be torn down and replaced, not painted. He asked me to talk to my brother and see if he could find someone to help with that and I agreed to do so. I needed an excuse to come back and I was pretty sure that he wanted us to come back.

An hour later, after Ms. Maloney was long gone and after I finished painting and cleaning up the mess I had made, I was ready to go. Saoirse said that when she reached a stopping point, we could leave. However, she wouldn't let me in her car until I cleaned myself up. Michael let me take a shower in the second bathroom and I put on the change of clothes I had brought with me, knowing that I would probably need them.

I commented on how clean the bathroom was, which was true. I thought to myself that it probably hadn't been cleaned in years before the aides came into the home, but I didn't say anything about that. Everything sparkled . . . clean as a whistle, as they say.

There was no doubt that Dr. McDuffy was being well taken care of. Even he had to acknowledge that, but he certainly was resistant to all the changes, and he definitely had questions about Kathleen and how she was involved in all of this. It had been a good day, and he was clearly glad to see us, saying that he looked forward to seeing us again next week.

In Sneem, we stopped at Kelly's for some ice cream. Having the scones with coffee had become a must when we arrived, and we decided to make having ice cream before departing a must-do thing, as well, unless, of course, we were to have a pint or two. We couldn't do both, not at the same time, at least. We sat outside and discussed our accomplishments of the day, as we enjoyed our cones.

When we were finished, I suggested that we go back to Killarney and visit other things there at the park, like the lakes or Muckross Castle, which we hadn't done before, although I really had little desire to do that. I just wanted to be with her, and if she wanted to, I was going. She decided against it.

The weather had made a change for the worse, too. The wind picked up, it got darker, and began to drizzle as we were finishing up. We decided to walk a few doors down to the Sneem Tavern and have some Irish coffee, waiting for it to subside some. That was something I rarely did, have Irish Coffee, that is. That was her idea, but it tasted good. Half an hour later, we were on the road headed back to Cork.

All in all, we were both proud of ourselves for what we had accomplished that day. I had finished painting the outside of the house and she had helped him clean out his shed. More importantly, he had taken a big step toward accepting the help that was being provided to him. We looked forward to reporting all of that to Dr. Delaney and Kathleen. They would tell Caitlin and her brother.

Before we left, Michael had given each of us an envelope with a hundred Euro note in it. That was good, too.

CHAPTER TWENTY-ONE

Problems Worsen

On Monday, when we assembled for our weekly meeting, Kathleen was delighted to hear all about what had happened on Saturday in Sneem. She was especially pleased to hear how Dr. McDuffy remembered her so fondly. "I wasn't sure that he would," she told us. "Please tell him that I send my love," she added.

We assured her that we would, but I asked her about how we should handle his questions, which I was sure were coming, about how and why all of this was happening. "He is puzzled by it all," I told her, "and he thinks that his daughter, Caitlin, is the one to start all of this. He doesn't quite understand how Saoirse and I know you. We told him that you were our teacher."

"And I'm fairly certain that he has no idea why the two of us happened to show up in his life. He still thinks that it was an accidental meeting. I think we have answered things to his satisfaction, so far, but he's going to have more questions. What should we do? What should we tell him?" I asked.

"Those are good questions, Brendan," she acknowledged, "and I don't want either of the two of you to have those conversations with him. I'd rather that Caitlin and Patrick do that. I'll talk to them about that."

"We spoke late last week when we had all of those problems with the people sent from the agency. Patrick is going to try to get here sooner than he had planned, but he's having trouble arranging his schedule, so just continue to dodge the questions as best you can until he gets here," she advised.

"In the meantime, just stay in touch with him. Try to see him once a week, if you can, and if you can't get there one weekend, call him just to say hello. Would you do that?" she asked.

We agreed to do so.

"And there's another big change that's about to be made in his home," she told us.

"What's that?" I asked.

"We're having a tele put in," she told us.

"I wondered about that. It's rare to find a home without one these days, but he doesn't. He listens to the radio alright, and he reads the Sunday papers, but no tele. I don't know why that is, but why are you doing it?" I asked.

"The people at the agency suggested it. Actually, they specifically requested that we do it. It's more for them than him, really, but it will be good for him to stay in touch with the world, as well."

"They didn't want to be there alone with him, without a distraction of some sort, don't you know? It's understandable. I can imagine that it could get pretty boring without it. They couldn't keep up a conversation with him for too long, now could they?"

"Especially if he didn't want them there in the first place. It could get rather unpleasant, couldn't it?" Saoirse responded.

"So, do you plan to be there this Saturday, Brendan?" she asked. When I told her that I was, she said, "That's grand. I'll set up the installation for this Saturday then. I want it to go smoothly, but I anticipate we'll have a problem with that. Any changes are going to cause problems, I'm afraid, and this will be a big change for him."

When she asked Saoirse if she could join me, I was pleased to hear her say, "I don't see why not. I've got some work to do down there helping him sort out his shed, but I can't spend all day."

"That's wonderful. You don't have to stay too long. I just want the two of you to be there when the men are there to put the tele in. Let's hope that Mrs. Maloney is still there. She's supposed to be. She seems to have passed the first few hurdles, thanks to the two of you, but that could change at any time, as I'm sure you're aware."

With that, she stood and said, "Alright then. I think we're done for now. Keep up the good work. We've made great progress. I think we're ready for what's to come . . . or as ready as we can be," she told us. "See you next week. If anything should happen between now and then, I'll let you know."

When she was gone, Saoirse turned to me and said, "Brendan, I'm not going to be able to do this every weekend. I'm interested in the case and all, and he's a nice old man, but I have other things to do on my weekends."

"I'm not sure what I'll do once the changes we keep hearing about start to happen. I'm not going to sit there with a man who can't talk to us or who is rude to us. I'm still planning on making this my thesis, or at the very least, maybe an article in one of the journals, but when it reaches the next stage, I'll have to reconsider all of this."

"It's an interesting case, without a doubt, and we got involved just at the right time, I think. Don't get me wrong . . . I am enjoying all of this, for now, but I'm not so sure that I'm ready for what is going to happen next."

I told her that I understood, and I agreed with her. "But maybe that's part of the job we've taken on, Saoirse," I told her. "Maybe these are things we'll have to do later on in our careers. It's not going to be all peaches and cream, is it?"

"Good point, Brendan," she answered. "I'm sure it will be good for us to see the whole progression, including the very worst, to the bitter end. That would be quite something, from a professional point of view, to experience that, but I'm not looking forward to it. I'll keep doing this for a while longer, as I said, and I'll go with you again this weekend. I told Kathleen I would and I will," she said. "Once I finish cleaning up his shed, what will I do? What will you do? I don't know," she added.

I knew that her interest in going down to Sneem had little to do with me, so I wasn't surprised by her comment. It was all about her career, which was fine. That was understandable, but for me, it was different. She could probably back out at any time without there being any problem whatsoever. I think I was stuck with the man, whether I liked it or not.

On the bright side, Sneem was my hometown, of course, and all of my family was there, except for my mother and grandmother, so that was good. I was spending more time with them than I had in years, but being with Saoirse had a lot to do with my interest in the case. I didn't want to see that end, and I didn't want to see the next stage in the progression of the disease arrive anytime soon, either. For now, things were good. I'd cross the next bridge when I came to it.

"We don't have to get there so early this time, do we?" she asked. "I like to sleep in on Saturdays," she said.

I figured that the tele would be coming from Cork, or maybe Killarney, as there was no place in Sneem that sold things like that. Because of that, I was as sure as I could be that the truck wouldn't arrive until later in the morning, so I agreed that we could meet at half eight and be there in plenty of time.

She surprised me when she said, "You can drive this time. It's a bit chilly in the Mustang these days. See you then."

I called Dr. McDuffy on Wednesday, and the phone rang six or seven times before he picked up. I told him that we would come down and help him with his shed, if he wanted us to. When he said that he'd like that, I told him that we would be there Saturday morning and that we could talk about the fence he wanted to put up while I was there.

"Oh, the fence . . . I'd forgotten all about that," he told me. "I do want your help with that, too. I'll see you then," and he hung up, somewhat abruptly.

It was an odd conversation, but I didn't think much of it. I realized that he probably didn't talk on the phone all that much. He didn't have many friends in Sneem, it seemed, or anyplace else, for that matter, from what I could tell.

When we arrived on Saturday, the van with the television was already there. Two men were standing outside, talking to Mrs. Maloney. When we approached, she said, "I'm glad you're here. These men were just about to leave. Dr. McDuffy won't let them in the house to do their work. Go talk to him, would you? See what you can do."

"The tele is sitting in the back of the van, still in the box. He's quite upset about all of this," she told us. "He's been ranting and raving for half an hour now ever since they got here. It's been all I could do to stop them from runnin' off."

We walked inside the house and saw Dr. McDuffy sitting in his chair, staring into the fire. He didn't greet us when we walked over to where he was and didn't even bother to get up. We sat down on the couch and Saoirse asked him in a soft, non-threatening tone of voice what was wrong.

"I don't want a tele in the house! That's what's wrong!" he told her. "But Caitlin does, apparently, though she didn't ask me about it first. This is all her doing. It seems as if I have no say in much of anything that's going on around here," he said somewhat angrily, though his displeasure wasn't directed at us.

When I asked why he didn't want the tele, he responded, "We never had one here while Marjorie was alive, and I don't need one now."

"Why not, Michael?" Saoirse asked. "There are so many fabulous shows on these days . . . about nature, history, famous people . . . all kinds of interesting things. I'd think a man like you would love to watch things like that, not the silly game shows and all," she told him.

He looked over at her and said, "We had five or six teles in Dublin. There was one in every bedroom, one in the kitchen . . . we even had a separate room we called the 'tele' room. They were everywhere, but when we came out here, she didn't want any."

"We'd read together or listen to music . . . we'd even dance over there, next to the fire, every so often," he said, pointing. "The quiet times were our best times. I want to keep it that way."

"Hmm, I see," Saoirse responded. "So that's it."

"We'd take turns reading to each other, actually. I miss those days. I don't need the noise and the bother. I don't want it!" he told us emphatically.

"Well, you don't have to turn it on, do you, Michael? You can leave it off when no one is here, but when your daughter comes to visit, she wants there to be a tele in the house. Why not let her do what she wants? Maybe she'll come more often," I said.

He turned to me and said, "I hadn't thought of that. You make a good point, Brendan."

"It sounds as if it would make your daughter happy," Saoirse added. "Let these men do what they have to do and make your daughter happy! There's no harm in that, is there now?" she added.

He looked over at us, studying us, and, after several moments, said, "I guess not. As long as I can turn it off and leave it off whenever I want to, that is."

We assured him that would be fine, and that seemed to appease him.

"Caitlin was quite insistent about it last night when we spoke. She became a bit cross with me over it. I didn't like that," he acknowledged. "I think I pampered her too much as a child. She seems to think I'll do whatever she wants. She always got her own way, I think, looking back."

"So, you'll let them in?" Saoirse asked. "We can go outside and I'll work with you on the shed until they're gone . . . how's that?"

When he agreed, I told him to get his work clothes on and we'd go to work. While he was changing, Saoirse and I walked outside to let the men know what had been decided. Saoirse told me that I was gaining his trust. I told her that we both were.

When we told the men that they could go in, one of them said, "He's a bleedin' tick, if you ask me."

"He's a fuking Amadan, I'd say," the other one added.

"A royal pain in the arse," the first man continued.

"Now, now, boys," Mrs. Maloney chided. "He's a well-respected gentleman, he is. He's just having a bad day. Thank you for being so patient with him."

"Patient indeed! If it weren't for you bein' here we'd be gone by now," the one said. "And we'd never come back, if it was up to me," the second one added.

I told them to wait until we were out of the house and he'd be out of their way. They were still grumbling as we ushered Michael out of the house and around to the shed.

About an hour later, after we'd combed through more debris and threw out most of what we found in there, organizing things as best we could, we heard the sound of the van driving off. Mrs. Maloney came out and told us that it was safe to come back inside.

"Your tea is ready," she said. "I thought the two of you might be coming today, so I brought some extra scones," she told us.

The three of us went back inside, and after washing our hands, per her instructions, we sat down for our morning tea.

"The elevenses is such a nice break in the day," Saoirse said. "I think it's an Irish thing, isn't it, Mrs. Maloney? Or are there other countries that do this as well?" she asked.

"It's an Irish thing alright," she told us. "And they do this in Australia and New Zealand, too, I'm told, but they're all Irish anyway, aren't they? Our 'friends' to the east have their 'tea-time,' but this is what we do. This is our time," she said.

We agreed and thanked her for what she'd done for us.

"Isn't this a treat, Michael?" Saoirse asked. "I think you're very lucky to have Mrs. Maloney here, don't you agree?"

We were pleased to hear him say that Mrs. Maloney wasn't all that bad after all or something to that effect. "I still don't think that I need all the attention I'm getting, but she's a very nice woman and I genuinely appreciate her help," he told us as he looked over at her and nodded, approvingly.

"Thank you for that, Dr. McDuffy," she responded. "You're a very nice man when you want to be," she told him, and we all laughed, even him.

When we were finished, as we were about to go back outside, Mrs. Maloney whispered to us and said, "Before you go back to whatever it was you were doing, I'll need some help setting this thing set up. They assembled it well enough, but I'd like for one of you to turn it on and get it running. I have no idea how to set up the remote control and all or which one to use," as she was holding up three separate hand-held devices.

"They told me there was nothin' to it and left. They said all I have to do is turn it on, but I'm not sure which one is which. One plays the movies and another one does the channels. I'm not sure what this third one does, so I don't have a clue about it."

"Will you help me with that?" she asked, "and more importantly, figure out how to explain it to the good doctor here so he'll know how to do it when I'm not here."

Saoirse told her that she'd be glad to do it, and she stayed inside with her while I went outside with Dr. McDuffy. We walked out toward the road to survey the rickety picket fence that was there and figure out exactly what he wanted done. It was obvious that the whole thing needed to be replaced. There was no fixing what was there.

"And I want it painted white, Brendan," he told me, "with some bushes and flowers here and there to spruce it up a bit. Marjorie would like that. She loves flowers."

I told him that I'd talk to my brother, Rory, about getting the materials and what it might cost. He was pleased to hear me say that he and I might be able to do it by ourselves. I knew that there were places that sold those kinds of things pre-assembled. If all we had to do was to dig a few holes and put some posts in the ground, even I could do that. I wasn't expecting much from him.

However, if carpentry was involved, that was a horse of a different color. I'd let Rory and his men do it. We walked around for over an hour, surveying the place, discussing what would be best. He kept saying what Marjorie would want to see done. That seemed to be the most important part of it all. He was more concerned about the flowers and the white paint than anything else.

When we were finished with that, we walked back over toward the shed. We saw Saoirse rustling around inside. When we got there, she held up a small box, and asked, "What's in here, Michael? It's locked."

"My goodness!" he exclaimed. "Look at that! I haven't seen that in years. I thought I lost it in the move somewhere along the line. I forgot all about it."

"What is it?" she asked.

He chuckled and said, "Don't be alarmed, but it's a gun."

"A gun!" she said. "Don't be alarmed, you say. Those are hard to come by, Michael. How is it you have one?" she asked.

"Years ago, when I was a young man, I belonged to a shooting club and I would go to a target range and shoot every now and again," he told us. "It was all legal. Nothing to worry about, lass."

"But you have to keep the licenses current and renew them every three years. I know all about that as me Da likes to do that. He has a gun, too," she said.

"Oh, I did everything I was supposed to do," he assured her. "Everything was Garda-approved, but Marjorie wouldn't let me keep it in the house. It had to be under lock and key and kept outside in the garage back then."

"When our children had gone off and left us, moving to America as they did, we sold our house in Dublin and rented an apartment. That's when we bought this place. It's a much smaller house than the one we had . . . much, much smaller. I was still working then, and we'd come out here on weekends.

"We were in and out of storage boxes for a long while. Somewhere along the line, I lost this. I had no idea where it was. I had forgotten all about it, to be honest. I haven't seen that gun in years," he told us.

"You probably should tell the Garda about it now, shouldn't you?" Saoirse asked.

"Maybe I should, but then again, maybe not. That would only cause trouble. It might be best to just leave it where it is."

"I have no idea where the key is. It probably doesn't work anymore anyway. I can't remember when I last fired it," he said. "Just leave it back over in that corner for now. I'll give it some thought and decide what to do. Maybe I'll ask Caitlin. She seems to be in charge of everything these days."

We looked at each other without saying anything. Then she shrugged her shoulders and said, "Okay, Michael. Whatever you say." We moved on to something else, and not long after, Mrs. Maloney was calling us in for lunch.

The tele was on a table, against the wall, not far from the fireplace, so Dr. McDuffy could sit in his chair and see it. The news was on as we walked in. He immediately said, "Would you please turn that thing off while we're eating?"

"Of course, I will, Dr. McDuffy," Mrs. Maloney answered, and she walked over to turn it off.

"It's a nice tele, isn't it? Look at that picture! It's as clear as a bell, as they say," Saoirse said.

"And it's easy to use," Mrs. Maloney told us as she picked up a bright, red device. She held it in front of Dr. McDuffy and said, "You just push this big green button here at the top to turn it on, and you go up or down the channels with these arrows down here at the bottom," holding the device in her hand and demonstrating how to use it, "and these other buttons on this side adjust the volume, see?" she asked him.

"Thank you, my dear," he said, condescendingly. "I know how to turn a tele on and off, thank you very much. I've been doing it since these things were invented."

"Not the remote controls, though," Saoirse offered. "They weren't around back then."

"That's true, but I know how to use them," he assured us. "I've agreed to allow it to be in the house, but that doesn't mean I have to use it, right, Brendan?" he asked, looking over at me. "That's what I agreed to, correct?" he asked again.

I confirmed that to be the case. That was my sales pitch, and that's what I had told him, so the television was turned off as we ate.

As it was the week before, the lunch was wonderful. When we finished eating, as we sat there chatting, Mrs. Maloney cleared the table, washed the dishes, and put them away. When she was finished, she told Dr. McDuffy that she would see him in the morning. He was much more polite and grateful this week than the week before and he thanked her for what she had done for us, with no complaints about her being there, which was good news to us.

Before leaving, however, she whispered something to Saoirse, who then followed her out to her car. When they left, I asked Dr. McDuffy if it would be alright to turn on the tele. I told him that there was a hurling match on that I was keen on seeing, and he agreed to allow me to do so. I had no idea if there was a game on or not, but I began flipping channels, commenting on how many good shows were on, like movies, sports, history, and other things.

He showed some interest in a replay of the Dublin versus Cork All-Ireland final that had been played a few weeks earlier, saying that he used to go to all the games back in his younger days. He had listened to the game, like most of the country, and knew the result. I asked if he wouldn't mind seeing some of it. I told him how I hadn't seen all that much of it, and he readily agreed. "I was rooting for the boys in blue," he told me.

We were sitting in front of the fire watching it when Saoirse returned. It was a typical Irish day which was now blustering, threatening rain, though it had been clear skies an hour earlier. I had no interest in working outside in those conditions and said so.

Saoirse leaned down and whispered in my ear that she really needed to get back to Cork and was ready to leave. I stood and said that was fine with me. I told Dr. McDuffy that I would talk to Rory about the fencing project and find out the cost of the supplies we'd need. We told him that we'd be back next week, if it was alright with him, to continue work on the shed, too. He was delighted to hear it.

As we were walking out the door, he handed each of us an envelope which had another one hundred euro note inside, thanking us for our help. "Caitlin says that I should pay the two of you whenever you come out here to help me, as you have today, and I have no problem doing so," he said.

We protested rather mildly, saying that it wasn't necessary, that we were glad to help, and that it was too much, but he insisted, saying, "The two of you don't need to be here, and I appreciate your help." We gladly kept the envelopes, thanking him for them, telling him that we would see him in a week.

Once we were in my car, headed back down Sea View Road to Sneem, I asked Saoirse what Mrs. Maloney had to say to her.

"She told me that Dr. McDuffy is on his best behavior when we are around, but that he's not nearly as good when he's by himself. She says he walks around the house aimlessly most of the time, getting in her way and jabbering about things she has no knowledge of, like Socrates and the ancient Greeks. The rest of the time, he spends in his room, resting, or he goes outside and walks around. She says that she needs a break. It's a little uncomfortable for her to be with him alone in his home, at times, her being a woman and all."

"She's not afraid of him, is she?" I asked.

"No, but she is concerned, saying that she wants us to find someone else to be with him, too. She doesn't want to be his only caregiver, and she can't be here every day, especially if the hours are going to increase. Her supervisors are aware of the situation, but she wanted us to know, too," she told me. "She knows that it could be a problem to find someone else who'll put up with him."

"She's not wanting to quit, is she?" I asked.

"No, but she wants help. She's been there every day, so far, and that has to stop. Plus, she says that there are times when she can't do all that needs to be done for him all by herself. I think she was talking about hygiene there . . . help with getting him dressed or bathing him. I wasn't sure exactly what she meant with that."

"She's hoping that the tele will help, and she's glad to have it, for herself, that is, but she thinks he's a lonely man who needs more companionship. Also, she's worried about what is likely to happen in the near future. After being with him for a full week, as she has, there's no doubt in her mind that he's suffering from dementia. She also told me that he's going to need more than just a housekeeper before too long."

"That's not good. What else did she say? Did she give you any examples of why that is?" I asked.

"She did. She told me about an incident that occurred yesterday. When she arrived, Dr. McDuffy was walking around outside the house in his pajamas, in the rain. He was soakin' wet . . . well, maybe not soakin' wet, but his clothes were wet from the rain and it was all she could do to get him to come inside and take a hot shower. He wasn't concerned about it at all. He was out by the road looking at the fence."

"She's not able to control him, physically, and she was concerned about what would happen if he fell and couldn't get up. He's a large man and she's a small woman."

"She's not able to do any of that, and that's part of it, I'm sure. Things are okay, for now, but she's concerned about what's in store for the man in the not too distant future."

"But that's part of her job, right?" I asked. "That's what she's supposed to do, right? Isn't that part of what this agency is to do for the man? This isn't just a house-cleaning company, is it?"

"I'm pretty sure they do it all. Kathleen wouldn't hire a company that just cleans houses, but we'll have to ask her," she responded.

"She's probably fine with little, old ladies, but Dr. McDuffy is just too big for her. I can see what she's saying and I agree with her. He probably weighs twice as much as she does. It could be a real problem for her, and for him," she added.

"But he's not going to want another man in his house, now is he?" I asked. "Not after what happened with that first fellow."

"Probably not," she agreed, "and that's why she wanted us to know about it, and for us to talk to Dr. O'Brien about it."

"Anything else?" I asked.

"Just little things, like forgetting where he put his glasses, finishing his sentences, or forgettin' what he was doing. He goes into a room and forgets what he went in there for . . . things like that. She has had to help him pick out clothes to wear and put them on. He wants to wear the same thing every day."

"Also, she says she's had to remind him to brush his teeth. His personal hygiene could be improved, too, she told me. Apparently, he doesn't use deodorant unless she tells him to."

"She's only been there a week, right? Is she saying that he's getting worse?" I asked.

"No, that's not it. She's just telling us what she's seen in a week. You and I have only seen him a few times, you more so than me. She's spent more time with him during the last week than we have in all the times we've been here over the last month, right?" she asked.

"That's true, but he's been so good when we've seen him, hasn't he? Like today?" I asked. "It's still hard for me to understand how he can be so different from one day to the next."

"He didn't start out so good today," she reminded me. "He was fine once we calmed him down, and she's telling us what he's like when we're not here," she said. "And you've seen him when he's not been so good, yes?" she added.

"That's true," I acknowledged.

"Like that time when you showed up at the door and he was out of sorts, right?" she asked. Again, I agreed.

"We'll talk to Kathleen about all of that. It's complicated, that's for sure. We don't know what's best for him, or someone like him, so we'll just have to ask her and see what she says," she concluded.

"Okay, that's enough about him for now," I said. "Let's talk about something else. Would you like to stop for a pint before we head back?" I asked.

She declined, saying she had things she had to do, which disappointed me, but we did stop for ice cream before leaving Sneem.

We talked about other things on the ride back, such as our classes, the changing weather, and other cases. Using my car made it much easier to talk. It wasn't nearly as noisy because of the hardtop.

She was going to a concert that night, undoubtedly with her boyfriend, but I didn't ask her about any of that. I didn't want to hear anything about him. I, on the other hand, had no plans and would probably spend the night watching the tele, just as Dr. McDuffy might be doing.

CHAPTER TWENTY-TWO

The Gun

That Monday, just as Saoirse was starting to tell her all about what Mrs. Maloney had told us, Kathleen stopped her and said, "I've read her report. I've talked to the owner of the business, and she has another woman in mind who might be able to handle the job."

"And get rid of Mrs. Maloney?" I asked.

"No, not get rid of her . . . in addition to her. She needs help, that's all. Mrs. Maloney is working out just fine."

"I've talked to Caitlin about it and she agrees completely. We knew that one person couldn't do what needs to be done all by herself. The problem will be, of course, what Dr. McDuffy has to say about the new person. We'll just have to wait and see about that," she told us.

"The woman is to start later this week, and she'll be there at the same time as Mrs. Maloney for a day or two so that Dr. McDuffy might feel less threatened. I'll tell them to arrange it so that she starts when the two of you can be there, too," she added.

"He's not going to like that, I expect, but he's got to understand that the woman can't be there all the time . . . she needs time off now and again," I said.

"The two of you being there should help with explaining that to him," she said, and then she added, gravely, "But it won't be long before someone will be with the man twenty-four hours a day, Brendan. Those days are coming. It's just a matter of when."

"I know that I've told you this before, but it's just so hard to believe," Saoirse said. "He's been so good most of the times we've been there . . . every time I've been there, actually. He was out of sorts when we first got there on Saturday, and the Saturday before that, but he settled down quite nicely both times. It's like a *Dr. Jekyll and Mr. Hyde* kind of thing, is it?" she asked.

Kathleen looked at her and said, "It's not like that, Saoirse, but as you've learned from the books you've read, the man will lose his self. It's not different personalities, he's the same person. He's losing himself, just like the title of the book I had you read."

"It's a gradual thing, but it's going to happen. He will no longer be the man you have met. He will have his lucid moments, but he's going to get worse, not better. You know that. We've talked about that several times now."

Saoirse and I looked at each other but didn't respond.

"You're quite fortunate, actually, to be seeing the man at this stage, especially you, Saoirse, if you're wanting to write your thesis about this dreadful disease. You'll be seeing him advance through the various stages. Not that many students have that opportunity. People like me have seen it happen more than they want to remember."

When we said nothing in response to that comment, she went on and said, "Also, I would caution you not to become too emotionally involved with the man, as I'm afraid you might be. You are becoming professionals and you must learn, the earlier the better, not to take these things too much to heart. You will have your heart broken over and over again if you don't."

"That's one of the reasons I'm not all that anxious to see him. I loved the man . . . I did. I still have deep feelings for him. I will hate to see him dragged into the dirt, as he will be before it's over, and I know better. He's been like a father, brother, and friend to me over the years," she said, "and I am doing what I am telling you not to do."

She pulled a tissue from her purse and dabbed her eyes. "I get emotional just thinking about that, and as I said, I know better. So, do as I say, not as I do," she repeated. "We're in for some rough times."

"What about him, Kathleen?" I asked.

"What about him?" she asked. "What do you mean?"

"How do you expect him to react to all of this?" I asked.

"He's losing his mind, Brendan. In the end, he's not going to remember much of anything. I don't understand what you're asking. What do you mean?" she asked again.

"Well, at some point, don't you think he's going to realize what's going on? And when he does, what do you think he's likely to do?" I asked.

"Oh, I see what you're asking. That's a good question, and that's something we may have to be concerned about. It could become a problem."

"To be honest, knowing all that I have learned about this disease, I truly don't know what I would do if I were in his shoes at the moment," I said. "I certainly wouldn't want to go through what he's about to go through, and I'm not sure how he will respond if he figures it out."

"Everyone is different," Kathleen told us, "but we, as Catholics, know what we must do, and that is what we, as professionals, say as well."

"He really doesn't have too many options, now does he?" I offered. "I guess he'll just have to accept the cards he's been dealt, won't he? Although I guess there are things he could do if he were so inclined."

She knew what I meant, although I didn't come right out and say it, and she responded by saying, "Yes, there are, Brendan, but keep in mind that we are Catholics, and although we are doing our best to separate the church from the government these days, the church forbids taking one's own life. To us, it is a sin . . . a mortal sin," she said, ominously, "and there are laws against it, too," she added, "so there is no doubt as to what position we must take in this matter. None whatsoever."

I chuckled and said, though I probably should have kept my big mouth shut, "That's true, there are laws against it, but there are no further penalties to be inflicted if one is successful, now are there?"

Kathleen wasn't amused, but she responded by saying, "I guess not, since once you're gone, you're gone and there's not much that can be done. They'd be answering to God then, wouldn't they? That could be a lot worse than anything we humans could do, now isn't it?"

"And keep in mind that if they tried and they weren't successful, that's when a person is put into an institution like ours, and I hate using that word . . . a hospital is what we are . . . because at that point, they have become a 'danger' to themselves. That's when the law steps in to prevent someone from doing just that," she told us.

"Why can't a person just end it?" I asked. "Why doesn't a person have the right to take his or her own life? I surely wouldn't want to go through what I've heard Stage Seven is all about."

"That's not a good question to be asking yourself, Brendan. Don't think like that. You know the law and we must follow it, even if we don't always agree with it, and I mean the law of the land, not to mention the laws of our church . . . both," she answered with a concerned look on her face. "And I suggest that you keep that kind of talk to yourself from now on. That's a little friendly advice from a friend," she said. "You wouldn't want Dr. Delaney to hear you say such a thing, now would you?" she asked. "It's unprofessional."

"Understood," I answered, and I thanked her for setting me straight on that point.

That's when Saoirse blurted out, "I found a gun."

Kathleen nearly jumped out of her seat upon hearing that, and asked, "You did what? When? Where? Why didn't you tell me!"

"On Saturday, when we were cleaning out his shed," she responded.

"Where is it now? Did you take it from him? He doesn't still have it, does he?" she asked, obviously disturbed by the news.

We explained how it was in a locked box and he had no idea where the key was, but that the box was still there in the shed.

"Maybe he'll forget about it," I said, half-jokingly.

"It's not a joking matter, Brendan," she told me, firmly. She sat silently for a few moments and then said, "I'll discuss it with the family and let you know what they decide to do with it. I'm not sure that I want either of the two of you taking it from him. I may have to discuss that with Dr. Delaney."

"It may be an heirloom or something that isn't operational, depending upon how old it is. I don't want to report it to the Garda just yet and get them involved, either, but I'm glad you mentioned it to me. My goodness! You scared me half to death when you told me that. How long has he had it? Where did he get it?" she asked.

We explained all that he had told us about that and how it came about that it was found.

"I have a vague recollection of that, now that you mention it. I remember how Marjorie refused to allow him to keep that in the house. That's been fifty years ago, or more, if it's the same gun. It probably doesn't even work anymore, but we can't chance it. I'll talk to Caitlin about it straight away."

Then she leaned back, let out a sigh, and said, "Holy Mary Mother of God! I'm glad you found it and told me about it as you did, Saoirse! It may be nothing to worry about, but it frightened me when you mentioned it. I'm definitely concerned about it."

She looked at her watch and said, "I think she's eight hours behind us there where she is in California, so she should be up by now. I'll do that before I leave today, for certain."

Then she said, "I'd best be going now as I have another meeting to attend, as usual, but we've made some more progress here this week. We now have a much better idea of what he's like on a day-to-day basis, and I think the tele will help. Finding the right person to assist Mrs. Maloney could be a bit dicey, but we'll just have to wait and see how that goes."

"In the meantime, you two keep up the good work. Is he paying you well for this nixer the two of you have taken on?" she asked.

"Oh, yes! Quite well, thank you," Saoirse replied.

"Well, that's no surprise, knowing the family as I do. They're both generous people, but I'm glad to hear it. You'll both be going out there again this Saturday, will you?"

We told her that we would be. I explained how Dr. McDuffy was wanting to fix up the fence at the front of his property and I was to help him with it and that Saoirse still had work to do in the shed. "It was rag order in there, for sure," she explained, "but it's better now."

"I'll let you know what to do about the gun before then," she told us. "I don't think that there's anything to be done between now and then, but I'll leave that up to Caitlin."

Then she stood and said, "I'm up to my ears in work these days, but this is my top priority. Thanks, again, for all of your help on this."

Once she was gone, I told Saoirse that it was a good thing she mentioned the gun. "I almost forgot about it, to tell you the truth. The only reason I mentioned it was because of what you said about how he might react if he should figure out what's happening to him."

"I think he's going to," I told her.

"I don't think it's a concern. He's a Catholic, like us. He wouldn't do somethin' like that! I'm sure of it," she said. Then she asked, "Would he? What do you think?"

"I'm not so sure," I responded. "I don't know what I'd do if I was him, like I said. Neither of the books we've read talk much about that, now do they? For me, it was my first thought as to how he might react."

"No, they don't mention that in the books or in my class," she answered. "Most people wouldn't think of such a thing, and neither would he, I'm sure."

Then she stood, saying, "See you on Saturday . . . same time, and you drive again. Your car is warmer," she said with a smile, "and I can doze off. I don't like getting up early on Saturdays, but I'll be there. See you then."

Mrs. Welch

Late Friday afternoon, Kathleen came down to my cubicle and told me that she had spoken to the two children and we were to pick up the gun and bring it back to her. We assured her that we would.

"Don't make a big fuss over it. See if you can't hide it from him so he won't know it's gone," she suggested. I told her that we'd do our best.

We were a little late in arriving on Saturday, and when we did, we saw that there was some wood and other supplies neatly stacked in the driveway, together with a post-hole digger and a hammer. I had mentioned it to Rory, but that was the last I'd heard of it.

We stopped outside the gate and I immediately called Rory. He apologized for not letting me know and said, "I dropped them off early this morning." He had spoken to Dr. McDuffy a few days ago and was sure that he and I could do it ourselves. I wasn't quite so confident, but it didn't seem to be all that difficult.

For the most part, it was pre-assembled, the fence part, that is. All he had to do was decide where to put the posts and then we could put them in the ground and attach the fence part to the posts. "Even you can do that, Bear. I'm sure of it!" he told me.

Just as soon as we parked, and as we were getting out of the car, Mrs. Maloney came hurrying out to greet us. "I'm so glad you're here. Dr. McDuffy is effin' and blindin' at the moment. He's in rare form, indeed. Mrs. Welch is about ready to leave," she told us.

A large, stout woman, much taller and heavier than Mrs. Maloney, came out not far behind her. She wasn't smiling. "I'll not put up with this abuse! I won't! Unless you can calm the man down immediately, I'll be leaving! The man's pure cracked!"

Saoirse and I walked hurriedly inside and saw Dr. McDuffy standing by the fire with a frown on his face. When we said good morning, he responded with, "This is utter shite, Brendan! Excuse my French, Ms. . . ."

"Saoirse," she told him.

"Yes, Saoirse. I apologize . . . but this is intolerable! I didn't want anyone to be here and now I have two people! Things are getting worse, not better! This is too much. I won't stand for it!" he protested.

The two women were standing in the doorway. Mrs. Welch had her arms folded in front of her. She had a scowl on her face. Mrs. Maloney had a look of confusion and frustration on hers.

I wasn't sure what to say. Saoirse came to the rescue, and in as sweet a voice as she could muster, said, "Before we get started, would it be alright if we had a cup of tea? The weather's a bit chilly here this morning and we've come a long way to get here. Would you mind?"

With that, the two women jumped into action and headed for the kitchen, saying that they would be glad to oblige. That gave us some time to talk to Michael.

We walked over and stood next to him by the fire, one on each side, and I asked, "What's this all about, Michael? It seems as if you've worked yourself up into a frenzy over all of this?"

Saoirse chimed in and asked, "It's not that bad, is it now?"

"What is it that these two well-meaning women did to get you all this upset?" I asked. "They're just doin' their jobs here, aren't they?"

The expression on his face changed some, but he didn't respond. Then I asked, "They're not teamin' up on ya with tag-team wrestlin', now are they? They're not related to Steven Casey himself, are they?"

That actually made him crack a wee bit of a smile. Steve Casey was the former world-champion professional wrestler decades ago who was from Sneem. The statue in the park there is of him. He knew who he was and responded by saying, "Christ almighty, Brendan! Whose side are you on, anyhow?"

"Yours, of course, Michael. You know that, but look at you . . . they tell us that you're shoutin' and roarin' to beat the band! Is it that bad?" I asked. "Have they been beatin' on ya?" I asked, again.

"Ugh! You're bein' scaldy now, Brendan! I'm serious about this," he told me.

"Now, now, Michael. Let's sit down, have a sip of tea these two nice ladies are making for us, and sort this out, shall we?" Saoirse asked.

The two of us sat down in our usual spots, and reluctantly, he joined us and sat in his chair. The two women served us our tea moments later. Mrs. Welch steered clear of Dr. McDuffy, who was still, obviously, quite agitated. Mrs. Maloney took care of him. Fortunately, it appeared as if he was still quite comfortable with her in his house. This was all about Mrs. Welch, which was not unexpected.

The tele was on, though turned down low, and Saoirse commented on the storm that was predicted to arrive later in the day. "We're not going to get too much work done today if the weathermen are correct," she said.

"They're the only people in the world who can get things right half the time and still keep their jobs," I said.

Saoirse laughed, as did the two women, but Dr. McDuffy was stoic. He wasn't making eye contact with any of us. I'd seen him angry before, but never quite like this.

When we had finished out tea, I said, "We'd better get to work pretty soon then if we're to get anythin' done. I see where Rory delivered the wood and all, and Saoirse here still has things to do in that shed of yours. Are you ready to go to work today, Michael? It's just you and me on the fence." I told him. "Rory told me that he's as sure as he can be that we can do this ourselves. Let's go do that, shall we?"

Somewhat reluctantly, he agreed, and when the three of us walked outside, he saw what was there and asked, "When did these get here?"

I told him of my conversation with Rory and he said, "They weren't here last night, I know that, and I haven't had my walk yet today, so this is the first I'm seeing of this. Do you think we can do this by ourselves, Brendan?"

"I do," I replied, and added, "Maybe we should let these two fine, young women go home a bit early before the weather arrives." That struck a nerve with Dr. McDuffy who said, "Now there's a good idea. I need to change my shoes before we get started. I've still got my slippers on."

"And I'll use the porcelain facilities while you're doing that," Saoirse said. "It was a long drive over and the coffee has worked its way through me system."

While they were doing that, I went back inside and spoke to the two women. At first, they said that they weren't allowed to leave early, but I assured them that it would be fine if they did.

"Don't worry yourselves over that. The two of you can get all the work done that needs to be done today in half the time, can't ya?" I asked. "And you're only here today to meet the man and get the lay of the land, aren't ya, Mrs. Welch? It's not about the work now is it?"

They looked at each other, and Mrs. Maloney said, "That's true enough. The two of us can do the work in no time at all. That's a fact. With her helpin' me, there won't be much for the both of us to do, just fixin' his lunch. He's had his breakfast already. I was able to do that for him before she arrived."

"So, let's do that. We all knew that this might be a bit of a problem today, now didn't we? He doesn't like any of these changes that are going on in his life. We all know that, and we know that it's because of his sickness. He's really a wonderful man, isn't he, Mrs. Maloney?" I asked. "Tell her."

"He is that. He's just going through some hard times, that's the truth," she responded. "It took a while for him to accept me into his house, it did," she added. "Now we're fine."

"Well, he certainly has shown his arse today," Mrs. Welch said. She was still clearly upset by all the commotion herself. "I'm not used to this!"

"Now, now, Margaret . . . you know how these people can be. He's just havin' a bad day, that's all. He'll get used to you soon enough. He wasn't too nice to me at first, either, and he went through two or three people before I came on, don't ya know?" she said.

"Aye. I heard about that," she confessed.

"So, are we agreed?" I asked.

The two women looked at each other, and then Mrs. Maloney said, "Well, I guess that will be alright. Let's do what else needs to be done and be on our way today. I don't care about the extra euros if they decide to cut our pay."

"Nor do I. I'd have left long ago if it weren't for you, Bridey. I'll go along with whatever you decide to do," she responded.

"I'll get him outside of the house and out of your hair and that should be the end of the problem for today. I'll talk to him about all of this and hope things will go better next time you come, Mrs. Welch," I told them.

"*If* I come back," she responded. "I'll have to give that some thought, I will."

"Well, we all hope that you will, but everyone will understand if you don't," I told her. "That's up to you. No one's going to force you."

"We'll fix you three some sandwiches after we're finished tidying things up a bit more, and then we'll be off if that's alright with you, Mr. Sullivan," Mrs. Maloney said.

I assured her that it was and just then, as we were finishing our conversation, Dr. McDuffy and Saoirse returned. He had calmed down considerably by then. Tea has that effect, at times, but that was Saoirse's doing, I think. She handled the situation well.

"Are we ready to get to work?" I asked.

"I am ready to get out of this house," he responded, "but I'm no carpenter, Brendan."

"Nor am I, but Rory thinks we can do this and I don't want to disappoint my big brother, so let's go see what we can do," I said. "We'll leave Saoirse to finish sorting out that shed while we're doing that."

The three of us walked outside, and before long, Dr. McDuffy and I were fully engaged in figuring out where and how to put up this picket fence he wanted. It wouldn't hold anything in or out, but it would make the place look much nicer. Saoirse went straight for the shed.

Rory had given us six pre-assembled sections of fence and all we had to do was dig a few holes, put in the posts, and nail them together. There really wasn't much to it and I was confident that the two of us were capable of doing it. Still, it would take some time.

Digging the holes would be the hardest part. As it is in most of the country, there were rocks in the ground, lots of them.

We were about halfway through the task when, about an hour or so later, the two women came out of the house, told us that lunch was on the table, said their goodbyes, and drove away. Not long after that, it began spittin' rain. I grabbed the tools and ran to put them in the shed. Then, the two of us hurried inside. Saoirse was already there by then.

Once inside, after shaking off the wet, we sat down to eat our lunch. When Dr. McDuffy got up to use the toilet, I asked her about the gun. I was shocked to hear that she hadn't been able to find it.

We talked about what to do and we agreed that we'd have to confront him about it. We couldn't go back to Kathleen and tell her that we didn't find it and he still had it. That wasn't an option. When he returned, she asked him.

He leaned back in his chair and said, nonchalantly, "Oh, I took it out of there and put it in a safe place. It's so old. It probably doesn't work anymore anyway."

"Have you found the key?" she asked.

"No, I haven't," he replied.

"So, you haven't been able to inspect it?" I asked.

"Not yet," he answered. He was clearly being a bit coy with his responses. He was acting like it was nothing to trouble ourselves about, but it was much more important than that to us, and we persisted in asking where it was and if we could see it.

After several minutes of back and forth without getting anywhere, I told him that we had to know. "Actually, your daughter wants us to get that from you, Michael. We can't leave without it."

"I'm sure she does," he answered. "I figured that there was a reason you were so curious about it. So, you told her about it, did you?" he asked.

"We did," Saoirse acknowledged. "It's against the law, you know. We felt it was our duty to tell someone."

"I see," he responded. "Your duty, you say?"

"Michael, what's up with the gun?" I asked. "Why are you acting this way? You understand why everyone is concerned."

He stood, walked over to the fireplace, and picked up a pipe. I'd never noticed it before and I asked, "Since when have you been smoking a pipe, Michael?"

"For years, Brendan. That was another thing Marjorie wouldn't allow me to do in the house . . . that and cigars. She said they were bad for my health and made the house smell awful. Now that she's no longer here, I can do as I please in that regard."

He laughed when he said that, and he added, "She's having a fit right now, but there's nothing she can do about it. I've just started back up with it again here recently and she doesn't like it at all."

Then he lit his pipe, drew in a few breaths to get the flame going, and said, "I think this is a good time for us to have a little chat . . ."

CHAPTER TWENTY-FOUR

Recognition

"Brendan . . . Saoirse . . . I appreciate all that the two of you have done to help me, and I know why you're here. Be sure to thank Kathleen O'Brien and send her my love. I have been giving a lot of thought to all of this, trying to figure out exactly why all of this is happening to me. I've also done some research and I think I now understand exactly why you're here, why these women were here today, why Caitlin showed up out of the blue as she did, and why Kathleen is involved in all of this."

"Although I guess I should have suspected something sooner, my first clue was when my daughter just happened to show up as she did after being away for so many years as she has been, ever since her mother died. I didn't think too much about it at the time, but she forced me to see that solicitor as soon as she got here. That was extremely unusual and I should have said something about it at the time, but I didn't."

"And by the way, Mr. Sullivan, I now remember when I first met you. It came to me when that Garda lady picked me up the other day. I recognized her face. Seeing her reminded me of that time in Kenmare, after she had taken me there, against my will. I knew that you looked familiar, but I couldn't place where and when we met. I remember now . . . it was at the Garda's station that day in Kenmare."

"I now realize that was why I saw that Dr. Doherty fellow. I didn't understand any of that at the time. And it was no coincidence when the two of you showed up at my doorstep that day with that other friend of yours, now was it?" he asked, looking over at the two of us.

When we didn't answer, he took a puff on his pipe, lowered his eyes, and said, "I feel a bit like my old friend, Socrates, after he'd been sentenced to death by his fellow Athenians. Do either of the two of you know anything about that?"

I confessed that I knew nothing about it, and Saoirse said she remembered learning something about it in school, but couldn't recall exactly how or why he died.

"Well, the circumstances are entirely different, actually, but I am under a death sentence, just as he was." He turned first to me, and then to Saoirse, looking both of us squarely in our eyes, and said, "Yes, I know what it is that I am suffering from. It pains me to say the words, but I must . . . Alzheimer's disease."

We didn't respond, and he went on, "Unlike Socrates, I have done nothing to deserve this fate. It's a quirk of nature if you will . . . a gene of some sort that has mutated or otherwise ceased to function properly. It can be argued, and it has been by many over the centuries, that Socrates did nothing wrong, either, but he was sentenced to death because of things that he said and ideas that he had."

"He was charged by those in power at the time with corrupting the youth of Athens with some of his more outlandish opinions and for failing to properly acknowledge a belief in the widely accepted deities of his time.

"He was convicted, after a trial by jury, and the sentence of death was imposed upon him by that same jury. If you can imagine this, and it truly is hard to believe, even for one such as me who has studied ancient civilizations as I have for decades . . . five hundred men were chosen, by lot, to hear and decide his case."

"Yes, that's right . . . a jury of five hundred men, all over the age of thirty, were the ones to decide his fate. It's still hard to imagine, but it's true. And those five hundred fellow Athenians decided, after a day-long trial, by a vote of two hundred and eighty to two hundred and twenty, that he was guilty of the charges. Plato, who was a student of Socrates at the time, was present at the trial, which was held in a building called the 'Peoples Court,' and wrote a summary of the ordeal.

"That same jury then voted on the penalty, after they found him guilty. As was his character, Socrates made light of the situation he was in. He suggested a penalty whereby he would be required to eat at the public health center for the rest of his life would be severe enough punishment. Obviously, he didn't take the matter quite as seriously as he should have."

"He was, reportedly, defiant and unapologetic. The men prosecuting the case argued for the death penalty. After much deliberation, a majority of jurors agreed with that recommendation."

Saoirse and I sat there silently, listening to his every word, not saying anything. He was giving us a lecture on a topic he had studied his entire adult life for fifty years or more. His tone was more conversational as if he was talking to friends about his friends, not as a professor to a class of university students. It was mesmerizing, but it was not the main topic of conversation . . . Alzheimer's disease and his recognition of it was, and we knew it. He was trying to explain himself to us.

"And keep in mind that Athens was the first community of peoples in the history of the world to choose a democratic form of government, not the United States, as some Americans like to think. They, unlike any other society in the history of the world before them, or any since up until the United States did so in the late eighteenth century, were also the most civilized in how they meted out justice. They tried diligently to administer justice in a fair way."

"The verdict was that Socrates was to die for his crimes, such as they were . . . and this is another unusual aspect of his case . . . he was to kill himself. That is where I find the similarity between my old friend and myself most striking. I am in much the same situation as he was back then," he told us, quite matter-of-factly. "I am killing myself."

We both had a physical reaction to his words. "You're not going to kill yourself, are you, Michael?" I asked in a loud voice that was nearly a shout.

"You wouldn't do that, would you?" Saoirse asked in what sounded more like a plea than a question.

He looked at us and said, "That's for me to decide, now isn't it, children? But that's not what I meant . . . my body is killing me . . .

my body is in the process of self-destructing, but I am the perpetrator, just like Socrates was, in a way, don't you see?"

At first, I was a bit offended by his use of the word "children" to address us, but then I realized that to him, we were children. He probably had grandchildren older than we were, or nearly as old, and we were definitely like children with regard to his years of experience and his intellect.

I was the first to respond, and said, "Not really, Michael, but I think that you need to give us that gun."

"I agree with Brendan," Saoirse said. "Please give us that gun, Michael!" she implored.

"I knew that was why you were asking, and I will do as you ask. I know that if I don't, you, Caitlin, Kathleen, or someone else will have the Garda here to search my house and seize it. I don't want that."

"I'll give it to you, but I wanted to have this conversation with you first. I want the two of you, and everyone else, to know that I know what's going on and that I will decide what is to become of me . . . not you, Kathleen, or anyone else, including my two children, who I love very much, and certainly not any judge or jury following some judicial proceeding, such as the one Socrates had to endure," he said.

I was relieved to hear him say that he would give us the gun, but that didn't solve the underlying problem. He knew he had Alzheimer's disease and he knew that he was facing death after suffering through what would be hell on earth. Based on all that I knew about the disease, I couldn't blame him if he did take his own life, even though I knew Kathleen and Saoirse were dead-set against that point of view, but I said, "You know it's a sin, right, Michael?"

"A mortal sin, at that," Saoirse added.

"I do, and I am much like Socrates in that respect, too. He didn't ascribe to what were the commonly accepted beliefs of his day. He, too, questioned some of the religious dogma of the society in which he lived, as do I," he responded. That was part of the reason why he was found guilty and sentenced to death.

"You question the teachings of our church, do you, Michael?" Saoirse asked.

He looked at her and said, "I guess I haven't had this discussion before, have I, Saoirse? I explained my thoughts on all of that to Brendan the other night, but you weren't here, so I'll explain it to you now."

"People all over the world, whether they be Christian, Hindu, Buddhist, Muslim, Sikh, Jewish, or a hundred other sects, including the Druids, have differed over that subject since the time human beings first arrived on this planet . . . and to answer your question, yes, I do question the teachings of our church in some respects. I don't accept all of the dogma."

"That said, I have spent my entire life as a member of the Catholic Church. I have chosen to believe what we have been taught. I have 'faith' in the teachings of our church and Jesus despite the fact that the term 'faith,' by definition, means that I am believing in things even though there is no objective proof of many of the most basic tenets of the church."

"And let's not forget, as if we ever could, we live in a land where two powerful Christian communities, Catholics and Protestants, have committed atrocities against each other for centuries. Without any doubt, it has been abominable what they have done to us, but we have retaliated, at times, and all of that occurred even though we share so many of the same beliefs, including going to the same heaven after we die. We are similar to them in so many ways, yet we kill each other because of our relatively minor theological differences."

"Relatively minor? I can't believe what I just heard you say! They rejected our pope and persecuted us as if we were vile human beings! Are you saying we should be forgiving them, after all that we've been through!" Saoirse responded. Clearly, she was more upset about that than anything else he'd said to us so far.

He chuckled a bit and replied, patting her on the knee, and said, "I might have gone a bit too far there, and I apologize if I did. Make no mistake, I am Irish to the core, Irish Catholic, that is, and I am a Catholic by choice. I will never deny either my homeland or my religion."

"I'm not denying Jesus Christ or our pope. All that I am saying, really, is that we are told that we may be going to the same 'heaven' with them when we die, that's all, and I do have questions about where any of us will go when we die," he said, gravely. "The point I am making is that the basic theology of both 'Christian' religions is relatively the same."

"But I'm not forgetting or forgiving them for what they've done to us over the centuries . . . I'm not. I'm talking about where we go after we die. I don't want any Protestants in the heaven I'm going to," he confirmed. "There's a special place in hell for them, as far as I'm concerned, make no mistake about that, lass, but my point is this . . . I don't believe that the whole world is going to the same place when we die. I realize that I may be entirely wrong, but that is what I choose to believe."

"Many Roman Catholics used to think, before Vatican II, which was in 1966, that only Catholics went to heaven. That was, and it is, poppycock. The church doesn't say that anymore. I read where our current pope, Francis, says that even atheists and agnostics can go to heaven."

"Who knows what 'heaven' is, if there is such a place? Nobody! So, I say that I get to decide what that place is to be like, now don't I?" he asked. "It's whatever I think it's going to be . . . whatever I want it to be . . . whatever I believe it to be, right?"

"I guess so," I responded, though I really didn't. "I never really thought about it all that much, to be honest. I just didn't want to go to the other place," I said.

"I think we go to heaven, Michael, if we're deserving, just like we're taught," Saoirse answered. "I don't think we get to make that decision."

"Of course, I do! We all get to decide what 'heaven' is or where it is. They don't tell us what happens after we enter the 'pearly gates,' now do they? Of course not! Nobody has been there and come back, have they? So, nobody knows what heaven is really like, now do they?"

"So, I get to decide, in my own mind, what that heaven is like, and so do you. Your idea of what heaven is like is, without a doubt, much different from mine, I'm sure. See what I mean?" he asked.

When we didn't respond, he went on, "I know what I want that heaven to be and that's where I believe I'll be going, and soon . . . one way or the other and it won't be long before I get there."

"We can't stop you, Michael," Saoirse responded, "as much as we might want to. If that's what you decide to do, that's what you're going to do, no matter what we might think or say, right? If I could, I would, though."

"Would you stop me if you could, Saoirse? Or you, Brendan?" he asked. "Would you sentence me to a death of however many months or years it will be until my body completely ceases to function properly?"

"Do you want to see me endure months and years of gradually losing my mental faculties? Losing my privacy and my inner self in the process? Would you want to see me suffer like that? Would you? he asked.

"Would you want that for yourselves or your family members, knowing as you do what awaits me?" he raised his voice ever so slightly as he spoke, looking back and forth at the two of us, straight into our eyes.

"Would you?" he asked again, awaiting a reply. After several more moments, when neither one of us responded, he continued, "Don't fret too long over that. It's a serious matter and it's not your concern . . . it's mine."

"You can rest assured . . . and you can tell Kathleen this . . . that I haven't made up my mind up at the moment. I'll talk to my children and do my best to make a decision before things get too bad. I don't want to wait too long and reach the point where I'm unable to make a rational decision or have the ability to do whatever it is I choose to do, but I'm not doing so badly at the moment, am I?" he asked.

"Well, you weren't too good earlier today, now were you, Michael?" I said.

He laughed and said, "I guess I did get carried away there, didn't I? I'm sure that it's hard for the two of you, and the others, to imagine or understand what it's like for me to be going through this. No one has to tell me that I'm having some difficulties. No one knows that better than I do."

"But that's what this is all about, isn't it? How bad is good 'ole Dr. McDuffy getting these days? Is he getting worse? Of course, I am! And it's going to continue to get worse, Brendan . . . you know it, Saoirse here knows it, Kathleen knows it, Caitlin knows it, and so does everyone else . . . and so do I," he told us. "Yes, I do, and yes it will! And don't think I don't know that!"

Then he stood, walked over to the cabinet next to the fireplace to put some more tobacco in his pipe, and said with a smile, "Besides, I've got a fence to fix. How can I leave now that we've got the place looking so good? The two of you, and others, like your brother and Seamus O'Reilly have done such a fine job of fixin' it up?" he asked. "That would be a shame to spoil things now, wouldn't it?"

"That it would, Michael," I agreed. "That it would. You can't leave us just yet."

"It's absolutely grand now, it is," Saoirse said. "You've got plenty of good years ahead of you, and you have women to wait on you hand and foot to make you as comfortable as could be. What could be wrong with that?" she asked.

He harrumphed when she said that and said, "Don't get me started on that, lass. You're as bad as he is. That's another matter altogether. That's not resolved yet, not by a long shot. That's part of the problem, actually."

"And 'plenty of good years,' you say? I don't think so, and I don't want to live like that, don't you understand?" he asked, plaintively. "That's what I'm trying to explain to you, but nobody seems to understand."

"We understand, Michael, but you really need the help that you're being given . . . you do, and that's a fact. You can't deny that this place is a hundred times better than it was before they came, with the food, the cleanliness, the washing, the drying . . . everything. There's no doubt that you need help with all of that . . . none whatsoever. Right?" I asked.

"There's no doubt about that, Michael, and it's for your own good," Saoirse added.

"For my own good, you say . . . with all due respect, I'll be the one to decide what's best for me, if it's all the same to the two of you," he responded. "Although my mind, or my brain, or both, if there is a difference, isn't what it once was, I am still capable of making my own decisions," he told us.

"However . . . and I'll be the first to agree on this . . . I am worried about what's happening to me, and I worry about how long I'll have that ability. As I said before, no one has to tell me that I'm doing things or failing to do things, that I should or shouldn't do. No one is more concerned about all of that than I am, you can both be sure of that."

"But we come back to the question of what's to be done with me, and we're not going to solve that problem today, now are we?" he asked. "You came for the gun, and I'm going to give it to you. When I do, my children and Kathleen will be pleased with that. That's what you've come to do, yes?"

"That's true," we acknowledged. "It is, but we can't make you do something you absolutely don't want to do," I said. "We want you to agree that what's being done is what's best for you."

"And we can't stop you from doing something you absolutely want to do, even if we totally disagree, but we'll try," Saoirse added.

"That's right, you can't. I am in charge of my body and my mind. I'm glad we've resolved that much," he said, still standing next to the fire, puffing on his pipe. For a moment, I had the feeling that this was a scene from a movie or a play. It was quite dramatic. We were at the core of a serious matter . . . a deadly serious matter, and we all knew it.

Saoirse asked, "Wasn't Plato with Socrates when he died? Didn't he try to stop him?"

"There's some debate about that, lass. He was definitely present throughout the trial, and he wrote a book about it that is quite famous, as I mentioned a few minutes ago. Some say that he helped with the defense of Socrates, but from all I know, as best I can tell, he was not there at the end, at the bitter end, that is," he answered, "but you're right, the people who were with him at the time, Socrates, that is, all tried to stop him from doing what he did."

"And what about Aristotle?" I asked. "Was he there, too?" I don't know why I did that. I knew so little about the Greeks. Those were the only three names I could remember, and I always heard the three of them mentioned in the same sentence, for the most part.

He looked at me in a kindly way, and responded, "No, Brendan, he wasn't. Plato was a pupil of Socrates and Aristotle was a pupil of

Plato. Aristotle was born many years after Socrates died. The three are forever linked in history, though."

I sat back, thought about all that I had heard this great man say, and asked, "So where will you go, Michael? Where is your heaven?"

"Elysium, of course," he answered without hesitation. "Marjorie is there, waiting for me now."

"Elysium?" Saoirse asked. "Where is that? And what is that?"

"It was heaven to the ancient Greeks and Romans," he answered. "To both the Greeks and the Romans, souls had to cross the river Styx to get there. It's not clear exactly where that was, but one had to journey quite a way before they arrived."

"And your Elysium . . . where is that?" Saoirse asked.

"Here in Ireland, of course . . . out in the Atlantic on one of our mystical islands," he answered with a smile on his face. "It's a magical place, intended only for the Irish," he answered. "Irish Catholics, that is," he added. "That's my heaven."

"But the point is this . . . according to the Greeks, the Romans, the Druids, and others, there is an afterlife, whether we call it heaven or something else, and I'll be goin' there sooner or later . . . and I look forward to it. I've done my best to be a good man, deserving of a place there, and I pray that I will be rewarded for my efforts in this lifetime."

"You've led a grand life, Dr. Martin Michael McDuffy . . . if anyone is deserving of going to heaven, it would be you, from all that I know about you," Saoirse said.

He smiled, thanked her, and said, "But that's enough of this gloomy and depressing conversation for now. I don't want to talk about it anymore if it's all the same to you. It looks as if the sun is coming out and it's time for all of us to go outside and enjoy this beautiful day."

He stood and said, "Those two women attacked me this morning before I had time to go for my morning walk. I need to get some fresh air and clear my head. No telling how many more of these beautiful days I might have, right? Carpe diem!"

"Who said that," I asked. "Which one of the Greeks was it?"

"Actually, that was a Roman . . . Horace, and he lived just before the time when Christ was born," he answered. "'Live for today' . . . and you two youngsters have a life-time ahead of you, full of hopes, dreams, and desires. I have had plenty of days such as this one in my life, more than my fair share, that's for sure. I've been very fortunate . . . very fortunate, indeed."

Then he started to wave his hands around in circles like he was shooing us out of his home. "Go on! Get out of here! Go live your lives to the fullest, that's my advice to the two of you . . . you've spent enough time with this moribund old man who speaks to you of death and dying! Get out of here! Go! Go! Get out and live your life!" he said, literally shooing us out of his home as he spoke.

"Alright! Alright! We're going, Michael," I said as I stood up and started to move to the door, with a laugh. He meant no ill toward us, I knew that, but he did want us out of his home and wanted us to go right then. He didn't want to talk to us anymore about his disease and the questions that were obviously tormenting him.

"But not before you give us that gun, Michael," Saoirse said.

I was glad she remembered. With all of the conversation about Socrates, Elysium, and the rest, I'd forgotten about it.

He laughed, reached behind him into a closed drawer, and handed her the box, which was still locked.

"That's right! Can't forget about that, can we now? We'd all be in trouble if you did," he said.

"I can't find the key, but either way, it doesn't matter. If it isn't in there, I don't have a gun, but if it is, I don't have a gun any longer. I'm as positive as I can be that it's in there. That's where I kept it for years," he assured her.

He went to shake my hand and thank me, but instinctively, I put my arms around him and gave him a hug. I'd never done that in my life, except to my father, and then that was only on a few rare occasions.

He towered over me, and my head was somewhere near the bottom of his chin, I believe. He hugged me back and said, "Thank you, Brendan. You've been brought into my life for a reason, and you have fulfilled your purpose. I'm grateful for that and I thank you."

Then Saoirse gave him a hug, as well, and he thanked her, too. I could see tears welling up in her eyes as she asked, "We will see you again, won't we, Michael? We're coming back next week. You'll be here to greet us, yes?"

"Of course, I will, my dear. I'll be here, in one form or another," he assured her.

"You promise?" she persisted.

"I promise," he answered.

"See you in a week, Michael," I said. "Take care of yourself between now and then, and don't give those women too much trouble, please! It will just cause all of us more problems, including you. You know that better than I do, right?"

"Marjorie agrees with you, Brendan. She still tells me what to do, and I do what she says, for the most part, except for this pipe, of course," he said with a laugh. "She's not happy about that."

"I'll do my best with those women, lad. Have a safe drive back to Cork. I'll see you next week, and please remember to give Kathleen my love," he said as he closed the door behind us.

CHAPTER TWENTY-FIVE

Socrates

We didn't talk much on the way back. At first, I tried to defend Michael, saying that I certainly wouldn't want to endure what he was going through, not only for myself, but for my family, my friends, and everyone who would support me or assist me, but she would hear none of it. She kept saying that it was wrong and I knew it. We had a bit of an argument over it, actually. We ended it by saying that we'd have to wait and see what Kathleen thought about it all.

That Monday, when we told Kathleen all about what had happened, the first thing she did was ask about the gun and where it was. I told her that it was still in the trunk of my car. I didn't dare bring it into the hospital for fear of setting off an alarm. Everyone, even the doctors, had to pass through security to get through. She said she'd take care of it straight away.

She was more concerned when I mentioned the business of how Socrates died. "You know how he killed himself, don't you?" she asked. Neither of us did.

"He swallowed some poison while surrounded by friends, and from all accounts, he died quickly and painlessly," she told us.

"Really?" I asked. "I thought if you took poison, it would burn your insides up and cause unbearable pain."

"Not according to Plato, who wasn't there, but he wrote about it and knew all of the people who were there. Reportedly, and much has been written about it since, Socrates was his own executioner, and he did so rather calmly while those around him wept openly."

"It is said that the effects of the poison were first noticeable in his lower extremities. His legs became numb and he was forced to sit down. Once the poison reached his heart, he was dead. Nowhere does it indicate that he experienced any pain or that he suffered."

"Socrates is considered to be the 'father' of western philosophy, and Plato was his most famous student. Socrates never wrote things down, and he wrote no books. Plato did that for him."

"Most of what is known about him comes from Plato. He is the one who told the world most of what Socrates thought and said," she told us. "And the casual student might think to give credit to him, Socrates, that is, for the ideals of equality and democracy, which the ancient Greeks were the first to espouse, but that wouldn't be quite accurate," she said.

"Really?" Saoirse interjected. "I learned of Greek civilization in a political science class, and I became familiar with Plato's Republic, but I never read where Socrates was anti-democratic. Is that true?" she asked.

"It is, in large part, and that was one of the main reasons he was sentenced to death. The charges against Socrates included one that accused him of 'corrupting the youth.' Another was that he should be punished for 'refusing to accept the gods recognized by his fellow citizens in Athens. One of the most significant complaints against Socrates was that he believed 'pure' or 'true' democracy was not the best political system," she told us.

"I didn't know that," Saoirse said. "I don't remember hearing anything about that, actually," Saoirse continued. Though she wasn't questioning Kathleen, she was clearly surprised to learn it.

I had no idea about it, myself. I hadn't taken any of those courses and knew little of Socrates views on democracy. I was more interested in the wars and the military history of the Greek civilization . . . Alexander the Great, Sparta, the Iliad, the Odyssey, and the creation of what became our modern-day Olympics . . . things like that.

"It's a fact, Saoirse, and you can google it right now if you'd like. He felt that only those people who were knowledgeable about politics should be allowed to vote. Quite famously, he likened the state of Athens . . . and back then, in Greece, the various cities ruled themselves, since Greece wasn't united, and . . ."

"Except for the Trojan War, right? They were united then, weren't they?" I asked, interrupting her as I did.

She looked over at me, with a kindly expression on her face, and said, "Most historians doubt that such a war ever took place, Brendan, though many believe that there might well have been some minor conflicts which provided a basis for that masterful tale, but as I was saying, he likened democracy to a sailing ship and asked, 'Who would you want onboard ship with you? Knowledgeable sailors or inexperienced ones?'"

"The answer was obvious, and to him, so was the answer to the whole concept of whether or not democracy was the best form of government. In fairness to him, that trial took place at a time when Athens was suffering from what was, without doubt, a most difficult period. Only four years prior to his death, Athens experienced a catastrophic defeat at the hands of Sparta and its allies, which ended the Peloponnesian War."

"A debate raged in Greece as to whether or not democracy was a better form of government than an oligarchy. The Athenians favored democracy and the Spartans and their allies did not. Socrates, though he was an Athenian, was on the wrong side of that debate, as far as his fellow citizens were concerned."

"The result of the war is what doomed Socrates, in my view, and that was due, in large part, to another of Socrates' students, a man named Alcibiades. He was a flamboyant leader, the son of a general who became a general himself. He was actively involved in the war and at the front of the debate regarding democracy at the same time, which must have been both difficult and precarious for him."

"As the leader of the country, he suspended all democratic institutions while he waged war. He was a demagogue and somewhat of a tyrant. He was rich, immoral, flamboyant, handsome, and was, according to all accounts, a fabulous orator."

"He had the ability to sway the masses and was enormously popular with many. I doubt that he was the leader Socrates would have desired. Rather, I expect that he was the leader Socrates most feared, one who could sway a majority of the less intelligent electorate, but he, Socrates, that is, was aligned with the man, historically speaking, because of the fact that the man was one of his students."

"Remember, although it was Plato who suggested that the rulers of a country should be 'philosopher kings,' he thought that a benign dictatorship was the best form of governance. That is what he wrote in his book, the *Republic*."

"Most historians believe he learned that from Socrates. Alcibiades was not that sort of ruler. He was a dictator and not all that benign. He was more interested in his own personal interests than he was in the welfare of the common man."

"Alcibiades' relationship to Socrates was one of student-teacher, and that would have been when he was a youth. He may have been a teenager when he first met Socrates who would have been in his thirties at the time. The views which both men had regarding a democracy, despite their differences, were, as I said, one of the main points against Socrates at his trial."

"You seem to know as much about all of that as Dr. McDuffy," Saoirse observed.

"I had a good teacher," she responded with a smile, "but he knows much, much more than I do or ever will know. I was a good student, and I remember much of what he taught me."

"As I was saying, Socrates was rather outspoken, and seldom held his tongue. He told people what he thought without regard to the consequences. In doing so, he was said to have been 'corrupting' the youth of Athens, and most importantly, siding with Sparta at a time when the two cities were at war with each other."

"We don't know what the two men actually thought of each other, though, once Alcibiades became a grown man and the leader of Greece. I don't think Socrates could have tolerated his behavior. Alcibiades is blamed for Athens' disastrous defeat at the hands of its bitter enemy and the loss of some fifty-thousand soldiers.

"Socrates suffered and ultimately died because of his perceived association with the man, rightly or wrongly. He was expressing his opinions, nothing more. He didn't openly support or provide aid to Sparta, but many Athenians were extremely unhappy with him after they lost the War, which is understandable."

"What about his views on the Athenian gods?" I asked. "Didn't you say his religious beliefs had something to do with it, too?"

She sighed and said, "Some say that he believed in only one god, not many, as the majority of Greeks did at the time. However, that is somewhat disputed because, as I said before, Socrates didn't write things down. Plato doesn't mention much about that, but none of this has anything to do with Dr. McDuffy's situation, mind you, Brendan, and I think we've spent enough time on the topic of Socrates, except for the business of how he died. Remember, he poisoned himself."

"Oh! So, you think Dr. McDuffy might try to poison himself!" I said as a light bulb went off in my head, finally connecting the dots.

Again, she turned to me, this time with a less kindly look on her face, and said, "That's right, Brendan . . . that's exactly what I'm saying. It's not the gun we have to worry about, it's poison."

"Think about it . . . isn't that exactly what a man who spent his entire life studying the ancient Greeks, who admired Socrates, Plato, and Aristotle so much, would do? It's a perfect ending, in a way, isn't it?" she asked.

"But it's contrary to the teachings of our church, Kathleen," Saoirse interjected. "You know that as well as I do. He wouldn't do that, would he?" she asked.

We both were staring at her, awaiting her response. This was, after all, exactly what we'd argued about days before. We both wanted to hear her answer. She didn't respond right away.

She reached her hands across the table and grabbed one of mine and one of Saoirse's, and said, "Alright, you two . . . you remember what I told you the other day . . . so you know exactly how I feel about all of this. However, I can't control Dr. McDuffy and I'm not about to have him put under lock and key to prevent him from doing what he 'might' do. The law won't allow it."

"That said, you know I do not, and never will, condone the taking of one's own life. I will never do that," she repeated.

"Can you imagine what Diarmud Martin, the Archbishop of Dublin, who's a dear friend of mine, would say? Good God Almighty! I might be excommunicated meself, just for thinkin' it, let alone sayin' it out loud!"

"So where does that leave us? The answer is plain, Brendan, isn't it? I can't do anything other than do all that I can to prevent the man from taking his own life . . . I can't, and neither can either of you."

She squeezed my hand harder and said, "But I'd be lyin' to the both of you if I didn't tell you that I am certainly worried about what the man might do. He didn't tell you that's what he's planning on doing, now did he? No, he didn't, but I will certainly discuss the issue with the two children, and with Dr. Delaney, but what more can I do?"

"Nothing, I'm afraid . . . nothing. I'm not going to suggest that a petition for involuntary hospitalization be filed because the man 'might' be a danger to himself, even though I suspect that he might be. Not unless he does something to actually try and do what we fear he might do."

"So! There you have it . . . I fear the worst but I don't think we have anywhere near enough information to do anything more than keep a close eye on him. It hurts me to say those things because I wish that there was something more that I could do for the man, but there isn't, I'm sad to say."

I could see tears continue to well up in her eyes as she spoke. We assured her that we do all that we could for the man and that we would report all that we saw and heard as best we could.

"He's between a rock and a hard place, or as he would say, between Charybdis and Scylla."

Saoirse and I looked at each other with blank looks on our faces, and she explained that Charybdis was a deadly, swirling whirlpool which no man could survive, and Scylla, a man-eating monster who dwelled in the cliffs above, who killed any who passed by him.

"It comes from Greek mythology. Dr. McDuffy knew them well and taught me all about them," she added. "It was one of his favorite expressions, in fact. He has no good options."

"I'll call Caitlin and her brother in a few hours, when they're likely to be awake, and explain the situation to them and see what they have to say about it. Suicide is such an anathema to me, and I'm sure it is to them, as well.

"Although from what I have read, the people on the west coast of the United States are quite open to such a thing . . . it's legal in some of their states, probably California, I'd wager. It's the most liberal place on the planet, I believe.

"So, who knows? They might approve of it in theory, though I doubt it, not when it comes to their father, I'm sure. But, let's wait and see what they have to say. Maybe they'll have some other ideas. Maybe they'll want to take some more drastic measures."

"More drastic than what they have so far? He's not going to like that one bit. I can guarantee you that!" I said. "Don't you agree, Saoirse?" I asked.

"Absolutely! He truly hates what's going on now, as we all know," she responded.

"There's no doubt about that," she agreed. "So, in the meantime, until we hear back from the children, we'll stay the course. Stay in contact with the man and be sure to submit your report, as you have done so well over these last couple of months now. We don't want anyone sayin' that we did anythin' but the best that we could."

"I'd say we've done the best that anyone could have done, without any doubt about it whatsoever. Everything is in place . . . he's prepared for what awaits him, whether he likes it or not, including the women who are there to help him," Saoirse offered.

"Thank you for that, Saoirse," she responded. "I've seen far too many of these cases over the last forty years to last a lifetime, but this one is a real sickner for me. That's for sure.

With that, she stood and said, "So that's it. You're going back there on Saturday, and I'll look forward to meeting with you again next week unless something important should come up in the meanwhile. If it does, you'll be hearing from me." She put a tissue to her eyes to dry some tears as she spoke.

"Wait!" I said, "Before you go, tell us what it was that killed him? What was the poison he used? What should we look for?"

"Hemlock oil," she responded, and then she asked me, "Just out of curiosity, did you happen to ask him where he's going when he dies?"

"We did. We talked about that," I told her.

"And what did he tell you?" she asked.

"Elysium," I answered.

"Of course," she replied, "to be with Marjorie, I'm sure. I'm not surprised." With that, she started to walk toward the door, but then turned back and asked, "But he didn't tell you he was going there right away, did he? You don't think he's going to do anything soon, do you?"

"No, no, no," we responded. "In fact, he promised us that he wouldn't," Saoirse said. "He said he'd see us this weekend, right, Brendan?" she asked.

"That's right, he did," I confirmed. "I'm not sure that he 'promised' us that he'd be there, but he said something like he couldn't leave now, not with the house bein' fixed up like it was, and he did say that he'd see us this weekend. I'm sure about that."

"That's good. Have a good week and, remember . . . don't take this to heart . . . let me do that. Just do your jobs. Whatever happens is not your responsibility, it's mine," she said as she walked out the door.

We sat there, somewhat stunned by what we had heard, not saying much of anything. I did a google search on hemlock oil and saw it was available for purchase on-line.

"Look here, Saoirse," I said, holding up my cellphone. "He could buy hemlock oil for less than ten euro online, right this very minute. He could have it within days. Can you believe that?" I asked.

"No! Is that a fact? Are you sure it's the poison?" she asked.

"It says so right on the bottle . . . poison," I told her.

"Should we tell Kathleen?" she asked.

"I expect she knows all about it, don't you?" I answered.

"That's true. If there was poison in the house, Mrs. Maloney would have found it and she would have said something about it, but she didn't. If she finds it, she'll tell us."

"We can talk to her about that on Saturday. Kathleen will tell the family and they'll decide. Kathleen will let us know what to do about all of that," she said. "Leave it up to her and them."

Then I asked, "I wonder what Socrates thought about God. Whatever it was, that's part of the reason why he was sentenced to death, apparently, but Kathleen didn't want to talk too much about that."

"Ask google," Saoirse responded, and I did.

"It doesn't really say . . . it says here that he might have believed in just one God, not all of the ones the Greeks worshipped," I told her. "But many people seem to question the accuracy of that, just like she told us. There's no proof one way or the other, from what I can tell," I said. "It says he might have been one of the first non-Jewish people to believe that there was just one god, not many, so she was right."

"Remember, he lived several centuries before Christ was born, and there were no Muslims back then. I don't know what the Persians and the rest believed," she responded.

"No one seems to know what Socrates truly believed, as best I can tell," I told her as I continued to read the various blurbs. "Looks like it was just what Kathleen told us . . . he believed in monotheism. It's mentioned in here a couple of times."

"I wonder if he believed in an after-life, like the others," she asked.

"It doesn't say, but whatever it was, it wasn't what his fellow Athenians believed, apparently," I answered.

"I wonder if there were many Jews in Greece back then or Rome for that matter," she asked.

"I have no idea, and it doesn't say anything about that," I answered, "but it doesn't seem as if people back then tolerated a difference of opinion all that well, does it?" I asked.

"Apparently not," she responded.

"Kind of like it is today, isn't it, Saoirse?" I asked.

"They didn't have Jesus Christ to teach them, as we do, did they?" she responded, "and don't you be forgettin' that, Brendan Sullivan," she told me in a semi-serious way, pointing her finger at me as she spoke. "We follow his teachings," she added somewhat emphatically. "All of them, not just the ones you want to."

"That's true," I agreed, but then I added, "I wonder what Jesus would have said to people about all of that back then. There were a lot of sick people around . . . leprosy and all. I don't remember anything about them ever getting any better. They lived by themselves in colonies, I guess, never getting any better. It was miraculous when he cured them. Were they supposed to live as beggars their whole lives and be happy about it? None of that is mentioned in any of the gospels, now is it?"

I don't know why I did that. I knew that would upset her, and it did.

"Don't be startin' that with me, Brendan Sullivan! It's wrong and you know it!" she told me, and she stood to leave. She was clearly not happy with me and my views on the subject. With that, she said, curtly, "I'll see you on Saturday. You're driving," and she left. A difference of opinion had blossomed into our first legitimate argument.

CHAPTER TWENTY-SIX

Thanatos

Early the next morning, not long after I arrived for work, a young woman, even younger than me, appeared at my cubicle and said, "Dr. O'Brien wishes to see you in her office. Please follow me."

I was in the middle of something that needed to be finished and asked if she meant right away. I was told that it was an urgent matter and that I was to come immediately. I followed her down the hall where she stopped at Saoirse's desk and told her to come along as well. Neither one of us had been to her office before, which was on the other side of the building, several hundred meters away.

When we arrived, we followed her straight into Kathleen's office, and saw her sitting in a chair, behind a desk, looking out a large, plate-glass window. Her back was to us.

"Have a seat," the woman told us, and she left, closing the door behind her.

When she turned around, we saw a woman who was barely recognizable. Every other time we had seen her, she had been dressed immaculately, well-coiffed, with make-up, lipstick, eye shadow, and the rest, but not this time. It looked as if she had slept in the clothes she had on and had just gotten out of bed. She looked awful, for her. It was obvious that she had been crying.

"I got a call early this morning from Caitlin," she told us, "and I don't know what time it was, because I was asleep. By the time I got to the phone, she had hung up. The message she left was that she was deeply concerned about her father and what he might do to himself. She asked me to call her as soon as I received her message no matter the hour. She had received a call from him minutes earlier that worried her and she wanted me to know about it immediately. She feared the worst."

"I called her right back, but the line was busy. She called me back fifteen minutes later. She had been talking to her brother. He, too, had received a call from him, and he was just as concerned as she was. Both of them had tried calling him, repeatedly, but neither one was able to reach him."

"She told me that she was as sure as she could be that her father was telling her, in his own way, goodbye. He didn't come right out and say it, but she knew that's what he was doing. Patrick hoped that he was just having a bad night, still upset at all the changes that were taking place in his life, but he, too, was worried that something terrible might happen, although he didn't think it was imminent. Caitlin thought it was more serious than that, and that something needed to be done immediately.

"She wanted me, personally, not either of the two of you or anyone else, to go to Sneem straight away and talk to him, to see what I thought. She'd read the report you submitted yesterday, so she knew all about what was going on. She had a gut-wrenching feeling about things. She was nearly hysterical on the phone with me, begging me to do what she was asking."

"Her brother told her that he would immediately make arrangements to get here as soon as he could, within the next week, at the latest. Caitlin was worried that he'd be too late by then, which was why she called me."

"When I looked at a clock, I saw that it was nearly five o'clock at that time, and I immediately called the Kenmare Garda office, hoping someone would be there. I knew that no one would be in Sneem. I spoke to a woman who told me that she'd see to it that an officer would go to the home and check on the man as soon one became available."

"She only did that after I explained to her who I was and how urgent I thought things were. She said she'd do her best, but she couldn't guarantee when that might be. She didn't think she couldn't get anyone there before eight, because that was when the day shift comes on."

"I wasn't going to be able to go back to sleep, not after hearing all of that. I was a nervous wreck. I walked aimlessly around my house, waiting for a call. I tried the agency, trying to locate Mrs. Maloney, but no one was there, either. I even tried Dr. Doherty, but I got his after-hours answer machine. I didn't know what else to do."

"I actually thought about getting in my car and driving there myself, but I didn't. I fixed myself some coffee and sat around, fretting, for an hour or two. Then, just as I was about to shower and get dressed for work, I received a call from Mrs. Maloney. She's the one who gave me the news."

"After calling Caitlin, I came in to do a few things that had to be done today, and to tell the two of you. I wanted to do that in person, not by phone. You deserve that," she told us. "You were an enormous help to the man in his final days, and the family appreciates that, as do I."

"I'll be the one who makes the arrangements with the parish priest for the funeral service and all. Caitlin and her brother, and as many of their children who can make it, are booking flights and will be here within the next few days. He'll be buried there in Sneem, next to his wife, in the cemetery beside the church, this Saturday, as long as the parish priest is agreeable. I haven't called him yet, but I assume that he will be."

"This comes at a bad time for me, as I have so much to do these days, but I'm not able to function too well at the moment. I'm sure you can understand why knowing what you do about the situation and my feelings for Dr. McDuffy and his family. I'll be leaving in a few minutes. I can't stay here, feeling the way I do."

She said with a hollow laugh, "I know I must look absolutely dreadful at the moment, and I hate to have people see me this way, but I felt that it was important for me to be the one to tell you what happened, as I said. Whether you know it or not, and I think you do, you were a great blessing to him there at the end. In fact, he left a note for you, Brendan."

"He did?" I asked. "What did it say?"

"I don't have it. Mrs. Maloney told me about it. It's in an envelope and she didn't open it. There was a note in his lap, as well," she told us.

"The note said, 'I've gone with Thanatos to be with Marjorie,'" she told us.

"Who's Thanatos? Or what is it?" I asked.

"Thanatos was the Greek god who carried humans off to the otherworld when their time on earth, as allotted to them by the 'fates,' had come to an end," she responded.

"I thought he was going to Elysium. That's what he told us," Saoirse said in a low, barely audible voice.

"He is," Kathleen responded. "Thanatos is the one who will take him there. Elysium was a special place . . . it wasn't, or it isn't, for everyone. Commoners didn't go there. It was the place where only 'heroes' went. It was, or it is, the place where the 'blessed' dead go, and that is where he belongs.

"At first, it was thought to be only for those who died in battle who were so brave and heroic that they gained immortality by their valor. Later, it was determined that it was also for those who deserved to be there as a result of a righteous life. If there is such a place, Dr. McDuffy is in Elysium as I speak."

"I'm so sorry to hear it," Saoirse said. "I can't believe he did it. What will the church have to say about it, I wonder?" she asked.

Dr. O'Brien stiffened, sniffled, put a tissue to her eyes and her nose, and said, "We'll just have to wait and see about that, now won't we? You're not to mention any of the details about this to anyone, understood? You're among the very first to learn of it, and you're to keep it to yourselves, please. Can you do that for me?"

We assured her that we would.

"Not to anyone, not even your colleague, Colin, and remember, not a word of our conversation yesterday to anyone, either. We'll let the authorities sort it out, but we won't be releasing our files to anyone unless we're required to do so. Understood?" she asked, looking squarely at us.

"Not a word," I responded.

"Me, neither," Saoirse agreed.

"Let me be the one to worry about all of that, and I will. It's a sad day for all of Ireland, that's for sure," she told us. "I guess I'll be the one to write his obituary, get them a picture, and all of that. I'll have to explain how it is he died, now won't I?" she asked, raising an eyebrow as she did. We didn't respond.

"You can always say it was something he ate or drank, can't you?" Saoirse offered.

"That I could," she responded. "Thank you, Saoirse. That's the truth, now, isn't it?" she asked.

"Or natural causes," I offered. "If it was the hemlock poison, that's the truth, too. It comes that way straight from the tree, doesn't it?" I asked. "That was it, wasn't it?"

She looked at me knowingly, and said, "Mrs. Maloney confirmed for me that he had received a package in the mail yesterday afternoon just before she left for the day, but she didn't know what was in it. I'm sure the Garda has it by now."

"She found him sittin' in his favorite chair, there by the fireplace. He was leanin' back, with his pipe still in his hand. She said that it appeared as if he died a peaceful death. There was no sign of any disturbance."

"When she tried to wake him and he didn't respond, the first thing she did was to call her office, and then she called me," she continued, "and that's when I called Caitlin to give her the news. She didn't take it well, though she wasn't surprised. Her suspicions were correct."

"We talked again just now, a few moments before the two of you came in, and she said that her brother, Patrick, was quite upset. He took it especially hard. He'd had a wonderful conversation with him on Sunday and was, according to her, devastated by the news, wishing he'd listened to her and done more to try and prevent it from happening."

"I wonder why he did it so suddenly," I asked. "He could have waited to see his son, couldn't he?"

"And he was still so brilliant. It was spellbinding for me to sit and listen to him talk, as I did those two or three times there before this. He'd had his bad moments . . . we all know that . . . but he was still having good times, too. He was fabulous to be with on those occasions," Saoirse added.

"I enjoyed that night I spent with Seamus and him at the bar, listening to them tell jokes, laughing as we did, as much as any I've ever had in my life," I told them. "I can't remember a time when I laughed so much or so hard . . . I can't. I will never forget that night. Why now? Why so suddenly?" I was near tears saying what I did.

"Sitting around the fire, listening to him tell us all about the Greeks, the Romans, world history, or the history of religion, among other things, as he did . . . I'll never forget those times. I think he still had many good months, if not years, to live. I just don't understand why he had to do it now, as he did, I don't. Why?" Saoirse asked.

"I agree with you both . . . why now? Things were going so well . . . I don't understand it, either, I don't," Kathleen said as she continued to sniffle and dab her eyes. "I haven't cried like this in a while. I apologize. This isn't like me at all," she sobbed. "Unfortunately, I've seen many people die over the years, but this one hits me especially hard, it does." She began to cry.

We sat in silence for a minute or two until she regained her composure and she continued, "The only thing I can say is that he was a proud man . . . a dignified man . . . and he didn't want to be dragged in the dirt as he would surely be. As to why he did it so suddenly, my only thought is that he didn't want pity, or condescending conversation . . . and he might have realized because of all that business surrounding the gun, that if he didn't do something then, as in right then, we would have done things to prevent him from doing what he did. I don't know . . . I really don't. Whatever his reasons, I wish we could have done something to stop him and change his mind."

There wasn't much either of us could do to comfort her, and we sat there, quietly, waiting for her to regain her composure. Moments later, she stood and said, "Well, I've got lots to do and it's not going to get done sitting here as I am. I should be going now. As I said, I wanted to be the one to tell you what had happened overnight, and now you know."

We stood when she did and she ushered us to the door, stopping to give us both big hugs along the way. "Thank you, again, for all you did to make Dr. McDuffy's last days on earth as pleasant as possible. I very much appreciate it, and so does his family," she assured us again.

"You'll let us know the details of when the funeral is to be, will you, Kathleen?" I asked.

"That I will," she told us, "just as soon as I'm able to make the arrangements. It will be sometime Saturday, I'm fairly certain, either late morning or early afternoon. Bye for now," she said as she closed the door behind us.

CHAPTER TWENTY-SEVEN

The Omega

The next day, Dr. McDuffy's obituary was front-page news in the Irish Times, the Irish Independent, the Irish Daily Star and, I expect, every paper throughout all of Ireland. That morning, Colin dropped the three big ones off on my desk first thing. "Thought you'd like to see these, Sully. He seemed like a nice, old codger. Sorry to see him go," he told me.

"But, that's the way all of those kinds of cases end up, isn't it? One way or another, sooner or later, and it's usually not soon enough, right? They aren't for me, mate, I'm going to help people who have other kinds of problems, like with alcohol and drugs . . . those are things I can relate to," he said with a laugh.

I thanked him, but it was no laughing matter. I know he was trying to make me feel better, but it didn't work. Actually, I thought it was inappropriate and insensitive on his part, to be honest.

I was seriously depressed by the news. He was no kin to me, but I had developed a fondness for the man. It was undeniable. I could understand why he did it, but I truly didn't understand why he had to do it so suddenly, and I was definitely going to miss him.

He slapped me on the back before walking away, and said, "Don't take it personally, Top Shillin'. You're just doin' your job, the one you chose to do. That's why we're here. Chin up, mate!"

When I saw Saoirse later in the morning and told her how I was feeling, she said she felt the same way. We made plans to attend the funeral, which was set for Saturday afternoon at 1:00. We read that in the papers. Neither of us had heard from Kathleen since yesterday morning.

She was quoted extensively throughout the articles, which featured a picture of him in his prime. He struck a fine pose, standing on the college green, in front of the archway leading into the college where he'd spent most of his life. Without a doubt, he was one of its most well-renowned figures in his day.

It was a fine piece of literature and covered most of two pages, including several other pictures of him with various government officials and world leaders from years past. We were sure that it was mostly Kathleen's work, though she hadn't written it, apparently. He was given much credit for his help in restoring Ireland's identity after it gained independence from England. We knew most of that, though there was much in there we didn't know.

Dr. Delaney called all three of us into his office—Colin, Saoirse, and me, that is, not Kathleen. He thanked us for our work on the case, telling us that we'd done a fine job. He expressed his sadness about how it ended but said things like that happen every now and again, though it's relatively rare.

"I want to make certain that none of you think that there was anything that you could have or should have done to prevent it from happening. I cannot stress that enough. You did all that was asked of you and more. I am quite pleased with the work all three of you have done on this case, and again, I thank you for it."

Saoirse and I made plans to drive separately to Sneem and meet there well before the service was to begin. We knew it would be well attended and that finding a place to sit might be difficult. Whoever arrived first would save a seat for the other.

I wanted to go to the internment as well as whatever was to take place after. She, not knowing anyone from Sneem, wasn't as interested in any of that, and didn't plan to stay long after the mass was over. Neither one of us wanted to attend the wake.

An Irish wake, by tradition, is supposed to take place before the funeral, and it was a time when mourners, usually the women, looked after the corpse until the person was buried. That's when they did their keening. I wasn't going to attend since it sounded like a time for mourning and crying.

I planned to drive over Saturday morning, attend the funeral, right up until the bitter end, when he was put into the grave. I expected that the family and a few close friends would go back to his house after that. If I was invited, I would attend that, too.

I figured that I'd be totally scuttered by the end of the day and I made arrangements to stay at my father's house that night. Saoirse had things to do in Dublin with her family that evening and would be going straight there from the funeral. Colin had no interest in attending any of it. He never connected with the man the way we did.

The next few days passed slowly as I had difficulty keeping my mind on work. My thoughts kept going back to Dr. McDuffy and the many conversations I'd had with the man. Some of the things he said to me were things I'd never heard of, or thought about before.

Meeting the man had been quite an educational experience for me, and I had become more emotionally involved than I realized, though I'd been taught and told not to do that. As I was learning, it's not an easy thing to do. Even though I couldn't think of anything I could have done or should have done to avoid what happened in the end, I still felt badly.

I read where the body of Dr. McDuffy would lie in repose on Friday night. That was something normally reserved for people of high standing, like government officials, when they die, and that was called lying in state. I had no interest in being there for that, either. I didn't want to see him like that.

When Saturday finally arrived, I left Cork mid-morning, allowing plenty of time to get to the church by 1:00. When I entered Sneem and turned onto Church Street, I saw where the lot in front of the church was full and a few men were directing people where to park. I went down and around and ended up at the Sneem Hotel, a kilometer away.

Though I was fifteen minutes early, there wasn't any room in any of the pews. I walked to my right and stood next to the far wall. I could see a casket, which was closed, sitting in the middle, just in front of the altar. A young boy and girl, in black robes, were walking behind it, lighting candles.

Saoirse, who was sitting in the second row, on the right side, way up in the front, saw me, and motioned for me to come up to where she was. She had saved a spot for me. I was glad she got there way before I did.

I was surprised to see my father and a few of my brothers and sisters as I walked by them, including Rory and his wife and kids. My family filled up a whole row. I didn't expect any of them to be there. I saw a number of familiar faces, and many more I didn't recognize.

Some were kneeling, saying prayers. Most were sitting there, silently, with rosaries in their hands. You could, as they say, have heard a pin drop. For some reason, my shoes seemed to be squeaking, making much more noise than they should have as I walked down the outside aisle to get to the front. I felt as if all eyes were on me as I did.

Everyone was dressed in black. Kathleen, who was in the row in front of us, had a long, black veil over her face. She was sitting next to a tall, distinguished-looking man, who I assumed was her husband, at the end of the row. We sat right behind her.

Next to them were two older couples with some young adults alongside. I recognized Caitlin and knew that one of the other men had to be her brother, Patrick. Their children, who seemed to be about the same age as Saoirse and me, sat on either side of them. There might have been as many as eight or ten of them, not including Kathleen and her husband.

When I sat down, after genuflecting and making the sign of the cross, Kathleen didn't turn to acknowledge me, at first, but when she did, she handed me an envelope without saying a word to me. My name was on the outside of it. I opened it immediately, holding it so that Saoirse couldn't see what it said. This was to me.

I read, "Find what interests you most, Brendan, and discover the bent of your mind. I thank you for your assistance in my final days. I wish you well. Carpe diem, my young friend." He signed it "Michael."

Below that, at the very bottom, he wrote, "When you find what you want, don't let it get away, lad." I was fairly certain that I knew what he meant and who and what he was talking about.

When Saoirse asked what it said, I told her, "He's gone to Elysium to be with Marjorie."

"I hope he's right," she responded, "but I'm not so sure of that myself, given what he's gone and done."

"Shhh!" I whispered. "None of that now, Saoirse! This is neither the time nor the place! Please . . ."

Just then, the organist, a woman named Flourinella McBride, who'd been playing there at the church long before I was born, began to play a song that I didn't recognize. When I asked, Saoirse told me that it was called "Carrigdonn," and that it was a sad song about an emigrant who mourns leaving his village in Ireland and going off to work overseas. Some people call it *Mountains of Mourne,* which are located near Dublin.

When it ended, I whispered how beautiful it was. She told me that it was one that is often played at funerals in Ireland. "I've been to many," she added, "more than I care to remember. My parents were forever dragging me along to them." I had been to a couple when two of my grandparents passed, but that was it, and I didn't remember much about them.

The church was totally silent for a minute or so, and then she began playing *On Raglan Road,* another mournful tune. It was one I'd heard many times in bars but never like this. It was played softly and slowly. It set the mood for what was to come. It was a melody about a romance won and lost. We both knew that one.

I looked at my cellphone to check the time and saw that it was still five minutes or so before the service was to begin. She began playing *Fields of Athenry,* one of my favorites. It was played at all the Cork City football club home games. Everyone sang along when it was, but not here. It was, like the first two, played much slower than I had ever heard it, and no singing.

Next, she played *Carrickfergus,* another sorrowful tune about a man looking back on his life, anguishing over the loss of most of his family and friends who were no longer alive. He is, according to the lyrics, drunk and seldom sober, and ready to "lay" himself down. I thought to myself that it might not have been the best choice for this occasion, but it was a popular tune that everyone knew and liked.

I could hear some people sniffling. I was sure many tears were being shed, and I hoped that I wouldn't be among those who did.

This was a sad occasion, and the music, the way it was being played, was appropriate.

This was, after all, a funeral for an Irishman of grand stature and much renown all across the land and these were all-too-familiar ballads for the Irish. All of these were more like anthems, national anthems, at that, deeply embedded into our culture. They were reminders of past wounds and losses, many that would never heal and never be forgotten.

When that one finished, I expected the mass to begin, but she kept playing, though it was now several minutes past the 1:00 hour. The next one was another one I hadn't heard before.

When I whispered that to Saoirse, she said, "That's *My Gallant Hero* or *Mo Guille Mear* in Gaelic. I love this song! It's perfect. He was a hero to our people."

"He certainly was to Kathleen, that's for sure," I responded. She agreed.

The next one was one that Saoirse didn't recognize. I whispered that it was one called *Kilkelly*. It was another sad one about people who died during the famine days. "It's a village in County Mayo," I told her.

"I know that, Brendan. I just didn't recognize the song," she said. "This is wonderful, just sitting here listening to the music," she whispered.

Beautiful flowers of all different colors, mostly purple, red, and white, were on the altar and scattered around the church, and in a moment between songs, I asked what kind of flowers they were.

"Chrysanthemums," she answered. "They're symbolic of death and grieving."

The church itself, one I knew well, having been there on most Sundays for over half of my life, was in good order. Everyone was dressed in their Sunday's finest and it looked as if the wood on the posts, walls, and pews was freshly polished. Despite the presence of hundreds of people, it was peaceful, calm, and otherwise quiet sitting there, waiting for the mass to begin.

Everyone was there to grieve the loss of a neighbor, countryman, and friend. I wondered how many actually knew the man. He didn't have many friends in Sneem that I knew of. I thought to myself that many of the people here probably came to every funeral no matter who the deceased was. Others, those that I didn't know, probably came here from Dublin and elsewhere, to pay their respects to the man.

I had learned early in life that the Irish seemed to relish an opportunity, any opportunity, to lament our heritage. No one needed to be reminded of the centuries of collective suffering the Irish have endured. Funerals were an especially opportune occasion for that.

I whispered to Saoirse that I didn't recognize the next song, and she whispered back that she didn't, either. Kathleen turned and said, "It's called *You Can Let Go Now, Daddy*. Caitlin asked the organist to play it. It's an American song." Apparently, she was able to hear our conversation and had been listening in. We didn't say anything in response.

I looked at my cellphone again and saw that it was now fifteen minutes past the hour. "Maybe the priest is enjoying this, too," I said in a voice loud enough for Kathleen to hear. She turned, acknowledging the comment, but didn't respond.

Then Flourinella played *Toora, Loora, Loora*. I could hear people crying while she did. That was the topper. When it ended, Father O'Flanagan walked in from the rear of the church with the young boy and girl who had been on the altar getting things ready several feet in front of him, holding single candles above their heads.

I was glad to see that it wouldn't be a "high" mass. I could tell that from the vestments and the number of candles on the altar. Those took much, much longer, but if everyone in the church received communion, as was likely, it would take a long time, regardless.

Plus, I figured that some people would probably speak, in addition to Father O'Flanagan, and that would take time, too. That would come at the end of the mass, though. I wasn't sure how he would address the fact that Dr. McDuffy took his own life. That was a "no-no," and there was no two ways about it, as far as the church was concerned.

The mass proceeded in the normal fashion and, other than the fact that Father O'Flanagan was wearing purple vestments while everyone else in the church was wearing black, one wouldn't have known it was a funeral mass. It was the same in all other respects. Everyone responded loudly and appropriately.

After he read the gospel, he chose to discuss, in his homily, the verse from Ecclesiastes about there being a time to be born and a time to die; a time to weep and a time to laugh; and a time to mourn and a time to dance.

"For everything there is a season," be began, "and a time for every matter under heaven. Today is a time for us to mourn. A few days ago, a member of our parish here at St. Michael's, and an esteemed member of Ireland's Catholic community, left us. We are all here to pray for the repose of the soul of a great man . . . Martin Michael McDuffy . . . with our fervent wish that he is going to a better place, as we all hope to do when our time comes."

As I sat there listening to him speak, waiting to hear what he had to say about Dr. McDuffy having taken his own life, I realized that most people in the church, and maybe even Father O'Flanagan, might not have known how he died. The true cause of death hadn't appeared in the obituary, only that he died of natural causes, so it probably wasn't public knowledge. We might have been among the very few people who knew any of that.

I knew that it usually takes the authorities a while to determine the cause of death and then it's only after an autopsy of the body if one was requested. There was no suggestion of foul play in this case, so it was possible that one would ever be done. Maybe no one would ever know, except for the two of us and a few others. No one needed to know and I certainly wasn't going to tell anyone.

He didn't speak for too long, as he often did, probably because he knew that others would be speaking after him, and he had to finish the mass, the burial, and the rest in time for the Vigil mass later that afternoon. He made mention of how Dr. McDuffy and his wife had made many financial contributions to the church over the years, including a sizable donation to help with recent renovations, such as padding on the kneelers and cushions on the pews. Not once did he mention the cause of his death. I thought to myself that he must not have known.

When he finished, he returned to his chair on the altar, observed several moments of silence, and then proceeded to bless the water and the wine, preparing to distribute the Eucharist to the faithful. As expected, everyone in the entire church received Holy Communion, it seemed. I didn't see anyone who remained in their seats. Fortunately, there were some eucharistic ministers, about half a dozen of them, so it didn't take nearly as long as it otherwise would have.

After everyone was back in their pews, most kneeling as I was, and the tabernacle was closed, Father O'Flanagan sat down. When he did, the sounds of kneelers being put back up, and people going from the kneeling to the sitting position, filled the church. Then all was quiet.

The organist began playing the *Parting Song* slowly and softly. When she was finished, Father O'Flanagan stood, walked to the center of the altar, and said, "The Mass is ended, go in peace to love and serve the Lord," and he made the sign of the cross over the congregation.

Then he said, "Now that the Mass is over, before we take the casket to the cemetery, the family has asked that they be allowed to give their eulogy at this time. Mrs. Caitlin McDuffy Golding, Dr. McDuffy's daughter, will be the first to speak.

Caitlin rose and started to walk toward the pulpit. As she was walking, Father O'Flanagan said, "You all are invited to join the family in the Parish Hall, afterward, for some fellowship and refreshments."

Once Caitlin reached the pulpit, Father O'Flanagan stepped back and then returned to his seat on the opposite side of the altar. She lifted her veil and began by introducing herself and thanking all who attended the service to honor her father. She spoke clearly and eloquently of her love for her father and how much he would be missed. She was, obviously, not one who was afraid of a microphone, though her voice quivered throughout.

She spoke for a good ten or fifteen minutes of her father's professional accomplishments and how much he had done for not only Trinity College, but also the Republic of Ireland. Without ever revealing how he died, or why, she talked about the dreadful disease, for which there was no cure, without specifically naming it, which was the true cause of his death. She said that she and her brother would be donating money to an organization to help fund research to find a remedy, and asked that any who cared to do so, do the same.

She concluded by saying, "My father knew that he was going to die, and just before he did, he wrote a note to my brother and me, saying, 'We can and must pray to the gods that our sojourn upon earth will continue happily beyond the grave. This is my prayer and may it come to pass. I love you both and your families, but the time has come for me to go to be with Marjorie.' My brother and I, and our families, pray that is where he is."

When she was finished, another woman, even older than Caitlin, went to the pulpit, who I didn't know and whose name I can't remember. She spoke of his undying love for his wife, Marjorie, and what a good husband, father, and friend he had been. As she spoke, I was able to figure out that she was one of Marjorie's sisters. She didn't mention the family's name, but I was sure I must have known some of her kin. I never thought to ask Dr. McDuffy about any of that and he never spoke of them.

His son, Patrick, who looked very much like his father, spoke next. He, like his sister, spoke clearly and articulately, telling of what a wonderful role model and father he had been. "I walked in his shadow my entire life," he told us.

"I should say that I basked in his shadow. He was a magnificent man . . . a true Irishman . . . one of whom we all can be proud to call a friend. I am proud to say that he was my father and I am his son. He was my best friend."

When I closed my eyes, it seemed to me as if it could have been Dr. McDuffy himself talking. Patrick was like a clone of his father. It was a bit eerie.

It made me smile to think that I might have been seeing what Michael looked like at that age. He, too, was unable to make it through without a few emotional breakdowns. He spoke of how his father was now reconnected with his mother, a woman who he loved and cherished.

Then, to my surprise, Kathleen spoke. I wasn't expecting that. She talked of how she, as one of his students, had admired him so and what a positive influence he was on her life and on the lives of all who knew him. She spoke of how much he was admired by his fellow faculty members and the alumnae at Trinity College Dublin, as well as all of those, like her, who had the opportunity to learn from him over the many decades he taught there. She provided the assembled with many more details of his professional accomplishments than either of his two children did.

She talked at length about how he had been such a large part of the movement to restore Ireland's native language, helping to make it a requirement that all students take courses to learn to speak Gaelic. She told how he had been a member of the Seanad Eirann for many years, which I didn't know much about. Fortunately, she explained that those were members of Parliament who weren't elected. They were selected by various methods, mostly by appointment. "He wasn't a politician, though. He was an educator," she said.

According to her, he was also instrumental in having the many signs put up all throughout the Republic, even into many places in the North, with Gaelic names on them, as well as the English translations. She said that he, along with her father and grandfathers, had been one of the most influential men in her life. She acknowledged her love and admiration for the man and how he truly was among the heroes of his generation, mentioning several of his contemporaries by name.

She concluded her remarks by saying that his most significant contribution to Ireland, though, was as a professor. She said that he was, without any doubt whatsoever, one of the leading authorities in the world on the ancient civilizations of Greece and Rome. She spoke of how much he admired Socrates, Plato, and Aristotle most of all. She told the audience that he had gone to Elysium, where others of his ilk now lived, to be with his wife.

"For those of you who aren't familiar with Elysium, it was, to him, the heaven of which Jesus spoke. He envisioned it to be the two islands far out in the Atlantic, off the southeastern coast of Kerry, the ones we call the Skelligs."

She stopped, looked around, and said, "He was, after all, an Irishman to the core. Where else would he go?"

That drew a chuckle from the crowd.

"He spoke of those two islands, especially Skellig Michael, quite frequently in his lectures. For any of you who have yet to visit them,

I encourage you to do so. If I didn't know of his fervent wish to be buried alongside his wife here at the cemetery at St. Michael's, I would have thought that he might want to he be cremated and have his ashes spread from the top of the mountain there on that tiny island. It is a magical and mystical place."

She paused, and then said, "Please join me as we pray for the repose of the soul of Martin Michael McDuffy. May he rest in eternal peace with his beloved wife, Marjorie."

When she returned to her seat, there was a pause for several moments, while Father O'Flanagan waited to see if anyone else would be speaking. When no one did, he stood, walked to the center of the main aisle just below the casket, and said, "We will now go to the cemetery. All are welcome to join us."

At that, Patrick and two young men, who were, I was sure, two of Dr. McDuffy's grandchildren, rose to carry the casket. Kathleen turned to me and said, "Go help them, Brendan." So I did. The four of us carried the casket out of the church as the organist began to play *Danny Boy*.

We walked a few hundred meters to the cemetery, where a lone bagpiper, dressed in the traditional kilts, stood. As we approached, he began playing *Hymn to the Sea*. It was all quite moving . . . perfect, actually.

We put the casket down on a cart next to the hole in the ground where it would, eventually, be placed, in a plot next to his wife's. Her headstone was already there. It made me cry just to think how fervently he believed that he would be with her now, forever. I'd made it that far without breaking down, but there at the end, I did. I couldn't prevent it from happening.

Father O'Flanagan said a few prayers with what seemed like everyone in the church circled around him. I don't think anyone left. He then concluded the ceremony and invited everyone, once again, to come to the Parish Hall. He then led the group in a slow walk back toward the church with the bagpiper playing his pipes the whole way.

I walked together with Saoirse back to the other side of the church, into the Parish Hall, where a group of four older men stood off in a corner playing *Finnegan's Wake*, but not nearly as loud as I normally heard it. The mood was very much subdued. There was a fiddler, a man with a guitar, another with a bodhran, and the last with a concertina. Moments later, the bagpiper was standing up next to them, playing along.

Saoirse and I stood in line, waiting to get some liquid refreshments, when Father O'Flanagan walked up to me and said, "Nice to see you again, Brendan. It's been a while."

I told him how I was now living in Cork, working to become a clinical psychologist, and assured him that I attended Mass regularly there, which wasn't entirely true, but I did go every now and again. After I introduced him to Saoirse, he said, "Shed the long face, lad . . . you know what we Irish believe, don't you?"

When I told him that I wasn't sure what he meant, he said, "He's gone to a better place. Believe that! If you do, you'll see that this is a reason for celebration. Remember that, and be happy for the man."

He was a nice, old man who reminded me of a little leprechaun, actually, much like Barry Fitzgerald, one of the stars in the *Quiet Man* movie. I had to smile when he said that, and it was true, but it surprised me to hear him say it. There was no doubt that he believed that. I wasn't quite so sure, but I agreed with him. I never argued with a priest; no Catholic ever does.

"He's going to a better place, Brendan," he repeated. "Remember that, whether it's heaven or Elysium, whatever you want to call it, and whatever you envision it to be . . . that's what we Catholics believe, and that's where he is. You know it as well as I do," he told me. "So be happy for the man!" he repeated.

Then he lowered his voice, grabbed my arm, looked me in the eye, and said, "At least, we pray that's where he is, right? No one knows for sure until we get there, don't you know?"

I wasn't so sure what he meant, to be honest. Maybe he knew the truth about how he died. Maybe not. I wasn't going to let on that I knew any different and simply agreed with him. I certainly was praying that he was in Elysium with Marjorie.

After a short while, when I looked around, everyone seemed to be smiling, and people were beginning to laugh, though not too loudly. The spell of the funeral, though still present, had been broken.

As time went by, and as the alcohol kicked in, the conversation and the laughter grew louder. I joined in.

At some point, we were surrounded by my father, brothers, sisters, nieces, and nephews. They were all anxious to meet this mysterious woman Rory had told them about. They made quite a fuss over her—they'd never known me to have a girdle before, despite the fact I told them, repeatedly, that she wasn't.

Caitlin came over, together with her brother, and introduced him to us. He thanked us for helping his father as we did. I told him how much I enjoyed meeting him and of a few of our special moments, like the night at Dan Murphy's Bar. Saoirse added a few of her favorite remembrances as well. He had read the reports and knew all about it.

After he left us, I thought to myself that maybe we shouldn't have said as much to him as we had. It was obvious that he was moved by what we'd told him. The thought occurred to me that he wished he could have seen him that way before he died. I really couldn't understand why Michael couldn't have waited until Patrick came to see him. I don't know why he didn't.

When I mentioned it to Saoirse, she said that Michael probably didn't want people to see him the way he was. "He was a proud man, Brendan, like Kathleen told us. He didn't want our sympathy or our pity! He didn't want to die a slow, agonizing death with people looking at him like he was a feeble, decrepit old man! In a way, I have to admire him for what he did."

I was surprised to hear her say that and told her so.

"I'm not condoning his actions, Brendan, but I have a better understanding of why he did what he did. I'm going to miss him, just like you are," she said, and I saw tears forming in her eyes as she spoke. "Thank you for allowing me to be a part of his care and treatment," she added as she put her arms around me and gave me a big hug. That caught me by surprise . . . a much-welcomed surprise at that.

Moments later, Caitlin came back over and introduced us to her children, a boy and a girl, who were about the same age as Saoirse and me, but maybe a year or two older. I couldn't tell. We connected with them quite quickly and soon were engaged in a conversation about what it was like living where each of us did. Shortly after that, Patrick's two children joined us.

We wanted to know what it was like to live in the US, of course, and they wanted to know all about living in Ireland. Though they weren't born here, they all seemed to feel as if they were as Irish as we were. It was enjoyable to chat with them all.

They couldn't have been nicer to us. We talked about all of us getting together again, after all of this was over with, either here in Ireland or over in the States. Saoirse was all excited about that.

I'd never even dreamed of such a thing, until then. They seemed to be sincere, too, as if they really meant it, talking about coming back over the Christmas holidays or over the summer. We exchanged contact information and promised to follow up on that.

There was plenty of food on the tables as well as more than enough liquor and beer to last a fortnight. It was the best party I'd ever been to in my life. Even though it was for a funeral, it seemed as if I had a smile on my face the entire time.

People kept coming up to me, asking me how I was and where I'd been. This was, after all, my hometown, even though I'd gone to live in Cork with my mother after the divorce. I didn't realize I had so many friends in Sneem.

Before long, I was in a different circle of people, separated from Saoirse and the four grandchildren, talking to old friends I'd known since childhood but hadn't seen in ages. She stayed talking to them for quite a while. She didn't know many people there, whereas it seemed as if I knew and talked to almost everyone in the entire building.

Even Seamus was there. I gave him a big hug, which caught him off guard. He told me a few more jokes and made me laugh, as he always did. He really was a funny fellow. It took me a few seconds to recognize him, though, all dressed up as he was.

He'd had his hair cut since I'd last seen him and looked to be an entirely different man. He was with a woman who was, I was sure, his wife, and was on his best behavior. Clearly, he wasn't comfortable dressed the way he was, with a tie around his neck.

Hours later, after the crowd had thinned some, the music stopped, and Father O'Flanagan took to the microphone to say that we were welcome to stay for a while longer, but that the Vigil Mass would be starting in half an hour, and at some point, we'd all have to leave. I thought to myself that I hoped another priest was there to say that one . . . he was in no shape to do so.

Then Caitlin came over and asked us to come and join the family at Michael's house. I accepted the invitation, but Saoirse said, apologetically, that she had to get to Dublin to be with her family for something and wouldn't be able to. She handed both of us an envelope and thanked us, again.

Then she said, in a low voice, so no one could hear what she was saying, "I know that you're wondering why my father decided to do what he did so abruptly, and I want to share this with you . . . he wrote my brother and me a note explaining to us that he was afraid that if he didn't do what he did right then and there, that he might not be able to do it later."

Although we didn't say anything, we were puzzled by that, or at least I was. She went on to say, "By that, he meant that the two of you, Kathleen, and the others would have done things to prevent him from doing what he did. Plus, he explained, he feared that his mind would falter and he wouldn't have the strength of mind to do what he did."

"Essentially, he was saying that he loved us and would miss us, but he wanted us to remember him as he was, not like what he was destined to become. Once he figured out what was causing all of his problems . . . that it was Alzheimer's Disease . . . and he realized what lay ahead for him, he knew what he had to do. The last thing in the world he wanted was pity."

"No one wants to be a burden and no one wants to go through what a person suffering from Alzheimer's must go through before death brings an end to the suffering. If he had any faults, and I am not saying that he did, one might be his pride. He took pride in who he was and what he had accomplished in his life. I guess you could say that his pride was his downfall."

"I honestly can't say that I blame him, though I will miss him terribly, as will my brother, but we understand why he did what he did. I certainly didn't want to watch him deteriorate. Maybe it shows strength of character, not weakness, to do what he did. I don't know, but I hope that helps the two of you understand it as well."

She squeezed our hands and gave us both a hug, thanking us, again, and telling me that she looked forward to chatting some more about things I had put in various reports, at his house, just before turning and walking away.

Her last words to us were, "I hope that the two of you will come visit us in America."

We were among the last to leave, and I walked Saoirse to her car. "Well, I'll see you back at the office, Saoirse," I told her. "I hate to see this chapter in our lives end, don't you? It's been a great experience, hasn't it?" I asked.

"That it has, truly memorable, and maybe even life-changing. Who knows?" she responded.

"It's been grand getting to know you and working together as we did," I told her. "It's pretty unlikely we'll ever get a case like this again, isn't it?" I asked.

"Highly unlikely," she told me. "This was a once-in-a-lifetime opportunity, I'd say. No doubt about that . . . none whatsoever."

"I agree," I responded, and then an awkward silence fell over us, neither of us knowing just what to say, I think. I didn't want to get too mushy and spoil everything. Then she handed me a business card, as she was getting in her car, and said, "My personal number is on the back. Give me a call sometime."

She'd never shared that with me before. "What about your boyfriend?" I asked.

"We've had a falling out," she told me with a smile as she started up the engine and began to back out.

I stood there, watching her drive away, stunned by what had just taken place, and then I thought to myself that a certain Martin Michael McDuffy might have had something to do with that, and I thanked him for it.

The End

About the Author

Pierce Kelley graduated from Tulane University, New Orleans, Louisiana, in 1969. He received a law degree from George Washington University, Washington, D.C., in 1973. He now lives in Fort White, Florida.

www.ingramcontent.com/pod-product-compliance
Lightning Source LLC
Chambersburg PA
CBHW061558190726
48288CB00007B/2080